THE HUNT OF NIGHT

KC KEAN

The Hunt of Night
Heirborn Academy #3
Copyright © 2024 KC Kean

The moral right of the author has been asserted.

Cover Design by Dark Imaginarium Art
Interior Formatting & Design by Wild Elegance Formatting
Editor - Encompass Editing Service
Proofreader - Sassi Edits

ISBN: 978-1-915203-49-6

The Hunt of Night/KC Kean – 1st ed.

To my inner child, my younger self, look how far you've come, girl.
Everything is worth it. If it amounts to this… It was worth every step.
I love you.
I love me.
I feel it, deep in my chest, and no matter how foreign it feels, how scared it makes me, I know what it is.
Hope.

I'd fall and stumble to watch you rise, to see you shine, to be in the presence of your greatness as you become who you were always meant to be.

– Brody

ADRIANNA

1

"So what will it be, Princess Adrianna? You, or little Princess Nora?"

The question hangs in the air, coiling around my limbs like an impenetrable wind that makes it impossible for me to move.

I knew coming to the academy and putting everything that I am on the line would come at a price. I was ready for it, expecting it even, but I didn't anticipate their desire to drag my sister into the same depths of Hell.

That was their mistake.

They can come for me and everything I stand for, but Nora? No fucking way. She's off limits.

My shoulders roll back, relishing the burn through my muscles as I focus on every detail of the room. All eyes are on me. Professors, council members, and the assholes who consume my every thought.

I take a deep breath, accepting the fire that rumbles in my chest as I do it again and again, all while casting my gaze over every single person here.

Kryll is closest to my left, a part of the circle that the guys and I create. His head is downcast, eyebrows furrowed as he looks up at me through hooded eyes. There's a darkness there. One I'm not familiar with, but it seems to have the ability to validate every ounce of my feelings that threaten to spread from my fingertips and take control of the room.

Cassian stands beside him, teeth bared and claws protruding from his knuckles, his wolf sits so close to the surface that I'm certain he's going to completely shift at any moment. His dark gaze is fixated on his father, a distaste for him that burns brighter than my own hatred for my mother blazing in his eyes.

Beside him, Brody stands with his shoulders slumped, a dejected energy vibrating from him as his finger taps on the sphere his hand is pressed against. *He knew. He knew. He knew.* I can't focus on that right now. Whether he knew or not, my attention must be on Nora, and her alone. The longer I stare at him, the harder it is, but I force myself to look to my right.

Raiden. Disgust has my teeth grinding together as I take in every inch of the vampire who stands as tall and sharp as ever. He looks just as he did the first day I met him, just like the day he stood in my bedroom, having tricked me with roses to break past Brody's spell. Arrogant. Self-righteous. The entire reason Nora is here.

I glance at my sister, my heart aching when I spy her eyebrows pinched with worry. Not for herself. *Never* for herself. Always for me.

It keeps me going, casting my stare to Raiden's mother, Professor Holloway, who stands poised, just as elegant as her son as she folds her arms over her chest and arches her brow at me, waiting expectantly for my answer.

My chest heaves, the inability to contain the fury that sparks through my veins revealing the truth of my feelings.

Fuck.

Sneering at Councilman Orenda, Brody's father, and the man whose magic dances in the air, I regard him with a solemn reality. His unkempt white hair and eyes filled with wisdom are a lie. There's a devilish evil inside of him, one that wants to bend me to his will, or my sister if I put up too much resistance.

I bite back a scoff, my nostrils flaring with rage as my gaze settles on the final person in the room.

Kenner.

Fucking Kenner.

Somehow, my hatred for this man seems to know no bounds, growing with every breath I take as he smirks. *Fucking* smirks. Like he has all of the power, all of the knowledge, *and* the right to reveal truths about myself. Truths he has no business knowing.

My eyes narrow, thoughts of my mother flashing through my mind as his words play on repeat. *Wolf. Kenner Wolf.*

I blink. Slowly.

"Tick. Tock, Adrianna," Kenner sings, but when I shift my stare again, it's to Nora. He doesn't deserve the satisfaction of harnessing my attention. "What will it be? You or Princess Nora?"

Yet again, the words fill the air, spiraling out of control, but this time, they don't pin me in place, they ignite the fuse, desperate to burn bright.

My shoulders drop, my knees loosening just the slightest touch as my fingers flex.

"I choose neither."

The words are nothing more than a whisper, but as quiet as they are, it's enough to trigger the power inside of me, forcing my hands into the air as my magic explodes from my palms.

I hear nothing but the pounding in my ears, and the visual I'm treated to is nothing but a sliver of delight.

Energy charges around me as Professor Holloway's mouth snaps open in horror, a presumed cry bursting from her lungs as she dodges my flames. She rolls across the floor, ducking behind a desk in the far corner of the room as quickly as her vampire speed will allow. My head tilts, searching along the tendril of power whipping from my other hand, cascading wicked winds toward councilman Orenda, whose lips move as he tries to hold my abilities back.

I watch the moment he realizes I'm stronger than he anticipated, the moment he understands that whatever he's muttering means nothing against the battering gale that swirls around him. Three beats of my pulse ringing in my ears and he's gone, opting to use a transport spell instead of a protection chant.

It's satisfying. *Almost.*

Turning my attention to Kenner, I retract my magic, letting it build in the palms of my hands. His eyes dance an unusual green, with flecks of gold dashed across his irises. A sense of déja vù washes over me. I've felt my magic rage like this before. I was staring him down then too.

My spine stiffens, dark memories threatening to consume me, fueled by the intrusive thoughts that claw at my resolve, penetrating my strength and leaving behind a lingering venom of self-doubt.

Not this time.

My back arches, struggling under the weight of the power that tingles over my fingertips, and I scream, the sound impossibly grating to hear, but the rumbles I feel in my chest at its shrieking, pain-filled sounds fuel my magic nonetheless.

Air and fire swirl as I take aim, projecting the magic at my target. A smirk tips the corner of my lips, watching as it barrels toward Kenner, but it's a second too late, and the relief of his demise is lost as he darts for the door before it explodes in his face.

My anger reaches new heights as the magic disperses and I'm left looking at my palms in disappointment.

"Addi." The word sounds distant. Lost. Hopeless. "Addi." There it is again. I blink. Again and again. My name is repeated, each time growing more urgent and concerned, bringing me back to reality. "Addi!"

My gaze falls to Nora, her voice loud and clear in my ears. Quickly darting my eyes around the room, I note there's no threat, except the four guys that stand in a mixture of disbelief and awe, so I rush to my sister.

Her arms drape around my neck as I fall to my knees beside her. My eyes drift closed for the briefest moment as I absorb every ounce of her. Her familiar lavender scent fills my nose, offering me the smallest comfort of home before the sound of footsteps pounding in the distance begins to inch closer and closer.

Rounding on my feet, I spin for the door, magic instantly at my fingertips as the sound of the kiss of Amethyst clattering to the floor dances in my ears.

Vallie's father steps through the open doorway, his face

red with fury as he snarls, instantly pointing a finger at me the second his eyes settle on mine.

"You," he growls, his canines elongating as his pupils dilate.

He takes one step toward me. One single, yet quick vampire step toward me, before I unleash my magic once more. Fire, fueled by a barrage of tornado winds, blasts toward him, exploding out in front of me in less than a second as haunting screams echo around the room.

His cries fall short as the red embers of fire die down, leaving the remains of his lifeless body in its wake.

ADRIANNA

2

The fall back to my knees feels like the longest route to relief, so much so I'm certain my knees will never collide with the floor, but to my surprise, the impact jolts through my bones reassuringly.

"Addi!" Nora yells, edging closer to me before her hands reach for my face. Her delicate, soft thumb grazes my cheek with a warm comfort that resembles the embracing glow of the sun on a perfect summer's morning.

It settles the warring rage inside of me as I blink up at her. The weight of the world still rides on my shoulders, there's no shifting that right now, but I need to channel every ounce of my being into protecting my sister. It's all I've done for as long as I can remember, but for the past few weeks I've done it from afar, and now, she's right in front of me, making any threat toward her feel even more imminent.

Taking a deep breath, I do it again, exhaling slowly as I sense four sets of eyes burning into my back. The smell of burnt flesh lingers in the air, making me cringe, especially when I see the distaste washing over Nora's face.

"Are you okay? Are you hurt anywhere? What happened?" I fire off, running my hands over my sister with a renewed sense of urgency as her wellbeing becomes my sole focus.

"I'm fine, Addi," she murmurs, but it doesn't stop me checking her to be sure. Once I've patted every inch of her body and inspected her mobility aid, coming up with nothing more than a scuff to the wood frame and the ratty knots in her hair that falls around her face, there's nothing to report. Thankfully. "See? I told you," she insists, giving me a pointed look, but instead of having its desired effect, it makes me grin.

"I've missed you."

"I mean, we could have met under better circumstances, but yeah, I guess I've missed you too," she breathes with a shrug, making my eyes narrow, and it's her turn to grin at me.

She's a witch. *My* witch. Her and my dad are—

"We need to find Dad," I whisper, feeling the color drain from my face as another level of panic tingles across my skin.

"They separated us," she admits, looking down at her lap, twisting her fingers, and I can feel the helplessness seeping from her.

Reaching for her arm, I give it a comforting squeeze, but it falls flat. "That's not your fault, Nora. We just have to find him."

"We can help," Kryll states from behind me, his tone slightly off, but when I glance over my shoulder, I can't get a read on him.

The four of them are standing together, no podium holding them in place like before as they observe Nora and me. "We're good," I grunt, rising to my feet as I dust off my pants.

Exhaustion clings to me. The fact that I have faced a trial, endured Vallie's vampire bite, and been healed by a mage isn't lost on me, yet my day is far from over after the mess that has unraveled here.

"Don't be petulant, Adrianna," Raiden starts, and I whirl around to him so fast the world continues to spin around me even after I come to a halt.

Jabbing a finger in his direction, I snarl at him. "Fuck you and fuck your petulance."

His jaw opens, and I instantly produce a ball of fire in my hand, aimed and ready to launch it at him if he so much as breathes wrong. To my surprise, he takes the warning, raising his hands in surrender as he quickly slams his mouth shut.

I glare at him, turning my anger toward Brody, Cassian, and Kryll as well, making sure they don't give me some bullshit either.

Satisfied, I turn my attention back to my sister. "Are you okay using me?" I ask, and her lips twist in concern instantly.

"Are you—"

"Don't ask questions you already know the answer to," I interject, aware that I have no clue how much time we actually have. It earns me a disgruntled glare, but she sighs, nodding before she holds out her hand.

I place my palm against hers, wrapping my fingers around her dainty wrist as I feel the familiar warmth rise between our touch. Her eyes fall closed as her lips part, and a ghost of a smile touches the corner of her mouth.

"What is she—"

"Shut. Up," Brody bites, interrupting Cassian's question as I try to block them all out, but I don't miss the sense of awe oozing from him.

"I can feel him," Nora breathes, my chest tightening with apprehension as I wait for more. She nods slightly, more to herself than anyone else before her eyebrows pinch together. "He's in some kind of cellar. He's not far, I just can't—"

"There's a small set of cells down in the cellar here,"

Brody states, and Nora's eyes widen as she releases my hand.

"Take us."

I look back at Brody, who nods in response. He inches toward the door, scrubbing at the back of his neck as he peeks his head out to check down the hallway.

"It might be better for me to use my magic to transport us in case there's someone waiting for us. We have no way of knowing if your father has anyone standing guard over him," he explains, and indecision wars inside of me.

I can either make it there on foot, with no certainty who I might bump into, or let him transport us there, unsure of what we will immediately walk into. Neither option sounds better than the other, apart from the fact that the transporting will be quicker.

Fuck.

"Transport us," Nora answers for us, making my eyebrows rise as she purposely avoids my gaze. I want to give her hell, but we don't have time, and realistically, it's the right option.

"You transport them, we'll use our speed to—"

"We don't need you as well," I grunt, glaring at Raiden, who waves his hands in frustration at me.

"You'll get what you're fucking given," Cassian grunts, speaking for the first time in what feels like forever, but I don't have the time to deal with his level of assholery right now.

Ignoring his remark, I place my hand in Nora's again as Brody steps toward us. He offers me his hand, a hint of uncertainty dancing in his eyes, but I ignore it, focusing on what needs to be done.

Before I can take a breath, the ground shifts beneath me, and a moment later I find myself in a dark and eerie space. It smells damp. The sound of dripping water rings around us, but it's quickly over trodden by the echo of a grunt in the distance, followed swiftly by a gurgled cry before silence falls over us again.

"What was that?" Nora asks, concern twinkling in her eyes.

"That was the unwanted wolf taking care of the security protecting your father," Cassian grumbles, appearing at the end of the hallway we're in.

"I'd say thanks, but I believe my sister didn't ask," Nora retorts, and I have to bite back a shit-eating grin at her sass as a grunt vibrates from the wolf in question.

I'm certain he's biting his tongue because if it was me who had spoken, he would be a snarling mound of fur and fangs. My sister, however, isn't blessed with the same grace as I would have been. It's almost impressive.

"Uh, follow me," Brody offers, cutting through the silence as he steps down the hallway toward Cassian while I assume my position behind Nora's wooden aid.

It feels nice pushing her, even though I know it drives her insane. It always has. She's too independent for any of it, but I love to be needed, especially by her. Anything for her.

"Did you miss the part where I said I took out the security detail on him? I already know where he is. You don't need to guide them," Cassian snaps, shaking his head in disbelief, making Nora snort back a laugh.

"Which one is the guy causing you stress in your life?" she asks as I hurry us down the hall, ignoring the bickering coming from Brody and Cassian, and I scoff.

"Only one?"

She laughs, head thrown back and straight from her stomach.

"That sounds about right for you, Addi."

She's going to be the death of me.

I glare at the back of her head, refusing to give her the satisfaction of a response.

Turning the corner, black wrought-iron bars come into view, outlining a row of five cells. Kryll and Raiden are waiting on the other side with four bodies at their feet while my father stands, mouth agape, in the center cell as he stares at Brody. The mage in question mutters a chant under his breath and after a few seconds, a clang echoes through the air from the cell door as it creaks open. Whatever magic was binding the steel closed is gone.

"Addi. Nora," he breathes, rushing toward us.

I'm in his arms a moment later, feet swept off the floor as he pins me to his chest. I feel his fingers tremble at my back as I wrap my arms around him, taking the strength I know he's offering before he slowly places me on the floor. He repeats the same motion with Nora, holding her tight and filling my heart with an overwhelming amount of love that only the two of them can offer me.

"Are you both okay?" he rasps, and when I turn to give him my full attention, I notice how drained he looks.

"We're fine. What did they do to you?" I ask, taking a step toward him, and a defeated sigh passes his lips. "Dad," I insist, knowing the look on his face all too well.

"I've been blessed with a gem," he murmurs, pointing at his back, and I frown in confusion.

"An amethyst? Dad, you can—"

"Not an amethyst, sunshine," he explains, shaking his head slowly. *Not an amethyst? What the fuck else is there?* He must sense my impending question and slowly turns, revealing an aquamarine crystal penetrating his flesh.

"What does that do?"

"Addi," he breathes, turning to face me with the most solemn look I have ever had the displeasure of witnessing in all of my life, and I've seen some looks.

"Dad. Spit it out."

He shakes his head, peering at Nora.

"Dad, whatever it is, you can tell us," she adds, proving the strength in her that so many tend to overlook.

His eyes continue to Brody, Kryll, Cassian, and Raiden, unsure whether to continue with them present or not, but their knowledge does nothing to the outcome of whatever that thing does.

"Just say it, Dad."

"The curse of the aquamarine is controlled by a dragon. An Aeternus dragon that no longer exists. It renders me powerless unless one was to magically reappear in the Floodborn Kingdom to remove it from my flesh."

ADRIANNA

3

I can't process what it is I'm feeling, my emotions myriad to the point of pain. My head. My chest. My heart. It seems life isn't done throwing sucker punches my way just yet. Now even my father is a victim of the damn council.

It makes me angrier. At least when it was me, I had a fake semblance of control over the situation, but now that it's him...the impossibility of his solution only leaves me helpless and spiraling.

I shake my head in disbelief. "A non-existent dragon can't be our only option."

My father's brows furrow deeper, unwavering pain settling deep into his eyes. "I wish it wasn't the case, Addi, but it seems every gem I banished as king has somehow found itself in the hands of the unsavory."

Unsavory isn't the word I would use.

"I refuse," I state, unwilling to give up without even trying.

My father's eyes find mine as Nora remains quiet, fingers laced together in her lap. "Addi, I would love to stay and continue this conversation with you, but our safety, especially yours, is the greatest priority. We must leave," he breathes, defeat thick in his voice as the weight of his words rings true in my mind.

Fuck.

I want to stomp my feet, raise my fists in the air, and throw the world's greatest tantrum that has ever existed. It's not fair. It's not right. It's against everything in the entire kingdom that I believe in, but that means nothing to those who still seem intent on controlling us all.

Sighing, my shoulders sag. "You're right."

I despise the taste of the words on my tongue, but they're true whether I like it or not.

There's so much I need to think about and process, but none of that can happen until my father and Nora are safe. I just need to figure out how the hell to make that happen because the veil they've hidden behind is no longer worth the magic it uses. It couldn't be fueled anyway, not with my father branded with the aquamarine gem of fucking death.

The sound of someone clearing their throat pulls me

from my head, and I glance over my shoulder to find Raiden rocking on his heels.

"I can—"

"You can shut the fuck up. Or better yet, just leave," I snap, interrupting whatever shit is about to spew from his mouth. I'll deal with him soon enough, but right now, he's just an unnecessary distraction.

"Addi," my father murmurs, the telling tone of his voice making my spine stiffen.

"Don't," I warn, but he tilts his head, giving me his look of wisdom, ignoring the caution from my lips.

"I think we should consider whatever he's offering," my father explains, arms falling relaxed at his sides as he acts calm and collected. Always calm and collected.

"It seems nothing he offers comes without a price. I'm good," I grumble, taking a step away from the vampire in question.

"Addi."

"Dad," I retort, eyes narrowed on him as he mirrors my stance.

"Addi."

"Dad," I repeat, knowing exactly where this is going as my teeth grind together.

"Princess Adrianna," he pushes, spiking the adrenaline in my veins.

"King August Reagan."

We're at a standstill. Ramrod straight spines, bunched muscles in our necks, with our hands balled into fists at our sides.

"What am I missing?" Raiden asks, igniting more irritation in my bones.

"This is what they do when they switch off the personal side," Nora explains, like we're not standing in front of them, aware of what's being said.

"What does that mean?" The curiosity in his voice annoys me more.

"It means he's making her see you through the eyes of a leader, without bias and prejudice. Whatever you have done to make her mad is taking her a lot to see past right now."

"So, you mean he's trying to get her to assess me without the rage vibrating from her?"

"You can see that?" Nora asks, her impressed tone only making me more agitated.

"Uh-huh."

"Well, yeah, that pretty much sums it up," Nora explains, as if she's offering a secret piece of me. We'll be having words about this eventually, but once again, his distraction isn't what I need right now.

Turning to face him, it's impossible to keep the glare from my face.

"That look doesn't seem to be working in my favor,"

he states, assessing me with a raised eyebrow.

"You're learning quick. You've got this, Fangs," Nora says with a beaming smile, like we're not in a crisis.

"Your sister called me that once," he replies, eyes narrowing while Nora snickers.

"Only once? That's embarrassing." His eyebrow rises farther. "What? It's a good nickname," she offers, like that's enough explanation.

"I have a name; a nickname isn't required," Raiden grumbles, and a knot in my stomach untangles at the amusement passing between the pair of them.

"Whatever you say, Fangs," Nora sings, turning to me with a ridiculous wink.

Brody breaks out into a full laugh, drawing my attention his way, but in the process, I notice Kryll frowning slightly and his gaze is aimed at my father.

This is all too much for me.

As if sensing my thoughts, Cassian grunts. "Are we getting a fucking move on, or are we going to remain where we all know it isn't safe?"

I hate that I agree with him. It gets under my skin even more than when he's being an asshole.

"I'll transport us," Brody offers, clearing his throat as he moves closer to my family. I flinch when he touches Nora and my father, uncertain of his intentions, but when his soft gaze turns my way, I relax a little.

Placing my hand on Nora's shoulder, I instantly feel a hand on my back. I turn, ready to give Raiden a piece of my mind, but it's not him I find; it's Kryll. He offers me a tight smile, one I focus on as the world shifts around us, and a moment later, worn tracks stand beneath my feet as trees blow in the distance.

The fresh air dances over my skin, sending a shiver down my spine. It's bliss. The earthy scent in the air has the ability to ground me, allowing me a moment of reprieve from the torrid panic battling inside of me.

My eyes fall closed as I take a few deep breaths, rolling my shoulders out with each exhale, and when I blink them open again, I feel a little stronger. I'm in no shape to move mountains right now, and I definitely still need to pass the fuck out, but I can focus more, at least.

That is until my eyes settle on my surroundings and everything becomes washed in a red haze. He brought us to the edge of the Heir Academy campus. Is he for real?

"Why the hell would you bring us here?" I bite, turning my attention to a startled Brody, whose eyes continue to widen the more he takes me in.

"I—"

"It's okay," Kryll interjects, waving a hand in front of me as he steps between Brody and me. "I can take them somewhere safe," he adds, the cords in his neck tightening ever so slightly as he stares deep into my eyes.

"There *is* nowhere safe," I mutter, pinching the bridge of my nose as my eyes fall to half-mast.

"Do you trust me?" he asks, using his thumb and index finger to tilt my chin up just enough that I'm forced to drop my hand from my nose and look at him.

I hesitate. I know he wants me to say yes, and I know even I want to be able to utter that single word, but it's still a hard thing to offer someone. Trust. Such a simple word yet so powerful in what it stands for, especially when it comes to my family.

"The fact that you didn't immediately say no gives me hope," he muses, his thumb stroking over my cheek as the corner of his mouth tips up. "I promise you, I would never put them at risk."

"I don't know that," I admit, my gut twisting as my hands clench at my sides.

"You know it in your heart." His words are nothing more than a whisper in the wind, yet they flutter around my stomach, sending a sharp gasp to burst from my lips. My heart races, my soul dances, and my breath catches as I try to find some kind of response. "Let me take them to safety. Trust me." It's a plea. The sincerity in his voice is like a gentle vice, coaxing my heart to calm down.

"You're asking me to trust you with everything that matters to me." My pulse rings in my ears as I sense everyone's eyes aimed in our direction, but I can't pay them any attention as I search deep into his irises, looking for something for me to cling to.

"And I would never risk a single hair on either of their heads knowing that fact. Trust me, Princess. No harm will come to them, I swear it."

His eyes soften, his touch delicate and his breath light against my lips.

It feels as if the ground shifts beneath my feet, the world altering around me without anyone's magic actually transporting me anywhere. That's because I'm not moving, but my soul is.

Taking a deep breath, I place my hand over his, leaning into his touch as I inhale the most determined deep breath I've ever taken.

"I trust you, Kryll. Do it. Take them somewhere safe."

RAIDEN

4

She's mad. She's *mad,* mad. I can feel it so strongly it leaves my nerve endings frazzled. I'm never frazzled. Not in any way, shape, or form. If the glares didn't show it, or the stiffness to her stance, then it would be the raw fury emitting from her, and here I am, crumbling under the anger that vibrates from her.

I can smell her rage, and I want to taste her fury, but something tells me I've got no chance in Hell right now. I can bide my time. That's fine. It fills me with irritation, but I'm learning it's just a new sensation that she brings out in me.

It takes more strength than I care to admit to hold back as she says goodbye to her family. I have questions and a lack of understanding, which heightens the tension inside of me.

For starters, I wouldn't care if my family was somewhere safe or not, just as they wouldn't care if I was. We may be connected by blood, but that doesn't generate an undeniable love or need to protect one another. We stand tall and proud together in public, to maintain appearances, of course, but we would never be bonded tightly like this.

King August Reagan stares at his eldest daughter in awe, his eyes glossy with a love I can't even begin to comprehend from a parent, while his bottom lip trembles whenever she's not looking at him. His worry is raw, his love real, and his helplessness overwhelming. Adrianna's bratty sister, Nora, is completely different. She beams at Adrianna, completely in wonder at everything her idol does. Despite the danger they're in, she continues to smile through it. It's almost impressive. Almost. It's mostly annoying, along with her snarky comments.

Adrianna, however, nips at her bottom lip with worry, constantly peering between her family members as they get ready to leave. I can feel her pain from here. It's almost as strong as her wrath. Who knew beneath her hard exterior is such a soft and delicate center?

Kryll whispers in her ear, and I'm a step too far away to catch wind of what he's saying, but a moment later, Adrianna nods, waving one last time to her sister and father before turning away from them. Brody edges toward them, and a moment later, August, Nora, Kryll, and the mage are gone.

Her pain amplifies, scrunching her face in discomfort as her knees buckle beneath her, but she somehow manages to remain on her feet. Her arms band around her waist, supporting herself as she leaves me more confused than ever. She's a blessing and a sin.

I glance at Cassian, who is staring at the woman before us just as intently as I was, but before either of us can say a word to her, she spins on her heels, storming toward the gate without a backward glance.

"Hold up," I holler, hurrying toward her. If she hears me, she doesn't acknowledge it, but that doesn't stop me from quickening my pace. Just as I'm about to grab her arm, she comes to a stop, spinning her attention to Cassian.

"Can you use that wolf speed of yours and get me the fuck out of here?" she asks, refusing to look my way.

"This feels too much like good entertainment," he retorts with a shrug, leaving her to gape at him in horror.

"You're an ass."

He shrugs. "This is not new information."

"Can we get back to me?" I grumble, throwing my arms out in desperation, finally earning Adrianna's attention, but the deathly glare she hurtles my way isn't reassuring.

"You don't want that," she snarls, nostrils flaring as she takes a step back.

"Why?" I push, taking a step toward her.

"Because I'm considering all the ways I could kill you

right now, some of which involve skinning you alive," she bites, eyes flashing with rage as her cheeks redden.

I cock an eyebrow at her. "That feels a little far fetched."

Her eyes widen, and I immediately understand we're not on the same page about the punishment she wishes to bestow upon me. Wagging her finger, she takes a step toward me before remembering herself and quickly inching away again.

"Far fetched? Far fetched is following someone without their knowledge and leading the enemy to her loved ones."

I rear back. "Is that what this is about?"

She scoffs, shaking her head in disbelief. "Your stalking almost got my family killed! What else would it be about?"

"I don't know, but I didn't ask to be followed," I point out, taking a step toward her, and she inches back.

"Neither did I," she snaps, her hands balling at her sides.

I wipe a hand down my face, trying to piece together how on Earth I can make it better when I had no control over it going wrong to begin with.

"How do we get past this?" I finally ask, hating that I have to, but I don't think I've ever felt this helpless in my entire life.

"There is no getting past anything," she retorts without skipping a beat.

I look to Cassian, hoping for help, but all I find is the asshole standing with his arms folded over his chest as he watches us intently, a ghost of a grin on his lips.

Fucker.

Turning back to Adrianna, I startle when I realize she has taken off again.

"Adrianna," I yell, but she doesn't stop, sauntering through the gates of Heir Academy in a flurry, and I rush to keep up. "Adrianna," I repeat, and I hear her scoff.

"Raiden," she retorts with an irritated tone.

This is bullshit.

Thankfully, the guards manning the gate pay us no mind, but I would still rather not have an audience. I wait until she's farther down the pathway before I try again, acutely aware that Cassian is maintaining a slow stroll behind me.

Asshole.

"Adrianna." Nothing. "Princess Adrianna," I repeat, trying a different tactic, and to my surprise, she whirls around with fire burning in her eyes.

"No. That doesn't work for you," she snarls, aware that I'm trying to replicate whatever her father did to get her to listen.

"Adrianna," I try again, dropping the title this time, but all she does is shake her head. When her eyes settle on mine, they feel void of everything, and it leaves a sickly feeling burning in my throat.

"How about you save yourself the effort and keep my name out of your mouth."

"I have to say, this is far more fun when it's not me getting this shit for a change," Cassian muses, coming to a stop beside me, breaking the moment.

I turn to glare at him, but he simply shrugs, unaware of the helplessness he's stoking inside of me. Looking back toward Addi, my chest tightens. "Where the fuck did she go?" I growl, earning a snicker from the asshole wolf I hate to call my friend.

"How about we head back and figure out what the fuck just happened while we give her some space to wrap her head around things?"

Since when did this fool start talking any kind of sense?

Fuck.

He might be right, though. Maybe she just needs a minute to think and realize that nothing I did was intentional. I am sorry it happened, but I'm not sorry I followed her.

Fuck.

Maybe I should have said sorry to her. It's too late for that now.

Sighing, I turn back to Cassian, who seems way too calm for my liking. "Fine, let's head back to my place and start with the secrets some of us were keeping," I grunt, stomping toward the pathways that lead to the origin buildings.

"You mean Brody?" he asks, and I scoff at his stupid question.

"Unless there are any other secrets I'm not aware of?"

BRODY

5

An uncomfortable tingle burns down my spine, reminding me of the shit that just went down and the mess that is yet to come. I pace back and forth, wearing down the grass beneath my boots as my knuckles turn white, anticipation clinging to me.

Kryll only let me bring him so far, and he's been gone for what feels like an eternity while I'm left here to simmer in my thoughts, in my mistakes, in my betrayals.

I feel like I'm in a waiting room, nervously listening for my name to be called. I don't know when it will be, and deep down, a part of me would like to be left suspended in this moment, the inevitable never arriving, but I won't be so lucky. I don't deserve to be.

I fucked up, and my father dropped me in it.

The truth should have come from my lips. That's what

makes this worse. That's what burns through my body more. The knowledge that I should have shared, but didn't.

Tilting my head back, I allow the heat of the sun to wash over me in an attempt to let it erase my sorrows, but there's no cure for the shit I'm feeling. By the time the guys are done with me, there will be no cure for what they put me through either.

Wings flap, once, twice, and it's the only warning I get as I turn to my right, watching Kryll shift as he lands beside me. He shakes off his cloak before ruffling his auburn hair. There's a lilt to the corner of his mouth, but it doesn't meet his eyes.

"All good?"

"It's perfect," he murmurs, rubbing at the back of his neck as he sighs.

"Where did you take them?" He finally looks my way, cocking a brow. "Fair enough," I grumble, taking the hint. "Are you ready to head back?"

"Are you ready to face everyone's wrath?"

I gulp, my spine stiffening as I meet the disappointment shining in his gaze. "No, but I don't have a choice."

He nods, silently agreeing with the downfall I know is coming.

Muttering the transportation enchantment under my breath, Kryll plants his hand firmly on my shoulder before the ground shifts beneath our feet. All too quickly, the fountain on campus comes into view, and the familiar surroundings take over.

My gaze flickers to the pathway that leads to the fae building before considering my usual path toward my room, but instead of going in either direction, I follow Kryll's heavy footsteps toward the vampire building.

The walk is quiet. Too quiet. There's only one way to get past this and it's to face it head on, and that starts with explaining myself. Well, attempting to explain myself, at least.

Stepping inside the vampire building, I take the stairs two at a time, cursing my father with every step. I want to blame it all on him, but my silence hasn't aided my innocence in all of this.

Is that a trait I get from him? Is that a part of him that runs through my veins? Am I just as foolish and tainted as him?

I fucking hope not.

All too quickly, Kryll raps his fist on Raiden's door, and it swings open a moment later.

"Oh, good, the liar is here," Raiden grunts, taking a step back to let us in.

"He is." Acknowledging myself as a liar is the first step to recovery, right?

"At least you're owning it, not even claiming some bullshit about omitting," Cassian adds, glaring at me as I step into Raiden's ridiculously large room.

I sink into the sofa closest to the door, bracing my elbows on my knees as I hide my face behind my hands. I need a minute. One whole second to gather my shit together before I force myself to sit back and meet their expectant stares.

"I don't think that would do me any good," I admit, making Raiden scoff as he collapses onto the sofa across from me.

"You'd be right." The bite to his tone and the sharpness of his jaw confirms he's beyond pissed, but it's no surprise.

"Are you actually this mad at him, or are you frustrated that Addi is mad at you, and you're redirecting all of that?" Cassian muses, perching himself on the arm of the sofa to my right, earning himself one of Raiden's signature death stares.

"You can shut the fuck up."

Touchy subject. Noted. Something clearly went down after we left, but I'm guessing now isn't the time for me to find out the details.

"How about we address one situation at a time?" Kryll asks, standing with his arms folded over his chest between the two sofas.

It's weird. I'm usually the one in his position, trying to calmly placate everyone, but not today, it seems. Today I'm the one in the hot seat.

"We can start with Brody," Raiden decides, completely shifting away from whatever drama he has with Addi right now.

All eyes turn to me, a heavy weight settling over the room before nestling itself deep into my gut. There's no point wasting more time with the thoughts that have been taking up far too much space at the back of my mind.

Taking a deep breath, I let the words slip from my lips. "I knew what they were planning with Vallie."

A weight shifts from my shoulders, but it doesn't leave entirely, confirming that expressing the truth now doesn't alleviate the mess I've created or my guilt.

"Why didn't you share that sooner?" Cassian asks, foot up on the sofa as he stares at me intently.

I rub my lips together, hating the fact that we're going to get deep on this, but there's no avoiding it. "Because I thought if I could just get my father to listen, he would realize how dumb it was."

Once upon a time, I told him everything. Once upon a time, he was an amazing father. Once upon a time feels like a distant dream, so far away that I question its authenticity now.

"But he wasn't listening," Kryll murmurs, and I hum. "No."

"So, why didn't you say something?" Raiden pushes, and I exhale, my breath deflating me as I avoid their gazes.

"Because I felt helpless."

The true weight of what I'd revealed shifts inside of me, the admission of a weakness lightening the world sitting on my shoulders. But what causes even more of a stir inside me is the calming silence that swirls around us.

I expect a jibe from Raiden or a grunt from Cassian. Shit, even a mutter from Kryll, but instead…there's none of that.

When I finally manage to lift my head, I find them all frowning, but there's no overwhelming outbursts of anger. Yet.

"You know this is all bullshit, right?" Kryll states, wiping a hand down his face. "Forcing fated mates is wrong," he adds for clarity, and I nod in agreement.

"Being mated to Vallie in any way at all is wrong," Raiden grunts, his jaw ticking even tighter.

"But to Addi?" Cassian asks, his words lingering in the air as a deeper silence descends over the room.

I can't deny the sense of hope that takes root in my chest. The idea of being connected to her in any way at all is consuming, but on that level? Fuck, that's something else entirely.

No one disagrees with his question. No one makes it sound absurd. Not even Kryll, the solitary shifter who refuses to admit anything when it comes to her.

But as much as the idea of connecting with Addi like

that offers me a blossom of hope, I know full well it's not an option. Especially not in the way they were attempting to make it happen. Forcing that on someone like Addi would only push her further away, which is the complete opposite of what I want with her.

It bundles my stomach in knots, but I express that fact to the guys. "Addi would never have responded well to that, especially under forced pretenses."

"Agreed," Cassian admits with a disgruntled sigh. "But she's hot when she's angry," he adds, making me snicker.

Raiden practically snorts. "She's hot when she's taking down the fucking council, not so hot when she's taking it out on me."

I jump at the opportunity to shift the topic of conversation, especially since they're not intent on burying me in my mistakes. Leaning forward again, I rub a hand through my hair. "I'm guessing she's pissed because you were followed while following her?" I ask, and his eyes widen.

"How did you figure that out?"

"How did you not?" I retort, brows pinching.

"It's beside the point," he grumbles, waving me off.

"It happened, and there's nothing we can do about it, but that doesn't change the fact that she's pissed at you," Kryll states, and Cassian nods in agreement.

"Facts."

Raiden glares at the wolf. "If we're airing all our secrets, it's probably Cassian's turn."

I turn to look at Cassian, noting the confusion on his face as he points at himself with a slack jaw.

"Me?"

"What were you doing on the Kenner compound with her last night?" Raiden asks, pushing to his feet. His shoulders roll back, his ego inflated by the height difference between him and Cassian since the latter is sitting.

Sometimes I can forgive Raiden for being a vampire. It wasn't his choice to be what he is, but in moments like this, when he uses classic vampire moves to flex his perceived superiority around him, it pisses me off.

"That's none of your business," Cassian bites, hands balling into fists on his lap. When no one turns away, he sighs. "She wanted to see her mother."

"She spoke with her?" I blurt in surprise, and he shakes his head.

"No."

"So what then?" Raiden pushes, and to my surprise, Cassian gives in.

"She just wanted to see her."

"She wanted to see her mother, who is apparently a wolf?" Kryll clarifies, and my gut twists, but before I can sink in my worry for Addi, I'm fixated on the way Cassian's shoulders sag and he dips his head.

"I noticed the lack of ears last night, but we hadn't put two and two together yet," he admits, making my chest clench.

"She's a half-breed," I murmur, and Cassian's gaze whips to me.

"Don't call her that." His jaw is clenched, anger vibrating in his eyes.

"I didn't."

"Just. Don't."

"She's a fae wolf. There's nothing wrong with that," I reiterate, and he rises to his feet.

"I didn't say there was."

I lift my hands in surrender, but it does nothing to calm him.

"I'm sorry." My words aren't much more than a whisper, but he must sense the truth in them because he, thankfully, takes a backward step.

Kryll clears his throat, taking a step toward the irritated wolf as I run my hands over my knees. "Did she say how she was feeling?" he asks, and Cassian shakes his head.

"All she said was how mad she was at Fangs over here."

"Will you stop calling me that?" Raiden grumbles, tugging at his hair. His distress is clear. Who would have thought it was because Addi was mad at him? It's half amusing, half concerning. Because I lied about something, and I get the feeling that doesn't put me in her good graces either.

"What do we do now?" I ask, wetting my dry lips as Kryll sighs.

"We give her space. Only a little, but we need to figure out how we push back on this. We all know that's not going to be the end of the trouble. But before all of that, we need it to be clear that we don't keep fucking secrets like this again," he states, eyes swirling, and I nod.

"How much space?" Raiden asks, eyebrows bunched in a mixture of dismay and anger.

"That's what you're focused on?"

He shrugs like there's nothing else to be concerned about, and it takes more than I care to admit to keep my snicker at bay.

"She gets until morning," Cassian decides, and no one disagrees.

"I can work with that," Raiden relents, making me scoff, despite my best efforts.

"Let's hope *she* can."

ADRIANNA

6

I shut the water off, my shoulders sagging with a defeat like I've never felt before. I don't even bother to lift my gaze from the tiled floor as I connect with my magic, effortlessly drying the beads of water from my body before I dress. My hair is twisted into a bun on top of my head as I step out of the stall into the communal bathroom.

The dripping of the shower is the only sound to comfort me and it does little to soothe the swirling emotions running rampant in my mind. Stepping toward the long vanity of sinks, I plant my palms on the marble as I lift my gaze.

The girl staring back at me in the mirror seems different. Is it possible to be more stressed than I already was? Apparently so. Shadows cast under my eyes, a reminder that my body is as exhausted as my mind.

Too much has happened in such a short period of time.

How has it only been a day? Not even. The sun has barely just set.

The trial.

Vallie's attack.

The kiss of death.

The Council.

Nora.

My father.

Fucking Nora.

My hands ball on the vanity, my knuckles growing whiter as I snarl at my reflection.

What the fuck have I caused?

The squeak of the bathroom door opening jars me from my thoughts, but it does nothing to rein in the anger flooding me.

"Get the fuck out," I roar, my face heating.

The door doesn't even open wide enough to reveal who is on the other side before it swings shut again. I'm certain I hear someone curse under their breath, but it doesn't register in my brain enough for me to care.

I try to take a deep breath, and another, and another.

Dropping my chin to my chest, I succumb to the helplessness consuming me.

They found them. They found my family, and it's all my fault.

I should have never given in and relented that day, not

even for a second. I didn't consider that I was putting them at risk. All I cared about was getting a glimpse of my sister and father, my two favorite people, and that selfishness drove them straight toward the chaos.

Fuck.

I should have never let my guard down. I had no idea Raiden was stalking me at the time, either, which is even more foolish of me.

Clenching my eyes closed, the muscles in my neck ache as tension locks in every limb.

Guilt.

Shame.

"Ahhh," I growl, bracing my arms over my head as my body tries to rid itself of the toxic feelings welling inside me, but it's useless. I'm going to feel them forever.

I hate it.

I hate that I can't go back and change it, just like the many other mistakes I've made in my life. Why do I continue to add to the list instead of learning from them?

Changing the past isn't an ability I have, but the future is still an option.

My muscles tighten, my arms cocooning me for a moment longer before I inhale sharply through my nose, holding my breath before I slowly exhale. I repeat the motion, only this time I drop my arms to my side, catching sight of my reflection again.

My family is safe now.

Safe from The Council...and me.

I trust that Kryll has taken them somewhere safe, and I trust that he will protect them. I'm not entirely sure why, but anything is better than being near me right now. I'm no good for them. I can't know where they are. It's not safe for them.

My heart aches, silently pleading with me to shift my perspective, just like my father taught me, but I need a minute longer to bask in the pain.

Wiping a hand down my face, I focus on the facts. They're not in danger now, which means I need to concentrate on the chaos closer to home instead.

Ice runs through my veins at the thought.

The Council...they tried to tether me to the guys.

Brody.

Cassian.

Kryll.

Raiden.

They wanted to force me to be fated mates with them.

Who the fuck does that? The Council, apparently.

And Brody knew? I can't even delve into that right now.

It doesn't matter who did and didn't know. What matters is that they were intent on doing it. Kenner's words echo in my mind and my fingers instinctively rise to my ears, running over the scars that have haunted me for as long as I can remember.

A vision of my mother flashes in my thoughts, making my stomach clench.

I'm a wolf. Or half of one, or so they told me. I don't know what to feel about that. I don't even know if I should believe it.

Does that mean Nora is too?

I look away from the mirror, hating the despair dancing in my eyes. A single thought of Nora triggers the self-loathing once again. The thought of what could have happened to my sister is a lasting pain I will never shake.

Turning from the vanity, I hurry for the door, slipping down the hall without interruption before I quickly shut my bedroom door behind me. Leaning back against it, I take short breaths as my eyelids fall closed.

I need to leave my emotions in the shower, keep my space clear of any negativity, but they still cling to my skin. I need to exert the energy that comes with feeling this way, but I'm too exhausted to truly do anything about it right now.

My hands clench as my eyes open. My chest rises and falls with an angry urgency as my gaze turns to the flash of red sitting on my desk.

The pretty petals taint my vision, turning everything crimson as rage takes over every part of me.

Flowers.

Raiden's fucking flowers.

A battle roar burns my lungs before it parts my lips, and I'm stomping across the room in the next moment.

Opening the window with a huff, the cool evening air does nothing to calm my rising temperature.

I can't think. I can only act.

My fingers press into the vase, and the pretty scent of the roses burns like acid, fueling the fire inside me before I launch them through the open window.

The telling sound of shattering glass swirls in my ears as I lean through the open space to look at the mess. Blinking, the rage-induced tint to my vision subsides as I watch the flowers roll down the path with the wind as the broken glass shimmers under the glow of the moon.

I had hoped to feel relief from the euphoric sound and the knowledge that Raiden was no longer in my space, but instead, all I'm left with is a deeper wave of sadness.

ADRIANNA

7

Cool air blows over my skin as I frown, exhaustion still clinging to my bones. Opening my eyes isn't easy, but after a few tries, the sun leaking in through my open bedroom window is finally bearable.

Groggily wiping the loose tendrils of hair off my face, I force myself to sit up, glancing at the time with a groan as my alarm starts to go off. I swing my legs over the side of the bed, swiftly turning off the treacherous noise, but the second the silence takes over the room, my mind is flooded with yesterday's events.

A purple glint from my nightstand draws my attention, but instead of reaching for it, I reach for the spot on my neck where the amethyst had pierced my flesh. I had considered putting it back in yesterday to maintain the fucked up charade, but I'm not playing these games any longer. Now that my family is safe, my priority has to be protecting myself, and if that means that Dean Bozzelli learns that I can get out of her hold, then so be it.

Today is going to leave me on edge, more so than usual, but at least I will have access to all of my powers.

The vibrating sound from the top drawer of my nightstand makes me pause before I slowly open it to see the intrusive device inside.

I shouldn't be surprised to see Nora's name flashing across my cell phone screen, but it somehow manages to send a shock through me. I consider the idea of ignoring her call, but the worry that something may be wrong wins, and I'm answering a moment later.

"Addi? Are you there? We're safe. He brought us—"

"Don't tell me," I blurt, cutting her off, and the sharp intake of breath that comes through the line tells me I've pissed her off.

"What?"

"I can't know, Nora," I murmur, pinching the bridge of my nose as I sense her irritation quickly rising.

"Why?"

"Because I put you in danger, I won't do that again," I state, sitting tall on my bed as I absorb my own words, willing them to become reality.

"That wasn't you, Ad—"

"Nora." The warning is clear, but so is her frustration.

"Get your head out of your ass, Addi. And whatever pointed look is on your face right now, drop it," she snaps, and I hear my father splutter over his breath in the background.

"Nora."

"What, Dad? She's doing that self-righteous crap she always pulls, and I'm not taking it. It will be no good doing all of this to protect me when I inevitably stop talking to you forever for being a bitch," she threatens, making my eyes widen in surprise as my father remains just as shocked at her straight-talking outburst.

"Nora."

"What? I'm not wrong," she insists, and I sigh.

"I love you, Nora," I breathe, earning a scoff through the line.

"If you loved me, you would hear me."

My head rears back. "I do."

"*No*. You *don't*."

I hear movement through the call, but since we're not video calling, I have no idea what's happening until my father clears his throat.

"Give her time, Addi."

Did she leave? Fuck.

"She's right," I breathe, willing to admit the truth. I'm definitely overprotective of her, forgetting that she does know how to handle herself.

"She always is," my father muses, making me roll my eyes.

I hate that she's that mad at me, but my mind drifts to the fact that it's just my father on the other end of the line right now. "While it's just you, there's something I want to ask."

"You can ask me anything, Addi," he offers softly, thankfully not on the same mission as Nora to tell me where he is.

Taking a deep breath, I swipe my tongue over my bottom lip as the words lodge in my throat. He waits patiently for me, like always, until I can gather enough strength to say it.

"Am I a half-breed?"

Silence greets me for what feels like an eternity until he speaks. "You are Princess Adrianna Reagan."

My lips purse. "I know that, but—"

"But nothing," he insists, giving me the same treatment I just gave Nora, and that makes me even more mad at myself.

"Dad."

"Addi."

"Don't hide this from me. Please."

My cell phone makes a noise, and I glance at the screen to see the request for a video call. A moment later, my father's face fills the screen, pained eyes and all.

I know it. I know it in every inch of his expression.

"I'm a wolf," I breathe, stirring something in my chest as he offers me a wobbly smile in return.

"I didn't know," he murmurs, glancing away from the screen.

"What?"

"*That* was the pinnacle of my downfall," he admits, shaking his head as he continues to avoid my stare.

"What was?"

"I was blinded by love." His eyes latch onto mine for a beat before he hangs his head.

"You're going to have to explain it a little straighter, Dad," I mutter, and he thankfully settles his eyes on me again.

"For a long time, it was declared that the royal bloodline would sign into an arranged marriage, forging fated mates to lead the kingdom with an almighty strength. It worked too, until me, because I fell in love with your mother." He looks away from the camera, but there's a wistful glint in his eyes. "She was shy, with a huge heart and pointed ears," he explains, making my chest tighten. "We were married quickly, the fated mates link connecting us together. It didn't take long for you to make your appearance," he muses, turning back to me.

"You're welcome. Imagine if you'd had all of Nora's sass first? I would never have existed," I tease, attempting to lighten the pain and darkness overwhelming him. The corner of his mouth tips up just enough to acknowledge my words, but it doesn't have the desired effect.

"It's only now, when I look back, that I can see that she became distant. Disappearing for long periods of time…I didn't know until that fateful night."

My hand lifts to touch my ears instinctively. "How?"

"Kenner came knocking," he breathes, and I lose his eye contact again.

"What for?" That's what I've never understood all this time, but now, it's slowly piecing together.

"He came for the power he felt he deserved after his plan had come to fruition."

"His plan?"

"To plant a Kenner wolf in the castle." His eyes pinch as he looks back at me. "She shifted before my eyes." I gape in surprise as a ghost of a smile touches his lips. "She was beautiful, but it was clear she wasn't mine. Not my Queen. Not anymore, maybe never at all. There was something different."

"Dad," I rasp, my chest aching at his pain.

"I asked her to come with me." He shakes his head. "I *begged* her."

"Dad," I whisper, choking on the truth.

"I had been aware there was a traitor in my inner circle, but the moment I realized it was her, I didn't care anymore.

We had to leave, and I was too blinded by my love for her and our family to see the kingdom crumbling around me. It was too late."

"And she didn't want to," I confirm, and he sags. "I'm sorry."

"Don't be, Addi. You never did anything but be you, just as I wished. But to answer your question, you are a half-breed, even though I despise that terminology. You are half fae, half wolf, and I've never been more proud." His words warm my aching heart, but there's still more to understand.

"Why haven't I ever—"

He offers me a soft smile. "Honestly, I don't know. I kept waiting, but nothing happened. Your mother always told me that it would come when you were ready, but I'm not sure if they did something to stop it from happening," he admits, making my spine stiffen.

I'm fed up with people doing things to my body without my consent.

A knock comes from my bedroom door, making my father clear his throat. "Go, focus on you. I've got us covered here. I'll see if I can find anything out for you."

"Thank you." I smile, despite the pain glistening in my eyes.

"I love you, Addi."

"I love you too."

The screen falls dark a breath later as another knock comes from my door.

Flora has no patience.

Connecting with my magic, I effortlessly change into my uniform, shoes and all, while shifting my hair into a tight braid. By the time I reach the door, I'm ready for the day. Even if it's only physically. Mentally, I'm not ready for anything.

I swing the door open, lips parted, ready to comment on her lack of patience, when I'm stalled in place.

There isn't one person.

There are four.

And none of them are Flora.

Brody.

Cassian.

Raiden.

Kryll.

Fuck this.

I'm not dealing with their shit before breakfast. Not today.

A breeze flutters over my body, reminding me my bedroom window is still wide open, and I decide to use it to my advantage.

Slamming my bedroom door shut behind me, I turn and run for the opening. The sensation of freefalling takes my breath as I hurtle toward the ground, but before I accidentally hurt myself, I connect with the wind around me and soften my fall. Landing safely on my feet, I straighten my cloak, glancing back at the fae building with a grin on my lips. I flick my wrist, channeling my magic to shut my bedroom window before I take off toward the academy.

Excitement tingles along my skin at escaping them, but it doesn't last long as the fountain has barely come into view when I'm stopped in my tracks.

"Adrianna Reagan. My office. Now."

ADRIANNA

8

My nostrils flare with irritation as my hands ball into fists. Bozzelli starts to saunter away without a backward glance, like she didn't spoil my already gloomy day. All the while, Fairbourne peers at me with his brows pinched together in concern. I can sense there's plenty he wants to say, but with Bozzelli in hearing range, it's not the best idea to discuss anything. Not even the weather.

He nods, the only signal to confirm I need to follow her command, before he moves to follow her.

I suppose I should do the same.

Fuck.

Running my tongue over my teeth, trying to hold back the snark threatening to burst from my lips, I glance over my shoulder to find a line of four men watching me intently.

Kryll. Raiden. Brody. Cassian.

My anger toward them shouldn't warm my veins. The lies and secrets that are intertwined between us all should turn me off, but they don't. Nothing about them should draw me in, yet there's a pull in my chest beckoning me closer.

Maybe stepping through the door instead of launching myself out of the window would have been the better option. It's too late to know for sure.

I can't seem to catch a break, regardless of which direction I take.

Before I can whip my gaze away and follow the dean to my impending doom, Raiden is blocking my path with his enhanced speed playing to his advantage. His back is to me, his arm twisted behind him so his fingers can grasp my wrist. I pull, needing out of his hold right the fuck now, but it only tightens his grip.

"Where are you taking her?" he snarls, earning a disgruntled sigh from the dean.

"That's none of your business, Mr. Holloway," she states, pausing her steps. She stands out like a neon sign in her vivid pink suit. She looks ready to work in an office with her pristine cut skirt and silk shirt, but the expression on her face resembles something only found on a battlefield.

"I beg to differ," Raiden snaps back, not faltering under her glare.

A flash of pink dances in the wind, and a moment later, the immaculate woman is right in front of him. She bares her teeth in anger as she presses two fingers firmly into the side of Raiden's head. His grip on my hand falls slack as he falls to his knees, crying out in pain. The noise is etched in horror for a split second as I gape in shock.

"What the fuck?" Cassian grunts, but before he can intercept, Raiden is pushing back.

His growl fills the air as he forces himself back to his feet. His hand finds my skin once again as he glares at Bozzelli.

"You can do what you want to me, but the last time you took Adrianna, you implanted a damn amethyst in her, and I won't give you the opportunity to do it again," he bites, and I feel a tremble at the feeling of his touch against my flesh.

"How dare you," Bozzelli snarls, lifting her hand again, but before she can touch him, I'm moving.

"Don't."

One single word from my lips. It's not a threat; it's a promise. One that catches me by surprise as much as it does Bozzelli. Even with my other hand in Raiden's hold, I stand unwavering, ready to defend the man that I truly hate right now.

Bozzelli's gaze latches on to my hand on her, not a single word slipping from her lips as I silently release my hold. Her jaw tightens with every passing second, her eyes drilling into mine as she turns a crimson shade of anger I've never seen before.

I hate that I defend him even when I despise him, but my hatred toward her surpasses it.

"Adri—"

"I'm here for that reason, Mr. Holloway," Fairbourne swiftly interjects, coming into view behind Bozzelli, who takes a small step back. It's clear there's retaliation dancing in her eyes, but having a staff member present seems to make her determination wane. For now, at least.

"You better be," the irritating vampire snarls, his fangs elongating as I gape at him. His eyes flash with a barely contained rage that makes my spine stiffen when he turns his attention to me. "I'll wait for you." The words are far softer, almost lost to the breeze that circles us, but instead of melting the walls I've put up to separate us, it only reinforces them.

"Don't."

I yank my wrist from his hold, stumbling back a step into Fairbourne, who quietly keeps me on my feet.

"Miss Reagan, let's go. Before punishments worsen," Bozzelli warns, her glare snapping between Raiden and me, begging for him to challenge her again, but this time, I march off with her, not daring to glance back over my shoulder as we hurry down the path.

I feel every ounce of distance as I place it between me and them. The four of them act as a faulty anchor that wants to hold me in place and keep me from getting lost in the waves, but it's too late for that. I have too many emotions swirling inside of me. Emotions I've never freaking felt before, and I don't know how to handle them.

I'm torn.

So fucking torn.

Tamping it down, I keep my gaze fixed ahead as I remain a step behind Bozzelli and Fairbourne, anticipation flickering over my skin as we wind our way through the corridors until Bozzelli's office comes into view.

I definitely should have stepped out of my bedroom door and dealt with the assholes that are plaguing my mind. It may have kept me from this moment a little longer. I hoped to not find myself here again, but it seems that's now out of my hands. Succumbing to this bitch is going to be the death of me, I'm certain.

The bleak walls feel like they're closing in on me as the door slams shut behind me. The seat I don't have fun memories of stands tall before me as my pulse rings in my ears. My fingers itch to run over my skin where the amethyst had rested, but I fight against it.

"Take a seat."

I purse my lips, glaring at the dean who does nothing but make my life hell as I consider my options. Take a seat on what can only be described as a death trap and get this bullshit over and done with, or drag this whole thing out while avoiding the tension rising inside of me.

As much as the latter appeals to me, the point of this meeting outweighs it all, and I'm acutely aware I'm on thin ice with Bozzelli right now since I put my hands on her only a few minutes ago.

Perching on the edge of the seat, bile burns in my throat, but it all goes unnoticed by Bozzelli, who laces her fingers together, bracing her elbows on the desk that separates us. Fairbourne remains silent as he leans against the wall beside the window that sits perfectly behind Bozzelli, casting a glow of light over the dean in an unholy shot straight for the devil.

"Would you like to explain what happened yesterday?"

Yesterday? Where the fuck do we even begin with the twenty-four hours that trampled on my life?

"Which part?" I ask with a scoff, making Bozzelli's glare darken as she leans forward.

"Do you find this funny?"

I lean back, despite the desire to run from the hot seat beneath me, as my eyes widen. "I find none of it funny, but I get the feeling you're asking me a specific question, and the entirety of my day yesterday was a clusterfuck, so I'm going to need you to help narrow it down for me."

Bozzelli shakes her head, disgust making her nostrils

flare and jaw tic. "Drama surrounds you, Adrianna. I don't care for the rest of your issues. I want to know why a highly regarded vampire is with the medical team fighting for her life after what you did to her."

"She's not dead?" I blurt, my eyes managing to widen even further as the dean's pupils dilate with unwavering anger.

"You should be thankful she isn't."

"I'm struggling to see how so," I admit with a shrug. Fairbourne wipes a hand down his face, disbelief flickering over his features as a twinkle of awe remains in the corner of his eyes. I'm certain there's a smirk hidden behind his hand, but I can't be certain.

"I won't allow a murderer to walk among us." Bozzelli's statement is clear but also bullshit, and she knows it.

"Isn't that half of the reason why we're here? The trial was literally set with the pretense that some may not make it out alive. I defended myself when attacked. I had to seek medical treatment from a mage yesterday, too," I snap, fingers pressing into the arm of the chair in a failed attempt to contain my emotions.

My admission only seems to please her more.

"Ah, I'm aware. You were taken off campus, which is also against the rules." She preens, pleased to be serving my ass on a platter of made-up rules that mean nothing right now.

"But it's not against the rules for Vallie to purposely attack me, so I would be taken to the council facility in a grand attempt to force me to be fated mates with some other students in attendance. Tell me, Dean Bozzelli, was that under your order or under your nose?"

Her knuckles whiten as she sits tall in her seat, a murderous stare burning bright in her eyes. "How preposterous."

I grin, unable to remain calm and collected as my father has always taught me. "That's a pretty big word for someone who likes to act dumb."

"How dare you," she snarls, launching to her feet. Her chair clatters to the floor behind her, coming to a stop beside Fairbourne, who plasters a hand over his mouth, failing to smother the smirk on his lips. "I put the amethyst in your body, don't think I won't…"

"What…this thing?" I ask, way too fucking sure of myself as I dig the purple gem from my pocket, twirling it between my fingers. I'm pushing my luck. I know I am. I saw what she was capable of doing to Raiden, and it's not a situation I want to find myself in.

"You could have it back, but I don't like the thought of knowing it will be placed in another student without their consent."

"You violated your punishment." She jabs a finger in my direction as I shake my head at her.

"No, you violated *me* when you placed this into my flesh." My heart beats rapidly in my chest, echoing in my ears. "Now, are you going to do anything other than throw your weight around because someone was injured during a trial, or are we done here?"

"I think we're done for now," Fairbourne declares, speaking for the first time, only to earn Bozzelli's rage. If looks could kill, we'd both be dead right now.

"This isn't the end of it, Miss Reagan," she promises, adjusting the lapels of her suit jacket, and I snicker, but there's not a single ounce of humor to it.

"I'm highly aware of that, but as always, I'll rise above it for the good of the kingdom."

ADRIANNA

9

The click of the door shutting behind me offers no refuge. I'm tense, wound tight with a bundle of emotions that I can't decipher enough to try and squash them.

I may have just placed an even bigger target on my back, one of my own doing with my reckless actions toward the dean herself, but I refuse to regret it. I won't falter. I won't show fear. I won't roll over for them anymore. Not after they put my family's safety in jeopardy. The same family that encourages me to take a calmer approach. My father's words of wisdom tingle the edge of my mind, but I'm done listening to the sensible option right now.

A bell rings, announcing the start of my first class, and I curse under my breath, straightening before I head down the hallway. I don't even make it to the corner to turn toward my classroom before I hear my name. The deep tone of a man makes me pause, but I quickly shake away my cloudy thoughts and turn to find Fairbourne heading toward me.

I can't stop myself from peering around him to make sure Bozzelli isn't also there, and I'm relieved to find him alone.

He nods for me to continue. "Let's not hang around long enough for her to change her mind," he mutters, falling into step beside me.

My eyebrows rise in question as I look up at him. He looks exhausted. The man needs a good night's sleep. Multiple, if the bags under his eyes are anything to go by. He looks about as shitty as I feel.

"Change her mind on what?" I ask when he doesn't immediately expand on his statement, earning a soft smile as he sighs.

"On letting us walk out of the damn office."

"She can't—"

"She can do whatever she pleases, Addi. Her chances of receiving any repercussions are slim to none; don't forget that," he warns, uncertainty making his eyebrows furrow.

"Why did she call me in there to talk about Vallie? I acted in self-defense. Is Vallie going to get questioned about this too?" Anger vibrates through my veins as I keep my gaze locked straight ahead. The few students that fill the hallways step aside, clearly sensing the fuck off vibes that dance over my skin.

"I think we both already know the answer to that." There's a hint of humor in Fairbourne's tone that catches me off guard. When I look at him, I find a huge grin stretching over his face, which is a stark contrast to the man who just followed me out of Bozzelli's office. I tilt my head in question, and he takes the hint. "Of all the Reagans before you, I swear, that was the best show of defiance I've ever seen. If your father were here, his jaw would be dragging along the floor in awe," he muses, making my heart skip a beat as I blink up at him.

"My father would likely give me a lecture about remaining calm and collected," I correct, and he shakes his head.

"There's a time and place for calm and collected, and there's a time and place for strength and defiance. You definitely have the gift of understanding when each is needed." I gape at him, speechless, as his words wash over me. "If you acted calm and collected in that room, you would have given her the upper hand, something she's had enough of, don't you agree?"

I nod, still unable to find my tongue as we come to a stop outside the class I need to be in. My lips twist as I peer up at him, a glimmer of pride shimmering in his eyes, and I don't know how to accept it. Distracting from the conversation, I redirect the topic to him.

"Do you want me to remove your kiss of death?"

His smile softens, no longer reaching his eyes as he shakes his head. "There will be a time and place for that too, and I don't think this is it yet."

"Soon," I promise, and he nods.

"Soon." He reaches a hand toward me in what almost looks like an attempt at an embrace, but I don't move and he quickly retracts his arm. "Let me explain to the professor why you're late so you don't have any trouble," he offers, turning on his heels and entering the room without a moment's pause, leaving me to scurry in after him.

My mind is still whirling from his comments as my gaze lands on Raiden's. The red cloak draped over his shoulders should be the only red flag I need with this guy, but it seems I have the ability to wave it away too easily.

"Are you okay?" he mouths, jaw tight as he rakes his eyes over the length of me a few times.

"I'm fine," I grumble, reminding myself that I definitely still hate his ass. One single thought of Nora and my heart is tight and drenched in horror, reaffirming my feelings toward him.

Flora gives me a slight wave, and I remember that she has no idea of everything that's happened in such a short span of time. It's a conversation I'm not dreading either. I know she will be the support I need, but not until I've been the support she needs. I haven't forgotten the beginning of the week and the weird vibe between her and Arlo.

"Take a seat, Miss Reed," the professor states as Fairbourne leaves the room, and I do just that, nestling between Brody and Kryll while avoiding both of their gazes.

Brody's arm instantly slinks around the back of my chair while a tatted arm inches closer to me on the desk. It's instinctive to push back, demand space, and put distance between us, but instead, I keep my mouth shut. Their proximity is almost…calming. I don't know what to make of it, but I decide being surrounded by them isn't a bad thing.

The professor proceeds with the class, discussing what the castle signifies to the kingdom and how its importance is in all of our hearts, rooting us to Floodborn. The words go in one ear and straight out of the other. Nothing sticks as I feel myself shrink in the room.

From the mighty fae that just stood toe to toe with Bozzelli to a crippled student among the masses in a matter of minutes.

The feeling doesn't shift either, weighing heavier and heavier on my shoulders as one class floats into another. The four walls that surround me change, but the feeling inside of me doesn't. Anything on the agenda today in these classes is lost on me as one becomes another and another.

I feel more out of place now than I did when my true identity was revealed to the academy. I know things I didn't then. Things that changed me at my core. Things I don't want to admit but can't stop myself from acknowledging.

With every passing moment, I feel myself disconnecting from the world around me, and my mind starts to play nasty tricks, consuming every part of me.

My mother is a wolf.

A Kenner wolf.

My father a fae.

A royal fae.

I'm...*what*?

A product of love? Impossible. Not with how everything unraveled from there.

A half-breed? The term alone makes my blood boil.

I'm still the same underneath it all. I know that deep down somewhere, but here, at this moment, with my mind tormenting my every breath, I don't feel the same.

I need to rid myself of these thoughts.

Clenching my eyes closed, I try to ground myself in the room, but nothing is sticking. The countdown to lunchtime looms, promising me a moment to breathe among the madness, but it feels as though time is standing still.

I don't know who I am. I don't know if the cloak draped

over my shoulders is the right color.

Gray.

Green.

Gray *and* green?

I don't know anything.

Fuck. Fuck. Fuck. Fuck. Fuck.

I've never truly felt like I belonged anywhere other than with my family, but now it's even worse. I don't know how to make it all better.

A hand clamps down on my thigh, startling me from my intrusive thoughts, and my head whips up to find Kryll offering me a soft smile, but I don't miss the way his eyebrows are furrowed together.

"Are you doing okay, Princess?" his voice is raspy as he whispers.

I try to gulp down the rising stress, but all I can do is shake my head. His grip on my thigh tightens, bringing me a little closer to the present, and I manage to take a deep breath, followed by another.

My lips part in an attempt to express what's going on in my mind, but my thoughts are cut off by the shrill bell that rings through the air.

I slump back in my seat, gasping with each rise and fall of my shoulders.

What the fuck is wrong with me?

I can't seem to get my tongue to work enough to ask it

out loud as Kryll rises to his feet. He offers me his hand, his swirling tattoos luring me in, and I'm acutely aware of Brody's presence beside me.

A flash of red in front of me confirms Raiden's close too and it's enough to push me over the brink I've been so desperately clinging to. But in the blink of an eye, a whoosh of green swipes across my vision.

Nausea radiates from my stomach, an all-too-familiar feeling at this point, and a moment later, the world is spinning around me as I stand on wobbly legs.

Blinking, it takes a few tries to get my gaze to settle on the tense jawline of an angry wolf.

Cassian.

"Let's talk, Alpha."

CASSIAN

10

My muscles twitch with an emotion I'm struggling to place or even contain, and the longer I stand still, taking no action, the worse it gets. Surely it will subside now. It has to.

I watched her trail after Bozzelli this morning, succumbing to whatever Hell she was ready to unleash upon her. I watched her return, shoulders slumped as if the weight she carries has increased. I didn't think that was possible. I've also watched her retreat into herself with every passing moment.

I'm done.

So fucking done with it.

Bracing my hands on the small of her back, I can't stop the sigh falling from my lips as I peer down at her. She's wavering in my hold, the motion affecting her like usual, and it's almost amusing.

"How sick are you feeling? Am I good to let go?"

"Don't mock me," she grumbles, pushing against my chest with a huff, but her fingers quickly curl into my t-shirt as she attempts to keep her balance.

"No mocking," I breathe, planting my hands on her hips to help steady her, but it only serves to earn me an eye roll.

She takes a step back, and with great reluctance, I let her go, lifting my hands slightly in surrender. Scrubbing a hand down her face, she lifts her face to the sky, a small break of the sunlight shining through the trees looming above.

"Didn't we have a conversation about how you should not do that to me anymore?" she states, lowering her gaze to quirk a brow at me.

I'm not encouraging the prolonging of her griping, so I shrug, turning away from her. "I don't recall."

"Of course you don't. Do you recall anything at all?" she snarks, continuing to push, but I see the falter in her eyes when my gaze whips to hers, heat burning in my irises.

"I recall how sweet your pussy is."

Her jaw hits the floor as she glares at me.

Good. She's present and alert. Her reactions are everything. Her demeanor is shifting. Long gone is the shell that encased the woman before me just moments ago, and in its place is a burning inferno.

A firecracker.

A warrior.

My alpha.

"What are we doing here, Cassian?" She peers around at the woods, the stone footpath a short distance away, and the familiar fallen log a step behind her.

"Take a seat."

"Why?" Her eyebrows pinch together in confusion as she looks to me for answers.

"Can you just take a damn seat?" I grumble, forever torn over the fact that she pushes back at me at every turn. There's a part of it that gets my dick hard, but the other part begs me to break her, to dominate her into submission. There's a fat chance of that ever happening. She's too strong, but maybe in the bedroom...

"Can you watch your tone?" she bites, pulling me back to the present, and I roll my eyes.

"No."

"Then maybe I can't take a damn seat," she spits, folding her arms over her chest as her gaze darkens.

I move before she can even acknowledge a single beat, cupping her pussy through her pants. Her gasp echoes in my ears and I relish in the sound. It has a way of igniting the wolf in me in a way nothing else ever has.

"Sit down, Alpha." I peer at her through my lashes, catching sight of her hands balling at her sides as she pouts her sweet fucking lips.

"Doesn't the alpha make the rules?"

"It's not a rule, it's an order."

Her pupils dilate, despite the contained rage glistening in her emerald eyes.

"I don't do too well with them," she warns, and I tighten my hold on her core.

"I recommend getting used to them," I breathe, my gaze flickering to her lips for a beat before locking back on her alluring eyes. She offers the promise of desire in those pools, yet whenever I get too close, one of us hesitates to jump.

"Or what, you'll keep grinding your palm against my clit? Oh, no." She lifts her hand to her lips, fake gasping as her eyes twinkle with mischief.

"It's a pity your mouth isn't as sweet as your pussy. Instead, you're full of sass. A little bitter if you ask me. Now, are you going to sit your ass down or not?" We're so close now that the tips of our noses ghost over one another.

She tilts her head, her lips grazing over mine as she talks.

"I'm bitter to the core, Cassian. Don't forget it."

I shiver at her words, my cock twitching to life, desperate to feel her. I lift my hand to her cheek, ready to take control, but she's out of my grasp instantly, lowering herself to the log with a smug grin touching her lips.

That beautiful, wicked—

Fuck.

I hate games, but hers...hers I live for.

I'm gone before I give in to my desires, instead focusing on completing the mission I set out for myself before I'm back in front of her, sandwiches in hand.

Two perfect turkey and Swiss sandwiches, warmed and wrapped in foil. One in each hand. I stare in amusement as she glances between them both.

"Lunch."

"Lunch," I repeat, offering one out to her as I take the spot to her right. She continues to look between the sandwich and me, but I'm too hungry for this cute stare-off. I unwrap my sandwich and take a bite, groaning at the deliciousness that always comes from Janie's.

Wordlessly, she follows suit. We sit in a comfortable silence that sparks a calmness through my body that I'm not all that familiar with. It's her, I know it is, but I don't know how or why, just that I only ever feel it in her presence.

Even then, it's fleeting. We spend most of our time angry or spent.

Mainly angry *and* spent.

In the best possible way there is.

"Why?" Her word is little more than a whisper on the breeze, one I'm not sure I would have heard without my enhanced hearing, but it's a question I don't have the answer to.

"I don't know," I admit, scrunching the foil remnants in my hand as I chance a glance at her out of the corner of my eye.

"You don't know." Her eyebrows are raised.

"Nope."

She presses her lips together, eyeing me with a level of uncertainty that is almost unsettling, and I haven't even opened my mouth to say what I brought her here to discuss yet.

"So, what's eating away at you?"

"You're asking *me* that? You?" she blusters, wiping the crumbs from her hands as her eyes remain locked on me. Instead of responding, I turn to her with a pointed look, earning me a sigh as she turns away. "Nothing."

"Bull. Shit."

She scoffs, shaking her head as she stares through the trees, intent on looking everywhere but at me. "Nothing I want to talk to you about."

"Well, I'm glad you clarified, but that doesn't mean I give a shit about who you would prefer to have this talk with."

"Good to know." I can't see her eyes, but I know she

rolled them to the back of her head. "So," I push when she doesn't miraculously unravel her torments on me.

"So," she repeats, clearing her throat as she slouches in her seat on the log.

"Dumb doesn't suit you."

"Thanks." She preens, lips twisting with amusement, but I don't focus on it, not when I can still see the shadow in her eyes.

"Is it worry over your family?"

Silence greets me.

"Is it Raiden being…Raiden?"

Her nose twitches, but still nothing.

"Is it whatever Bozzelli said?"

It's a long shot, but the stillness that continues to greet me confirms that she didn't falter under that bitch's threats.

My jaw tics, the options diminishing to almost nothing as I assess her. I'm shocked I've come up with so many reasons already, but thinking of any others is growing even more difficult. Except for one thought.

"Is it the whole wolf thing?" Her spine stiffens, confirming what's gotten under her skin the most. "It's the wolf thing." She looks off into the distance, avoiding my gaze even more. I try to see the situation through her eyes, but I can't see past the end of my own fucking nose. There's no point wasting further time on it when I could just ask her instead. "What about it is causing you issues?"

She snickers, her nostrils flaring as she shakes her head. "What part *isn't* causing me issues might be the easier question," she grumbles, and I grip her chin, immediately pulling her gaze to mine. Her eyelids fall to half-mast, sadness seeping from her, so I tighten my hold, forcing her to look me in the eyes.

"Whatever you're worrying about, we can make it all go away. Talk to me and maybe it will help you wrap your head around it." It makes sense in my head, but saying it out loud...fuck.

"How am I supposed to wrap my head around the fact that my mother is a wolf, making me...whatever I am? It changes everything about me." I can't tell if the words are directed at me or herself. Her eyes might be on mine, but she's not focused.

"How?" I grunt, desperate to bring her back to the present.

"What?"

"How does it change everything about you?"

She blinks. Once. Twice. Her eyes settle on mine, a frown pulling her eyebrows together. "It just does."

"Be specific," I push, watching her nostrils flare with irritation.

"Back off, Cassian." She knocks my hand away, but her success is short-lived when my hold comes back stronger.

"I'm not going anywhere until you tell me what the

issue is." My grip on her chin tightens, making her jaw fall slack, but she still doesn't falter.

"I'm not saying there's an issue. I'm saying the rug has been pulled out from under me and I don't know how to stand on my own two feet right now. Apparently, I'm half-wolf, yet it's never triggered anything inside of me. How is that even possible? Where am I even supposed to find my place here, at the academy?"

There it is. It hangs heavy on her shoulders, tainting the air around her.

My teeth grind together. "You think somebody did something on purpose?"

She shrugs. "It's the only option I can come up with, and my father was even more unsure," she admits, lowering her internal walls just an inch.

"He knew?"

"He knew," she whispers, a small hint of disappointment on her tongue.

"How does that make you feel?" I want to know. I want to make it better. I want to take it all away.

Despite the burning desire inside of me, she shakes her head. "I can't delve into that as well when I'm already hanging on by a thread."

"If you leaned on me, maybe it wouldn't feel so heavy," I murmur, my pulse ringing in my ears as my claws sit just beneath the surface, desperate to rip the answers from her.

"The level of stability you think you have is almost amusing," she says with a scoff, jaw tightening beneath my grip.

"Don't disregard this, Addi. Don't disregard me."

The air thickens around us, my words hang in the air as I silently plead for more from her, but it's not words I get.

It's her lips.

ADRIANNA

11

I don't know whether I want him to shut up or if I just want the press of his lips against mine, but here I am, losing myself to him once again.

Not because of his growly presence.

Not because of the way he grips my pussy oh so perfectly.

Not because of the burning in his eyes that vibrates through the grip he has on my chin.

No.

It's because of his fucking words.

Cassian's. Words.

It can't be real, but it's impossible not to deepen our kiss.

His grip on my chin tightens as his free hand finds its way to my core again, parting my thighs, even from this angle, rendering me powerless in his hold as our lips meld together.

There's nothing light about each pass of our mouths, but they somehow get stronger, harsher, needier.

My palms press against his chest, his pecs firm beneath my touch as my fingers curl into his t-shirt. I should push him away, that's what my brain is saying, but my body has a different idea altogether.

More. More. More.

Heat consumes me as Cassian's grip on my chin finally loosens, but it's only so he can wrap his hand around the back of my neck, controlling me even more.

His teeth rake over my bottom lip, earning a desperate groan from my lips as I try to nip him back but fail miserably. It doesn't stop me from attempting again and again, powerless to his strength as he snickers.

"You're feral, just like a wolf. Hot to the core, just like a wolf. Mine. Just like a wolf. It all makes sense now," he rasps, making my heart race as I force my eyes open, sluggishly blinking at him in confusion.

"What does?"

"You. Me. Fae. Wolf. Half-wolf." He cements each word with his lips on mine, melting what little of my brain was working.

"Can you say that in a complete sentence? I don't understand caveman, or cavewolf in your case."

His gaze latches onto mine, his tongue sweeping across his bottom lip, making my thighs press together as I wait expectantly in my lust-induced haze for a response.

"It makes sense why you're my alpha."

"I'm not your alpha."

"You are…in here."

Before I can decipher where *here* is, exactly, he crushes his lips to mine.

We're all hands and mouths, claiming, accepting, tugging desperately at one another as the world melts away.

All of my problems, my concerns, and my darkness fall away.

The first press of his hand underneath my t-shirt raises goosebumps in his wake, and a moment later, my back hits the ground with a thud, but the pain doesn't register as I continue to deepen our connection.

There's no gentleness, no sweetness, no delicacy, just raw desire and need.

My cloak twists awkwardly around my neck, stuttering my breaths as I gasp. Cassian eases up on my lips as he hovers above me, the feel of the prickly grass beneath me finally registering. His gaze is dark and heated, but it's not fixed on me. He's staring at my pebbled nipples that are begging for attention.

He lowers his head slowly, a complete contrast to the man ravaging me moments earlier, but the bite around my taut peaks is something sinister. I cry out, my back arching up off the ground as I scramble to hold on. To what, I don't know, but every time I sink my fingers into the grass, I tug too hard, leaving the green blades in my palms.

"That's it, Alpha. Show me how much you want me," he breathes, earning a glare.

"I don't," I grumble, lying despite my actions, and he knows it.

His palm is curled around my pussy in the next breath, grinding against my needy clit, and my eyes roll back with pleasure. "I bet if I remove the fabric between us right now, I'd find you wet and wanting."

I shake my head, unable to draw the lie from my lips, but the grin that curls the corner of his mouth tells me he's more than willing to prove me wrong.

Using his enhanced abilities, I barely take a breath before a cool breeze drifts over my exposed skin, and I realize my pants are gone, along with my boots and panties. He stares at me, hunger burning bright in his forest-green eyes as I lay naked from the waist down.

"The devil shouldn't look this tempting," he murmurs, his Adam's apple bobbing as he devours me with his eyes.

Unclasping my cloak, I miss the sharp pull against my skin, but it's worth it to rid the rest of the clothes from my body. I don't care where we are. I'm done being far too dressed when it comes to this man playing my body to the perfect tune. I'm ready for my sweet harmony to pour through my veins with my skin flush against his.

I tug my t-shirt over my head and discard the lace bra barely containing my breasts and lay in all of my glory, watching as his stare turns feral.

His fingers press into my hips, flipping me in one swift move. He doesn't give me a chance to adjust myself as he places me like a doll, moving my legs and arms until I'm in the exact position he wants.

My thighs tremble with anticipation, my knees shoulder-width apart as I brace on my elbows. Peering over my shoulder at him, I find he's discarded every inch of material that draped his skin moments earlier. My vision zones in on his thick cock, jutting in my direction, eager for the attention I so desperately want to give.

"You look like a wolf ready to pounce, Alpha." I shiver at his words, my breath lodging in my chest as I peer at him. "Tell me, do you want to feel the wolf that lives deep inside of you?" His eyes are fixed on mine as he slowly rolls a condom down the length of his dick. It makes my mouth dry, and my ability to respond is long gone. "Answer me."

It takes more strength than I care to admit to lift my gaze to meet his. "There's only one wolf I want to feel inside of me right now, and if you don't hurry up, I'll—"

My words are lost as he lines up his cock with my entrance and slams deep inside of me. It's impossible to adjust to him at first. My fingers dig deep into the ground, going beyond the grass as I search for the soil to keep me in place.

"You'll what?" he goads, flexing his hips slightly to circle his cock deep into my core.

I have no words, no response, nothing to give him, and he knows it.

My head dips, my hair grazing the grass as I try to move, but he holds me in place, forcing me to submit.

"Look at you, knees buried in the ground, hands smeared with mud. You truly are a feral little wolf itching to come out to play. I wonder how dirty we can make you?"

I turn, glaring at him over my shoulder, but he doesn't get to feel the wrath of it because he starts to move and I succumb to his touch.

He fucks me.

Hard. Fast. Primal.

His fingers dig deliciously hard into my flesh, marking me as proof of this moment as I struggle to keep myself propped up.

I match every swing of his hips with one of my own, falling apart with every pass, but I falter when his hands release me, and with his next thrust, I fall forward. He doesn't stop, tumbling with me as he fucks me into the ground.

The earth beneath me presses into my skin, dirtying

me, just like he wants.

His grunts ring in my ears as ecstasy coats my skin, and a moment later, his hands are back on me, but this time, there's something on his fingertips.

He draws shapes along my back while his thrusts remain just as relentless and unhinged.

I can't see what he's doing, and that's only adding to the bliss coiling in my core. My pussy clenches around his length, in need of release as my clit brushes against the ground with every slam of his hips.

"That's it, Alpha. Take from me. Come on my cock and mark me as yours. That's what I am, aren't I? *Yours*. Say it. Fucking say it," he rasps as his hand presses down on the side of my face, pushing me even further into the grass and soil beneath me.

I gasp and moan, but the words don't come out.

"Say it, Addi. Say it now," he bites, his other hand coming down on my ass with a harsh slap.

My body explodes, the impending need inside of me taking over as wave after wave of frenzied desire courses through me. My vision blurs, my muscles coiling tight to obliterate at his touch.

"Say it!" he barks, his moves coming more jagged as he leans over me, pressing his chest against my back as he claims every inch of me. "I need the words, Alpha. Take me over the edge with you."

It's a plea. One I can't seem to deny.

"You're mine."

"Again."

"You're *mine*, Cassian."

His hips stop as the pulse of his cock inside me vibrates my walls, and I find myself shivering around him once again. His climax takes me over another peak of pleasure, leaving me drenched in mud, but not his release, a thought that feels like a twinge of disappointment, even in my sex-induced haze.

My pulse rings in my ears, my mind refusing to acknowledge what I said and how much I meant it.

I'm gone for him, for them, and there's nothing I can do about it.

BRODY

12

Dragging my fork across my plate, I prod at the food, my appetite not quite there. I know why. I know it without a doubt, and all it does is sour my mood more. The empty seat across from me is adding to it with every passing second, reconfirming with every fleeting glance that the company I would like to be keeping isn't here. A whole dining hall of people, and the one I want to see the most is off somewhere with the annoying wolf I happen to call my friend.

"How long are we supposed to just let him have her to himself?" I grumble, dramatically dropping my fork as a huff echoes in my ears.

Flora scoffs, earning my glare, but she continues to smother her grin, unfazed by my silent threat.

"What?"

She shakes her head, the amusement dancing in her eyes as she turns to peer at me. "Do you hear yourself?"

"What's your point?"

"Don't take it out on her," Arlo interjects from the other side of her, eyes narrowed as his jaw tics. I don't need his bullshit on top of my own.

"Alright, Arlo, calm yourself. He's good," Kryll states, waving him off, and to my surprise, he does relax at his words. Kryll to the rescue. Who knew?

Flora clears her throat, and I turn my gaze back to her. "I'm saying, why does Cassian get to whisk her away without care for the rest of us?" It's the truth. It's irritating and petty, but I don't care.

"Shouldn't you be considering what's best for Addi?" she retorts, cocking her brow as she takes a sip of her water.

I roll my eyes at her. "We all know I'm the least growly. I *am* what's best for her." *Duh.*

"Is that so?" Raiden grumbles, not lifting his gaze from his plate as he scoffs at me.

"I like it," Flora states, wagging her finger at me, and I shrug.

"You say that like *she's* going to like it."

"Oh, she's definitely not. That's what makes me like it," Flora retorts, wagging her eyebrows at me.

"That sounds mean."

"Mean? Please, she's my best friend. I'd stand against

any of you if that's what she wanted or even needed, but I'm realistic and…a dreamer, and she needs the four of you just as much as you need her."

"You think?" Raiden whips his stare to Addi's friend, a sense of hope drifting from him, just as it does me. Yet all Flora does is shrug like it's no big deal.

"How do you know that?" I push, giving her my full attention now.

"I don't know for sure," she replies with a gulp, slightly backtracking, and there's no way in Hell we're doing that. Not after what she just said.

"Don't give me false promises and try to take them away," Raiden grunts with a shake of his head while Kryll silently observes Flora, forever quiet and watching.

"How do I make her love me?" The words blurt from my mouth by mistake. I want to backtrack now, pretend I didn't say it, but the way her eyebrows rise, silently questioning me, I know there's no chance of that now.

"Is that what you want?" she asks, softer than I expect. There's no mocking, no making fun of me. There's suddenly a kindness that seeps deep into my bones.

"Yeah, Brody, is that what you want?" Kryll interjects with a snicker.

I glare at him across the table. "Fuck you, asshole."

"Dick isn't my preference, but thanks," he retorts like he thinks he's funny.

"Raidy, baby. I was waiting for you to come and see me."

The table falls silent and still as a shadow casts over us. The familiar voice makes my muscles bunch together in a mixture of anger and frustration as my gaze lands on the vile vampire.

Her blonde hair is pin-straight, making her eyes seem even more narrow. There's a slight discoloring to her right cheek, but otherwise, she looks every inch the bitch that she is.

"Back the fuck up from the table right now before I put you through it." Raiden's voice is dark, deadly, and the sneer on his lips reveals his protruding fangs as he promises her downfall.

Anyone else would scurry away, wilting at his stare alone, but not Vallie.

Never fucking Vallie.

"Raiden Holloway, you promised me—"

"I didn't promise you shit. Now, get the fuck away from me before I finish what Adrianna started."

Vallie stomps her foot, balling her hands into fists at her sides as she bites back a squeal of frustration.

"Are you still thinking about her? Look at what she did to me!" she rages, wincing as she adjusts her cloak and lifts her t-shirt to reveal bandages littering her chest and sides. "You need to keep away from her, Raiden. She's a lunatic."

"You're a fucking mess, Vallie. Do us all a favor and go irritate someone else," I grunt, completely losing every ounce of my appetite. Her gaze fixes on me as her bottom lip juts out.

"Don't fucking speak to me, you lowly fucking mage. I'm above you. Remember that."

Raiden's fists slam on the table, shaking the entire thing as he rises to his feet. He inches toward the enemy until he's looming over her. His eyes are blacker than black, an endless pit of darkness with the tips of his fangs desperate to pierce something...anything.

"Did it feel good? Attacking Adrianna in the trial so your father's plan could come together?"

She smirks, *fucking* smirks. "I don't know what you're talking about."

"Do you know what your father's plan was?"

"I've been researching a lot about fated mates, Raidy. I'm going to be so good at it," she promises, lifting her hand to press against his chest, but he catches it before she can actually touch him. His knuckles instantly turn white as they lock around her wrist.

"You don't know, do you." It's not a question, I can see the hope that still resonates in her eyes, and I'm more than happy to diminish it after everything she's done to Addi.

"Didn't I tell you not to speak to me, mage?"

"Is that how you would speak to one of your fated?" I

ask, cocking a brow at her before shaking my head. "Ah, shit, that's right. I forgot. The plan changed, and the center for our parents' plans is no longer you...is it?"

She rolls her eyes, flipping her hair over her shoulder as she turns her attention back to Raiden. "What bullshit is he talking about, Raidy?"

He smirks, but there's not a hint of kindness to it. It's rotten to the core.

"The plan is for Adrianna. You know, her royal heritage makes her a more viable option. Didn't your father explain to you why they needed her there?"

She takes a step back, and another, shaking her head dismissively with every move. "You're lying."

Raiden shrugs. "I don't care what you think. I would tell you to go ask your father, but well... his lack of breathing will make that a little difficult."

My eyes bug out of my head as I gape at him, but he doesn't falter under the surprise announcement that just parted her lips. Vallie, however, the color drains from her face, her eyebrows raising in horror as her bottom lip quivers.

"No," she breathes, the word whooshing from her mouth.

"Yes," Raiden insists with a nod, the promise lingers in the air before she hurries from the room. A few people continue to stare at us, confirming that she garnered an audience, but we don't pay them any mind as Raiden slowly retakes his seat.

I exhale, wiping a hand down my face as I try to alleviate the tension rising in my temples.

"What was that all about?" Flora asks, but before I can answer her, my cell phone vibrates in my pocket.

Happy to take the distraction so I don't have to answer her question, I reach for it, only to find my father's name flashing across the screen.

Fuck that.

Disregarding the call, I place my cell phone on the table and watch it. As predicted, it comes to life once again a few moments later.

"How many times has he tried to reach out?" Kryll asks from across the table, his gaze locked on the screen, and I shrug.

It disconnects, and not five seconds go by before it goes off again. The same name is highlighted on the screen.

"Answer. It shuts them up," Raiden explains, sighing with a sense of defeat I can relate to.

"Are you talking from experience?"

"I'm ignoring my mother right now, but she can find me without a cell phone," he states with a shake of his head. His mother is the head of the vampire-origin students on campus. I'm surprised she hasn't come looking for him yet.

I purse my lips as my cell phone falls silent before dancing across the table again, and I relent.

Answering the call, I lift it to my ear. There's a strange static noise that comes through the line first, but my father's voice isn't far behind.

"Brody? Finally, the plan is ready for the next steps, and I need your help."

ADRIANNA

13

The reflection staring back at me is not the same one that I found this morning. It feels like a lifetime ago that I jumped out the window, yet it was merely a few hours.

I made the right decision not to go back to class looking like this. I look…a complete mess.

Mud is everywhere. It clings to my hair, it's smeared across my face, splattered across my breasts, and smudged with grass stains on my knees.

It's hot.

Hotter than it should be.

This isn't where I anticipated finding myself today. Not when I tried to escape the four of them, not when Bozzelli had me in her office, and definitely not when Cassian whisked me away.

It was reckless, yet exactly what I needed.

My thighs clench, the delicious ache still clinging to my limbs as I brace my palms on the vanity. Exhaustion seeps into my muscles, but I need to shower away the mud before I can pass out. Then eat. Eating needs to be high on my agenda too.

Taking a deep breath, I push up off the vanity and step into one of the shower stalls. Just as my hand wraps around the handle, a bang echoes from outside the communal bathroom. I frown, considering my options, but when I hear my name being hollered a moment later, I pause my shower and slip out into the hallway.

"What are you doing?"

Wild blue eyes find mine.

"Hey."

Clearing my throat, I let the door fall shut behind me as I fold my arms over my chest. "Hey."

He gapes at me, eyes raking from head to toe. Slowly, his head tilts to the side. "What happened to you?"

"Why are you here, Brody?" I ask, trying to redirect the situation, but it's disregarded.

"What happened to you?" he repeats, taking a step toward me, and I look away. He sweeps a loose tendril of hair back off my face, revealing more dirt clinging to my skin, and I feel his grin before I hear a soft chuckle come from his lips. "Cassian happened, huh?"

"Something like that," I mutter, shaking my hair back into place as I look at him.

Worry crinkles the corner of his eyes, making my chest tighten with a panic that doesn't feel like my own. Before I can question him on it, he cups my cheek delicately.

"Can we talk?"

"What about?" I've already done the whole talking thing with one of these assholes today and now look at the state of me. I don't think I'm in any position to do it again.

He wets his lips, nerves revealing themselves in the twitch of his nose. "Are you mad at me?" The question is soft on his tongue, and I frown at him.

"Why would I be mad at you?"

"For knowing," he admits, scrubbing the back of his neck.

It takes a minute for me to figure out what he's talking about, but the reminder of everything that unfolded at The Council comes flooding back to my mind.

"About what they were planning."

"Yeah." Guilt gnaws at him. It's visible in his every breath.

I shake my head. "I don't get the feeling that you knew they were going to do it like that."

"I didn't." He exhales, but the struggle he's dealing with doesn't budge. I nod nervously, unsure what it is he wants me to say. "But that doesn't mean I shouldn't have explained what I did know," he adds, a tight smile on his lips.

"Why would you explain it to me?" Did he technically omit things? Yes, but we've all done it.

"Because…" He gives me a pointed look, like that explains it.

"Because? I didn't tell you I was Princess Adrianna Reagan," I state, and he scoffs.

"That's different." I cock a brow at him, but he doesn't falter. "It is."

"If you say so."

"So, you're not mad at me?"

"There's no reason for you to tell me things like that. About Vallie, about your father—"

"What if I want there to be a reason?"

My head dips as his hand slips from my face. "I can't handle this conversation right now."

"Well, I'm slightly impressed. I feel like we tested the waters of your feelings and emotions a little more than last time. Progress, right?"

I frown, trying to recall what he means, and the memory of us in the forest together, after my secret was revealed, floods my vision. I don't know if I'm all that progressed, but I'm not going to correct him.

Clearing my throat, I force myself to lift my head up and stand strong. "Is this what you came here for?"

"No. I came because of my father."

"I thought I just said—"

"I know what you said, but this feels important, and since we all now know it involves you, you have a right to know." How ominous. Perfect. I raise my eyebrows at him in question. "They're going to try again, Addi." I gulp. My nostrils flare, and my heart rate increases. "They don't care about anything but their own goals, and unfortunately, I don't know what those goals are. I just know that I will never lose what little of your trust I might have."

"What's their plan?" I ask, trying to keep my growing concern shielded, but something tells me I'm doing a terrible job of it.

"I don't know for sure, but he told me to keep you close and be prepared."

Wow.

Instinctively, I take a step back. Brody reaches for me, but it only makes me inch back farther.

"Dagger, I—"

"Sorry," I blurt, hating the concern that washes over his features, but I just need a little space to think.

"It's okay, I just…I'm telling you this because I want you to trust me and realize that I'm not a threat. Fuck, I want you close because I want you, not because of my father, but I can imagine that those lines are blurred on your end right now."

A warmth spreads through my body as he offers me a soft smile, and despite my inner torment, I return it.

"When did you get so wise?"

"I'm a mage, remember? I was born wise."

"There he is," I say with a snicker, shaking my head in relief that the fun guy is still in there.

"Who?"

"Brody the big-talking asshole. He's still able to make an appearance," I muse, and he winks. The tension that suffocated the air moments ago dissipates.

"So you understand?" he asks, hope in his gaze, and I shake my head, making myself dizzy with how many times I've done it in such a short span of time. "I didn't think you would. I'll give you some space, but just know, Dagger, we're not done—far from it."

ADRIANNA

14

The dirt is gone, but the heat touching my skin remains. I can still feel Cassian everywhere, and now it's mixed with Brody's heated stare. The shower was exactly what I needed, but my reflection doesn't seem any different as I look myself over.

My hips are mottled with fingertip-sized bruises and my ear is still red from Cassian pushing my face into the ground.

I love it.

I don't love the fact that classes are done for the day and I don't know what to do with myself. Usually, down time like this would instantly have me considering a run, but I think I've already worked up enough of a sweat for the day. I need to head back to my room and consider some alternatives.

Feeling fresher than earlier, I fix the towel around my chest as tightly as I can, silently berating myself for not grabbing clothes before stepping in here. It's either the towel walk of shame or putting the filthy clothes back on, and that's not an option. I *could* use my magic to clean them and dry them, but it feels like a waste.

Thankfully, I make it back to my room uninterrupted, letting the door click closed behind me with a resounding thud.

I freeze in place; my jaw slacks as I gape at the vase that sits proudly on my desk. It's not the same one, but the dozen red roses that stand tall inside it look familiar.

What the fuck?

My nostrils flare as my fingers ball into fists, gripping the towel like my life depends on it.

I need to get dressed before I overreact. I need to check my fucking room to make sure no one is here because I sure as fuck threw them through my window last night. I know I did.

Using my magic, I drop the towel and swiftly slip into my underwear, a white top, and a loose pair of black joggers. I do a quick scan of my small space, confirming no one is hiding under my bed or tucked in my walk-in closet, before I finally let my shoulders sag, releasing the built-up tension.

My gaze circles back to the bright roses beckoning me

closer, and my lips purse as I try to contain the desire to touch them.

I fail.

Hovering by them, my index finger runs over the delicate petals, making my heart sing as my earth magic flares to life.

Fuck.

My chest aches with a tension that only worsens with every second I stare at them.

A lot of shit went down because of Raiden, and these link back to him. They offer him access to my room. I don't know how the fuck he managed to get inside here after I tossed them out in a fit of rage last night, but here they are.

My instinctive reaction is to toss them to their same demise, but the magic swirling inside of me pleads with an intense fury not to.

I'm torn.

Again.

At the hands of these men.

Raiden. Cassian. Brody. Kryll.

All so different, yet all equally under my skin. There's no denying it any longer.

Four men, even more feelings.

They're my fucking kryptonite. Just like Nora, my father, and even Flora, but in a different way altogether. I can't explain it, which is probably because no matter what

I do to fight it, I find myself back here time and time again.

My kryptonites.

My kryptos.

My utter downfall.

Grabbing the vase, I take a step toward the window, struggling to control my emotions as they threaten to consume me. I shouldn't feel like this. Not when I'm alone. It's ridiculous.

I just need to throw these stupid thornless beauties out of the window and put an end to it.

Mind made up, I swing my window open, but before I take the final step to lean outside, a knock sounds from my door.

I pause, glaring at the offending wood like it holds the secret to my problems.

I'm too in my head to answer the door right now, especially when it's likely to be one of my Kryptos. That's the last thing I need. Settling on my decision to ignore it, my grip on the vase tightens when another knock follows a moment later.

Lowering the offensive flowers back to my desk, I decide throwing them out will only confirm I'm here, and that's the last thing I want to do. I just need to remain quiet, and they will eventually leave.

"Hey, it's Flora. I know you're in there."

My stress calms at the sound of her voice, and before

I can think better of it, I hurry over to the door. I open it just enough to see her red hair and green eyes waiting expectantly on the other side.

"Hey," I breathe, and she offers me a small smile.

"Let me in."

"What?"

She cocks a brow at me and my eyes narrow, observing the bags in her hand. I can't tell what's going on, but I relent nonetheless.

Pulling her inside, I quickly shut the door behind her and she murmurs her thanks.

Wordlessly, she dumps the bags on my bed before planting her hands on her hips as she assesses my space.

"What's going on?" I ask, but she shakes her head.

"I don't know what you think you've done with this room, but it's lacking. Those cute roses are your only saving grace. Otherwise, I'd think it was a morgue or something."

My eyebrows rise to my hairline.

"Uh, I didn't realize I was letting you in to be judgy."

She turns to me with a grin. "Oh, if you think this is judgy, you haven't seen anything yet." All I can do is gape at her. She must sense that she's caught me completely off-guard because she turns to face me properly as her smile softens. "We're having a sleepover."

"Sleepover? But it's not Friday."

She shrugs, digging into one of the bags to pull out a

bag of candy. "I know, but Brody said you needed me. So, I shifted it to now."

"Brody did what?" My head rears back, confusion racing through my mind as she beams at me.

"He didn't offer an explanation, but…"

"But?"

"I could read the sincerity coming from him," she offers, tapping her temple to confirm her magic is what made that assessment.

My heart warms against my will. I refuse to acknowledge how it makes me feel that he went in search of my friend to be here for me when I can't seem to accept him doing the same thing.

Shaking my head, my shoulders begin to relax, and I didn't even realize they were coiled so tight. "This sleepover is supposed to be for you. That's why I agreed in the first place."

"For me?" Her nose crinkles in confusion as I nod.

"I could sense something was off with you after the weekend."

Her smiles are her expressions. I can read her by her mouth, and it's only confirmed more when her smile drops, etched in sadness.

Clearing her throat, she tucks a loose tendril of hair behind her ear as she peers at me. "How about we make this for both of us then? It feels like we've both had a lot going on."

I scoff. "That feels so vague yet *so* accurate all at once," I admit, making her lips curl up a little again.

"Agreed. Now, help me set this stuff up." She sweeps her hand over the bed, indicating the bags she brought in, and I nod, silently following her order.

Strangely, it's almost therapeutic handing the reins over to someone else, not having to think as she throws an array of items at me, specifying exactly where she wants them.

Throws and fluffy pillows scatter across my bed, adding a splash of pastel yellow and lilac to the otherwise 'morgue-like' room. She strategically lays out face masks, hand masks, and even feet masks on my nightstand while I pile chips, candy, and popcorn in the middle of the bed, ready for us to dive into.

What catches me by surprise the most is the small white box she sticks to my ceiling. Before I can question her on it, the familiar menu screen of *The Office* projects onto my far wall.

"Wow."

"Right? This was Arlo's idea. I think it's because he thought it might earn him an invite," she states with a roll of her eyes.

"Poor guy. Excellent idea, though." I take stock of my room. It barely looks familiar, especially as she closes my window, draws my curtains closed, and drapes a string of fairy lights over them. "Is there anything you didn't think of?"

"Food, but Brody said he would bring pizza."

As if hearing her admission, a knock sounds from my door. Pressing my lips together, I edge toward it with caution, finding a stack of four pizza boxes thrust in my direction. Brody's head appears over the top with a nervous smile on his lips.

"I wasn't sure what to get, so I got you a mixture," he explains, shoving them closer.

"Thank you."

"It's just pizza," he mutters, his nerves still visible in his eyes.

"Not just for that."

His smile spreads further across his face, victory flashing in his eyes, and it's the sexiest I think he's ever looked. Leaning forward, trying to avoid crushing the pizza boxes, my lips press against his without a single thought.

It's small, but the warmth that explodes through my body is huge.

His hand cups my cheek, burning me even brighter, but all too quickly, he takes a step back.

"Have fun, Dagger," he breathes, offering me a salute before he disappears from view.

Balancing the pizza boxes with one hand, my fingertips

ghost over my lips as I stare at the empty spot.

"Stop hoarding the pizzas," Flora hollers, pulling me back to the present.

Kicking the door shut behind me, I slump on the bed, strategically placing the pizza boxes between us. I reach for a slice of classic margherita while Flora delves into the meat feast. We're three slices deep when she clears her throat.

"So, who wants to go first?" She clicks a remote, starting the next episode of *The Office* as I point at her.

"You. Definitely you. You're always here for me, and I want to offer you the same."

She gives me an appraising look. "Who knew you could be so cute and sweet under all of that harsh exterior?" she muses, earning a glare, but she doesn't acknowledge it.

"Don't tell anyone," I relent, making her snicker.

"Pinky swear." Silence descends over us as she looks off toward the twinkling lights. It takes everything in me to remain quiet, giving her a moment to think until she finally blurts it out. "He kissed me."

My eyebrows rise. "Arlo?"

"Yeah."

"That's fantastic, right?" They're step-siblings, long in love before their parents decided to start bumping uglies, and that's not her fault.

She shrugs. "I don't know. In the moment, it was

everything; even now, my body reacts to the memory, but just as quickly as it started, it stopped. He left immediately and hasn't spoken a word about it, and I don't really know what to do." That little shit.

"I'll fight him."

"I'm sure you would," she snickers, shaking her head at me.

"The least I could do is cause him a little pain," I push, considering how best to do it, and she sighs.

"I don't know. I can see the pain in his eyes already."

Well then. Looking at her, I see the nerves flickering in her expression. "But you can't bring yourself to ask him," I murmur, earning a nod as I speak her truth. "Men," I grumble with a sigh, earning another burst of laughter.

"Yes, plural, definitely in your case," she muses, effectively redirecting the conversation, and I let her.

"I don't even know which one of them is the worst." I slump back against the headboard, certain there's no room for any more pizza in my stomach.

"Definitely Raiden or Cassian," she declares, and I scoff.

"That's accurate."

I feel her eyes on me, assessing, searching, until she finally just asks. "What's changed this week?"

Peering at her out of the corner of my eye, I sigh before I unleash everything. The trial, Vallie, The Council,

Raiden, Nora. Everything.

"I'll fight them," she blurts, using my words, and I grin. "All of them," she adds, nodding in agreement with herself. "You might need to help me because we both know I'm lacking, but—"

"We're good. I think I'm struggling with the reality that I care." I don't know where the words come from, but they floor me nonetheless.

"About?" She knows, I can see it in her eyes. She just wants me to say it.

"Them." It's barely more than a whisper.

"You're blushing." Her pointed finger is aimed at the heat I feel in my neck, and I turn away from her as if that's going to make a difference.

"I am not."

"If you say so," she mutters, and I pretend I'm focused on the screen. "It explains why Vallie was a bitch at lunch," she adds, effectively earning my attention again.

"She's back?"

"Like she never left. I wouldn't have even known if you hadn't just explained."

"What did she do?"

"Nothing different from usual. She overused that dumb nickname for Raiden that makes bile burn my throat, but it was excellent. Raiden threatened to destroy her." Her hands are animated as she giddily explains everything that happened, then her face suddenly drops. "He may have also said some things."

"Some things?"

"Like that her father is dead."

Fuck. Of course he did.

"How delighted was he to share the fact?" I murmur, my nails biting into my palms as I exhale slowly, and Flora snickers.

"Too much. Although, is it too much when it's still a classic expectation from Raiden at this stage?" she asks with a quirk of her brow, and I scoff.

"Does that mean there's a psycho vampire bitch on the hunt for me now?"

Flora's nose crinkles as she smiles at me. "He didn't mention your name, but even if it wasn't you, I think we would find you at the end of her wrath anyway," she admits, and I hum in agreement.

At least now she actually has a reason to put a target on my head, I guess. But one fact remains, and it lingers deep into the night, swirling in my mind on repeat. Somebody has to destroy her.

And all I can hope for is that I will get to do the honors, just like I did with her father.

ADRIANNA

15

After the best sleepover ever, the weekend finally arrived and passed by in such a blur that it feels wasted.

It's not, I remind myself. One thing I learned while becoming a hermit was that last week's mess was wreaking far too much havoc on me, and the only person who can stop it is little old me.

Even without a pep talk from my father, I've got a new mantra that echoes in my mind.

No more fading out in classes.

No more losing sight of what's important.

No more free falling into dark thoughts and feelings.

Focus. That's my new mantra. Just focus.

I gave myself the weekend to get over myself, and now here I am, Monday morning, all sweaty and panting from my early morning run. I anticipated Raiden or Cassian making an appearance and spoiling my mood, but to my surprise, it was a complete success on my end.

The perfect start to the day. Accomplished. *Focused.*

Stepping into the shower, I hurry through the mundane task of washing the workout away before I dress in my gray combat pants and long-sleeved tee. Fixing my cloak in place, I'm slightly impressed with myself for remembering to bring my fresh clothes into the communal bathroom with me.

Another sign that today is going to be a good day.

I'm just finishing up twisting my hair into a crown braid when the door opens and Flora sticks her head in.

"Hey, are you ready?"

"If I say no, can we watch the final season of *The Office* instead?" I pout, silently pleading. We really did watch that much at our sleepover, and now she's prolonging the inevitable, even though she has a new series lined up for us after this—something called *Brooklyn 99*. I'm taking her word on it being good.

"But once you've watched it, you know you can't rewatch it, right?"

I roll my eyes at the same line she's given me all weekend. I threatened to watch it alone, but we both know I would never. "The alternative you're giving me is to never watch it at all."

She ignores my pointed look, waving for me to follow her out into the hall. Arlo is waiting against the wall, knee bent and foot propped behind him. He doesn't see me. His eyes are fixed on the sassy red head right beside me.

I bite back my smile, turning for the stairs. Stepping outside, I'm relieved when I'm not bombarded with any of my Kryptos or professors eager to drag me into an unnecessary meeting and piss me off. Instead, the three of us fall into a comfortable calm that adds a spring to each step I take.

My Kryptos. I shake my head. They're not *my* anything, and I need to remember that. Especially since I've managed to avoid them all weekend.

"What drama are we anticipating this week, ladies?" Arlo asks, smirking as his gaze settles on me. I glare at him, but that only seems to make his grin grow wider. Ass.

"We're anticipating none. We're focused completely on what we're at the academy to do and what we want the future to look like," I reply, pleased with myself once again, but the nod he gives me tells me I'm either full of shit or delusional.

As we pass the fountain and head toward the academy building, the pathway fills with more students. My stomach grumbles, reminding me I need to eat.

Heading into the dining hall, I immediately feel four sets of eyes fall in my direction. I'm acutely aware of them. From where their gazes touch my skin to the way they make my heart react. My head pleads with me to turn toward the food counter, while my body leans toward them.

Despite my efforts, I turn in their direction, casting my gaze over each of them one at a time.

It's like I've been starved going so long without seeing them, and now I'm finally being nurtured again.

Brody's blond hair is messy, matching his crazy personality. His eyes shimmer with a jolt of excitement that I feel running down my spine. Cassian sits beside him, jaw tight and eyes narrowed at me. At this stage, I'm aware this is his default look, and it really shouldn't be so hot. Kryll peers over his shoulder, his stare assessing while his features work extra hard at giving nothing away. The smallest tell I can find is the shift of his twitchy tattooed fingers as he clenches them on the tabletop. Raiden, the usual aggressor, looks pale, distant, and almost...small in his seat.

I turn away, quickly reminded that I hate him right now, but before I can go to choose my food, an arm drapes around my shoulders.

"Good morning, Dagger. I'm glad you're no longer hiding. Now, come on, I have food for you."

My lips twist as I turn toward Brody. I consider declining, but my feet move on their own as he pulls me along to the table.

He pulls out my usual chair between Kryll and Raiden before hurrying around to his spot. I glance back to look for Flora and Arlo, only to find them huddled close, talking about something as they wait for food.

Someone clears their throat and I turn back to the table, finding a plate piled high with pancakes, bacon, and maple syrup.

"Who expects me to eat all of this?"

"Have you eaten anything at all over the weekend?" Cassian grunts, pointing his fork at me accusingly.

"I've eaten," I rasp, caught by surprise, but the nod he gives me tells me he doesn't believe me.

When he doesn't bark another question at me, I turn my attention to my plate and dive in. I can still feel them all looking at me, and I all but pray that I at least half look like I'm not faltering under their gazes.

"You've been avoiding us," Kryll states when I place my cutlery down, having devoured half of the plate, I can't stomach a single bite more.

I look up, catching sight of Flora and Arlo watching me intently. I was working so hard to avoid the distracting men around me that I didn't even realize they had joined us.

Focus, Addi.

"Why is that?" Brody adds, eager for an answer.

I sigh. "Because I need a minute to think."

"About what?" Raiden chimes in, swiping his tongue over his bottom lip as he quirks a brow at me.

"About whatever I want."

"Which is?"

"None of your business," I bite, unable to contain my irritation.

He growls, the sound low and deep, worming its way to my core as he rises to his feet. Anger vibrates through him, but it does nothing to shift the despair in his eyes. He stares down at me, eyebrows furrowing before he suddenly spins for the exit, storming off without a backward glance.

I watch him.

Every. Step.

Right up until he gets to the door and pauses.

My heart lurches in my chest as he turns just as suddenly as he stopped, marching back to me with purpose. I'm rooted to the spot, watching his strides until he's right back in front of me. His hands slam down on the table with force, rattling the cutlery, and his eyes narrow on mine.

"Do you know how worried I was about you?"

I gape at him, keenly aware that there are more eyes on us than just those at our table.

"I'm going to take your silence as a no, but let me lay it out for you. Your friend, she told me I had to give you space, and I did, I fucking did, but here you are, with your damn sass, cold shoulder, and beautiful, *beautiful* face."

His nostrils flare, his dark hair unkempt as he runs his fingers through the ends. My tongue is frozen in my mouth as my brain short-circuits, and before I can function at all, he waltzes around again, barreling toward the exit.

A mixture of emotions strike me.

The desire to race after him takes hold, but remembering seeing Nora in The Council's grasp renders me motionless in my seat.

"So…class?"

I look at Flora, a small glimmer of contentment blossoming in my gut as I nod, eager to take her offer.

"Yeah."

Hurrying to my feet, I keep my eyes fixed on the exit, not slowing my stride until the fresh air hits me. I give myself the opportunity to take in three deep breaths, failing to calm myself. Apparently, a weekend hiding away leads to a Monday morning of awkwardness, and I don't know what to do about it.

Fuck.

So much for focus.

Straightening my spine and rolling back my shoulders, I silently give myself a pep talk before I feel someone come to a stop beside me. Assuming it's Flora, I take off, thankful for her silent company, only to peer up at Kryll after a few steps. I falter, and the tight smile he offers resonates inside of me.

"Have you heard from your family?" he asks softly, turning away from me as we keep in step.

"Yeah," I manage, my blood spiking at the mention of my loved ones.

"Are they okay?"

I nod, clearing my throat. "I'm sorry, I feel like I haven't thanked you properly for—"

He lifts his hand, waving me off. "It's not necessary."

"Well, I appreciate it," I murmur, biting back a smile.

I glance up at him, only to find him already looking at me.

"If you ever change your mind about knowing where—"

"I won't," I snap, a little too harshly, cutting him off.

His brows knit together. "But—"

"I won't, Kryll," I bite, my pulse ringing in my ears as my face heats.

This time, when he lifts his hands, it's in surrender. "Whatever you say, Princess." Without another word, he takes off, the classroom coming into view, and he makes a beeline for his brother.

"Kryll, I didn't..." My words trail off, his attention focused elsewhere, and I come to a stop at the edge of the growing group of students.

Helplessly looking around, I spot Raiden, but a bubble of embarrassment has me turning away.

What the hell is wrong with me?

Desperation has me glancing back over my shoulder, considering a swift exit despite the little mantras I worked on all weekend. Flora raises an eyebrow at me and I sigh, folding my arms over my chest as I look at her pleadingly.

"Am I being a bitch or just repelling the assholes in my life?" The words taste weird on my tongue, but they need to be spoken. I'm not sure why I suddenly care, but here I am, lost in them even more than I thought.

"A mixture." There's not a single ounce of uncertainty in her answer, and it makes me cringe.

"You're supposed to be on my side, Flora," I grumble, my arms tightening around my middle.

"That's why I'm giving you the truth, bestie," she promises, making Arlo scoff.

"This is what happens when she loves you, Addi. Get used to it," he muses, and I roll my eyes.

"Fine, but I'm not saying I like it."

Although, her truth settles something inside of me.

"Good morning, my least favorite group of assholes," Professor Tora hollers, calling everyone's attention to him. I spot Kryll rolling his eyes at his brother's choice of addressing us, and it makes me smirk. Just a little. "I hope you're all up for an adventure."

"The last time you said that, I was almost killed." Vallie's shrill voice fills the air as she comes into view. The desire and need to do it all over again vibrates through me, but a hand clamps down on my shoulder as I take a step.

"Not yet." The gruff order comes from Cassian, his fingers curling tighter, forcing me to stop.

I appreciate that he didn't say *no* and went with *not yet* instead.

"I don't care if you live or die, Miss Prissy," Tora shouts, giving her a pointed look before turning his attention to the rest of the group. "Buckle up. We're off to Glacial Lake."

ADRIANNA

16

The ground shifts beneath my feet, transforming the blades of grass and warm sun into a thin layer of compact snow, with thick clouds slowly drifting across the sky.

I shiver, instinctively drawing my cloak tighter around my body as Cassian steps in closer. He presses his front against my back, attempting to shield me from the icy air.

"Why would you even bring us here?" Vallie whines, stomping her foot in disbelief as her teeth chatter.

"Why would you even bother attending the academy if you're just here to ask dumb questions like that?" Professor Tora retorts with a cock of his brow, and it takes all my effort to smother my grin, but the chuckle that slips between my lips doesn't go unnoticed.

Vallie's laser-sharp gaze snaps my way. Her lip curls

in disgust at the mere sight of me, and the promise of war burns in her eyes. How fun. Her mouth parts as her finger aims in my direction, but before she can utter a word, Tora continues.

"For all those actually interested in making a difference to the Floodborn Kingdom, I've brought us to Glacial Lake today because it is a part of what matters. Every town, every city, every inch of this kingdom matters, or it should, to the heir." I feel his gaze cast my way for what feels like a split second longer than everyone else, but I shake it off, not inflating my own ego that much so early in the day. "Take a look around, we're just on the outskirts, but we'll press forward, farther into town in a few moments. I recommend staying in pairs at a minimum. The snow beneath your feet is covering ice, and if that breaks…let's just say the cold you're feeling now will pale in comparison." A wicked smirk tugs at his lips as he turns away from everyone, muttering with a woman beside him as he taps away on the device in his hand.

"How funny is it that Kryll and Tora are brothers, made from the same DNA combination, yet they're so different?" Cassian murmurs, his lips brushing against my ear with every word, making me shiver at the contact.

I hum in agreement, unable to find my tongue.

Focus, Addi.

Dammit.

Clearing my throat, it takes every ounce of my strength to take a step forward, putting some distance between us. Thankfully, he doesn't follow, giving me a little space as I take in the area, as Tora advised.

I keep my movement steady and my feet shoulder-width apart, acutely aware of the ice that lies beneath me. Emptiness surrounds us, except for a tree line in the distance with a clifftop peeking down at us from the west.

Everything feels still, quiet, calm. Only the chatter from our class fills the air.

A flurry blows, whipping soft flecks of snow into the air, and it dances majestically around us. It's mesmerizing. A stark contrast to the weather we're used to. I've never been here, to Glacial Lake. Not that I can remember, at least, but my father has spoken of it many times in his bid to educate me.

I recall mentions of battles that took place here, but nothing specific comes to mind, and if I'm right, the main origin to inhabit the area is mages. The cold keeps the brain alive, and the calmness allows the mages the ability to think uninterrupted.

"It's magical, isn't it?" The whisper is one of awe, and I tilt my head to Brody, who stands shoulder to shoulder with me as he gapes at our surroundings.

"It's something," I answer honestly, not overly keen on the cold chill that's starting to cling to my skin, but it is breathtaking. The snow glistens in every direction, offering a whimsical feel to the air despite the hidden sun.

"I grew up here," he offers, making my eyebrows rise in surprise.

"You did?"

"Yeah. Until my father was accepted onto The Council, at least. Then everything changed." The thought seems to cast a haze over his eyes, the brightness dimming as he relives whatever seems to plague him.

"The forming of The Council seems to have changed a lot of things for a lot of people," I admit, earning a hum of agreement.

"I know one of my best friends is a vampire, but they're no good for the kingdom either, not when they're running rampant as they are."

My brows furrow. "It's strange. Since we joined the academy, I feel like I've heard nothing about it, seen nothing worth noting, or even felt the fear and panic like I used to when trolling the streets of the city," I admit. He turns to me with a soft smile, but before he can speak, Kryll appears.

"I said the same thing. I can't decide if it's simply because we don't have access to the media outlets like we usually would or if it's something the academy is purposely keeping from us. There's no denying that it still has to be going on. We've experienced enough of it. It can't have simply stopped altogether because they created the academy."

"I wouldn't be shocked if it had stopped exactly for that reason. It would only create the illusion that the idea of an heir is working already," Raiden muses as he decides to join us too.

Fuck…that wouldn't be the case, would it?

"I think there's more to it than that. More that involves my father," Cassian adds, his voice coming from over my shoulder, and the others nod in agreement.

"Addi told me everything, and I couldn't agree more. That man is shifty as fuck, but my mother has been telling me that the vampire attacks are still causing fear among the citizens of Floodborn," Flora chirps in, earning everyone's attention. She blushes under the steady gaze of her audience, quickly taking a step back, and Arlo's arm immediately goes around her, holding her in place.

"What use are we to the kingdom if we're not being kept in the loop about everything happening *within* the kingdom?" Arlo asks, making a valid point.

"Maybe it is because it's been considered that your focus should be on your studies." Professor Tora's voice cuts through the confusion thickening around us, turning everyone's attention to him as he stares at us with a cocked eyebrow, waiting expectantly for a response. Or was it rhetorical?

Before I can decipher his tone, Arlo is already scoffing at him. "Please, Professor Tora, with all due respect, an heir would want to learn everything the academy has to offer *while* also understanding the turmoil the kingdom finds itself in. That's exactly what would be required from our leader when the position is filled. Would it not?"

My gaze pivots between the two of them, a tinge of awe and astonishment flickering in my chest at Arlo's outburst. Who knew he had it in him? I wholeheartedly agree with every word out of his mouth, but I'm intrigued to see Tora's response.

I blink, and blink again, certain he's turned to stone as he stares at Arlo, but before I can look to Kryll with concern, his brother takes a step forward, offering Arlo his hand. "You would be correct, Mr. Zeller. Let's see to it that the lack of information is rectified going forward, shall we?"

"We should," Arlo breathes effortlessly, taking the hand offered.

Tora then stalks away without a backward glance as I turn to Arlo. "Holy fucking shit, Arlo. Who the fuck are you, and where is the quiet guy from day one?" The words leave my mouth so fast I'm certain he doesn't process any of it, but to my surprise, he smirks.

"I'm a fae. I know my place, but I also know my beliefs." He shrugs matter-of-factly, leaving me to scoff.

"You're impressive. No one ever stands tall like that to my brother. Sometimes, not even me," Kryll states, making Arlo beam with pride as Flora's cheeks turn pink on his behalf.

"Flora told you in the beginning, Addi. She's here to learn how best to support the future kingdom. I'm here because she is. I think we all silently know that when we say support the kingdom, she means you. So, you've guessed it, that means I support you too. I need to start making myself useful, otherwise, when the time comes, and you slaughter every other fucker in the academy, you won't see my value. And I can't have that now, can I?"

He says it so direct and to the point he leaves no room for doubt. As much as his words catch me off guard, I completely understand what he's trying to say; it's just taking my brain a hot minute to realize it's all in relation to me.

"That's enough chit-chat; let's begin, shall we?" Professor Tora calls out, saving me from having to come up with a response, but the smile Arlo offers me is enough to know that a reply wasn't needed or expected.

Holy fuck.

An arm bands around me, pinning my own to my sides as I'm pulled against a hard chest, and I peer up to find it's Kryll. Startled by the fact that he's the one technically man-handling me, I fall into step with him without an ounce of argument.

"If I didn't know he had the hots for his dear little step-sister, then I would have been worried he was into you," he states, not looking at me as he speaks. Which means he certainly doesn't see my jaw fall slack as I balk.

What the fuck?

"You're insane, you know that? I don't know why it would matter to you anyway," I mutter, my body tensing from head to toe as the words part my lips, and he snickers.

"Of course not. That's why your heart rate kicked up a notch as you lied. Please, Princess, carry on," he muses, peering down at me through hooded eyes.

My lips twist. I hate being called on my bullshit. It's irritating because there's no denying it.

Shaking out of his hold, like the petulant child that I'm pretending not to be, I hurry my pace, falling into step with Flora and Arlo. They both look at me in amusement, but I give them the stink eye and focus dead ahead instead of acknowledging any of it.

"The water we're walking on is the central point of Glacial Lake. In the warmer months, it draws in so much wildlife that mages use their abilities to put a sound bubble over the area. That way, the beauty and nature don't become a distraction to their otherwise peaceful and quiet life," Tora explains, throwing his hands out in magnificence at our surroundings.

"That's true," Brody hollers without prompt, making a small grin touch the corners of my mouth.

The lady walking beside Tora throws her arms out, murmuring a soft chant under her breath before the ground moves beneath us, but this time, the surroundings don't exactly change, we just grow closer to the clifftop.

Standing beneath it, I crane my neck back, staring up dauntingly at the peak. Snow doesn't glisten from this angle. It's dark, with an air of danger as jagged icicles dangle in our direction. One falls at the opposite end to where we are, hitting the ground with a thud, making it rumble beneath our feet as shards of ice cascade in every direction.

Holy fuck.

"I don't think it's safe here," someone in a cream cloak states, taking a nervous step back, and Professor Tora shakes his head.

"It's not safe anywhere."

"It's definitely not safe when a student kills people for the fun of it." The barked words come from Vallie, freezing me in place as I turn to find her stare already settled on me. My tongue flicks out over my bottom lip, adrenaline skimming over my skin as I anticipate whatever is going to come next from the psycho bitch.

"Miss. Drummer—"

"No, Professor Tora, I refuse to pretend as though

everything is okay when that cunt killed my father. I deserve vengeance, and she deserves to die."

"But—"

"Watch out!"

I don't know who calls it, but my gaze darts up and I see the ice tumbling down at an insane speed toward me. Not just me. Flora and Arlo too.

Shit.

My heart lurches, lodging in my throat. Without thinking, I shove at Flora, sending her straight into Arlo, and the pair of them hit the deck, sliding through the snow just as I hoped. Before I can consider joining them, the ice hits the ground exactly where they stood a moment earlier, crashing through the ice beneath my feet.

Plunging into the ice-cold water, my body stiffens. My muscles instantly ache from the tension, almost overriding the shock of the chill that seeps down my bones. Panic sets in, the weight of the water pushing down on my shoulders as I will my body to move.

I need to raise my arms and kick my feet, but it's easier said than done.

I'm locked in, coiled tight. My mind may be alive, but my body…it's preparing for the worst.

Blinking up at the world above me, I consider the fact that this is the end, but it's as if my subconscious laughs at me. When I go, it will be more painful than this.

As the fleeting thought enters my mind, something falls into the water, beelining straight for me. I can't see with all the bubbles, but a moment later, hands grab my waist, tugging me toward the light.

Certain it's the afterlife that awaits me, I choke on my first breath as I'm wrenched from the icy depths of Hell and thrown onto snowy land.

"You're okay. You're okay, Addi. Everything's going to be okay."

The words of reassurance are barely audible over the sound of chattering, which I acknowledge a moment later is my damn teeth. It hurts to breathe. It hurts to move. It hurts to fucking think.

"She'll pay for this. She better fucking pay." The snarl comes from Raiden. I know that for certain, even if I can't see him.

"W-w-who?"

My body racks with pain, but I manage to slip the stuttered words past my lips. It's so quiet that I'm certain he hasn't heard me, but after a beat, I feel his breath against my skin.

"Vallie will pay for this. I swear it, Adrianna. She'll pay."

ADRIANNA

17

I shiver. I'm not even cold. It's just my body reminding me of the pain it's been put through at the hands of Vallie.

Fucking Vallie.

Fucking ice.

Fucking Glacier Lake.

Remind me never to go there again.

Rising from my bed, the sheets tousled since I've spent the rest of my day nestled in their warmth, I pace back and forth in front of my window. I'm fine now. I was fine soon after it happened, but no one would hear it.

Bed rest, as ordered by Professor Tora.

The smug look on Vallie's face as I was carted away will forever be imprinted in my mind until I seek my revenge. My father would tell me to calm down, not react or show emotion, but we're long past that now.

Kryll brought me back here, and thank goodness it was him because anyone else would have forced their presence on me. Not him. No. He heard the sincerity in my voice and respected my space, like always, giving me time to heal alone. How that man is a virgin is beyond me. I don't think I'll ever understand.

That was then, though, and this is now.

I'm going insane.

Staying on campus, surrounded by people like Vallie and Bozzelli, who are hell-bent on making my life difficult, is suffocating. At this point, it's more than making my life difficult; they want to write me off altogether.

I plant my hands on my hips, sighing with irritation when my gaze lands on the crimson roses that are still perched on my desk.

Fuck.

That's enough. I need to get out of here.

With my mind made up, I know exactly where I want to go. Changing into a black pair of joggers with holsters fastened around my thighs, I tuck a loose black tee into the waistline before clipping my dagger-lined waistcoat over the top. Satisfied, I lace up my combat boots and opt for my black cloak. With the hood perfectly secured over my head, I make my way outside.

The sun set almost an hour ago, leaving the shadows

free for me to roam as I avoid everyone else on campus and head for a route off-site. I can't go for the usual gates, of course; they wouldn't allow it. Not at this time, and simply because of who I am, so I take the jogging path like usual, spying the small break in the barrier walls that work as armor for the campus.

I press my back against the brick wall, peering around every inch of space around me, making sure no one is watching before I heave myself up to where the wrought-iron bars are twisted out of place. I'm surprised to find there's no additional magic noticeable in the air, and when I glance over the other side of the wall, I see the little river that runs along to the main entry gate.

Jumping, my fall is silent, but I still press my back to the wall, holding my breath to make sure I haven't attracted any attention. A beat passes, and no guards come looking, so I take that as a win and head along the perimeter.

When I near the cobbled bridge that offers access to the academy, I connect with my magic, both air and water. Letting it run through my veins, I part the slow-flowing river and use the air around me to lift me off my feet, just an inch, as I glide to the other side without a sound.

Slipping behind a tree, I glance back toward the academy to see four guards patrolling the area. Each of them is none the wiser to my presence. Grinning in success, I don't waste time hanging around. I get the hell out of there.

My feet carry me on their own accord, my body melding into the City of Harrows with every corner I turn. Every step earns me a clearer breath, a lighter weight against my shoulders, and a sense of relief I didn't realize I was chasing.

The academy may be what will lead me to the future I'm fighting for, but it's also the main source of pain that's trying to destroy me in the process.

I don't stop until I hear the chime as I open the door and step inside. Familiar scents tingle at my nose, making me groan as one of my favorite people comes into view. She smiles as her gaze tracks over me from head to toe, not in the least bit startled by me bolting through the door like that.

"I thought I might be seeing you, kid. Take a seat. I'll bring it over." She smiles softly at me like there's something she knows that I don't, but I let it slide as I make my way to my usual spot in the back. I try to avoid the other customers' curious stares, but their eyes linger longer than necessary. Thankfully, once the whirlwind dressed in black slips into her seat, hiding from everyone, they quickly redirect their attention. "Soda. Your steak will be a few. Everything okay?"

Pulling my hood down, I smile up at Pearl, but the way her eyes crinkle tells me it wasn't all that convincing.

"That's great, thank you. I'm good, how's business?" The small talk tastes like acid on my tongue, and she knows it.

"I'll take that as a no then," she muses, winking as she sashays back to the kitchen.

Called out for what feels like the thousandth time today, I frown down at my soda before taking a few gulps, attempting to wash away the problems that trail after me despite my best efforts.

A shadow casts over my table a few moments later and I tilt my gaze up to give Pearl a pointed look before she can say anything else, but it's not her that I find.

I gulp, wetting my dry lips as I stare up at my unwanted guest.

His dark, pensive stare is locked on mine as he pulls out the chair across from me and fills it in one swift move.

"Ah, what are the chances of my stalker being here too?" I cock a brow at him. "What are you doing here, Raiden?"

Gone is his academy-issued red cloak. Gone is any cloak at all. Instead, he's dressed in a deep-blue suit with a crisp white shirt underneath. The top button is undone, making him look even hotter than is necessary.

"I could ask you the same question, Adrianna. You're supposed to be resting." His words are murmured; curious, yet demanding.

"I don't have to explain myself to you," I grumble,

focusing back on my soda so I can't allow myself to be distracted by him, but his voice still manages to vibrate through me, even in anger.

"Don't have to explain yourself? No one's asking you to. I get you have this cute sense of independence, shit, you rock it, but I literally had to watch you fall into that icy water today, Adrianna. I am not okay."

"Imagine being the one doing the falling," I retort, immediately hating how I sound. I can sound like a bitch, that doesn't faze me, but acting like the world revolves around me, my feelings and emotions, fuck, that doesn't sit right. "I didn't mean that," I quickly add, shaking my head dismissively as I continue to avoid his gaze.

"You can mean whatever you want, Adrianna. I don't care, but we're not leaving Pearl's until we've hashed this shit out."

My eyes snap to his, my nostrils flaring in annoyance. "I'd rather we didn't."

"I'd rather I didn't give a shit, but here I am," he says, lifting his hands in defeat.

"No one asked you to." I sink my teeth into my tongue, hating that I just did it again. It's hard. He instantly makes me defensive, and I'm madder than mad right now with him.

"I'm well aware. Now. Can we get to the groveling part? This silent treatment is causing us nothing but issues."

"You? Grovel?" I mock, lifting my hand to my chest, but all he does is shrug.

"I don't know how, but for you, I'm willing to try just about anything." His words hang in the air like a sunkissed promise, making my stomach clench.

"Why?" I breathe, revealing my intrigue more than I should.

"Why?" he repeats, just as Pearl appears with two plates. Two. That woman knew. *Dammit, Pearl.*

"Is there an echo in here, Pearl? I've never noticed it before," I smart as Pearl purses her lips, hiding a knowing smile, but the moment she glances at Raiden, her features soften.

"Be nice to him. I don't know what he's done, but he's been glum this past week," she explains, placing our plates in front of us, and I scoff.

"He put my family in danger," I blurt, pointing an accusatory finger at him.

"Ah, dammit, Raiden," Pearl hisses, shaking her head. "I know what they mean to her. There's no way I can save you from her wrath," she states, lifting her hands in surrender before backing away without another word.

"I'll take her wrath. It's better than her silence," he hollers, loud enough so the other customers can hear, and I glare at him.

"You want my wrath?" I growl, my frustration rushing

179

to the surface.

"Hit me."

I feel the sting against my palm as I connect with his cheek before I even realize I'm moving.

"Not literally," he grunts, placing his palm over the reddening spot as I quickly retreat. "Do you feel better?" he asks, rubbing at it as I roll my lips.

"No, your jaw is made of steel," I mutter, curling my fingers together in my lap.

"Thanks," he says with a smirk, preening as though it's a compliment.

With my eyes narrowed, I sigh, focusing on the food in front of me instead of the devilish vampire intruding upon my brooding.

"Carry on being mad at me," he murmurs, and I shake my head.

"This isn't a joke, you know."

"I'm well aware."

"Are you though?" I stab my fork in his direction, avoiding actually making any contact as he takes a mouthful of his food.

"I fucked up. Royally. I had no idea I was being followed, otherwise I would have never allowed any of that to happen. I wouldn't have risked your snarky sister or your father either."

My head rears back. "Snarky sister?" I bite. No, he

fucking didn't just say that.

"Don't give me that look. I'm half certain she's got a sharper tongue than you." He gives me a pointed look and it, along with his words, instantly deflates my anger.

"That's accurate." I agree, stuffing my face with food before I can say something half nice.

Raiden scrubs at his neck nervously, looking down at his plate like it may hold all of the answers. I can't help but watch him. The slight mess to the front of his hair, the pinch at his eyes, the twitch to his fingers. It's all...not the usual Raiden. When he finally glances back at me, I expect him to call me out for catching me staring so intently, but instead, a dam seems to break, and his eyes soften so painfully that my heart lodges in my throat.

"You're making me…"

I wait, and I wait, and I wait, but this man does not continue his sentence. "I'm making you what?" I rasp, desperate to know what else rests on the tip of his tongue.

He shakes his head, making my chest tighten as I realize just how much the distance I placed between the two of us hurts me as well.

Fuck.

"You're making me see past the end of my own nose," he mutters with a sigh, and my eyebrows pinch in confusion.

"What does that mean?"

"It means I've spent my whole life with one thing in mind…me."

I scoff at the well-known fact everyone is aware of. "Okay."

"And now you," he adds, sending a shiver down my spine.

"Me."

"You make me consider how things would affect people that aren't me. By people, I mean you."

I feel light-headed, lost to his words, but I naturally shift to tamp down his affect on me with the humor I'm eager to hide behind.

"Aww, you're growing," I joke, hearing the patronizing tone to my voice, but he doesn't acknowledge it.

"Growing? I feel like I'm falling."

"Falling?"

"For you."

RAIDEN

18

I don't think Adrianna ever looks as beautiful as she does when she's left speechless. I love her fire and sass, but watching her jaw fall slack as her lashes flutter with every blink does something to me. Her cheeks turn the palest shade of pink as her pupils dilate, searching my stare for answers I'm more than willing to give her if only she would ask the damn questions.

My heart races as the silence stretches between us, despite my appreciation for her in this state. I shouldn't have said that. Just because I'd decided to come to terms with it myself doesn't mean she was ready to hear it.

I can handle this silence, though. It's the deadly silent treatment she delivers that's driving me insane. There's no way in Hell I can handle another moment more of it. Especially not after today. There are no words that can describe the heart-lurching feeling that rippled through my body at the sight of her falling through the ice.

She took a piece of me with her.

That's why I dove right in after her, giving Cassian, Brody, and Kryll no chance to consider their options. It *had* to be me. I had to save her. After I led the damn council to her, I knew deep in my bones that I had to be the one to do it, with the weight of impending guilt if I didn't. But that's not the case. She's here. *Right* here, and I'm done wasting time letting her be mad at me. Well, she can stay mad, but I'm done staying away.

"Raiden, I—"

I wave her off, not wanting whatever bullshit is about to fall from her sweet fucking lips. "All I need to know from you right now is whether you can forgive me or not." She blinks at me, mouth moving with no words coming out. "I told you I'll figure out how to grovel, but just tell me that you can." It's a plea, one that would have had me rolling on the floor in a mixture of embarrassment and disgust before, but for her, it's worth it. I know it.

She leans back in her seat, her gaze assessing as she searches my eyes. "How did the roses end up back in my room?"

My eyebrows rise. That's not where I was expecting her to start.

Scrubbing the back of my neck, I know I just have

to be straight with her. "Wow, you're going straight to it, huh?" I murmur, earning a pointed look from her. "While you weren't there, I snuck in and hid the roses in the back of your closet and replaced the ones on your desk with standard roses. No blood involved."

Frown lines form on her forehead as her lip pulls into a thin line. "So I threw normal roses?"

She's mad.

Clearing my throat, I quickly adjust in my seat to brace my elbows on the table between us. "The shattering could have been heard from here, so if it makes you feel any better, I gathered them, and they're in my room."

Her body relaxes, the relief for the roses prominent, before she frowns back at me again.

"So you've still had access to my room this whole time?"

I should feel guilty, but I don't. I predicted her moves and kept myself one step ahead. That's who I am. That won't change, especially when it comes to her.

"I snuck back in to move the roses, but that's it," I offer, but the mention of sneaking in again definitely doesn't work in my favor.

"That's it? You're not supposed to sneak in *anywhere*, Raiden," she hisses, and I shake my head at her.

"Do you know how tempting it is to know I could sneak in and watch you sleep? To consider lying beside you?" I ask, watching as she gapes at me. She doesn't offer a response, but that doesn't mean I'm done. "Well, it's tempting, *very* tempting, I might add, but I haven't, so that should count for something." I lean back, folding my arms over my chest as I wait for her response.

"My steaks better not be getting cold over here," Pearl interrupts, giving us both a pointed look before she saunters off. We wordlessly dig into the steaks on our plates before she comes back to tell us off again.

A silence descends over us, but this time it feels comforting, like there's hope that everything just might be okay. Once we're done, I leave some money on the table for Pearl. I always over-tip, and she always tells me off, but this time, I manage to slip out before there's a chance. She's too busy murmuring something to Adrianna to pay me any mind.

I use the moment of calmness to come up with a game plan with Adrianna, but the moment the thoughts start running through my head, I know I'm approaching it wrong. I need her to forgive me, but every path to that goal that I come up with is only me forcing her into something that will make her hate me more.

Pearl's words from the other day ring in my mind and my spine stiffens.

"She needs to see your vulnerable side, Raiden."

"I don't have one."

Or do I?

I wasn't raised to have one; that's the issue. Pearl is a human, wearing her emotions on her sleeve like so many others do, but that's not something that's passed through the vampire line.

The door swings open, the usual chime ringing through the night air, and I turn to see Adrianna lift her black hood over her head.

"What now?" she asks, turning to me awkwardly.

"That's up to you," I breathe, silently pleading for her not to take off without a backward glance.

To my surprise, she nods and takes off down the narrow cobbled road. I keep in step with her, relieved that she's still here, even if it is in silence, but to my surprise, she cocks a brow at me a moment later. "Is this what you usually wear to visit Pearl's?"

She's far too observant for her own good.

"No, this is what I wear to visit my father," I admit, the moon offering enough light for me to see her eyebrows lift at my honesty. "He didn't know about my mother's involvement in the whole fated mates situation, but he didn't seem upset by it either," I add, offering her full transparency even though she didn't specifically ask for it.

"How does that make you feel?" she asks, catching me off guard.

My brows bunch together, uncertainty clawing up my

spine as my pulse throbs. My fingers itch to massage my temples, but I tuck them into my pant pockets instead. "Honestly? Like a pawn in someone else's game."

"I know that feeling," she replies, her words barely more than a whisper, but the truth in them hits me square in the gut.

"Enough about me. Well, in this sense, at least. How about you tell me how I can get the groveling in full swing," I offer, praying for her to go along with the change in subject.

Curious eyes sparkle as she stares up at me.

"What does groveling look like to you, Raiden?"

Damn.

"I don't know, but it definitely starts with me on my knees," I muse, raking my eyes over the length of her. She may be hidden behind her black cloak, but I know those hot curves that are concealed right now.

"Your knees?" she breathes, and I'm moving before I can think.

Reaching for her waist, I tug her toward me, circling around the stone wall into a shadowed alcove obscured from view. Plastering her back against the wall, I hear the sharp intake of breath that renders her speechless as I drop to my knees before her.

"Raiden..." I don't know whether it's a warning, a plea, or a promise, but it goes straight to my cock.

"Fuck, I never thought you'd say my name again," I admit, running my fingers over her thighs. The telltale trace of a sharp object beneath her joggers confirms this crazy-ass woman has daggers pinned to her flesh.

Hot. As. Fuck.

"What are you doing?" she asks, her hands falling to my shoulders as I inch higher, curling my fingers beneath her waistband.

"Groveling."

"How?" she squeaks, making me grin as I pull down her pants to reveal the silver at her thighs glistening in the darkness. Focusing my stare on the lace that covers her pussy, I grin.

"With my tongue. Possibly my fingers too, but definitely not my cock because this is all about you," I ramble, unable to cut the words off as I lean closer.

"An orgasm isn't going to make everything better," she murmurs, and I look up at her through hooded eyes, a grin on my lips.

"I know, but it will help," I state before snapping my teeth on the lace blocking me from my target. It snags easily, tearing at her hip as I use a little of my advanced speed. I watch with satisfaction as the material scatters, lost to the soft breeze in the air as I feast my eyes on her center.

Her fingers curl into my shoulders with anticipation,

not pushing me away like I half expect, and I dive in.

Running my tongue from her center to her clit, a soft moan escapes from her mouth as her head falls back.

"That's it, Adrianna. Tell me how much you want this," I breathe, repeating the motion, but this time I rake my teeth over her sensitive nub.

"Fuck, Raiden," she rasps, so I do it again. And again and again.

Desperate to feel her clench around me in any way I can, I line up two fingers at her core, diving inside as I swirl my tongue around her clit, and she writhes against the stone behind her. Her walls pulse around me as I curl my fingers inside her.

Fuck.

Nothing has ever tasted as sweet as her.

She's addicting, intoxicating, and everything I vowed never to want.

But now I can't breathe without her.

Eager to taste her release, I double down my efforts, pressing the tips of my fingers against her g-spot as she grinds against me. With a final nip of her clit, she cries out, her fingers moving to my hair as she tugs at the ends.

I lap at her core, not wanting to waste a drop of her ecstasy as she sags, spent, against the wall.

"Fuck, Raiden," she repeats, her fingers leisurely stroking through the strands of my hair, and I smile, just as satisfied, despite my cock pressing against the waistband of my pants.

Standing, I fix her joggers into place and peer down at her, but she barely moves. She's exhausted. She's had one hell of a day, so I'm not surprised.

"I'm going to move us, Adrianna," I murmur, tugging her against me, and she sags in my hold, surprising me when she doesn't argue.

Clinging to her, I move us as quickly as possible, and a beat later, we're in her room. Fairy lights hang at the window and a smattering of yellow cushions litter her bed. Something tells me this has something to do with Flora, but it suits her still.

Even when I kick the door shut behind me, she keeps her face nestled against my chest, making my body warm at our connection. Shuffling closer to her bed, I tug the cover back before gently lifting her in the air and placing her on the sheets. When I unclip her cloak, she rolls over, allowing me to tug the material away. I place it over the chair at her desk and turn back to her.

"Goodnight, Adrianna," I whisper, fighting the desire to stay as I move toward the door. But as my fingers curl around the handle, I hear one single word.

"Stay."

"Stay?"

"Such a parrot," she grumbles, making me scoff as my

heart gallops in my chest.

"You're one to talk," I retort, earning a snicker as she peers over her shoulder at me. Her eyes are barely open as sleep threatens to take over.

"Are you staying or not?"

She doesn't need to ask me again.

Undressing as quickly as I can, I slip beneath her sheets in just my boxers, and she nestles back against me.

Holy. Fucking. Shit.

This is something so small, so simple, yet so fucking euphoric it leaves me breathless.

I know I'm not through the woods with her yet, but fuck, there's a chance, and that's all that matters.

ADRIANNA

19

I cling to the edge of sleep, desperate for it to envelop me in its dark and warm embrace. But the extra warm embrace that actually lingers around my waist quickly transports me to the present, denying the plea of my dreams.

Shifting, I quickly realize there's an entire body pressed against mine, and last night swiftly comes back to mind. The hand engulfing my hip clenches, their fingertips digging into the sheet that falls over my flesh, and I shiver.

Groggily, I peer over my shoulder into the deep and heated eyes of Raiden. His smolder is back in full force as he strokes his thumb over my cheek.

"Good morning," he murmurs, his voice thick and rich, like whiskey without a single drop of ice. Not that I would know, but I remember reading that in a book once, and this moment seems fitting of that exact term.

"Good morning." I lean into his touch, acutely aware that he needs a reminder that all is not forgiven, but that can wait for the time being. My eyelids threaten to close, but the sun that drifts from my bedroom window makes me pause.

Glancing at the time, I startle, throwing him off me as I push to sit up.

"What the fuck! Why didn't my alarm go off?" I splutter, swinging my legs over the side of the bed, and Raiden's hand clamps down on my shoulder.

"You looked cute sleeping. I didn't want to disturb you," he offers, making my spine stiffen as my eyes widen.

"We're going to be late."

"We're good. I picked up food."

I gape at him, a part of me wanting to shake some sense into him, but the smell of chocolatey goodness fills my senses as he lifts a chocolate croissant in my direction.

"Thank you," I manage, taking the pastry from his grasp, ignoring the grin that spreads across his face as I sink my teeth into the deliciousness. I groan, basking in the sweet start to my morning.

"No problem," he rasps, trying to discreetly adjust himself beneath his pants. It's only then that I notice he's fully dressed. It would make sense with the breakfast in my hands, but my brain is slow to start this morning.

He reaches behind him, and a moment later there's a hot mug of coffee being wafted in front of me. Holy fuck, yeah. I take it, gulping down the slightly too-hot gift from the coffee gods before I murmur my thanks.

"You've been busy," I state, cocking a brow at him, and he grins.

"I had someone to be busy for." He says it so casually, like there's barely any weight to those words, but I feel them. Every ounce.

A knock echoes from my bedroom door, making me frown as I glare at it.

"Ignore them," Raiden grumbles with a sigh, and I pause.

"Them?"

"They're not happy that I'm in here, and they're out there," he offers, like it makes total sense, but my eyebrows gather even more.

"Who?"

"Who do you think?" he says with a scoff, and I'm up on my feet in the next breath.

I make sure to swallow down the remainder of my croissant before I pry the door open to reveal three very irritated men.

Kryll, Brody, and Cassian.

They each quickly try to shield their emotions, masking their harsh expressions with a soft grin, but it's too late. I saw. It's almost creepy to see Cassian smile like that; it's so unnatural it makes me cringe. A frown rests on his face at all times. I can't adjust to this. At least Brody and Kryll have experience with their lips twitching upward.

"What are you doing here?" I ask, opting to ignore their poor acting.

"Making sure you're okay," Kryll explains, swiping an inked hand through his red hair, and I grin.

"I'm fine."

A snicker comes from behind me. One look back, and it's clear Raiden is loving this. "Yeah, but he flies past your window every morning and had a real shock when he saw me lying beside you," he offers, making my jaw fall slack as I almost drop my coffee in surprise.

"You do what?" I squeak, turning back to the shifter in question, who blinks at me in shock before glaring at the vampire over my shoulder.

"Ignore him," he growls, baring his teeth, but I think I'm entitled to more information with regard to this.

Before I can push for more, someone's cell phone goes off, and luckily for Kryll, it's his.

"Fuck," he grunts, glaring down at the device as he takes a step back, giving Cassian the opportunity to edge forward and take his place.

"Hello? Yeah...Yeah...Okay...Yeah, thanks, asshole." He ends the call, sighing as he tucks his cell phone away.

"What's going on?" Brody asks, a sense of uncertainty drifting from him like he can tell something's going on.

"That was my brother. A heads up that there's going to be another practice trial today."

Damn. Already? I haven't recovered from the last one, and I'm barely making do after yesterday, but the kingdom waits for no one, and that includes me.

"Are you going to be up for it after yesterday?" Raiden asks, immediately behind me, his fingers gliding down my spine with a sense of comfort as he looks down at me with worried eyes.

"Of course."

"If you're not—"

"I am," I interject, refusing to bow down or look weak in front of anyone. Including them.

"Can I check?" Brody asks, eyebrows rising in hope before I shake my head.

"You already did when you healed me yesterday, remember?" I give him a pointed look and his gaze drops to the floor in defeat.

Raiden clamps his hand on my shoulder, giving me a little shake as he clears his throat, spreading a wide smile across his face.

"It's fine. She's fine. It's all fine because we're sticking together this time."

.

ADRIANNA

20

The walk to the open field for our first class feels like the longest walk of my life. It might have something to do with the fact that Flora is right beside me, a knowing smirk on her lips as she glances at me out of the corner of her eye, but I choose to ignore it.

Anything that involves me and these Krypto assholes has her preening like a peacock. I'm quite sure my life has become a new television show for her at this stage. Who needs a subscription to watch the drama unfold when it's right here for free?

Professor Tora stands tall as we approach the gathering students, observing the crowd who seem no wiser to what is coming today. Our luxury is the heads-up he gave Kryll, but he didn't offer any specifics or any kind of hint or tip to prepare us for the madness. Just that it was happening.

It counts for something, I guess; I'm just not sure what yet.

Vallie stands across the crowd of students, smirking in my direction as her friends giggle around her. Anger vibrates through my body, pleading with me to retaliate, but I know deep down that biding my time will be worth the rage I feel right now. It has to count the next time I respond to her because she sure as shit isn't taking the hint.

She bounces back quicker than a damn ping pong ball, and I'm done with it.

"Miss Reagan, a moment," Tora barks, making the murmurs and conversations in the group dwindle to nothing as all eyes fall my way.

Thanks for that.

Sneaking a glance at Kryll, I raise an eyebrow, but he simply shrugs, no wiser to what his brother wants from me than I am.

"Do you want me to come with you?" Flora asks quietly, and I shake my head. That would only paint me as weak in front of everyone, and that's the last thing I am.

"I'm good, but thanks," I breathe, fixing my cloak around my body as I step toward Tora. He waves for me to follow him, coming to a stop a few steps away from everyone else. Once I'm close enough to him, he reaches for my shoulder, making me frown, but the touch isn't harsh.

"It's so I can keep our conversation private," he

explains, and I nod, gulping back my uncertainty.

I never know how to feel around him. On one hand, he's Kryll's brother, which should make him safe, but on the other hand, he's a professor, a little ruthless, and under Bozzelli's leadership. Keeping him at arm's length is the best option, but it's a little difficult when he's standing this close, looming his unspoken power over me.

"Why would it need to be private?"

"I mean, it's for your protection, not mine, unless you would like everyone here to know whether you're in full health or not." He cocks a knowing brow at me and I fight back an eye roll.

"I'm fine."

"I'm sure you are. How many fingers am I holding up?" he asks, raising three fingers on his free hand.

"Three."

"Great. Follow the tip of my finger," he orders, moving it from side to side, and I sigh.

"Is this necessary?"

"I'm making sure you don't have a concussion," he explains, and I scoff as my eyebrows bunch together.

"You probably should have done that yesterday."

"I did, and you *did* have a concussion." The pointed look he offers me could murder a man, and even I have to refrain from shrinking beneath it.

"I'm all healed now," I grumble, dampening my

embarrassment at the fact that he did this yesterday and I have no recollection.

"So it seems," he states, dropping his free hand.

"Can you contain yourself during today's lesson?"

"*Me*? I'm not the one hell-bent on causing a scene at every opportunity."

"Well the groups are the same as last time we had to work in teams," he explains, and I blink, confusion clouding my thoughts for a beat until I remember the team I was on last time.

Kryll. Raiden. Grant. Vallie.

Ah, fuck.

"Containing myself feels like you're asking a lot of me."

"Good," he states, releasing his hand from my shoulder as he takes a step back.

"You're confusing," I grumble, and he grins.

"You're a handful."

I narrow my stare. "Are we done?"

He nods, but his eyebrows furrow just a fraction, stopping me from stepping away just yet.

"Stay close to Kryll," he breathes, his words a whisper in the wind so no one else can hear him now that his privacy magic is gone.

"Why?" I ask, but he's already turning away to face the gathered students.

"Good morning. I hope you're all ready for an adventure because we're going to be running another practice trial today," he announces, and the audible gasps that echo around us confirm everyone else is caught by surprise.

A few groans and mumbles of concern ring out as I head back toward Flora, Arlo, and my newly named Kryptos. As soon as I come to a stop beside my favorite red-headed fae and favorite red-headed shifter, Vallie's shrill voice comes to life.

"Are we forgetting what happened to me the last time we did this? What that bitch did?" she hisses, pointing a finger at me, and before I can bottle my frustration, I take a step forward.

"That *bitch* defended herself against some frenzied fucking vampire who was hell-bent on killing me with her thirst for blood," I snarl, hearing my father's voice in my head, reminding me to remain calm and collected, but there's no chance of that right now.

"Please, I would never—"

"You did," Brody blurts, appearing at my side a moment later. "I healed the gaping fucking hole in her neck," he adds, pointing at the exact spot on my skin, and I shiver at the reminder. The remnants of pain ricochet through my body and it takes everything in me to shake it off and act unfazed.

Vallie stomps her foot, her cheeks heating as she glares

at the mage beside me. "I never—"

"We're done with your drama," Professor Tora interjects, and Vallie folds her arms over her chest with a huff. "Today, we are going to work in teams to reach the peak. The same teams you were placed in when we did the trail in Evermore."

"You say a lot of *we* when you're not the one participating," Grant, my least favorite human, states, cocking a brow at the professor with far more swagger than he actually has.

Tora swipes his tongue over his bottom lip as he stares him down.

"Beau," Kryll murmurs, fingers flexing at his sides as he takes a step toward his brother. Thankfully, he seems to pull Tora from whatever he was thinking and he clears his throat.

"*You* will work in your preassigned teams to try to reach the peak. Better?"

"What peak?" Grant grunts, matching Vallie's stance with his arms folded over his chest. Who the fuck does this guy suddenly think he is? And are those muscles bulging beneath his tight, long-sleeved tee? Where did those come from?

A mage professor makes her way over to Tora, who nods at her, and that one wordless command has the ground shifting beneath our feet.

I startle, struggling to fucking breathe when a chill blows around me, and I look down at my feet to find snow.

Fucking snow. *Again.*

"What the fuck are we doing back here?" Raiden grunts, coming to stand in front of me a moment later.

"Are you okay?" Flora whispers, and I nod, despite the lump lodged in my throat.

I can rise above this. I can rise above this. I can rise above this.

"Make it to the top. The first team wins," Tora announces, ignoring Raiden's outburst, and Grant scoffs.

"But those that have wings or speed are obviously going to beat everyone else. What's the point in that?"

He does have a point, but life isn't fair, and the teams are blended so we're just going to have to deal with it. Maybe he's worried about the vampire's speed again. He was a little…green from it last time, and that's saying something coming from me.

"Ah, good reminder. Maybe you are useful in your whining," Tora states, nodding at the woman once again. Nothing noticeable happens as she chants under her breath, the words lost in the wind as I strain to listen. It takes me a moment to spot the carved wooden object in her hands.

"What is that?" I murmur, peering at Brody, who follows my line of sight.

"Ah, that's a…ah fuck."

"Everyone, thank Grant for the fact that you're saying goodbye to your abilities for the next few hours," he declares, sending a chill down my spine as I gape at him before joining everyone else in glaring beside the stupid fucking idiot that made the entire thing harder for everyone.

"It's an artifact that empowers the mage to gather the powers of those in the surrounding area. There's only one of them in existence that I'm aware of, and I'm slightly shocked they're using it so carelessly. It's called The Engraved Obliviosus."

"I'm going to kill that fucker," Cassian grunts, the snarl on his lips making me believe him.

He at least has the nerve to look a little sheepish as Tora chuckles under his breath.

"The quicker you make it to the top, the quicker you get them back."

ADRIANNA

21

Tora disappears with the mage without any further guidance, and I shake my head in disbelief. Of course he would give us nothing to go on. It's irritating right now, but my subconscious takes on my father's voice, reminding me that if I were the leader of the kingdom, I wouldn't get a heads-up either.

Damn.

"What now?" Raiden asks as everyone floats between the gathered students to form the groups previously assigned. I sense Vallie getting closer, but I keep my stare fixed on my preferred vampire.

"Now, we reach the top," Kryll states, like it's simply going to be as easy as that, but something in my gut promises the day will be more eventful than a casual stroll up a snowy mountain top.

"With no abilities," Raiden grinds back, irritation seeping from him.

I take a moment, centering myself as I focus on my magic, but all I feel is…nothing.

Fuck. That little speech wasn't just for show then.

"Apparently," Kryll confirms, still downplaying the inconvenience of it all.

"This is a joke," Raiden gripes, nostrils flaring in irritation, and as much as I agree with him, this mindset isn't going to help get us anywhere.

"It's life," I state, rolling my shoulders back as I shake the negativity off.

"I can't do anything," he continues, making me roll my eyes.

"Oh, you big baby, you're going to be just fine," I chuckle, trying not to jab his eyes out in frustration, and thankfully, my words seem to relax him a little, even if he's still pouting

"What's this whiny fuck complaining about?" Cassian grunts, appearing at my side, and Kryll scoffs.

"What do you think?" he retorts with his eyebrows raised.

"Fangs is probably sad because he can't use his pokey peggys," Brody muses, nudging him with his shoulder, which only makes his pout grow tighter.

"Don't call me Fangs, and my teeth are deadly.

Remember that," he grunts, straightening his cloak as he stands tall.

"Are you always this mean to my Raidy? You're lucky he doesn't kill you. It's not like you all don't deserve to be dead!" Vallie exclaims, cocking her hip as she glares daggers at me.

My hands ball into fists at my sides, rage brimming through my veins as I take an instinctive step toward her. I'm more than happy to finally address this bullshit with her, but Raiden beats me to it.

"I'm not your anything. You're lucky I don't kill *you*," Raiden snarls. "Now, take a step back because these groups might be predetermined and out of my control, but that doesn't mean I want you in my proximity," he adds, turning a dark stare her way. His jaw ticks as his teeth bare, and I hate how good he looks.

Clearing my throat, I take a step back, aware of Flora grinning at me from my left. She definitely caught my instinctive reaction, but if I avoid her stare, I won't have to acknowledge it to her.

"Well, it looks like we're doing this as a giant group because I'm not leaving you in danger," Cassian states, cutting through the vampire stare off to meet my gaze.

Vallie snickers. "Would you look at that? The princess needs an army to defend her. You didn't give my father the same grace now, did you?"

This bitch is so dumb. My fist forms again, and this time I'm ready to smash it into her face, but the second I take a step toward her, Flora speaks, halting my rash decision.

"You're just salty no one's defending you, Vallie."

"Listen here, you little—"

My fingers are around her throat in the next breath, choking off the bullshit about to come from her lips.

"Please, finish that shit that's about to spew out of your mouth so I have a reason to remove your tongue and slap the shit out of you with it. You're going to make my goddamn fucking day." My teeth grind together as I snarl at her, my fingers flexing against her flesh as I ready my free hand to give her face the pounding she so desperately deserves.

Hands clamp on my arms, restricting my movement before I'm dragged back a step. My hold falls slack and I drop my grip on the heinous bitch.

"Adrianna, we would never allow you to get your hands dirty when we're right here," Raiden murmurs against my ear, a hint of delight and humor in his voice as I watch Vallie shrink under his unspoken threat.

"You're all ridiculous," I mutter, shaking out of his grip. Tightening my cloak around my body, I dart for Flora, who falls into step beside me, Arlo right beside her, as we head toward the bottom of the mountain range that peaks into the clifftop.

The quicker we get off this damn thin ice, the better.

Wordlessly, the others follow us, and after a few minutes, I heave a sigh of relief when the snow thickens beneath my feet. Looking up at the top of the cliff, I shiver, the chill in the air growing harsher as I start up the slight incline.

Flora rubs her hands together, blowing warm air against her reddening fingertips.

Was it this cold yesterday?

Damn.

Pressing my lips together, I continue forward, refusing to be defeated by the cold weather, but it doesn't stop my teeth from chattering and my ears from aching.

"Hey, are you cold?" Cassian asks, drawing my attention to where he walks a step behind me.

I open my mouth, ready to deny any such thing, but before I can stop my teeth from rattling together, Kryll is at my side, pulling me in close against him. His warmth envelops me, easing the building tension in my muscles just enough for me to exhale a short, steamy breath.

"I'm hot-blooded. Stay close," he breathes, his voice completely unfazed by the temperature. Maybe this is what Tora meant by staying close to him.

Glancing around the entire group, I notice the fae, mages, and humans shivering just like me. My gaze lands on Cassian, who must see the realization in my eyes.

"All wolves and shifters, share your warmth with those beside you. Fae, mages, and humans," he grunts, barking out his command.

"No thanks," Grant grunts, continuing to make an issue out of every little thing, even as his lips turn blue.

"We make it there as a team, or we don't make it at all. Get over yourself," Cassian retorts, not even bothering to glance in his direction.

The students gathered from our three groups follow Cassian's command as he wraps his arm cautiously around Flora while a wolf girl does the same to Arlo.

"Does anyone have a good sense of direction?" I ask, nestling deeper against Kryll's chest, soaking in his heat enough to be able to bear the icy climate.

"Sense of direction? All we have to do is get to the top of the cliff. It looks pretty straightforward to me," Brody states, offering me a confused smile, and my eyebrows furrow.

"What do you mean? There are trees everywhere." I look toward the steep incline, reconfirming the snow-topped pine trees.

"What are you talking about? It's a clear path," Kryll murmurs against my hair, and this time when I shiver, it's not from the cold.

Frowning, I start to question whether crazy is something

else to add to my personality list until Flora clears her throat.

"I see the trees," she breathes, but it doesn't offer much comfort when I see others gaping at us in confusion.

"I see them too," Grant murmurs, lips pursed as he nods toward the incline.

"Me too," rings out from surrounding fae and human members of our group.

"Are you sure? There's nothing here at all," Raiden states, taking a few steps ahead of everyone.

"Wait," I holler, waving my hand. "There's one right there."

I've never seen someone roll their eyes as dramatically as he does before he continues on his path like I didn't just warn him. Two seconds pass, and right on time, he slams straight into the tree I told him to pause for, stumbling backward as he grasps his nose.

"What the fuck?" he grunts, glaring at the offending tree, but I get the feeling he still can't see it.

"Okay then. Fae and humans lead the way, but the shifters, wolves, and vampires need to stay close to keep them warm; otherwise, we're never going to make it through this invisible fortress," I declare, heading for the treeline before anyone can decline my order.

Stepping between the pines, the world grows darker, the bleak, pale sky shrouded by the looming treetops.

Thankfully, the silence that blankets us is comforting and calm despite the fact that Vallie leaves me on a level of high alert in a way that only she can bring out in me.

Seconds turn into minutes which morph into hours, until a bright glow slips through the trees ahead. "Is that a clearing?" I ask, glancing back to where Flora waivers a little, but Cassian keeps her propped up, warm, and moving. I owe him a thank you later, but for now, I need someone to confirm I'm not seeing something else.

"I think so," Arlo breathes as Flora smiles.

I will my body to move faster, but the altitude doesn't make it any easier, so my pace remains the same. Moving through the opening, I heave a sigh of relief at the clearing in front of us that stretches all the way to the peak of the mountain.

Everyone gathers, staring at the snowy expanse that stretches between us and our end goal. We're so close. The major uphill graft is behind us and now we're into the homestretch.

Relief has my muscles relaxing as the remaining tension leaves my body.

"How do we get around that?" Kryll asks, pointing a finger at the clear path ahead of us.

"Get around what?" I murmur, hearing the same lacing of confusion in my voice as I had hours earlier.

"That." He gulps, tilting his head slightly as he analyzes

something I clearly can't see.

"I have no idea what you're talking about," I admit, instantly disliking being the one at a disadvantage.

Grant shakes out of the warmth of the shifter keeping him above freezing, glancing back and forth across the space as he searches for something he can't see either.

"Shh," Raiden snarls, taking a step toward Grant, but he stops himself from going too close.

"Why?" Grant grunts, glancing back with a frown etched into his forehead.

"There's a—"

An almighty roar burns through the air and I whip my head around, searching for the source, but I come up empty.

"What is it?"

"A fucking dragon," Raiden breathes, his words a mixture of nerves and awe.

"There are eggs," Kryll mutters, his eyebrows pinched in concern as he looks between the open space and me.

"It's okay. Go."

I nudge at his arm, encouraging him toward the issue. He offers me a tight smile before carefully stepping forward, and Cassian quickly wraps his free arm around my shoulders, holding me close to Flora.

"I can't see anything, can you?" I ask Cassian, and he shakes his head.

"Raise your hand if you see the dragon," Kryll states,

turning back to look at us from his spot beside Raiden, and I watch as every vampire and shifter raises their hand.

Fuck. This trial is really making us work as one and lean on each other.

"Wolves, double up on the fae and humans so the shifters and vampires can guide us around whatever the hell we're up against," Cassian grunts, his nostrils flaring, and I quickly realize he hasn't been able to see anything so far. He's had to put his trust in others, just as the other wolves have, and I'm sure it's eating away at him.

"Everyone, follow the outer path. That includes you, asshole," Raiden orders, directing the latter at Grant, who rolls his eyes at him but eventually obeys.

Raiden and Kryll take off ahead, leading the way and making sure everyone stays back. I can't decide how I feel about being led blindly around a dragon protecting its nest. It sounded ferocious.

Curling into Cassian, I take a deep breath as his warmth bleeds into me.

They make us walk out wide, and when we slowly begin to come away from the edge leading toward the treacherous depths below, hope blossoms in my gut. We just need to get past this damn—

"Ahh, oh shit." The yelp makes me pause, and when I search out the sound, I find Grant flailing his arms at his side.

"What the fuck is he doing?" I murmur, confused as to why he's rocking as if he's on the edge when his feet are firmly on flat ground.

"Oh, don't be so dramatic," Vallie grumbles, stepping toward him with a huff. She raises her hands and pushes against his chest, making him scream as he falls. It's slow, excruciatingly slow, and when his back hits the snow, he slips across the glistening surface off toward the center of the empty space.

"Fuck," Kryll grunts as another roar rattles through the air, making my bones stiffen in fear.

I blink, watching in horror as Grant flies through the air once, twice, three times. Blood gushes everywhere, staining the pristine white snow as everyone gapes in horror.

My instinct to react is halted by the fact that I can't see the danger. That doesn't matter to Cassian as he bands his arm tighter around me and takes off running to where Raiden and Kryll start waving to everyone.

There's no saving Grant. He's gone, and if we don't move, more will join him.

The strain and struggle to move quickly, with Cassian and Flora holding me back, is too much to bear, and I slip out of his hold. "Run with her, you'll be quicker," I state, and Cassian shakes his head.

"I'm not going anywhere without you," he grunts,

refusing to see past me.

"I'm fine, I'll be fine. Take her," I yell, taking off ahead before he can say another word. The peak is almost beneath my feet when Grant's body finally falls limp. The quiet that echoes around us lasts a whole four seconds before another screech rents the air.

"Run!" Vallie screams, and everyone cries out, running as fast as they can, despite the climate toward the peak of the mountain top that tapers off into a point.

I'm panting and out of breath as I all but fall into Raiden's arms when I reach the top. In the blink of an eye, the ground shifts, and the air warms around me, revealing the campus.

"Well done," Professor Tora declares from behind me as more and more students from our oversized group fall through the magic that draws us back to the academy.

I land with a thud on my ass, along with Raiden, as we both try to catch our breaths. I watch as his fangs extend and his eyes go wide with relief, and I quickly use the moment to check in with myself, too.

My worry dissolves as I feel my magic tingle through my veins, and I sag with a mixture of relief and exhaustion as I let the warm afternoon sun cast down on me.

What the fuck was all of that? Invisible trees? Invisible dragons? What else could there be out there that we haven't faced yet? It can't get worse, can it?

My mind is spinning with the insanity of it all. Working as a team, seeing everyone have different strengths over one another, swirls something inside of me, something that awakened a part of me I was too afraid to consider.

Something I need to explore.

My wolf.

ADRIANNA

22

The dining hall buzzes around me, unaware of the turmoil that's taken root in my gut. I'm quiet, I can sense it. I don't have the mental capacity to engage in unnecessary conversation, and the glances I keep getting from everyone around the table confirm they can sense it, too.

I shiver. The cold chill still hasn't quite left my bones yet. I think it might take the rest of the week to warm me up again. I might even go in search of a second blanket for bed tonight. Otherwise, I know I'll be pummeled by icy nightmares, and I'm not about to succumb to that.

"What's on your mind, Alpha?" I startle at the deep rumble of Cassian's voice, slightly surprised by him using his apparent nickname for me in public.

"Nothing," I breathe, unwilling to lift my gaze from

my plate, where I continue to move my peas around the porcelain instead of actually eating them.

"You're a shit liar," Brody states with a scoff, and I do manage to lift my stare this time, only to give him a dirty look. When he doesn't falter under my irritation, I roll my eyes, turning away from him once again.

I can hear Flora giggle softly from beside him, making me sink my teeth into my bottom lip as I keep my emotions in check.

"So, what is it?" Kryll asks, capitalizing on the moment, and I shake my head.

"Do you need girl talk?" Brody offers, and my gaze flicks to Flora, who smiles softly at me, making it abundantly clear that if that's what I need, then she's here for me.

"No," I admit, offering her a tight smile in response, and she nods.

"But you need to talk," Raiden chimes in from my left, his stare burning the side of my face as I hum. "With who?" he pushes, unrelenting, and I sigh.

The quicker I give them an answer, the quicker they'll back off. That's clear. Irritating, but clear.

"With a wolf."

I catch sight of Cassian throwing his arms in the air at my admission, drawing everyone's attention his way.

"Would you look at that?" His eyes are narrowed, but

there's a glint there that tells me he's all ears.

"I'm considering if there's anyone else first," I admit, looking back down at my plate to avoid the wrath I know is coming. Instead, the feeling in the air is more butt-hurt than anything.

"What's wrong with me?" he asks. I shrug, acutely aware that the entire table is waiting for another answer, but I pretend the peas on my plate are too riveting to shy away from. "Addi." There's a warning in his tone, and I sigh, tilting my head to meet his pointed stare.

"I don't...maybe Janie might help," I grumble, watching as his brows gather and his jaw tics.

"Janie? I mean, for sure, she would, but what's wrong with me?"

I'm locked in a stare-off with him, unable to look away as I struggle to give him an answer, when Flora snickers.

"You don't come with a vagina."

I splutter on my next breath as the table erupts in a round of laughter and her cheeks turn pink from the attention.

"So?" Cassian is not backing down from this. Maybe he *could* help. I know he would, but there's a part of me holding back. Likely the part that knows something is growing between us, between all of us, and I'm scrambling to push the pause button, but it's futile at this stage.

"You're also hot-headed and she might need a softer approach," Brody muses, wagging his finger at Cassian, who huffs.

"And just hot in general, she's going to struggle with that too," Flora adds, earning another chuckle as I gape at her. She's definitely a handful. I can't handle her and Nora together. Ever. I wouldn't stand a chance with these smart comments.

I chance a glance at the wolf in question to find his heated stare still focused on me.

Fuck.

This is exactly what she's talking about, and I hate that she's right.

"Are you two still together?"

I frown, glancing at the girl suddenly appearing at the end of the table, and my spine stiffens. One of these days I'm going to get to eat a meal in peace, but it's clear my chances are slim. Looking at her, really looking at her, it takes me five seconds to get my read on her, and shock, horror, it's not good.

Her green cloak says enough, and the way the corner of her lip flicks up on a sneer leads me to believe I know exactly where this shit is going.

"Excuse me?" I plaster the fakest smile I can muster on my lips, relaxing my shoulders back as if my mind isn't mush.

She runs her tongue over her teeth, flicking her brown hair over her shoulder in a way that has me questioning if she's been taking lessons from Vallie. "I mean, are you still laying claim to our man?"

Our man? *Our man?* Our fucking man?

It spikes a level of anger through my veins that I can't make sense of, or I refuse to, but either way, my nails dig into my palms as I fight back the immediate urge to knock her the fuck out.

"Again, excuse me?" I repeat, tilting my head and fluttering my eyelashes like I have no idea what she's hinting at.

"Don't play dumb," she seethes, and I snicker.

"But I do it so well." My eyes narrow as my nostrils flare. My anger is no longer hideable.

"Has anyone challenged you since the new moon?" she asks, pressing her palms flat on the table beside Cassian, and I hate how close she's standing to him.

"I have no idea what moon we're on," I grunt with a shrug, watching her inch closer to him.

"She was forced into a duel the other week. Pretty certain we're still on the same one," Brody states with a bored tone, but she's unfazed by his lack of excitement at her presence.

"This can't go on any longer," she snaps, baring her teeth at me.

"Says who?" Raiden chimes in, leaning back in his seat as he drapes his arm over the back of my chair. She catches the movement, gulping as she turns to the vampire, which clearly sets a level of uncertainty running through her.

"Says me." There's a slight falter to her voice.

"And?" The corner of his mouth confirms he loves the reaction he's garnering from her by simply staring her down.

Flustering, she pushes up from the table and folds her arms over her chest. "Someone better step up to a duel."

I frown. "Wait, you want to duel for Cassian, right?"

"You're playing dumb again," she snaps, loud enough to draw a few stares from others around the dining hall. Perfect, what we need more than anything else right now is a growing audience. It's exhausting.

"Who else are you going to be able to duel for him if not me? Come back when the new moon comes," I grumble, slightly excited by the fact that I can get my hands on her. It's a pity it's not today, I need something to exert all of this pent-up stress on, and she would make the perfect target.

She shakes her head, a glint of something in her eyes as a sneering smile spreads across her face.

"No. Not when I can duel with the wolf instead."

ADRIANNA

23

"Is this a joke?" It has to be.

Glancing around the hall, I look for a sign that this bullshit is just for shits and giggles, but I come up empty-handed. The scrape of a chair along the floor has my gaze whipping back to the table to find Cassian rising from his seat.

"Unfortunately not," he grunts, resignation in his tone, and I shake my head in disbelief.

What in the actual fuck?

"You're not going to fight her," I blurt, watching as the bitch steps back with a wide grin. She's far too pleased with herself, leaving me desperate to wipe the damn look off her face.

"I will when she calls it," he states, cracking his neck from side to side as I continue to shake my head. Surely it's going to fall from my shoulders any time, but I can't seem to stop.

"I refuse," I declare, standing with him, and he offers me what can only be described as a softening look. For him, at least. The corners of his eyes relax, the tension slipping from his features as the tips of his lips curl up.

What the hell is going on right now?

"It doesn't quite work like that, Alpha. You've done a few of these now to know," he muses, unclipping his cloak from around his neck. Brody takes it from his hands without a word while Cassian casts a look of disdain toward the bitch interrupting our lunch. "Let's take it outside."

"Let's take it nowhere," I retort, scrambling for a way to make this stop, but he starts toward the door without a backward glance.

Half of the hall rises to do the same, confirming we have a bigger audience than I realized, and I sigh.

"What are you panicking for? He's got this," Raiden states as Kryll slips his arm around my shoulders.

"That's not my concern," I grumble as we hurry to catch up with everyone.

"Then what is?" Kryll asks, intrigue flashing in his eyes as he peers down at me, and I gape at him, unable to find an answer.

"I don't know," I finally admit as we step outside, and Brody suddenly appears in front of me.

"Oh, you don't want your wolf to get injured?" he fake pouts, stroking my arm with fake concern, and I snatch my arm back out of his reach.

"Not my wolf," I mutter, the words heavy on my tongue as Brody snickers.

"If you say so."

Glaring at him, I feel my blood simmer with annoyance. "Your charm doesn't shine through when you're being an ass."

His head falls back with a full laugh before he settles his gaze on mine. "It doesn't need to. You like me either way," he states, turning toward the focal point of everyone's attention as the wolf, whose name I don't even know, starts to circle Cassian. The latter stands still, bored and inconvenienced, as he glances at the time.

"Call it out, Crystal. Let's get this over with," he grumbles, but Crystal stands tall, making sure she's got everyone's attention as she makes her announcement.

"I challenge Cassian Kenner to a duel for him."

It doesn't even sound right, I think, as Flora appears at my left side, nudging my arm with hers.

"She's actually going to try and take down the man she wants to win over. How the fuck is that real?"

I scoff, unable to calm the nerves running rampant inside of me. "I don't even know anymore," I admit, inching a little closer so I can have a full view.

"These wolves are weird," Kryll mutters under his breath, offering me a little relief. At least a shifter sees it too.

"I know," I mutter, *and apparently, it runs in my veins.*

He must sense the unspoken words as he draws me in closer. "You're not weird."

I bite back a smile, despite the circumstances, as I turn away from him to focus on Cassian. "If you say so."

"You've got this, Crystal," someone hollers from the crowd, igniting a fire inside me that's ready to build into an unstoppable inferno.

"What's going on here?"

The entire gathering falls silent at the professor's voice, and I peer through the crowd to see Professor Whitlock standing tall among the students. His eyebrow is cocked as he folds his arms over his chest, waiting for an answer. A sense of relief washes over me, ready to bring this whole mess to a stop.

"Crystal has challenged me to a duel, Whitlock. We may be a few minutes late to our next class," Cassian states, and instead of shaking his head and calling it all off, the professor nods.

"As you were."

He saunters off without a single look back at the mess he's leaving behind, and I gape at him in disbelief.

This entire thing is fucking madness.

"Somebody call it," Raiden hollers, clapping his hands to move the duel along, and I know, despite my preference, it's going to happen whether I like it or not.

"Let the duel commence," a wolf shouts from the crowd, and Crystal takes off, charging toward Cassian with a devilish glint in her eyes.

My heart pounds wildly in my chest as panic creeps up my spine, but the moment she comes within arm's length of him, he knocks her away. She stumbles to the side, slowing to spin around. She manages to find me in the crowd, her smile splitting her face in two before she takes off for him again.

Bitch.

"He's being gentle," Kryll murmurs as we watch him redirect her again, and I scoff.

"Cassian? Not possible," I grumble, hands balling into fists with agitation, and he must hear my words because his dangerous dark eyes find mine.

I can't look away, I can't blink, I can't do anything but lose myself to him until a claw rips through the air and cuts his cheek. I gasp, moving to take a step toward him, but Kryll holds me back.

Blood drips down Cassian's cheek from the three slits that now mark his face.

That bitch. I'm going to destroy her.

"Focus, Cass," Raiden grinds out in annoyance as I try

to swallow past the lump in my throat, but it's impossible.

Cassian rolls his eyes as he swipes a hand over the blood before turning to face Crystal. She charges at him again, an extra leap to her movements as she edges closer to him, but just as she goes to reach for him again, his fist rises, smashing her in the face.

I shy away from the sight. Duel or not, and under these conditions or not, a man hitting a woman is not a visual I'm open to. I peer through my fingers in time to watch her limp body fall to the floor with a collective gasp echoing around us.

Holy fuck.

She's completely passed out on the ground.

Brody sighs as another wolf calls the duel to a close. The tension seeps from my body as Cassian turns to look at me.

"Well, that was a little anticlimactic after the big game she just talked," Brody mutters, disappointment thick in his tone as I gape at him.

Flora snickers, but I shake my head in disbelief at the whole thing.

"He went easy on her, Princess. Remember that," Kryll whispers against my ear, and I nod. I know that. I do.

"Is she dead?" someone asks, and Cassian shakes his head, leaning down to lay his challenger in the recovery position before sauntering toward me with a prowl that leaves me rooted to the spot.

"No, but I'm going to take her silence as surrender," Cassian states.

"What now?" Kryll asks, somehow making Cassian's eyes narrow on me even further as blood continues to trickle down his cheek.

"Now I need cleaning up. Alpha, help me."

ADRIANNA

24

Alpha, help me.

Alpha. Help. Me?

If I wasn't so damn concerned about the gash on his freaking face, I'm certain I'd attack him myself. But I can't. It's impossible to deny that my worry for him outweighs my anger at the request and his lack of manners. He can make it up to me later.

Shaking my head, I sigh, keeping in step with the growly wolf as he directs us toward the wolf building. No one follows after us, not even Brody or Raiden who always seem to oversee everything.

It's just the two of us, wandering in silence, and with every passing beat of my heart, the tightness eases. With every step, I know with raw, annoying certainty that the anger burning through my body is misdirected.

Cassian isn't my true target; he's not who I'm mad at. I'm mad at fucking Crystal.

Dumb bitch.

Apart from Janie, every wolf I've encountered has been hell-bent on making my life difficult, removing me from the board by defeating me in the challenge. Crystal is now closing in on Vallie at the front of the line, high on my target list, but since she's not here, everything centers around Cassian.

"What's the scowl for?" The wolf in question's gruff voice cuts through the air, and I feel his eyes dancing over the side of my face as he stares me down.

"Nothing," I mutter through clenched teeth, and he scoffs. *Fucker.*

"Does it have something to do with your white knuckles?" he asks, a hint of amusement vibrating through his heavy tone. To drive his point home, he lifts his hand, pulling mine along with him, and it's only then that I realize our fingers are intertwined. Not only that, but my knuckles are like snowy peaks on a winter morning.

I groan, easing my hold and forcing my fingers to relax, but he doesn't like that.

"Nah, bring it back." His grasp on my hand tightens, making my fingers ache with the way he clings to me, and I gape at him.

"Hey!" My attempts to retract my hand from his

are wasted. His hold is like steel, and I'm apparently an unwilling victim locked in place.

Meeting his stare, my lips part, ready to give him a piece of my mind, but when my eyes latch onto his, he leaves me gaping instead.

Speechless.

His eyes swirl with fire and ice as he takes me in.

Anger and joy.

Destruction and harmony.

"If I tell you to pull away, will you squeeze tighter? I don't really have the capacity to work backward right now, but it seems I'll do just about anything for you," he mutters, raising a questioning eyebrow at me.

We pass the fountain that redirects the pathways to each origin building, and we take the wolf path without hesitation. My gaze steals a peek at the gash on the side of his face and I cringe. It doesn't look good. Hopefully, it's just superficial, but he's acting like nothing is out of place.

The sight of his pain has me complying. Again. Once to his initial command, now to this. What is he doing to me? Flexing my fingers around his, he relaxes his tight grip just a smidge so it's comfortable.

"Actions speak louder than words, Alpha, and this…I like it." He nods down at our joined hands with a pleased grin on his face, and I sigh.

"Of course you do."

He doesn't treat me to a smart remark or even a sliver of snark. Instead, he swings open the main door to the wolf building and leads me inside. It's eerily quiet since everyone else is likely in class. Our footsteps echo around us as we march to his room, and by the time he kicks his bedroom door shut behind us, my pulse is thundering in my ears.

Swiping my tongue over my bottom lip, I wiggle my fingers between his, and he thankfully releases his hold. I take the distance and double it, tilting my head back as I inhale a deep breath. When I finally feel centered enough to deal with this infuriating man, I glance around his room to find him perched on the side of his bed.

His elbows are braced on his thighs, his fingers laced together as his eyes track my every move.

"Why did you do that?" I ask, my eyebrows pinching with confusion. Every situation we find ourselves in only seems to go from bad to worse, and today is no different.

"Do what?"

"Duel," I say with a gasp, waving my hand at the door like that helps.

"Why wouldn't I?" He leans back, switching his elbows for his hands on his knees as he continues to assess me.

"Why didn't you mention that *you* could fulfill the challenge?" I push, pursing my lips.

He shrugs. "Because it didn't matter."

"It didn't matter that someone might attack you?" My head rears back, horror dancing in my eyes as I gape at him, and all this ass can do is shrug. Again.

"Just like someone might attack you?" He quirks a brow, turning the situation back around to me, and I shake my head.

"That's different."

"How?"

Fuck.

Exhaling slowly, my hands clench at my sides. My right hand wraps around fabric, reminding me I still have hold of Cassian's green cloak. I quickly toss it on his bed like it's on fire and step toward him.

His thighs spread wider and I enter his proximity with bated breath. Reaching for his face, my thumb grazes over the bloody mess down his cheek, avoiding the main damage.

"She could have done much worse," I murmur, squinting at the wound as if an adjustment to my eyesight can help me gauge how deep the three cuts are.

He tilts his head to the side, leaning into my touch. My heart races, my throat dries, and my eyes blink in wonder at him. "I was distracted by your beauty, and she's lucky she got away with this," he murmurs, a smirk touching the corner of his lips, and I shake my head again.

"I shouldn't be a distraction."

That's what I'm struggling with. More than the remnants of her attack, more than the duel in general, I hate the fact that his guard slipped because of me. Being a distraction wasn't my intention, but here I am, causing chaos for those around me.

"Get over it," he grumbles, replicating my touch on his face, only his thumb strokes in wide swipes across my cheek, leaving goosebumps in his wake.

"Cassian." His name slips from my lips. A prayer? A curse? A plea?

"Addi, I would take more than a slash to the face for you. This?" He points at his face with his free hand, driving his point home. "This is nothing."

I blink at him. Once. Twice. Three times, until he suddenly shakes his head, shifting my hands from his face as he sighs.

"Fuck. I didn't just say that," he mutters under his breath.

"You did," I whisper, my eyes searching his as he tilts his head back.

"Did I?"

I frown, beyond confused, and he must sense it.

"Do you want to admit it, too?"

My eyebrows furrow even deeper. "I…"

"I can't hear you," he says with a smirk, dropping his gaze from mine as he takes a deep breath. When his gaze meets mine again, I exhale, noting the shift in his stormy eyes.

"Let's get you cleaned up, shall we?" I offer, silently pleading to change the subject, and he offers me a small smile as he nods.

"Whatever you say, Alpha." He stands, leaving me rooted to the spot as he slips into his bathroom, reappearing moments later with somewhat of a first aid kit.

"Stop calling me that," I mumble, pressing my fingertips into my temples as I try to ease the tension that's rising in me.

He shrugs. "No. It's true," he states, all matter of factly like there's no question to it at all.

"What is?" I persist, and he gives me a pointed look as he retakes his seat on the bed, caging me in with his wide-spread thighs once again.

"I feel like we just agreed that we're not admitting anything right now."

"We're not," I agree, an ache in my chest growing against my will as my stomach ties itself in knots.

He nods, a knowing glint in his eye that confirms he knew I would say that. "When you're ready, we'll get into it properly, but for now, you can help patch me up."

"What makes you think I'm any good at that? Why didn't you just ask Brody to heal you with his powers?" I ask, more than happy to change the subject.

"I don't know if you're any good at this, but I needed a minute, and I wanted that minute with you. Don't ask why; you don't want to get too deep. I just did, and I don't need Brody all up in my space about this. It will do more harm than good," he adds with a grunt, nudging the first aid kit toward me.

Wordlessly, I pry it open and glance at the supplies. Running my fingers lightly around his open wounds, I cringe when the blood continues to drip down his cheek, running over my fingers.

"It's deep," I admit, pushing at his chin to tilt his head back to give me better access.

"Does it make me look all rugged and shit?" he asks, and I snicker at him.

One stupid question and the tension coiling in my muscles eases enough for my shoulders to relax.

Unable to keep the soft smile from my lips, I look closer, slowly running my fingertips down the side of his face. "I think it makes you look—"

"Why is your touch so warm?" he asks, making me freeze as my eyes narrow on him.

"I don't…" My words trail off, taking any kind of rationale with it as I gape in shock.

"Oh my gosh," I breathe, my eyes so wide they're on the verge of pain. I'm too scared to blink for fear of missing it.

"It's healing, isn't it? I fucking knew it would." Cassian's grin spreads from ear to ear. I'm sure I've never seen him look so pleased, and I can likely count on one hand the amount of times I have, so there's not much to go off.

"You knew it would?" I whisper, watching as the holes in his flesh knit together beside my fingertips. I can't decide if I'm impressed or creeped the fuck out, but I couldn't move my hand away even if I wanted to.

"I hoped," he admits with a shrug, and I shake my head in disbelief.

"How?"

"Because you're my Alpha." My gaze darts to his as my heart races so fast I'm sure I'm going to pass out.

"Cassian."

I still can't decipher if it's a prayer, a curse, or a plea, but the weight of it is heavy on my tongue. My fingertips only fall from his face when not a single mark remains, and he swipes a hand over his cheek to confirm it for himself before he offers me a response.

"The duel. *The one you're fighting for is the only one who can heal you.*" I remember him telling me those exact same words after I had my first duel. We were in Raiden's room, the words heavy in the night as he healed me too. Except...

"But you weren't fighting for me. You were fighting

for you."

That's what he said. That's what he means. It still doesn't explain how I did this. I look down at my hands, searching for an answer in the creases of my palms, but it's Cassian's next words that give me the understanding I wasn't prepared for.

"Addi," he breathes, waiting until he has my gaze. "I'm *always* fighting for you."

.

CASSIAN
25

My heart ricochets in my chest as I stare up at the fucking wonder that is Adrianna Reagan.

In the beginning, I wanted to hate her for so many reasons. Simply breathing being one of them. I wanted to despise the fact that she was fae, more so because she's royal, but it's impossible. So much has changed since then, and it's not even because she's part wolf. It's more than that.

It's her. *Just* her. Irrevocably, undoubtedly her.

A shiver runs down my spine. Imagine if I'd harmed her, written her out of my fate before I even got a peek beneath the layers she holds so guarded.

Fuck.

The mere thought of her has the power to bring me to my knees. There's no fucking way I could ever do anything that may have a negative impact on this woman ever again.

I'm sure she could give me a long ass list of all the ways I've fucked her over already. I'll deny it out loud, but in my head, I'm free to admit that I will spend the rest of my life repairing every last piece I put out of place. My feelings are desperate to be released because they're so strong, so fierce, and I don't know how to contain them.

Growing up on the compound as a Kenner taught me that you fight for your own, you fight for your family, and you fight for your compound. I believe in all of those values; I just don't believe in the Kenner name. Not when I've borne witness to what it's capable of.

There's not a family-rooted bone in my father's body. He's selfish, strategic, and reckless; none of which a true alpha should be. Instead, he has all of a vampire's traits in a wolf's body, and he's going to lead everyone to slaughter.

Yet, when I look into the emerald eyes that peer down at me like an angel from above, I know those values can still be ingrained in me. Except my family, my compound, isn't the Kenners; it's mine.

There was a reason Raiden, Brody, Kryll, and I were all meant to find each other and start an unwavering friendship. It was for her. They're more than my friends now, they're the family I had no idea I was searching for, let alone needed so desperately. Now we have our center, the piece to hold us all together.

I gulp, desperate to find the words to express what brews inside of me without scaring her away with the first syllable.

She's my Alpha. My fucking queen. And she healed me, just as any Alpha would. If there wasn't a dormant wolf lying deep in her veins, there's no way she could have aided me just now.

But I don't know how to do any of this shit. I don't know how to do anything other than isolate myself. Even my friends don't get the full version of me, but with Addi, fuck…I want to feel everything instead of tampering it all down.

Yet all I know how to do is worship her using my body. At least I know I can show her how I feel that way.

My mind grows quiet as my body comes alive.

Instinctively reaching for her, my hands splayed across the side of her thighs as I inch my way up to her waist, I watch as her pupils dilate, inviting me in deeper.

My fingers run under the hem of her t-shirt, revealing her toned abdomen as I stroke across her skin in awe.

"Cassian," she breathes, a rasp taking root in her words as she shivers.

"Shh." I look up at her for a beat as I swipe my tongue over my bottom lip before focusing back on her body again.

Inching the material higher, I spread my hands wide

across her skin, watching as goosebumps rise in my wake. My breath is lodged in my throat, desire curling through every fiber of my body as I try to calm the thundering pulse in my ears, but it's futile. The pent-up need in my bones won't calm until I've taken a piece of what's mine.

The smallest distance remains between us, and with one stilted breath, I erase it, skimming my lips over her exposed stomach as my fingers wrap around her waist.

She gasps, stilling at the soft touch, and when I trail my lips around her belly button, eyes fixated on hers, her gasps turn to moans.

With her hands clamped down on my shoulders, she blinks down at me, anticipation rooting her to the spot, and I know I have her exactly where I want her.

Fuck.

Sweeping my tongue over her goosebumps, I release my hold on her waist to reach for the fastening of the cloak draped over her shoulders. It falls to the floor in one swift breath, somehow taking all of the oxygen with it as I gape up at her with need.

"I can't fucking breathe," she rasps, confirming exactly how I feel too, and I hum in agreement as I reach for the hem of her t-shirt once again, only this time, she helps me slip it from her body.

Her pebbled nipples are the first thing to draw my attention, tight and needy behind the black lace that fails to cover them from my view. I don't move for them, even though I'm desperate to. Instead, I slip my hands beneath the waistband of her pants and slowly trail them down her thighs.

She remains balanced, hands on my shoulders as I make quick work of removing everything until she's standing in her black lace bra and matching panties.

Fuck me.

An angel has never looked so sinful.

Finally removing my mouth from her skin, I lean back to get a good look at the woman who claims every inch of me without even trying. She doesn't shy away from my gaze as I rake my eyes from head to toe. Her confidence only seems to blossom as she stands taller, preening under my appraisal.

When my gaze pauses at the apex of her thighs, I can't stop myself. My hand shoots out, cupping that sweet pussy that brings me to my knees. She moans, her cries far more muted than I want, but it's instantly rectified by the way she grinds against my palm, eager for more.

"This pussy just loves to be punished," I breathe, and her teeth sink into her bottom lip as she bites back another groan.

With my free hand, I blindly search the bed beside me, finding the material I'm after before draping it over her shoulders. She doesn't balk, she doesn't push me away, she doesn't put an end to anything.

It takes everything in me to release her pussy so I can secure it around her neck, but when I do, it's oh-so fucking worth it.

"You look good in green, Alpha," I state, relishing in my origin-issued cloak draped around her.

I cup her pussy again, my favorite thing to do, as I watch her eyes widen and swirl with a mixture of emotions I can't quite decipher.

She's thinking too much.

"Are you ready to venture into your wolf, Addi? Not now. Right now you're all fucking mine, but soon?"

The words hang in the air, leaving me on bated breath with my cloak around her shoulders and her pussy warming the palm of my hand.

She nods.

One single nod and that's all I need.

"Good. Now put that thought away for later. You're thinking too much and I'm going to put an end to that. All I want my Alpha to do is feel."

I replace my palm with my mouth in the next moment, nipping at her through the dark lace and eliciting a sweet moan from her parted lips. Her legs immediately tremble, so I stand, grabbing her waist and depositing her on my sheets as I loom over her.

As much as I like seeing her standing tall for me,

watching her beneath my frame is something else entirely.

Reaching for her face, I swoop a hand down her cheek, along her jawline, down her elongated throat as she arches beneath me. Down between the sweet crevice of her breasts, I edge the lace that shields her from me, tugging just enough at the material to reveal her nipples that plead for my attention.

It's not in me to disappoint right now, so her taut peak is in my mouth in the next breath, my hands continuing to trail over her exposed skin. As I swirl my tongue, I tug at her panties, feeling the material snag in my grasp, and I discard it without care.

One less barrier between us is exactly what I need.

Moving to her other needy nipple, I sink my teeth into the pebbled flesh as she groans, writhing beneath me, and I can't contain my grin.

Look at us getting along. It's always the case when we keep our mouths shut and let our bodies do the talking.

Trailing my lips down her stomach, swirling around her belly button, I press my palms against her thighs, spreading her wide, ready for the onslaught we both know is coming.

The first swipe of my tongue, from her core to her clit, has her practically leaping off the bed as a pleasured cry breaks from her lips.

I want more.

I need more.

I have to have her falling apart at my touch. Now.

Clamping my teeth around her swollen nub, I thrust two fingers into her core, relishing in the noises that come from her mouth as her fingers dig into my green cloak that lies beneath her.

I twist my finger inside, feeling her walls clench around me as I rake my teeth over her clit. Her hips move, her pussy grinding against my face as she takes as much as I give.

"Cass. Cass. Cass." Her chants are fucking ecstasy through my veins as she moves, each grind of her hips searching for the release I'm so desperate to give her.

"Come for me, Alpha. Let me taste you."

I don't relent in my efforts, letting the rhythm take control as her fingers find their way into my hair, taking the last nudge she needs to tumble over the edge of ecstasy. Her cries grow louder, her movements erratic as spasm after spasm rocks through her limbs.

Lapping her release, her sweetness coats my tongue as my dick grows impossibly hard. The neglect it feels is warranted, but it's all for a good cause.

With my need now pounding throughout my entire body, I remove my fingers from Addi's core and hover above her. I'm out of my clothes as quick as my next breath, unable to stand the material between us any longer.

"Now I'm going to make you mine," I rasp, nudging at her entrance with my cock, when a knock sounds from the door. "Fuck."

"Ignore it, Cass," she breathes, pleading as she wraps her legs around my waist, encouraging me deeper.

I nod in agreement but push back so I can't feel her pussy against my cock. It's too much. She's too much. "Condom," I grunt, sliding open my nightstand drawer to retrieve one. I can sense the refusal on her lips before she even utters a word. Shaking my head, I sheath my cock as I offer her a clipped explanation. "If I come in you bare, Alpha, I'll fucking mark you, seal us together, and make you my fated mate. I don't think we can make decisions like that in a state like this."

It probably doesn't make any sense to her, it doesn't in my own ears, but she doesn't argue when I realign myself at her entrance with the condom securely in place.

Another knock.

Fuck.

"Please, Cassian," she pleads, fingers reaching for my arms, nails digging into my biceps as I groan.

"Not before I've had my fill of your sweet cunt," I bite, thrusting into her with one swift move. My eyes roll to the back of my head as I fill her.

Gripping her chin with one hand, I fist the other in the cloak and sheets that are spread beneath her, desperate for leverage as I thrust into her again and again, unrelenting as the sound of skin on skin slaps around the room.

She claws at my back, hands making their way to my throat as she cries out louder with every pass of my hips, and I see stars. Her legs release from around my waist as she plants her feet on the mattress and shifts her hips, matching my movements as we collide together again and again.

"That's it, Alpha. Fuck me."

Her back arches off the bed as she takes every inch of me. Her blond hair scatters across my sheets, across my space, my cloak beneath her providing the perfect contrast, and I can't take it anymore.

"Come with me," I growl as euphoria dances over my skin, coiling my muscles tight. Ecstasy claims me. *She* claims me. I feel her pussy clamp down around my cock, riding another orgasm at my touch, and it makes me pulse again.

Another knock at the door, followed by the sound of Kryll's voice, ends the hope of being left to swim in the pool of our afterglow.

"You good?" I stroke a loose tendril of hair back off her face as she smiles whimsically up at me with a nod.

"Better than good. But we better get that before they start trying to break the door down," she muses, reaching up to cup my face. "I can't believe I healed you," she whispers, still in awe at what she does to me, and I smile down at her, my heart beating wildly as the truth slips from my lips.

"You heal every part of me."

ADRIANNA

26

The reflection in the mirror staring back at me looks...disheveled, and that's putting it nicely. My panties are tattered, and the pair of boxers that Cassian offered as an alternative rests on the vanity beside me. I'd have to turn the waistband on them at least five times, so it's not worth the effort.

Commando it is. It's not the most scandalous thing ever, but it's different. If anything, it feels quite fitting for what just happened out there. Not that I can find the words for what just happened in the confines of Cassian's room, but the longer I linger in his bathroom, the harder it is to leave.

I healed him. I fucking *healed* him. And then he fucked me like it was a goddamn omen, and I'm powerless to resist his hold.

His heated gaze, his soft touch, his fucking cloak. All of it. I succumbed to all of it, all while admitting there's a part of me that wants to understand more about my wolf, more about me.

Using my magic, I fix my hair, making myself a little more presentable as I hear the guys talking on the other side of the door. Cassian at least had the decency to let me slink away in here, but I know he answered his door in just his boxers, confirming what was going on.

It shouldn't matter. It doesn't matter. But the blush continues to bloom on my cheeks nonetheless.

Taking a deep breath, I straighten my gray cloak and head for the door. As soon as I open it, four sets of eyes look my way.

Kryll sinks his teeth into his bottom lip. Raiden scowls at me with a heated twist to his stare, while Cassian grins with amusement. Brody, however, takes a step toward me, humor dancing in his eyes as he taps a finger against his chin.

"It smells like sex in here," he declares, making the heat intensify on my cheeks, and Cassian scoffs.

"I wonder why?" he mumbles with a barely contained grin.

"I'm glad at least someone was having fun while we were fending off the professors," Raiden grumbles, wiping a hand down his face as my eyebrows pinch in confusion.

One quick glance at Cassian and I see the same look reflecting my own on his face.

"Why?" he asks, folding his arms over his chest, still in just his boxers.

"Because you knocked a girl out," Raiden retorts with a pointed look.

My gut twists.

"I didn't want to," Cassian states with a shrug.

"We know that. Them? Not so much," Kryll explains, an apologetic smile on his lips as his gaze swoops over me.

"Well fuck them," Cassian grunts, waving his hand dismissively before slipping back into his clothes, unfazed as everyone watches him.

"I think you've done enough fucking," Brody adds, a snicker on his tongue as he winks at me. I just shake my head at his antics.

"For real, though, they're waiting to grill you," Kryll comments, scrubbing at the back of his neck with a hint of nerves that leaves me confused.

"Of course they are," Cassian snipes with a huff of irritation, but Raiden shakes his head, making everyone pause.

"No, not you, asshole…Addi."

My spine stiffens as irritation creeps through my bones, leaving me to gape at him in a mixture of confusion and horror. *What the fuck?*

"What the fuck?" Cassian barks, mirroring my own thoughts as he takes a protective step toward me.

"This really shouldn't shock me," I murmur, pressing my fingers into my temples in a failed attempt at calming the raging headache that threatens to take over.

"That's bullshit," Cassian snaps, refusing to let it drop, but there's no point. I have to assume this is Bozzelli's doing, and when it comes to her, nothing surprises me. All of my troubles lead back to her.

"It's life," I state with a sigh, rolling my shoulders back as I take a step toward the door, but I don't make it two strides before Cassian's arm whips out, halting me in place.

"Well, I'm going instead."

I shake my head at him, but before I can protest, Raiden speaks. "We thought you might say that."

"But—"

"No buts, where do I need to go?" Cassian interjects, cutting off my words as he glares down at me.

"Bozzelli," Brody offers, and I shake my head. Again. These Kryptos are going to give me goddamn whiplash.

"No." I go unheard. My hands clench at my sides, the desire to stomp my foot like a child taking hold of me as tension grapples inside of my chest.

"I'll slip Addi back to the fae building," Kryll offers, continuing to ignore my protest, and I reach my limit.

"Can you all stop talking over me!" I snap, eyes wide

with unleashed irritation.

Raiden tuts, sighing down at me with a pointed look. "No, because if we give you a chance to speak, you're going to say some bullshit, and we're already handling the situation," he states, like that makes total sense.

"*I* can handle it," I grind out, certain I'm going to explode. But a hand cups my face, drawing my attention to its owner, Kryll.

"You can handle yourself and your shit all alone, Princess, we know, but give us a chance, yeah? We all know that you're not the one they should be calling on. They've never called on you when you have actually been in a duel on campus. This is some twisted bullshit, a trap, and we can't risk you walking in there if we can avoid it."

I blink up at him, lost for words, and somewhere deep inside, it's because there's a part of me that agrees with what he's saying.

Fuck.

"Besides," Brody hollers, shouldering his way through Cassian and Raiden to stand side by side with Kryll. "Do you really want to go to Bozzelli with eau de sex clinging to you?" he asks with a quirk of his brow, and my nose crinkles in distaste.

"It's only going to delay the inevitable." I meet each of their stares, seeing the same knowledge in their eyes, but Cassian still shakes his head.

"It won't. I'll make sure of it," he promises, leaning in to kiss the corner of my mouth with a delicate touch before he steps back, heading for the door.

"Oh, are those on offer?" Brody asks, swooping in for a kiss too. His lips are gone just as quickly as they plant against mine, leaving me to gape at him in surprise.

With my lips parted, Raiden takes his chance, leaning in to rake his teeth over my bottom lip. "Delicious," he breathes, his hooded eyes peering into my soul as he takes a step back, swiping his tongue along his lips as he goes.

And just like that, they're gone.

The sound of the door closing solidifies it, leaving me with Kryll. I stare up at him, my jaw moving, but no words come out as I stare around the room in disbelief.

"What the fuck just happened?"

"I missed out, apparently," he murmurs, looking down at me with need burning bright in his eyes. Turning to face him properly, I shake my head, still in a state of confusion.

"Why would I leave you out?"

His grin spreads across his face as he leans in close so we're nose to nose. "Oh, thanks," he mutters before clinching the moment and pressing his lips to mine.

Fuck.

Gasping, my fingers fist his t-shirt as I get lost in his touch.

"Fuck, Princess," he rasps, taking a sudden step back

as he swipes a hand down his face. "Let's get you out of here before they come looking," he adds, pointing at the door behind him.

I press at my temples again, willing myself to focus, but it seems futile surrounded by these men.

"If you know they're going to come looking for me, why am I not just going to Bozzelli now to cut the bullshit?" I ask, following him out of Cassian's room on wobbly legs.

"I know this may come as a shock to you, Princess, but we fucking care about what happens to you, especially where Bozzelli is concerned."

My chest aches at his words, the feeling foreign in my limbs as I stare at him. Is this what Nora always feels like when I railroad her into doing what I say so I can protect her? Damn. I don't think I like it, but I understand the motive behind it.

As we step outside, the surrounding areas are still quiet since everyone else remains in class, and I sigh. "If they're going to come looking for me, they're going to head to my room first, right?"

My gut twists, feeling as though I'm running from a situation no matter how much I tell myself I'm not. If Cassian wants his moment to shine, he can have it. It will only prove me right in the long run, and then we won't end up in this situation again. Today is a lesson, this moment is proving to me that handing the reins over to someone else doesn't deflect attention away from me. All it will show them is that they can't step in whenever they think they're needed and magically fix everything.

My discomfort eases at my thoughts as Kryll purses his lips. "Possibly, but they could also be watching for you in class," he offers, and I nod in agreement.

"Maybe we could just go for a walk?"

He nods, and we take the pathway that leads down toward the forest. We walk in step with one another, and the farther away from the main buildings we get, the more I let the current situation sit on the back burner as I rake my eyes over the tatted hunk of a man beside me. His hair almost looks brown without the sun kissing his strands, which somehow has the ability to make him look darker, more dangerous, and more reckless.

Raking my teeth over my bottom lip, I wonder what the ink looks like beneath his clothes. The curls and thick lines leave me itching to be distracted.

"Don't give me that look, Princess. You're tempting, and as much as I would love to get lost in you, I don't want my first time to—"

I wave a hand, pulling my thoughts from the pits of desire as I focus on him. "You don't have to explain yourself to me."

His gaze meets mine as we continue walking. He is searching for something, but what? I'm not entirely sure, but he nods a moment later before turning to face forward again.

"What else can we talk about?" I offer, completely aware that if I can't be distracted by his body, I'm going to need his words to keep me out of my head.

"Your family?" he offers, peering out of the corner of his eye at me, and I immediately shake my head.

"No."

"But—"

"No, Kryll," I bite, no longer looking for a distraction as worry settles in my veins at the mention of those I love more than anything else in the world.

"I could make some plans for you to go and see them," he pushes, ignoring the irritation in my tone.

"They've checked in. I know they're okay. That's all I need," I mutter tersely, folding my arms over my chest as I stare straight ahead. I'd rather be dealing with Bozzelli than this conversation right now.

"Are you sure?"

"Yes," I snap, effectively stopping his pushing as silence descends over us, or so I think. As the silence stretches out between us, I know he's waiting with bated breath with something else to say. Glaring up at him, I give him a pointed look as we come out of the forest and continue along the pathway heading the long way back to the fountain. "What?"

He purses his lips, looking down at me like he's unsure he wants to say whatever is on his tongue, and I would leave it there until the end of time at this point, but he finally speaks. "It's just…I get the vibe that they're the most important thing in the world to you."

I rear back. "They are."

"Then why wouldn't you want to see them?" he asks, his brows furrowing with so much confusion that it worms under my skin too.

"Because it's complicated," I grumble, nostrils flaring as I fight to keep my emotions at bay. It used to be so easy, yet now, it's a daily struggle.

"Says who?" he asks, refusing to relent when he doesn't understand, and I shake my head in frustration. I need some space from him, from this topic, and it's not something I can handle right now.

Rounding the corner, the fountain comes into view. It's on the tip of my tongue to part ways when Raiden and Brody appear.

"Bozzelli has called a gathering," Brody states, making Raiden glare at the fact that he beat him to it.

I sigh, my irritation transferring from one subject to another. I hold back my 'I told you so.' It will be worth saving for when they're all here.

There goes the calm we were looking for. It doesn't exist, no matter what we do.

"Do you think Cassian managed to talk with her?" Kryll asks, concern etched near his eyes as he looks down at me, and I shrug.

"We're about to find out."

CASSIAN

27

I storm through the academy building. A man on a mission. Raiden and Brody stay one step behind me as I prowl through the halls until Bozzelli's office looms up ahead. I could use my speed and get it over and done with quicker, but fuck that. This bitch can stew on it for a few more moments, expecting Addi to appear at her command.

Over. My. Dead. Body.

It was me who was involved in that duel. I was forced to lay her out even though I really didn't want to, but I didn't have a choice. Crystal herself took that choice away from me, and there's no way in Hell Addi is paying the consequences for my actions. She already has to live with enough at the hands of my family; I refuse to add more to it.

As I reach the open door of Bozzelli's office, I signal for the guys to wait outside and I step into the room, not bothering to knock. The dean's gaze finds mine immediately, and I watch as it narrows with distaste.

"I do believe I summoned Miss Reagan," she states, steepling her fingers together on her desk as Professor Fairbourne, the professor to the fae, stands behind her. A small grin spreads across his face at my arrival, and he nods as though his approval matters to me.

"And I do believe you gave the wrong order," I bite back, kicking the door shut behind me as I saunter across the room and take the chair across from her.

She looks down her nose at me while I try not to cringe at the garish neon green dress and matching blazer she's wearing. She's a goddamn walking highlighter. For a vampire, she sure doesn't dress as a dark and mysterious weapon that lurks in the night. She demands attention, and her attire projects that.

"I'm struggling to see how you think I care what you believe," she states, cocking a brow at me, and I shrug.

Tilting my head at her, I narrow my gaze. "Is it because you were worried you might upset my father if you called me here?" I ask, watching as she balks at the accusation, but I see the smallest flicker in her eyes that confirms my assumption. That, and the fact that she wanted some bullshit excuse to have Addi in her grasp.

Fuck that.

She shakes her head with a sneer. "I would never—"

"Are you sure?" I interject, leaning forward as I match her sneer. "You don't look sure," I goad, watching her eyes widen, her jaw ticking as her irritation comes to life. Getting under her skin is easier than I thought.

"Mr. Kenner. I am the dean of this academy because I do not waver to anyone else who believes they should make the rules," she snaps, rising to her feet as she presses her palms flat against the desk that separates us.

"If you say so," I muse, rolling my eyes as I lean back in my chair. Fairbourne remains tight-lipped from his spot behind her, but the amusement on his face is clear.

"Don't push me," Bozzelli warns, and I shrug.

"Let's stay on track then, shall we? Am I here because of the duel I took part in at lunchtime?" I ask, getting straight to the point, only to have her tsk me as she straightens her suit jacket.

"Need I remind you, Mr. Kenner? You were not called for."

My gaze narrows. "Why would you require Miss Reagan's presence?" Intrigue coils around me, waiting for whatever bullshit she's about to come out with.

"That is no business of yours." Or no bullshit at all, it seems. Should I have expected her to share?

"I think it is," I push, ready to prove to this woman what

it actually looks like to be unaffected by others' attempts at power.

"I've already told you: I don't care what you think," she grinds out through clenched teeth, and I wag my finger at her.

"No. No. No. You said you don't care what I *believe*," I reiterate, and she huffs in irritation.

"They're the same thing but different words."

"You seem flustered, Dean Bozzelli. Are you okay?" I feel every inch the gaslighter I am in the moment, and it feels so fucking good to worm my way under her skin. She fucking deserves it.

"Get out of my office. Now. And send for Miss Reagan immediately." She directs the latter to Fairbourne, waving off my presence with a flick of her hand.

Like the fool he is, Fairbourne stands tall. "Yes—"

"No," I interrupt, and Bozzelli spins around to give me a deathly stare.

"Do you need a reminder of who I am?" There's that fire, the exact one I saw in her gaze before she hurt Raiden the other day. But she's never been punished at the hands of my father. I don't fear anything she may try and throw at me, and I think she knows it. That's why she doesn't want me here; she wants Addi.

"There we are. Do you get off on throwing your weight around? Is that why you wanted Addi? Is that why you applied for this position? Does it make you feel good?" Every word that leaves my lips comes out darker as my eyes narrow.

"I'm not engaging in this conversation with you," she states, lifting her hand to stop my pestering.

I stand, matching her stance. "Understandable, but I'm still intrigued by why you're calling for Miss Reagan," I persist, and Bozzelli throws her arms out wide.

"Because she will pay for her actions today," she blurts, no longer able to contain her anger.

"She didn't take any actions." It's a fact and she knows it, but she gives me a pointed look nonetheless.

"That's not what I've been told."

"And what is it you've been wrongly told?"

She stands tall, running her hands over her dress as she blinks profusely, only confirming the bullshit that spills from her mouth. "That she knocked a wolf unconscious outside the main academy building. A whole audience saw."

"That was me." I say the words slowly so she understands, yet she shakes her head like it's me who needs the gentle approach.

"Covering for her won't negate her punishment," she promises, causing me to pull my brows together in confusion.

"I'm trying to figure out this little vendetta you have here."

"I don't have a vendetta," she insists, wetting her lips

nervously, but Fairbourne nods subtly behind her. Pity he can't open his mouth and put her in her place instead of leaving a student to do it.

"Well, what would you call it? Is it because she's the former king's daughter? Is it because she's simply a fae, or does her strength leave you feeling threatened?"

That's the straw. I know it. I've pushed until I can push no more.

"Excuse me?" she bites, venom laced in each word.

"Oh, you're excused," I retort, folding my arms over my chest as I give her a pointed look.

She waves me off, slipping behind her mask of indifference, as a malicious grin spreads across her face. "It doesn't matter. I have the perfect consequence in place anyway. I'll kill two birds with one stone."

"What does that mean?" I can't hold back the question. I can see the chaos swirling in her eyes, and I know it involves Addi.

"You may follow me," she orders, rounding the desk, and I scoff.

"I'd rather not," I grunt, but she continues to wave me along. I hate the fact that my intrigue pulls me to trail after her.

"Summon the students," she murmurs to a member of staff I don't recognize, and they scurry off. Brody and Raiden hear the same words, and instead of getting answers from me, they take off. I know they've gone in search of Addi, and I would have done the same.

Following her outside, I'm not surprised to see the masses gathering already by the time we get there. Fairbourne remains beside me, but his lack of protection over Addi is wearing thin on me, so I don't even bother to acknowledge his existence.

I spot Addi first, then the guys, and I leave Bozzelli's trail to join them.

"What's going on?" Kryll asks, and I shake my head.

"Fuck if I know," I admit, hating that I don't have the answers to the concern growing in Addi's gaze.

Bozzelli doesn't waste a beat, though, drawing everyone's attention to her in the next moment. "Good afternoon, students. It has been brought to my attention that there are people here on campus who feel they should know more about what's happening outside of our protected walls to better understand the dangers we face. After some consideration, I agree with this statement, and what better way to gain knowledge than to receive it firsthand," she offers.

I frown. Where the fuck is she going with this? It has nothing to do with what we were discussing in her office. She's playing games, but I can't figure out the rules just yet.

"Where is she going with this?" Raiden asks, but I

don't have the answer, so I continue to stare the dean down expectantly.

"Field trips will be prepared for each class to take turns experiencing the frenzied vampires that roam the streets at night. We'll begin this evening with Professor Thornhill's homeroom."

"That's us," Flora blurts, and I startle at her arrival, unsure when she and Arlo joined us, but nonetheless, she's right.

We're up first.

Bozzelli's eyes settle on mine, the corners of her mouth tilting up in a wicked grin as she delivers the blow she intended.

"Do make sure you don't get yourselves injured, won't you?"

ADRIANNA

28

Who knew one finalizing comment from Bozzelli could cause such a stir? A stir big enough that we're all holed up in Raiden's room. If you can even call it that. It's more like an apartment. Either way, his sofas are filled, feet pace back and forth around the coffee table, and the chatter is starting to reach new heights.

Even Flora and Arlo are here. Their attention keeps spanning from the awe at the mere size of Raiden's room to the assholes yelling at each other. It would be amusing if I weren't the topic of conversation.

"I know Bozzelli's words were aimed at us, aimed at Adrianna, so I know what I'm telling you now is to keep her safe," Cassian growls, his fists balling tight at his sides. I'm certain his claws are going to protrude at any moment, his rage is soaring.

"And I'm saying there are other ways, not just yours, wolf," Raiden snarls, eyes flashing red with fury as he squares off with his friend. All while my gaze ping-pongs back and forth between them as they fight for control of the situation that is beyond their purview.

This bullshit has been going on for a solid thirty minutes, and my disbelief at their crap has reached an all-time high. When Raiden and Cassian both start yelling at the same time, I've had enough.

"Quiet!"

The irritation is clear in my voice. I can sense Flora and Arlo staring at me with wide eyes, likely amused at my outburst more than anything, while Cassian and Raiden both sigh at me.

"Not now, Addi," Cassian mutters, pinching the bridge of his nose like the weight of the world rests on his shoulders alone, and I scoff.

"Did you just fucking 'not now' me like I'm a child?" I bite, my magic flooding my veins, ready to unleash with the anger now consuming me.

His jaw falls slack as his eyes pinch at the corners. "No, I—"

I wave my hand, halting whatever is about to come out of his goddamn mouth. "You've done enough talking," I snarl, aiming my finger at him before turning it on Raiden.

Brody and Kryll have mostly remained quiet and not tried to take control of the situation, but with one wrong word, I'll be jabbing my fingertip in their direction too. "I'm a grown-ass woman who has taken care of herself long enough to know how to handle things. I've faced three duels because of *you*." My attention focuses back to Cassian, who doesn't so much as wince under my disapproving glare. "I've fought off The Council when they tried to force me to become fucking fated mates with you all, Vallie's constant bullshit, and everything else that has been tossed my way, I've handled. This is no different. I can handle it all the same." My shoulders sag, the truth coming to the forefront of my mind. "I want this, fuck, I *need* this. I need to prove I can defend the kingdom, and seeing this through is going to aid me, and us, in the future. If something happens, then something fucking happens. That's what I live for. I *like* the trials. I *like* the tests. I *like* all of the action."

Understanding settles in Kryll's stare while Brody looks at me in wonder. Raiden and Cassian, however, are not on the same page. The latter steps forward, hand reaching for me, but I swipe it away.

"I know that, but Bozzelli—"

"Fuck Bozzelli. I'm here to win, Cassian. W. I. N. Against Bozzelli's liking, against Vallie, against every wolf, every vampire, or any other origin who desperately wants my head on a spike. I'm here to win against all of you. Whatever it takes. Including whatever this is." My chest heaves with every breath, bursting for someone to acknowledge that and respect it.

"But she's going to do something," Raiden murmurs, his harsh tone wavering slightly as I shake my head.

"That doesn't surprise me, but letting her get to me is not on my to-do list for today," I state. It weighs heavy on me as I look around the room at everyone, Arlo and Flora included. "I need you to respect me and my decisions in moments like this because this is who I am. If you can't, I get it. If that is the case, then we need to draw a line in the sand on whatever the fuck this is right now because I will *not* continue to have these conversations with you."

Silence descends over the room, and I watch as some nod eagerly straight away while others scrunch their faces in distaste. I wait it out. My shoulders are relaxed, my breathing is easing, and I feel lighter for getting this off my chest.

"I think it's admirable, Dagger." I turn to Brody, noting the smirk at the corner of his mouth before he continues to speak. "That you are willing to acknowledge there is something here between all of us. It's a big step. I'm proud."

I roll my eyes at him, but the snickers that come from the sofa tell me Arlo and Flora are enjoying his humor after our blunt conversation, and it eases the tension in the room.

"Thanks, Brody. Not what I was going for, but I'll take it," I mutter in response, earning a wink from the mage himself.

Kryll clears his throat, cutting the short distance between us to plant his hand on my shoulder, offering me a comforting squeeze along with his soft smile. "Whatever you need, Princess. I'm here. Now, are we done? Everyone will be gathering," he states, turning his attention to Cassian and Raiden, who are both still riddled with tension.

"I'm good," Raiden relents first, taking a step toward the door. He gives me the smallest nod, but I take it.

"Me too," Cassian rasps, eyes boring into mine as his brows furrow with concern.

"The queen has spoken. Let's go," Flora declares, standing with a grin.

"Of course you take her side," Raiden grunts, giving her a disapproving look, and she rounds on him with a quirked brow in place.

"There are no sides. She's right, and you're wrong. Oh, maybe there are sides."

I chuckle at her, failing to smother it with my hand as I head for the door. I scurry down the opulent stairs without a backward glance. The fresh air hits me like a soothing blanket as the sun starts to set in the distance.

Flora links her arm through mine, Arlo right beside her, and I watch as the four Kryptos who influence my every move and consume my every thought circle around me. Kryll and Raiden upfront. Brody and Cassian are behind.

I know it's their protective formation, and as much as I want to give them hell over it, at least it gives me a moment to clear my head with them focusing on that instead of me directly.

Fuckers.

Anticipation coils through my bones as we turn down the pathway to find Professor Tora standing by the entryway to the campus. The rest of Thornhill's students are gathered around him, Vallie included, and the air around the space feels thick. A sense of unease vibrates through the atmosphere. Even when Tora hollers for everyone to follow him, it remains.

The gates separating us from the outside world open, and all too quickly, the cobbled streets are underfoot. They feel familiar as we head under the archway and through the square, and for the first time in my life, I'm not hiding beneath my black cloak. My gray academy-issued cloak is draped over my shoulders and the hood remains down. I take the view in without a shadow cast over me. There's something about this place that takes purchase in my chest, warming my limbs and fueling my heart.

I spy the castle looming in the distance and my chest

tightens. This is our home, this is *my* home, and I no longer want to live in the shadows and hide from it all. I want to prove I'm worthy. I want to *be* worthy, and that all starts now.

Professor Tora leads us toward the clock tower, and we climb the stairs, one stone slab at a time, until we reach the top. The view of the city is even more spectacular from here, which means the vantage point when the vampires show up will be perfect.

"Now what?" Vallie asks with her hands on her hips, pulling me from my thoughts.

"Now we wait," Tora offers, the curl to his lips overshadowed by the furrow of his brows.

"For what?"

He glances around the group and shrugs. "For chaos."

ADRIANNA

29

Someone stifles a yawn. I'm not entirely sure who, but it sets off a ripple through the group and I have to clamp my hand over my mouth to refrain from doing the same.

We have to remain alert. Vigilant. Just because there's no immediate threat doesn't mean we won't need to act at any given moment.

Rolling my shoulders back, I move from my spot, doing a slow, measured patrol around the limited space we have. It earns me a few deathly glares from other students, but it didn't bother me the first time they were inconvenienced by my surveillance, so it doesn't bother me now. Especially when there's a likely chance I'll observe the city below just like this in the near future.

I have to prove I can handle situations like this. Not to

the academy. Not even to Professor Tora. But to myself. Particularly after the shitshow that went down in Raiden's room. I can handle my Kryptos' desire to help, but their need to overstep is not going to be tolerated, and I meant every word I said.

"Anything new?" Flora asks as I settle back into the space I had occupied moments earlier, and I shake my head with a sigh.

"It's weird. In one sense, I want to see them right now, but in the other, I hope they don't show up at all so the civilians will remain safe."

Flora offers me a soft smile as she nods in agreement. Her hands band around her waist as she holds back a slight tremor. It's getting colder now that the sun has settled, and the moon glistens in the sky. Arlo must notice the same shiver because he wraps his arm around her shoulder a moment later. Flora leans into him, and I wonder if they've figured things out, but a heavy sigh cuts through the air, disturbing the peace.

"Professor Tora, don't you think it's safe to call it a night?" The whine comes from Vallie as she pouts, rocking on her feet and fluttering her eyelashes.

"Does she think that look is going to work in her favor?" Brody whispers against the shell of my ear, and I grin, fighting back a snicker. At least I'm not the only one put off by her shit. "Now, if you were to do that, I—"

"I would never," I interject, peering over my shoulder at him with a pointed look, and he chuckles, the sound thankfully muted by Tora's sharp words.

"Vallie, please walk yourself back to the academy if you don't have the stamina and patience to perform a proper patrol. It's not like it's for the good of our kingdom or anything," he snarls, and when I turn to see him among the crowd, I find a deathly glare on his face.

Vallie flusters, throwing her hands out at her sides as her leg bounces, and I'm certain a foot stomp is due at any moment. "We've been waiting almost four hours. They're not coming," she insists.

I tilt my head as I look at her. She seems certain of the fact. Her eyes are wide, pupils filled with truth as she nods profusely.

Why?

Why would she be so certain? How?

Confused, I turn, glancing over my shoulder at Cassian, Raiden, Kryll, and Brody, and I find my vampire staring at her with narrowed eyes.

I shake my head. He's not *my* anything.

Fuck.

"Raiden?" His name is a breath on my tongue, and his gaze whips to mine. I look back to Vallie and then to him, and when our gazes connect again, he nods. Once. That's all it needs to be for now. We can discuss it in more detail later, but it's clear he senses what I do.

"I don't care if we stand here until dawn and no one shows. It's for our kingdom," Tora bites, the words rattling inside me as they take purchase, settling deep in my gut.

He's right.

The hairs on the back of my neck suddenly stand, making me freeze as my magic shoots to the surface. Closing my eyes, I try to focus on the air as it whips around us. Something has shifted. But what?

"But, Professor—"

"Quiet," I rasp, and Vallie's shrill voice surprisingly pauses. Turning, I let my body guide me, but I've barely taken two steps before she makes her presence known again.

"Excuse me. Don't you—"

"Shut the fuck up," I growl, my irritation clear this time as I turn to her with a pointed look. She gapes in disgust, a scoff parting her lips, and that's when I hear it. *Truly* hear it.

My heart lurches before kicking into overdrive, and I rush to the north-facing point of the tower.

"You can't speak to me like that," Vallie persists, and I bare my teeth at her as I turn on a snarl.

"Be quiet, or I'll offer you as bait."

She frowns, along with many others, which is ridiculous. Especially since she's a vampire. Her hearing should be alerting her to this.

"They're coming," Kryll states, appearing at my side a moment later. His fingers flex on my shoulder as he plants his hand on my cloak, squeezing in comfort.

Not two seconds later does the visual match the sounds I could hear.

A stampede.

A fucking stampede of frenzied vampires.

I watch in horror as at least forty of them flood the streets below us. Their eyes are wild, and their movements are off, but I can practically smell their need from here.

Lifting my foot up onto the wall that shields us, Kryll's hand tightens, halting me in place.

"Let go," I murmur, trying to keep my voice low, but it still manages to garner Professor Tora's attention.

"We're not taking action. We're observing," he states, his tone almost bored, a complete contrast to the man giving Vallie a mouthful moments earlier.

"What?" I turn to him, noting his expressionless face in the moon's glow, and I frown.

"That's the order," he offers with a shrug, and my stomach twists in panic.

"They're going to kill people." A woman's cry echoes from below, sharpening my point, but he still makes no move to take action.

"That's what the soldiers are for."

"And they're *not* here," I push back, shaking my head in disbelief. I thought we were here to fight, to protect our kingdom.

"Not my problem. I have my orders," Professor Tora offers, offering me a dismissive wave as he turns away, but I can't calm the burning rage inside of me.

"Your orders are bullshit," I growl, shaking out of Kryll's hold as I push up onto the wall.

"Where are you going?" Tora asks as gasps ring out from the other students, who seem to be more than happy to just sit back and watch.

I glance back over my shoulder, determination fueling every breath I take.

"To protect my kingdom," I declare before I fall into the night.

ADRIANNA

30

I lose my breath as the air rushes past me, but all it serves to do is fuel my adrenaline.

My air magic comes to life before I hit the ground, softening my fall as it guides me firmly onto my feet.

There's no time to take a deep breath and ready myself. It's carnage down here. Civilians rush for cover, but if their doors are already unlatched, it's too late.

I take one step forward when a hand lands on my shoulder. In my chaos-induced haze, I turn, ready to attack, to see it's Cassian.

"Together."

I gape at him, lost for words, but there's no time to hesitate so I nod.

"Together."

Raiden, Brody, and Kryll descend beside us. "Together,"

they say in unison, bolstering the insanity I know I'm exuding right now, but for the good of my kingdom, I'll do whatever it takes.

One word.

One word, and we're on the same page.

A rarity for us, but we're going to need to make the most of it.

A man's scream of horror rips through the air, spinning all of our attention to the destruction unraveling around us, and we're off.

No more words. No more observing. No more thinking.

Just action.

I run, barreling toward two vampires as they try to break down the wooden door to a storefront. The owners are on the other side of the glass, sobbing in fear. The terror in their eyes tells my soul they're humans. Defenseless.

Fuck.

Quickening my pace, I shove up my t-shirt to reveal eight of my daggers. Blindly grabbing one in each hand, I lunge the rest of the distance, stabbing both of the fuckers in the throat.

Wild eyes meet mine, and both of them reach for me at the same time, eager to exact their revenge, but I twist the handles, driving home the venom exuding from the silver tips. Their movements sag, the pair dropping to the ground on their hands and knees. As they struggle to find their last breath, I conjure the air around me, using it to my advantage as I sheath both of my blades and use my bare hands to snap their necks.

I ease my magic, the air no longer adding to my strength to get the job done. Kicking them both over, I make sure they're both *dead* dead before I glance at the humans inside the store. The woman's hand is pressed against her chest, eyes wide under the light of the moon as she hyperventilates with every breath. The man beside her, however, stands ramrod straight, lips in a tight line as he looks from me to the dead vampires.

"Do you have a barricade?" I ask, stepping up to the glass, and the man shakes his head. Fuck. "You need one. Let me in," I blurt, and he shakes his head. Taking a deep breath, I flex my hands at my sides. "I'm trying to help you."

"I don't want no help."

It's on the tip of my tongue to point out his use of a double negative, but I fight against it, scanning my surroundings to see what there is. A crash echoes behind me and I glance over my shoulder in time to see a wrought-iron gate fall beneath three vampires.

What the fuck are they even doing?

Shaking my head, I focus. Summoning my magic to my fingertips, I use the air around me to bring the mangled metal toward me. When there's enough, I use fire, desperate to be released from my touch, to weld the metal together.

Pulling and stretching, I morph the searing-hot iron as quickly as I can before dousing it with water in an attempt to cool it. There's no water source nearby, so I work on transforming the steam from the heat into water droplets until the chaos behind me reaches new heights and I have to stop.

"I'm going to leave this here. It should be enough to withstand any further attack, but it would be better from the inside," I state, my gaze locked on the man on the other side of the glass, who doesn't utter a word in response.

The woman beside him, however, nods her head profusely. "Thank you. Thank you. Thank you."

Satisfied, I turn to the carnage that continues to unravel around us. The numbers we're up against are dwindling. We're taking them down. One at a time. The next one falls, the distinct sound of their neck cracking ricocheting off the walls as a flash of red hair makes me pause.

"Flora?"

I gape, watching as she presses her fingertips into the skull of a vampire on his knees at her feet. He falls in a heap a moment later, lifeless, as she smiles at me.

"Hey."

"What are you doing?" I balk, earning a side eye from her as Arlo saunters up beside her.

"Getting a manicure. What does it look like I'm doing?"

she retorts, making Arlo snicker. She winks, a proud glint in her eyes before she takes off toward the remaining vampires with Arlo at her side.

Holy fuck.

A dozen or so vampires take off down the narrow pathway to the left, wreaking havoc and leaving chaos in their wake, and I follow after them, acutely aware that they'll be nearing Pearl's in a matter of seconds.

"I'm right with you, Dagger," Brody hollers from behind me, his boots pounding the ground with urgency as we take off into the night, chasing vampires like it's a casual affair.

"Like we've practiced," Raiden snarls, his deep voice cutting through the night air making me frown in confusion, but I can't stop to ask what he means. I can't let the vampires get away. Especially not when I see the entryway to Pearl's come into view.

I need to act, and I need to act now.

"Praesidium. Tutela. Praemunitio. Arx. Umbra. Praesidium. Tutela. Praemunitio. Arx. Umbra. Praesidium. Tutela. Praemunitio. Arx. Umbra." Brody's chant flickers through the air, casting darkness around us with every word he mutters.

Suddenly, Pearl's is no longer in view. Nothing is. Just an inky darkness that touches everywhere around the five of us, and the vampires intent on destroying the city.

"Now," Raiden grunts, and Cassian takes off running. He leaps through the air before he reaches the vampires, and I watch in awe as he shifts before my eyes, a hulk of a wolf in his place as he hits the ground.

His teeth are bared, his eyes narrowed, and his body coiled tight, ready to unleash his pent-up adrenaline on the enemy.

He charges for the closest vampires, his teeth sinking into their throat as he grapples with them. Blood splatters everywhere, marking the inky darkness with a deep-crimson hue.

My view is quickly blocked by a vampire tearing toward me with purpose. Instinctively, my hands twirl around the handles of two daggers again, and when he lurches forward, arms out to grab me, I duck, slicing the poisoned silver into his thighs.

He howls in pain as his blood splatters across my face. He drops to the ground in a heap but quickly rises to his feet, ready to charge me again as the poison slowly takes hold.

Before he can take another step toward me, Kryll is behind him; hands clamped down on either side of his head before he twists. The sound of snapping bones resounds in my chest with every breath I take, leaving me to gape with my lungs heaving as Kryll winks and moves on to the next target.

Fuck.

Sheathing my daggers, I reach for two more, silently thanking the trinket gods that I had a few viles of the vampire toxin in my possession.

Blood seeps into my clothes, causing it to cling to my limbs, staining my skin. I swipe at my face, but it's futile. All I'm doing is spreading the mess. I can worry about the state of me once I'm done here.

Settling my gaze on the next vampire, I take off, approaching from behind before I pierce him from either side, wedging my blade between his ribcage to cause the most damage.

"You bitch," he snarls in a choked voice, his gaze locked on mine as he sinks to his knees, and I twist the blades for good measure, just like I did earlier. His blood drips from my fingers as I retract my blades, returning them to my holster before I use my air magic to aid the satisfying sound of his neck snapping.

I shouldn't like the sound of it. It should make me recoil, but it's the sound of justice.

"Two more, Adrianna. Are you with me?"

I peer at Raiden, surprise tainting my vision as I blink at him. He cocks a brow like he expected an instant answer, but I'm too startled.

"What happened to the asshole from earlier? The one adamant that I needed defending at all costs? The one believing I couldn't do this?" Now isn't the time to be asking, but I can't help myself. The man standing before me, hand outstretched, inviting me to slaughter the remaining vampires, is a complete contrast to earlier.

"That man was an asshole. An asshole desperate to protect you from the world and completely forgetting that you don't need protection from anyone or anything. You're a fucking warrior, Troublemaker. Now, are you going to do me the honors or not?"

Well, when he puts it like that.

I nod, taking his hand at the exact same time a flash of white blinks from behind him, and teeth sink into his neck a moment later.

My eyes widen, terror bleeding through me as I watch Raiden's body tense under the bite of a frenzied vampire. My breath lodges in my throat, adrenaline coursing through my limbs with such force that it takes me a second to remember how to move.

"No!" I croak, like the word will make him stop, but it goes unnoticed as I bolt toward them.

I can't grab a blade quick enough, so I drop my shoulder and throw myself into the assailant with the wind behind me. Freefalling through the air, the force of the magic making it more drastic than necessary, but I don't have the strength to retract in time.

Thankfully, I knock the fucker away from Raiden,

toppling him to the ground. Braced above him, he squirms beneath me, bucking and twisting to get me off him as he snaps his bloody teeth in my direction. I scramble to keep the upper hand, fumbling for my two remaining poison-tipped blades before plunging them into his eyes.

I yank them out, repeating the motion again and again, plunging without care as I scream, the pent-up tension needing a release from my body.

My throat burns, and my actions are relentless. Even when he stops trying to fight me off, even when he's dead, I can't stop.

If he hurt Raiden…

No.

He can't.

I refuse.

Raiden.

I stop abruptly, daggers raised and ready as the panic still sounds in my voice and my cries continue.

"Troublemaker." The nickname cuts through the pounding of my pulse in my ears as I search desperately for the source, but the darkness Brody created is hazed by a red glaze over my eyes.

Relief floods my body as Raiden's face comes into view, but the sight of blood gushing from the open wound at his neck is enough to set my panic into full force again.

"Raiden," I rasp, cutting the distance between us as

my daggers fall to the ground. I band my arms around his neck, clinging to him as I try to calm the racing of my heart, but it's easier said than done.

"Take the alley. We'll clear this up," Kryll states, but before I can understand what he means, Raiden is moving.

A moment later, my back is plastered against a stone wall as my vampire hovers above me. His hand is clamped down on his neck, his fingers dripping with blood as it streams down his body.

"How can I help? Tell me how to help!" I choke, placing my hand over his as I peer around our new surroundings. We're down a small dead end. One I'm familiar with, two turns from Pearl's.

We should be safe here. But there's nothing I can use to aid him.

Fuck. Fuck. Fuck. Fuck. Fuck.

I need to stop being a distraction to these men. Look at him. This is all my fault.

"We need to get you help, Raiden. Fast. How?" My voice is getting louder, the alarm clear in my tone as he smiles down at me. He fucking *smiles* like he's not bleeding everywhere.

"All I need is you."

I gape at him. He can't be real right now.

"I'm the last thing you need right now," I retort, anger coursing through my veins as I peer up at him. "I'm the reason Cassian was cut today and the reason you're bleeding from the neck," I snap, trying to wrap my head around the fact that I've been through this twice in one fucking day.

I need a break.

Fuck.

"Adri—"

"No, Raiden. Don't give me any of this shit right now. Help me help you," I growl, and his free hand grips my chin, squeezing for good measure as he forces me to look up at him.

Blood is smeared over every inch of him, glistening along the strands of his otherwise dark hair. I can't imagine what I look like, but that doesn't seem to matter to him.

"Give me a minute, Troublemaker. I'll be fine." His voice is dark, husky, tired.

"A minute? Fucking minute? Raiden your—"

My words are cut off and forgotten as he effectively shuts me up with his bloody lips crushing against mine.

RAIDEN

31

I want her.

I need her.

I have to have her.

Her lips are soft yet firm against mine as I slam my own against them, and something settles in my soul as we fuse together.

Easing my grip on her chin, I cup her face with both hands, tilting her head back to the perfect angle to part her lips and taste her sweetness on my tongue.

"Raiden," she rasps against my lips, a moan etched with concern, and it's enough to tear me from her mouth to see what's wrong. "Your neck," she gasps, instinctively reaching out for the open wound as blood trickles down my collar.

"It's fine, Adrianna," I murmur, declining to mention

the wooziness that is slightly dimming my vision and leaving my head a little light.

"It definitely doesn't look fine," she grumbles with a pointed look, and I grin. I would bleed out right now if it meant I got to kiss her again. "We need to get this seen to. Where's Brody?" she asks, her fingers curling tighter around my neck as she tries to apply pressure while her gaze flits to the opening of the alley in hopes the mage will magically appear.

If he does, I'll kill him.

"Troublemaker…Troublemaker…" Two breaths of her nickname and a squeeze at her chin again so she's finally looking back at me. Certain I have her full attention, I lean closer. "I'll heal on my own…eventually. Until it passes, it's just me and you." My tone drops deeper, darker, and needier as I peer into her eyes.

Her tongue sweeps out over her bottom lip and her gaze drops to my lips.

"When? It looks bad," she whispers, taking a slight peek at where her hand presses against my throat. I don't need to look to know her fingers are going to be coated in blood. My blood. That only turns me on more.

"It's fine. It'll be even better if you kiss me again."

She shakes her head at me in disbelief, but I'm deadly serious. I need her more than my next breath. The tremble that vibrates through my veins has nothing to do with the wound at my neck and everything to do with her proximity.

"Raiden, now isn't the time to—"

I slam my mouth against hers, raking my teeth over her bottom lip as she groans, but I swallow each little cry for myself. Her protests are wasted on me, but her moans... they're exactly what I'm living for.

Releasing her again, her head slumps back against the stone wall behind her as she tries to catch her breath. Her fingers don't move from my neck, warming my icy veins as I stare at her in wonder.

"Do you realize how fucking phenomenal you are?" I breathe, catching her eyebrows pinching in confusion, leaving me to be the one to shake my head in disbelief this time.

"Raiden, I—"

I press my thumb against her lips, cutting off her next words. "The next time my name leaves your lips, it's going to be with a moan. Ideally, with your cum dripping down my fingers or, preferably, my cock. Understood?"

Even under the moonlit night, I can see her pupils dilate, the rhythm of her heartbeat kicking up a notch as she stares at me in a mixture of desire and confusion. To save her any more bewilderment, I spell it out to her.

"Adrianna, there are never going to be enough apologies that leave my lips to make up for ever doubting you. Tonight, you left me awestruck. Your fearlessness, resilience, and brilliance—I want all of it. And if I tell you a little secret, you can't tell a soul, do you hear me?" She nods, eyes wide as she hangs on my every word. I want to see her reaction to my words, but keeping them as quiet as possible is more important. Her hearing them surpasses anything else, which is why I lean in, pressing my lips to the shell of her ear as I offer her my secret. "I walked through the doors of the academy with one thing in mind: become the next leader, the new heir, the royal I know I can be." My chest tightens, aware that I'm no longer the same man who walked through those doors such a short time ago, and it's all because of her. "But if it comes down to it, if it was just me and you at the end of the race…I'd fall and stumble to watch you rise, to see you shine, to be in the presence of your greatness as you reclaim who you were always meant to be."

Leaning back, the first thing I notice is how blown her pupils are, the crimson stains of blood laced across her face drying with every passing moment.

"I would never ask you to do that," she manages, her voice nothing more than a croak, and I shake my head with a smirk.

"You wouldn't have to."

She tugs at my neck, eliminating the distance between us as she takes the reins, crushing our lips together.

All sentiments are gone, every word disappearing

along with them as our bodies do the talking.

I blindly reach for the waistband of her pants, slipping beneath the material to find no further barriers.

Fuck.

Has she been like this all day?

Or just since she spent some time with Cassian today?

Fuck.

Slipping my fingers through her core, I'm met with overwhelming heat, and as I tease my pads at her entrance, her desire coats my skin.

I rest my forehead against hers, watching as her eyes roll back at my touch. Her pussy clamps down around my fingers as I fuck her slowly. Every move is punctuated, deliberate, as her back arches off the wall.

Using my free hand, I slip my palm under the hem of her t-shirt, but the weight of the fabric throws me off.

"I'm drenched in blood, Raiden," she rasps, her breath whispering against my lips, and I grin.

"You say that like it's a bad thing."

"It is."

"I think you're forgetting what I fucking am, Troublemaker."

Her breath hitches and I wrap my fingers around her wrist, tugging her hold away from my throat. It takes a second for her to trust me, but a moment later, she realizes what I already know.

"It stopped."

I nod, aware that the reminder of the wound still coats my skin and hers. Unbuttoning my pants, I tug them open just enough to relieve my cock from the tension of being imprisoned behind the fabric.

With her hand in mine, I wrap her bloodied fingers around my length, groaning at the contact as she gasps. "Paint my dick red, Adrianna."

She blinks at me, testing the weight of my cock in her grasp as I release her hand. I want to feel her, touch her, have her. I slip back into her pants, finding her core once again, and I waste no time making it mine.

The first thrust of my fingers has her hand tightening around my dick, making me gasp, and she must like to tease me because she does it again and again with every thrust of my fingers.

Our breaths mingle between us as we stare down at where we're connected, but the sight of my cock painted in my blood does something to me, especially with her fingers locked on me.

"I'm going to come, Troublemaker, and I want to do that inside you," I rasp, continuing to fuck her with my fingers as I use my other hand to pull a condom from my pocket.

"Please," she whispers, her eyes pleading just as strongly.

Sinking my teeth into my bottom lip, I lean into my abilities, and before she can blink again, my cock is sheathed in protection, her pants are dangling from one leg, and her back is against the wall, suspended in the air with my dick lined up, ready to slide home.

"Please," she repeats, breathless, as our gazes settle on one another.

I don't need asking again.

My fingers dig into her thighs as I tilt her just a little more before thrusting deep into her core. Our moans morph into one between us as I take a second to adjust to her heat.

"You're my everything, Adrianna," I rasp, desperate to give her everything I have the ability to offer while claiming every last ounce of her for myself. "You're mine, you know that, right? Fucking mine." Her eyes pierce mine with a ferocity that sets my veins on fire. "Say it."

She swipes her tongue over her lips, and I thrust into her harder, faster, desperately, encouraging her words.

"I'm yours."

Two words, barely more than a whisper, and I'm ready to crumble to my knees. My cock twitches, ready to explode at the declaration, but I bite it back, refusing to go over the edge before she comes on my cock.

"That's it, Troublemaker. You're mine, and I'm yours. I know those fuckers are a part of this too, and I promise you I will worship the ground you walk on, but don't *ever* threaten to leave me again. Not like you did earlier. Not ever."

My movements become brutal as I pound each word into her. The reminder of her threatening to walk away back in my room was enough to make me see sense. Never again will those words leave her lips. Not in my direction anyway.

"You're mine," she breathes, wonder in her tone as she gapes at me, and I grin.

"Yes, yes, I am."

Our lips fuse together, words no longer needed, as I feel her pussy squeeze desperately around my cock. The second she sinks her teeth into my bottom lip, stifling back her cries of ecstasy, I chase her over the edge.

Panting, I'm lost to the spasms that ripple through my body, and just when I think they're done, she shivers, another wave rushing through her, and it seeps into me, too.

"Fuck, Raiden," she rasps, warming my whole fucking being, soul and all.

Lowering her feet to the ground, I fix her pants before rolling the condom off my cock. I take a step back with a sigh, a strange feeling clinging to my lips.

"What does it mean if I feel weightless? Like, my heart is calm, my soul full, and my entire body is serene?"

She offers me the sweetest fucking smile I've ever

seen as she takes a step toward me. Squeezing my arm, she tilts her head. "I'm quite sure that's how I would describe feeling content."

Content.

Huh.

"That's how you make me feel," I blurt, and her smile somehow gets cuter, warmer, happier.

"When you're not an erratic lunatic of a vampire, you make me feel that way too. Sometimes."

"Sometimes? I can take that, Troublemaker. I want to make you feel all of those things. Always," I say, cupping her cheek as I lean my forehead against hers again.

The warmth only seems to grow hotter as I bask in her, this moment forever searing itself into my memory.

"I like you, Raiden."

"I like you too, Adrianna. A lot."

"A lot," she repeats, a giddiness to her tone, and I smirk down at her.

"Let's get out of here, get you cleaned up, and I'll happily show you how much a lot is," I promise, vibrating with delight at the sound of another giggle.

The sweet sound is cut short as she lurches to the side, her humor turning into a grunt of pain as she slams into the stone wall where I just fucked her, and my heart crinkles in my chest.

Alert, I growl as I find Vallie standing at the opening

of the alleyway. Her snarl is aimed at my fucking Troublemaker and I don't like it. Not one bit. The way her chest heaves and her arms roll back, I know she's the reason Adrianna is no longer in my grasp.

Fucker.

"You were boring the fuck out of me," she states, flicking her hair over her shoulder with a sigh as her stare turns to me.

"You're just asking to meet your end, Vallie," I snap, and she rolls her eyes at me.

"If you say so. Let's go and see what your father says about that, shall we?"

"Why the fuck would I do that?"

"Raiden?" Adrianna's soft voice cuts through the air as the pounding of footsteps echoes off the walls.

A moment later, Kryll, Brody, and Cassian stand behind my least favorite vampire with disgruntled expressions.

"Raiden, what the fuck is going on?" Cass asks, pointing over his shoulder to reveal my father's men lining up behind them.

"He's being summoned. Come, little pet," Vallie hollers with a wicked snicker.

Fuck.

Glancing down at Adrianna, my heart aches, but I know what I need to do. Her eyebrows pinch as she meets my stare, and I hope she can see the smallest flicker in my eyes before I lock my emotions down.

"Go home. I'll meet you there."

"But—" I wave Brody's protest off as I turn for Vallie and my father's men.

"I have somewhere to be."

RAIDEN

32

Crimson stains splatter my clothes and skin, but it does nothing to halt my swagger as I swing the door to my father's manor open. The gaudy finish to the entire space only serves to piss me off even more.

I don't want to be here. I shouldn't fucking be here, but against my better judgment, I wanted to make sure I kept Adrianna as far away as possible from the fucked up mess that is the vampire origin.

Mahogany wood covers the floors, the bottom half of the walls, and the grand staircase, which I bypass in search of my father's office. It's where he'll be. It's where he *always* is.

The fleur de lis pattern on the wallpaper shimmers in gold under the glowing yellow lights fixed to the walls. It's like a damn mausoleum in this place, not a house. I don't know how I've never really considered that comparison until now. But it seems every interaction I have with Adrianna is one step into the truth that is my life. She helps me remove the rose-tinted glasses that were firmly lodged in place, and now I have the unfortunate reality of seeing everything for what it truly is.

Dead.

The desire to swipe a hand down my face itches at my fingertips, but I refuse to offer even a glimpse of uncertainty. Not when Vallie is a step behind me, my father's men one further, and fuck knows how many more cameras the old man has installed since I was last here.

He's obsessive, possessive, and slightly deranged. Yet, it's still my mother who is the one you should be careful of.

As much as I despise being here, I'm eager for answers as to why the fuck his men showed up tonight, with Vallie no less. We were already dealing with enough bullshit, and then he had to come and interrupt the most perfect fucking moment with my woman.

The door to the kitchen is open, the slightest trickle of sunlight threatening to break the dawn over the darkened hills in the distance. My mind is drawn from the present and I wonder if Adrianna is seeing it too.

Tonight she was...fuck, she was everything and more.

Fearless. Resilient.

She was a goddamn heir.

I meant every word I said to her, and I was ready to give her more until we were rudely interrupted.

"I can stop all of this from happening, you know." Vallie's shrill voice cuts through my thoughts and irritation coils through my tired limbs.

Sneering, I don't even bother to turn in her direction as I bite out my retort. "You can't stop the bullshit that comes from your mouth, so I don't have high hopes for anything else, and that's a particularly low bar. Besides, the last thing I would ever want or need is your help."

She clears her throat, disdain evident in the move. "She's changed you."

I don't need to glance her way to know she will have tilted her head back and looked down her nose as she spoke those words. It's a given. "Hmm."

"Aren't you going to ask who?" she pushes, far too eager to cause a scene as we turn down the hallway, my father's office coming into view.

"I'm not a fool. You are referring to Princess Adrianna Reagan." I bite back the smile on my lips as I use Adrianna's true, full title, earning a scoff from Vallie, just as I expect.

"You mean Addi Reed," she snaps with a huff, and I finally tilt my stare to the left to meet her gaze.

"I didn't stutter, and you know it."

Her lips purse, anger swirling in her eyes as she subtly

shakes her head. "When will you realize that she is no good for you?"

It's my turn to huff. "Oh, I already know she is. In my family's eyes, at least. But the reality is, *I'm* no good for *her*. It's an easy thing to admit when you look at a situation through selfless eyes. You wouldn't know the meaning of it, so I know it's a stretch asking you to even consider that as an option."

"We could be—"

I raise my hand, shutting down whatever bullshit is about to slip from her lips. "Nothing. We have been and will always be nothing." Exhaustion clings to every word. I'm sick and tired of doing this with her. It's as if she thinks she's going to wear me down eventually, but that's never been the case.

Maybe it was my fault for going along with what our parents wanted for so long, but even then, that was only in the public eye. I never touched her—not even my hand on the small of her back as we entered a room. Nothing.

I have no desire to even glance in her direction, while Adrianna...fuck, she captures my attention without even trying, all while hating me, and that's saying something considering how much she hated me when we first met.

It's addicting. *She's* addicting.

"Son." My father's voice cuts through the air and I pause at the open doorway to his office, assessing the state of him. Maybe I'm as hopeless as Vallie is because I assess him every time, hoping to gauge what mood he's in, but it's impossible. He's unpredictable, and that's the way he likes it.

A plush maroon dressing gown wraps around his shoulders, the golden emblem of the family crest stitched into the pocket at his breast. There's a crystal glass filled with a brown liquid, which I'm certain is his favorite bourbon, in his right hand and a cigar in the left. Frameless glasses are perched on his nose, and his silvery hair is swept back off his face.

But beneath all that, I see the crinkles at his eyes, the exhaustion on his face, and the pinch to his jaw.

"Care to explain why your summons came through her?" I ask, stepping into the dated room with a pointed finger aimed in Vallie's direction.

"I have a name," she scoffs, and I glare at her.

"You don't want me to use the one I'm thinking of," I grunt, her desire to stick around irking me. "You can leave now."

"I'm good where I am, thanks," she smarts, folding her arms over her chest as she gives me a pointed look.

"Blood? I know we're vampires, son, but did you have to be so...tasteless in your feast," my father murmurs before taking a sip of the good stuff, and I turn my irritation his way.

"Unfortunately, this isn't from a sampling with my teeth, more with my fists. The frenzied managed to get a bite of me." I point to my neck. Even though it's mostly healed now, I know there will be enough remnants for him to catch my drift.

His eyebrows furrow for a moment before he quickly shakes it off. "You must be depleted. Do you need—"

"I'm good," I interject, waving my hand dismissively. "Inconvenienced by whatever this is, but I'm sure you'll get to the point eventually."

"Take a seat," he offers, pointing at the deep red and gold loveseat facing his desk. I shake my head as Vallie makes herself comfortable.

"Like I said, to the point so I can find more…satisfactory company."

My father nods, swirling the glass in his hand as he looks from me to Vallie and back again. "I'm not entirely sure why you're here," he admits, and I know he will hate to admit that. Especially with an audience.

It goes straight over Vallie's head, however, when she offers him an explanation. "Because he leaped in to fight against the frenzied."

His eyebrows pinch as he wags his cigar between the two of us.

"Why were you off campus?"

"To look for the frenzied, as instructed by the dean,

remember?" I offer, and Vallie sneers.

"Look. That's all it was supposed to be. We delay the frenzied as long as possible, later than the usual time, and—"

"Wait, wait, wait," I interrupt, my pulse thundering in my ears as I stare at Vallie. "Do you want to start that again," I rasp, my brain slowly piecing together what she's saying.

She rolls her eyes at the inconvenience, but I don't fucking care. "I'm sure you're not hard of hearing, Raidy baby, keep up." *Bitch.*

"We're controlling this," I breathe, letting the truth slip from my tongue, and it earns me another eye roll from the bitch herself.

"Of course we are."

"How hadn't I considered that?" My thought slips from my lips before I can rein it in, and my father sighs, lifting his glass to his lips.

"Your mother has a way of harnessing her control, son. But why does that bring you to me, Miss Drummer?" He finally takes a sip, two to be precise, which is never quite a good sign because as liquid-smooth as that bourbon is, it still burns like a bitch.

"My uncle insisted. Since my father was killed in cold blood, he's taken the reins." The sneer on her lips does nothing to my conscience and the lack of care I have for her father's demise. If anything, I want to hunt out a party popper and fucking celebrate.

"Your uncle," I repeat like a fucking parrot as she somehow sits taller in her seat, glossing over the fact that Adrianna was the one to bbq her father with her magic.

"Since you won't be fated mates with me, my uncle is a little less lenient with the errors you're making," she explains slowly, like I'm a child who can't keep up.

"I'm struggling to see the errors I'm making," I insist with a shrug, and she gives me a pointed look with a flat smile that has no intention of meeting her eyes.

"Of course, you wouldn't, but if you need me to spell it out for you, you're hooked on fae pussy, and it's going to be your demise."

"Wow. A bit brash don't you think?" my father says with a snort, opting for a drag on his cigar this time, and I roll my eyes.

"Brash as always," I state, and my father's drawn brows turn back to the thorn in my side.

"It's unbecoming, Vallie. If your uncle insisted on this, consider my son thoroughly scolded." He waves her off, but her lips twist in distaste as she rises to her feet.

"You haven't—"

Her words fall off as my father discards his glass and cigar, letting them tumble to the floor as he charges. There's no time to avoid his rage, and there's no point delaying the inevitable as the room thickens with trepidation at the sound of his glass shattering.

The sound ricochets around the room at the exact time his hand finds its way to my throat. His nails pierce into my flesh, giving him leverage as he lifts me off my feet.

I can't breathe, I can't think, I can't do anything but feel his wrath, all while trying to act as unfazed as possible.

"Don't interrupt the frenzied again. That's an order." His dark and sinister voice booms around us, and I hear Vallie gasp before my father discards me just as quickly as he approached.

I fall to the floor, my knees hitting the ground with a thud, and brace my hands against the awful rug beneath me as I try to catch my breath.

"There you are. You can be on your way now," my father declares.

"Let's go, Raidy," Vallie says with a sniffle. Like this is deeply upsetting to her when it only happened because she wanted it to.

"I'm good," I rasp, my throat burning, and she scoffs in confusion.

"You can't want to stay here with a man that harms you so effortlessly."

"Trust me, out of the two options I have right now, it's still my preferred," I grunt, pushing to my feet and meeting her stare with a bored expression.

Predictably, she rolls her eyes. "Whatever. I'll see you in the morning," she states, heading for the door.

"Preferably not," I mutter as she saunters from the room without a backward glance.

The door clicks shut behind her and I sag on the spot.

"I'm sorry, son."

I peer at my father, watching as his lips pinch with sadness and his eyes remain fixated on the floor.

"It's fine," I breathe, rubbing at my neck as he shakes his head.

"It's not, and no words of apology will stop the pain I've caused. Any of it."

"I'm sure—"

"Do you want a vial?" he offers, swooping over to the cabinet in the far corner where he keeps a ridiculous amount of blood available to him.

"I'm good."

"I can sense you're weak," he pushes, concern flickering between his eyes as he assesses me, but I shake my head.

"I'm fine."

"Nothing is ever fine with you. The use of it twice in such a short span of time is concerning, to say the least."

I rub my lips together. As much pain as I'm in, I'm not as tormented as the man before me. I see it now more than ever, but it's not something I'm even remotely ready to dive into.

"Where's mother?" I ask, earning a sigh.

"Where do you think?"

"With Vallie's uncle, most likely," I say, and he nods. That's another topic not for today, too, it seems. Clearing my throat, I circle back to the surprise I felt earlier. "Are we really controlling them?"

"Of course," he replies, his voice seeped in disappointment and despair.

"All this time?"

His gaze meets mine. "From the very beginning."

Fuck. "Why?"

"You know why," he mutters with a pointed look.

"How are frenzied vampires going to earn us the castle, the kingdom?" My eyebrows pinch in confusion.

"The same way it gets the vampires everything else… fear."

ADRIANNA

33

Staring at the empty spot where Raiden had stood moments ago, I brace myself against the stone wall behind me as I try to wrap my head around what the fuck just happened.

We went from fighting the frenzied to fucking to… leaving?

"Are you sure he's going to be okay?" I murmur, concern swarming my gut as I wipe a hand down my bloodied face.

A part of my brain reminds me that I'm not supposed to care, but there's no denying it anymore. Not after that. Not that I can even explain what *that* was.

I'm so screwed.

"He's a big boy. He can handle himself," Brody answers, crouching down beside me. A soft smile touches the corner of his mouth as fatigue swirls in his eyes.

"I know that. He just…"

"He just fucked you so good, you don't want the high to end yet?" he says with a smirk.

"Fuck off," I grumble, unable to hide the smile from my face as I shove at his shoulder. The second I do, I wince, my nose scrunching with the sudden pain that shoots down my arm.

"Are you hurt?" He leans forward, forgetting the humor as seriousness washes over him.

"I'm fine," I mumble just before he presses against the top of my arm and my face makes the same expression again.

"That look says otherwise," he points out with a knowing stare, and I sigh.

"Is our fae princess acting all stubborn and… princessy?" Kryll asks, and my gaze narrows on him as he stands with his hands tucked in his pocket. Blood stains his cloak, but for the most part, he's clean. Not as clean as Brody, who doesn't have a single drop on him.

"That's rude," I say with a pout, and Brody snickers.

"That's cute," he retorts, booping my nose with a grin before offering me his hand. "Let's get you home so we can take a look at your arm."

My stomach turns as I take his hand with my other arm and stand. "That's going to mean nausea, isn't it?" The thought of moving anywhere above the speed of a snail is completely off-putting right now.

"No, I've got you, Dagger," he breathes, stroking a loose tendril of hair back off my face. Thank goodness for his badass mage abilities. I like him even more now.

He pulls me in close, ready to move us, when I plant a hand on his chest. "Wait, what about Flora and Arlo?" I balk, remembering their involvement, but I've been so caught up in myself that I don't even know where they are, and that doesn't sit well with me.

"They're both good. They returned to the academy with Tora and the spectating assholes," Cassian grunts, making his presence known as his gaze rakes over me from head to toe.

I roll my eyes at the mention of the students who quite happily did nothing before my mind drifts back to seeing Flora in action.

"She was unreal," I mutter, and Brody squeezes my good arm in comfort.

"She was awesome."

"She was," I confirm, beaming at the strength Flora showed. A *lowly fucking fae* doing far more than anyone else.

"So was he," Kryll adds, referring to Arlo, and I nod as Cassian rolls his eyes.

"Sure," he grumbles, not appreciating the praise going

anywhere else.

"But—"

"Not as awesome as you, Princess," Kryll states, interrupting my retort and distracting me altogether.

"Stop," I grumble, waving him off, and he grins.

Before anyone can say another word, the ground shifts beneath our feet and Cassian steps in, touching my neck and Brody's arm as Kryll reaches for the wolf. When the world stills around us again, I quickly recognize the room we're in.

"Cassian's?" I ask as everyone takes a step back, and the man himself shrugs.

"It's the biggest we've got access to since Raiden's not here," he offers, and the mention of my vampire has my gut clenching with worry and fear all over again.

"He was bleeding bad," I murmur, my hand lifting to my neck instinctively.

"But it stopped, so don't worry. What you need to worry about is how he's going to replenish himself," Cassian says, an almost snicker at his lips, and I frown.

"What?"

"You know," Brody interrupts, snapping his teeth together before pretending to suck from his wrist and rub his belly in delight.

I gulp, recalling the ferocious pain that burned through my body when Vallie did the exact same thing to me, and it sends a shiver down my spine.

"I worry for his victim," I admit, shaking my head when Cassian gives me a surprised look.

"I thought you would be a willing target."

My head rears back. "After Vallie's attack? No fucking way."

Brody leans in, cupping my cheek and arching my face to stare into his eyes. "I mean, she let her pointy tips poison you. That's what I was healing. Raiden wouldn't do that. Besides, I've been told it's quite an experience," he offers, wagging his eyebrows and leaving my brain like mush.

"That sounds like someone has experienced it to know," I blurt, raising my eyebrows at him, but he just shrugs. *Fucking* shrugs.

"Jealous?" he asks, booping my nose again, and I sigh. "Very."

"Of it being done, or—"

"Of someone doing it to you," I snap, my irritation hard to hide as the green-eyed monster takes hold of me.

"Noted," he replies with a smirk, and Kryll smacks him across the back of the head.

"Don't get smug," he grumbles, making Brody smile wider.

"I would never."

He's full of shit, and we all know it.

"The bath is run for you," Cassian states, and I turn to

him with wide eyes.

"Bath?"

"You don't have a bath?" Kryll asks, frowning at me, and I realize the only time he's been in my room was the moment he entered the window and rolled straight out of the door because of the ward Brody put in place.

"We have a communal shower area. I'm surprised Cassian hasn't told you about it. He has so much experience in there," I muse, appreciating the shift in conversation to lighter topics. Especially when Cassian rolls his eyes at me.

"Of course he does," Brody grumbles, a flicker of jealousy shining in his eyes as he places his hand on my back. "Let's get you in there so I can look at your arm, shall we?"

"It's fine," I insist as we head into the marbled bathroom, and I'm left gaping in wonder again. It's just as stunning as the last time I was in here, and a far cry from the bathroom stalls in the fae building.

"Of course it is," Brody states, and I pout.

"I'm not lying."

"Of course you're not."

Turning my attention from the cream marble surfaces that touch every inch of the bathroom to the mage beside me, I stand tall. "I'm not. Look."

I move my arm, lifting it beside me, but I don't manage

more than a few inches before I lower it again with a wince.

"You're a terrible liar, Dagger," he says with a chuckle, and I roll my eyes at him.

"Whatever," I grumble under my breath, the topic long forgotten as he helps me out of my blood-stained clothes.

Each layer of material hits the floor with a slap, and I cringe as I catch sight of my red-smeared hair that no longer looks all blonde and golden after tonight's events.

Brody wastes no time guiding me to the huge bath as soon as I'm undressed, and I groan with delight as the hot water coats my skin. As soon as I'm seated, he hollers for Kryll, who appears a moment later.

"Watch her while I run to get what I need," he orders, and I shake my head.

"I don't need—"

"Shh," he murmurs, planting a kiss on my temple. "I won't be long, Dagger," he adds before rushing from the room.

I sink lower in the water, letting the bubbles float around me as I try to let the strain and tension ease from my limbs. A calmness settles over me, one I never thought I'd feel again after the adrenaline coursed through my veins earlier, and I sigh with contentment.

"You were fearless out there," Kryll states, leaning back against the ornate vanity, the black ink along his neck flashing in his reflection in the mirror behind him.

I shrug, faltering at the compliment. "I was just acting on instinct."

"Well, those are some unbelievable instincts," he insists, making me smile as I hum in acknowledgment.

"How mad is your brother going to be tomorrow?"

"You mean today?" he states, pointing at the window, and I startle at the first glimpse of the sun shining through the frosted glass.

"We have to face lessons today," I say with a gasp, weariness making my body ache at the prospect.

"Oh, fuck no. His anger will hold a day," Kryll replies with a shake of his head, and my body relaxes at his outburst.

"But he will be mad," I reiterate, and he sighs.

"Internally, he'll be mad he couldn't join us. Externally, he'll be furious," he admits, but I can't seem to be upset over the anticipation of it. We did what was right, and I don't care what anyone else says.

"Sounds fun," I muse, and he smirks.

"It won't be, but we can rest and take the day. We're exhausted from protecting the kingdom. They can deal with it," he insists, and I can't deny the fact that I like the sound of that.

With a soft curl to my lips, I let my eyes fall closed as I enjoy this moment to relax.

"I'm back. Miss me?" Brody asks, stepping into the

bathroom, and Kryll scoffs.

"Like a hole in the head."

Brody doesn't even acknowledge the remark as he drops to his knees beside the bathtub. "I think I have what I need here," he explains to me, jingling a few vials and trinkets in front of him as he starts a soft chant.

"Sano. Consano. Sano. Consano. Sano. Consano. Sano. Consano. Sano. Consano."

Warmth spreads across my arms as he brushes the surface with a few sprigs of sage dipped in a powder. As the heat recedes, I lift my arm, feeling no pain or resistance.

"Thank you."

His smile hits me straight in the chest. "You're welcome. Now, let's get you in bed."

At his words, Cassian appears at the doorway with an oversized t-shirt in his hand.

"That's not my—"

"Shut up and get in it, Alpha," he retorts before I can continue to argue, and I don't have it in me to push.

Brody and Kryll step out of the room as Cassian approaches with the t-shirt in one hand and a fluffy towel in the other. He stands patiently beside me as I dry myself off, my magic eager to take over, but feeling his eyes on me as I use the towel overcomes everything else.

All too quickly, I reach for the t-shirt, our fingers touching just enough to send a shiver down my spine, but my core protests. It's been battered in the best possible way in the past twenty-four hours by two of my Kryptos. She needs a break, despite the rest of my body being eager for attention.

"Any news from Raiden?" I ask, trying to pull my head from the gutter, and he shakes his head.

"Not yet," he says, tugging the hem of his t-shirt in place at my thighs before taking my hand and leading me into the bedroom. He doesn't stop until I'm perched on the side of his bed, his sheets soft beneath me.

"And you expect me to sleep?" I retort, suppressing a yawn, and he shakes his head again.

"No, I expect you to rest."

I shuffle until my back hits the headboard, and Brody appears to pull the sheets back.

"That means letting my guard down," I mutter, uncertainty curling in my throat.

Brody leans in, cupping my cheek. The softness of his smile doesn't match the ferocity in his gaze as he speaks. "Dagger, let's be real. I think you've already done that."

ADRIANNA

34

Muttering vibrates through the room, stirring me from the depths of darkness. My head instantly aches with the onslaught of an irritating migraine and my vision blurs for what feels like an eternity as I try to focus on my surroundings. Exhaustion clings to me, leaving me fuzzy until I hear the distinct sound of a grumpy vampire.

My focus sharpens, revealing Raiden and Cassian standing at the foot of the bed, where I lay with Kryll on one side and Brody on the other. They're both passed out cold. Brody's leg is thrown over mine while Kryll's palm rests at my waist.

"Hey," I murmur, garnering the attention of the two hotheads at the foot of the bed. Cassian's jaw ticks as he glares deeper at Raiden, who turns to me with a brilliant smile spread across his face.

"I told you not to wake her," Cassian snarls, but Raiden waves him off without a glance.

The blood is gone and the wound at his neck is no longer visible, which settles something inside of me.

"Troublemaker."

I sigh, intent to listen to him use my nickname again and again.

"You look…good," I mutter, still taking stock of him from head to toe, making sure there's nothing out of place.

"I know," he retorts with a wink, making me narrow my eyes.

"Uh, so you're back to yourself then," I state, making him rock back on his heels with a wicked smirk. As annoying as it is, it only serves to calm the worry that was wreaking havoc on my body.

I try to shake off his effect on me and continue unfazed, but I fail, and his gaze darkens, forcing my thighs to clench as I hold his heated stare.

"Miss me so soon?" he asks, nodding at Kryll and Brody at my sides, and I shrug.

"Jealous?" I breathe, struggling to hold back a grin as his gaze continues to deepen, his pupils dilating before my very eyes.

"Very," he rasps, making a show of adjusting his dick behind his pants, and Cassian scoffs at his little performance.

"Well, *she* was jealous of *me* earlier, so beat that," Brody grumbles, wrapping his leg further around me as he nuzzles his face into the crook of my neck. Kryll's fingers flex at my waist, confirming he's awake too, but none of that seems to matter to the vampire.

"Well, I was deep inside her earlier, so—"

"That's enough," Cassian interjects, his face reddening with agitation, and I take the awkwardness in the air as my cue to slip out for a minute.

"I don't think so," Raiden retorts, more than happy to keep pushing like he usually does.

I instantly miss the heat from Brody and Kryll as I slip from between them, earning a groan of complaint from them both as I go. I mutter about using the bathroom as I avoid Raiden's outstretched hand and Cassian's stare, quickly shutting the door behind me.

Taking a deep breath, I wipe a hand down my face. I think this is the first time I've woken up surrounded by them all. It's definitely the first time I've woken up sandwiched between two of them, and the distraction it's offering isn't exactly working in my favor.

I make quick work of relieving my bladder and washing my hands before I finally dare to take a look at myself in the mirror. My blonde hair is sticking up in every direction, my eyes are puffier than a damn puffer fish, and my skin looks pale. I'm quite sure I could camouflage as a bottle of milk or a corpse right now, neither of which sound appealing. Not when there are four men on the other side of the door. Four men who I can no longer deny my need for.

Sighing, I shake my arms out, trying to lose the irritation creeping up my spine, but it's unavoidable. I'm in here, thinking about dick—multiple dicks, to be specific, when I should be considering the kingdom. Now isn't the time for me to be selfish.

With my mind jumbled over my current situation, I focus on myself first. Without a desirable audience, I use my magic to tame my hair into a crown braid around my head before splashing water on my face, hoping it will wash my puffy eyes away, but it's not as easy as my hair.

"Troublemaker, I brought you some clothes. They're on the shelves," Raiden hollers from the other side of the door with a little rap of his knuckles.

"Thanks," I murmur, frowning as I find exactly what he's talking about. "Did you go to my room without me?" I ask.

"Would it make you mad if I did?" he asks, a hint of uncertainty in his tone.

"Yes."

"Even if it was to get you some clothes to save you from doing the walk of shame?"

"I had clothes," I retort, recalling what I was wearing last night, and he scoffs.

"I'm quite sure Cassian burned them. There was no coming back from that much blood," he explains, making my lips purse as I quickly dress.

"You have to stop going in my room, Raiden," I state, swinging the door open to find him right in front of me. There's not even a hint of apology on his face, which reminds me I may need to consider tossing those goddamn roses away. For good this time.

"I'm sorry."

"No you're not."

He shrugs, wetting his lips to hide the grin on his face, and it annoys the hell out of me. I'm too tired for this.

I press my fingertips into my temples, wincing against the headache that begins to pound louder. "What time is it?"

"Eleven," Kryll answers, perched on the side of the bed with a tight smile on his face.

My eyes widen in surprise. It feels like I barely slept, and even though only a handful of hours have passed, it somehow feels like most of the day has passed.

"You must be hungry," Brody murmurs, and I shake my head.

"I need to think before I eat."

"About what?" Raiden asks, confusion knitting his

eyebrows together, and I sigh.

"I don't know where to start." It's the truth, and that's what is causing even more of a headache.

"That's what we're here for," Brody offers as Cassian stands with his arms folded over his chest, staring at me intently.

I shake my head, and Brody is in front of me in the next breath. "Don't you dare put your guards back up," he warns, tilting my chin back as Kryll sighs from his spot beside the bed.

"They already are," Kryll adds, and I hate how they always have the ability to see through me. Façade or not, it's a power I wish no one had over me.

"What do you need, Princess?" Kryll asks, cutting through everyone even though he's the farthest away.

"To think," I admit, a strange feeling tightening my chest. I don't like having to explain myself to anyone, but this doesn't feel like that. This feels…reassuring, I think. I don't fucking know. I need to think about this too.

"Where?" he asks, his demeanor remaining relaxed as I sense tension from the other three.

"Not here," I admit, exhaling harshly as I feel judgmental eyes fixate on me even more.

"Okay," he answers, and I slip past Raiden toward my saving grace among the craziness that are my Kryptos, but that doesn't stop the hot headed vampire from trying to interject.

"Okay? Definitely not okay," he grunts, hands balling into fists at his sides, firing anger into my veins again.

I pinch the bridge of my nose, trying to hold back my agitation, when Kryll speaks.

"You're making it worse." He's not fucking wrong.

"How could it possibly be worse?" Raiden snaps, his own irritation coming to the surface. "I learned the vampires are controlling the frenzied vampires. On top of the fact that the head vampires are also in cahoots with the other leading assholes intent on forcing us to be fated mates. All while some of us are having to hide family members for safety so they aren't used against us. Again."

"That sounds heavy, but now that you mention it, it's surprising, just not all that shocking for the vampires" Brody muses, brows gathering in concern as he looks from Kryll to Raiden and then to me.

"It is heavy," he retorts, and I sigh, lifting a hand to interrupt.

"The fated mates thing…maybe that's done with. They would have acted by now, surely."

Raiden looks at me like a second head has sprouted from my neck as he shakes his in disbelief. "They've waited this long, biding their time. They're not known for their patience, Adrianna. They'll make a move again. And soon, I can guarantee it."

"My father did say," Brody mutters, reminding me of the conversation we had. It feels like forever ago, but it's been barely any time at all.

Pressing into my temples again, the pounding only worsens.

"You're making me think out of sequence and it's ruining my brain," I grumble.

"What?" Cassian mutters, confusion etched into the single word.

"I need to compartmentalize, and you're only looking at the whole picture. I need to assess each individual issue first before I piece it all together. Otherwise, it gets too much for me."

Kryll's hands come down on my shoulders, forcing my gaze to his. His eyes are soft and calming, but his lips are set in a flat line. "Go. Think."

"No. Do not go and think. If last night taught us anything, fuck, if the past few *weeks* have taught us anything, it's that she's not safe," Raiden gripes, sending a cold chill down my spine.

"And I thought I proved last night that I can handle myself. Not only that, I fucking warned you what would come if you kept undermining me like that."

"Oh, I have no doubt about your abilities, Adrianna. That's not my issue, but if we can avoid danger, I think we should. And don't even get me started on that goddamn threat. I told you as much last night." His warning rings louder than mine, and I gulp. For a split second, I falter, until his words repeat in my mind and the restraint I was holding on to slips between my fingers.

"*You* think?"

"Yes." He nods vigorously, and I scoff.

"Guys," Brody warns as if sensing the anger that I can feel in the air around me.

"No, please, continue. What else do *you* think?"

Kryll's hands drop from my shoulders as I turn to stare down Raiden head-on. The vampire lifts his hands in surrender, but the determination doesn't leave his eyes.

"I'm not looking to pick a fight, Adrianna."

"No, you're looking to have me trail after you, nodding in agreement with whatever *you* think," I snap, unable to contain the pure rage his words have created inside of me.

"No, I—"

"Save it," I bite, turning for the door.

I need out of here right now. I can't breathe, and a small part of me can't decide if I'm overreacting or not. Some fresh air will give me the balance I'm looking for, and that's only going to piss him off. But so be it. I'm my own fucking person.

"Wait," he calls, and I half expect to feel his grasp on me in the next breath, but it doesn't come.

"Let her go, Raiden," Cassian mutters, his quietness

in all of this a little unnerving, but it surprises me even more when I peer over my shoulder to find him restraining Raiden from moving toward me. It's just a hand on his shoulder, but it seems to do the trick.

"If anything happens to her, it's you I'll blame," he snarls, turning his words to Kryll, who nods at his friend before signaling for me to get the hell out of there.

The door slams behind me as I scurry down the stairs and straight out the front door. I can't decide if he has a point or is insane, but either way, all of this is ridiculous.

Before I realize it, I'm at the fountain with a fork in the road, considering my options. I can take a walk, I can go for food, or I can hurry to my room. Despite the other options, the latter sounds the most appealing. As much as I need space, annoyingly, he's not wrong, and my ward will serve to protect me.

With my mind made up, I march toward the fae building, my pace quickening even more when it comes into view. I grasp the door handle and twist, but freeze when movement sounds from the tall bushes to my left.

My pulse rings in my ears as my gaze darts everywhere. When movement ruffles the leaves, I stand tall, ready to defend myself.

One final flurry has someone stepping out into the open, and my heart stutters in my chest.

"Hello, Adrianna."

Fuck.

"Mother."

ADRIANNA

35

Her gaze caresses over me, assessing every detail as her eyes sparkle in the late morning sun, while I grind my teeth together to make sure my jaw doesn't fall slack and reveal my surprise. Uncertainty zings up my spine, making my fingers flex at my sides as I offer the same eye scan.

I can't get a sense of her feelings or emotions. She's got them locked down and bolted, which only serves to leave me on higher alert. Of all the dangers Raiden could have warned me about, I doubt this would've been one of them.

Even though her presence pisses me off, it grates on me more that Raiden is right. *Nowhere* is safe. That doesn't mean I don't know how to handle myself, though.

Her hair is pulled back in a slick ponytail. She's

wearing jeans, a white t-shirt, and a plaid shirt. In all of my memories as a child, she didn't look like this in any of them, but I guess that's because she wasn't really herself then. Not like she is now.

Clearing my throat, I keep my lips in a flat line as I cock a brow at her. "Why are you here?"

"To see you," she admits, twisting her fingers together as her head dips, but she keeps her gaze on mine, peering at me through her lashes like she's vulnerable.

I can't bite back the scoff that burns from my throat as I shake my head. "You've seen. Anything else?" She presses her lips together and takes a tentative step toward me, but I lift my hand, pausing her next move as I continue to shake my head. "You're good where you are."

She nods, unlinking her fingers as she shakes them out at her sides. She stands taller, taking a deep breath, and my chest tightens as I watch her brush off the vulnerability, hiding her weaknesses just as quickly as she revealed them. It's not the fact that she's putting walls in place that bothers me; it's the fact that I've seen the same reaction in myself. Admitting there's anything similar between us swirls like poison in my gut.

"Sorry, I…I just…" Her words trail off as she tries to find the right level of bullshit to get through to me, but I'm not dealing with any of it.

"You just what?" I push, ready to get the fuck out of

here. Why the hell am I not just leaving her here and going to my room?

Fuck.

I can't bring myself to move, and that agitates me even more. Curiosity wins out.

"I wanted to see you." The words are a whisper on her tongue.

I tilt my gaze, trying to assess her from a different angle, but I don't come up with anything different. "I don't believe you."

"I can't imagine you would," she replies with a tight smile. I open my mouth but nothing comes out, and the reality is, it's because I have nothing to say to her.

I manage to take a deep breath, keeping the irritation from my tone as I twist the door handle. "Anything else?"

Her eyebrows pinch, her gaze darting over me. I can sense her brain whirling with the need to keep talking.

"How is Nora?"

I see red. Crimson *fucking* red. I step toward her, finger aimed in her direction as I snap. "You keep her fucking name out of your mouth." She gapes at me in shock, and I scoff. "Shocked? You shouldn't be. Did you expect this to be some sweet reunion? Newsflash, it isn't." I can feel my chest heating from my rising blood pressure, creeping up my neck and tingling down my arms to the tips of my fingers.

"I just…" Her words trail off once again and my nostrils flare with anger.

"You just can't seem to finish that sentence, and I honestly have no desire to know what's on the tip of your tongue," I bite, pushing the door to the fae building open.

"Adrianna, I'm sorry," she blurts, garnering my attention once again. Her hand is flat against her chest as her lip wobbles.

"For?"

"E-Everything," she stutters, and I shake my head.

"I feel like you have a colossal list of shit you should be sorry for. You're going to need to get a little more specific if you think I'm going to even remotely believe anything that you say." Even then, I know I won't. She doesn't deserve my forgiveness. She doesn't even deserve my time, yet here I am, still giving it to her.

Her hands twist in her white t-shirt, coiling around the material until her knuckles are the same color. Unshed tears line the bottom of her eyes, but it does nothing to produce even an ounce of sympathy.

"I shouldn't have come," she says, trying to swallow back the emotion, and I nod.

"You're right."

Her eyebrows crinkle with pain at my words. "I miss you."

I scoff. "You can't miss me. You don't know me," I

retort, making her eyes widen as she holds her hands toward me.

"I did, I—"

"You left. You left Nora and me without a care for anyone but yourself. Everything that followed changed the both of us. So, no, you don't know me, and you most definitely don't know her, because the day our lives came crumbling down, at your hands no less, those girls went with it."

"N-No," she stumbles again, tears rolling down her cheeks as she blubbers, and I snarl.

"Yes."

The venom on my tongue is real and I don't like it. I don't like the darkness that sweeps through my limbs or the level of anger that courses through me, because I can't control it. I can't control myself in her presence, and it makes me feel more vulnerable than ever before.

Calm and collected. Calm and collected. Calm and collected.

"I left to protect you," she insists, and I huff, refusing to believe any of the bullshit she's saying.

"How's that going for you?"

The pain in her eyes burns into my memory and I nod to myself, happy to keep it there as a reminder. She did this. She did this to us. She did this to herself.

She has no idea of the emotions she's stirring in me,

and I worry the longer I stick around, the closer she may get to finding out. "We're done here."

"Please, Adrianna—"

"You don't want to feel the wrath of the emotions coiling through my body right now," I warn, my jaw drawn tight with tension.

"Emotions?"

"Not the good kind," I repeat, and she nods.

Just put one foot in front of the other, Addi, and get the fuck out of here.

I take a backward step, eyes still fixed on her as she swipes her tongue over her bottom lip.

"Has your wolf…"

Her words trail off once again as my blood runs cold.

"My wolf," I repeat, my voice void of emotion as darkness creeps up my spine.

She clears her throat and nods. "Have you shifted?"

Is this some kind of sick and twisted game for her? "No," I admit, hating myself the moment I let her know the truth, especially when she offers me a sad smile as some kind of condolence. Fuck. "I'm going to assume I have you to thank for that," I add, satisfying the dark urge inside me to destroy her. To my surprise, she nods, her smile growing tighter as she bites back emotions I don't care to identify. "I think I'll withhold my appreciation for that," I snap as she stuffs her hand into the back pocket of her jeans.

"This is for you," she mutters with a sniff, revealing an envelope.

I look down at it with a frown as she waits for me to take it. "I don't want it."

"You might change your mind," she pushes, her grip tightening on it as she pushes it in my direction.

"*You* never did," I bite, my gaze rushing back to hers. Guilt swarms in her eyes as frustration takes root in my bones. Not at her; at myself. I'm literally fucking annoying myself in her presence, and it needs to stop. Now.

"Please take it, just in case," she encourages, her plea desperate.

"And you'll leave?"

Her face scrunches with pain before she nods. "If you take it, I'll leave."

Right now, I will do just about anything to put some much-needed space between us. Her being here doesn't make sense. None of it does.

Before I can talk myself out of it, I grab the envelope, but she doesn't release her hold. Instead, she tugs it closer, bringing me along with it.

"Be safe, Adrianna," she whispers, the pain in her voice matching the swirl of terror in her eyes. "He's coming, and try as I might, there's nothing I can seem to do about it," she adds, tears tracking down her face.

I rear back with a frown. "Who?" The second I say it, I

know, but she confirms it for me anyway.

"Kenner."

"Does he know you're here?" I bite, eyes wide with rage when a thick, dark voice cuts through the air.

"He didn't." My body stills as my mother balks with panic. I blink over her shoulder to find the man in question stepping out of the bushes she appeared from a few moments ago. A sneer spreads across his lips, making him look even more sinister than usual as adrenaline burns through my body. "And I can't say I'm all that pleased now that I do."

KRYLL

36

"Why would you just let her leave like that?" Raiden grinds out, the chords in his forearms coiled tight as he clenches his fists. I get it. I do. But the reality is we're dealing with a special fucking woman who is not going to react well to being told what to do.

"Because trying to contain her will only push her away," I state, the words not doing justice to what we're up against with her. If anything, it's our fault for getting all desperate and needy over the strongest, most independent woman I've ever met in my life.

I wouldn't change a damn thing, but the reality is, this is out of our comfort zone.

Raiden growls as Brody sighs.

"Kryll's right. I'm sure the way you and Cass give her

those asshole unhinged vibes gets her all fucking hot for you, but those feelings are only going to get you so far," he states with a shrug, and Cassian scoffs.

"They get me far enough."

Brody gives him a pointed look, turning it to all of us before he speaks. "I want more with her. Do you?" It's weird seeing him like this. He's usually the lady's man. The guy with too many girls crying over him, yet he's the first to take everyone else off the table to have Adrianna. He's quieter, but it doesn't feel like it's from sadness. More…contentment.

My animal swirls inside of me, eager for the same feeling that it knows will come from her, and I rub at my chest, trying to will the ache away.

"More?" Raiden asks with his eyebrow raised in question, and Brody rolls his eyes.

"Love, dumbass."

The vampire scoffs, but it's cut short as he frowns, looking down at his hands in confusion. "I'll go and find her," he blurts, swiftly rising to his feet, but I move faster.

"No, I will," Cassian grunts, hurrying for the door, shoulder-barging me as he goes.

"Wait. Wait. Wait," Brody hollers, swinging his arms around in panic as my chest warms.

One word. Four letters and my animal wins out.

"No, you won't. I will go. What she needs right now is

a calm approach. Someone that is actually going to listen to her, and we all know that's me." The words leave my lips with a surety I didn't know I had, taking root in my core as I take strength from them. It's not lost on me that it wasn't so long ago that we were in a similar position, and I refused to claim her.

That was then. This is now.

"Fuck you, Kryll," Raiden grumbles, his lips setting in a thin line as his nostrils flare. "What we need is a plan because we're just waiting around for the next attack aimed our way, and I don't care for being on the defensive all the time. Last night reminded us of that. She needs to understand all of this as well as everything we're feeling."

"Agreed, but she needs to be equal to us, or shit, above us, because anything less than that will only put distance between us, and that's the last thing we want. Right?" My body thrums with anticipation as I practically bounce on the balls of my feet, waiting for their response.

"Fine, you go," Cassian mutters, stepping away from the door with a sigh.

"We'll meet you at the dining hall. She needs to eat," Brody orders, and I nod, rushing out of the door before anyone can change their mind. Especially Raiden, since he kept his lips shut.

I hurry down the stairs of the wolf building, basking in the silence since everyone else is in class, but the moment

I step out into the fresh air, my confidence falters. Have we really given her long enough to think? The time I promised her? The likelihood of her being pissed at my appearance feels pretty damn high, and that's not going to help us.

Fuck.

I reach the fountain quicker than I can make a decision when a thought comes to mind. Maybe I should fly by her window and see how she's looking first. That would give me a head start when I actually knock on her door. If she's actually gone back to her room.

Fuck.

I didn't think of that.

Swooping past her window first seems like the best option. Then, if she's not there, I can scour the surrounding areas on campus.

With my mind made up, I make sure no one is around before I dart into the air, shifting the moment my feet leave the ground. The tension I hadn't realized was rippling through my body eases as my animal takes over, enjoying the rush as I soar through the air.

With them close to the surface now, their thoughts intertwine with mine, and everything I feel toward Adrianna increases tenfold.

I can't sleep without her in my dreams, I can't think without her in my thoughts, and I can't hear without her voice echoing in my ears.

She's everywhere.

Gliding toward the fae building, I frown when I hear Adrianna's voice. This time, I know it's not in my head. I can actually hear her.

My gaze narrows as I look toward her building, and she quickly comes into view. My eyes turn to slits as I realize she's not alone.

Is that her mother? And...Kenner.

Double fuck.

There's no time to tell the others. All I can do is act. But they can't see me like this.

Not just because Adrianna is playing this little game with me, questioning what I am, but because Kenner can *never* fucking know.

Shit.

My heart leaps into my throat as a wolf's snarl rings through the air, and I descend, barreling toward the ground behind the back of the fae building as quickly as I can. My animal burns through my body, desperate to remain as present as he is now, and it takes every ounce of my control to keep him at bay.

I shift just in time for my feet to hit the patch of grass before I take off running as the telltale sound of Adrianna crying out in pain hits my ears.

Fuck. No.

Darting around the corner, I roar with rage when I find

Addi on the ground, Kenner in his wolf form on top of her with his fangs locked on her upper arm while her mother cowers against the fae building wall, doing nothing to interject.

I see nothing but my woman.

Charging at them, I launch at Kenner, wrapping my arms around his neck as my legs twist around his middle. He snarls and snaps, releasing Addi from his grasp, and I quickly roll him away from her. I can't see a fucking thing with his fur all in my face, but I tighten my grip, refusing to let him get anywhere near her again.

If only I was in my animal form. I would slaughter him right now.

As if sensing my thought, his teeth graze over my forearm, the swipe drawing blood instantly, and it weakens my grip on him. He's out of my grasp before I can do anything, but he doesn't race at Addi again. To my surprise, he takes off, darting between the shrubs that surround the fae building, leaving nothing but a trickled trail of blood in his wake.

My mind and body war with one another.

Stay and help Addi or chase that motherfucker down and bring him to his demise.

"Kryll?"

One word from my princess and my answer is sealed. I rush to my feet, only to slam down to my knees at her side a moment later. "I'm here, Addi. I'm here."

Unshed tears well in her eyes as she stares down at her mangled arm, bestowing panic into my bones as I watch the color start to drain from her face.

Fuck.

"Is she okay? I didn't know he was here. I swear. I swear," her mother sobs, whipping my gaze to hers as I snarl.

"Get the fuck out of here before I do something we'll both regret."

She doesn't pause to consider my words. She instantly bobs her head and gets the fuck out of here, and it's no surprise that she follows the same path as Kenner.

With my nostrils flared and my jaw set in stone, I turn my attention back to Addi. "Is there anywhere else that hurts, Princess?" I ask, stroking a fingertip down her cheek as I try to reassure her.

"I can't catch my breath," she rasps, her breathing coming in wheezy pants. Her pupils are nothing more than pinpricks. There's something I'm not seeing, something more than the mangled arm at her side.

I need to protect her, but it's clear she's not safe here. The last time Brody took her off-campus in an attempt to heal her, we only found ourselves in deeper shit.

There's only one place I trust with her, and I'm not entirely sure she won't hate me for it. But if the choice is between her health and how she feels about me, her health is going to win every time.

"Please don't hate me," I murmur, tentatively scooping her up in my arms the best I can. She winces, a strangled cry bursting from her lips as I try my best to cradle her injured arm against my chest.

"Hate you?" she whispers in confusion, pinching her eyebrows. I offer her a soft smile as I stand, one hand around her back, the other under her thighs.

"Just rest. I've got you. I'm going to take you somewhere safe," I promise, and before I can change my mind and risk her safety once more, I shift, darting toward the sky with my wings fully spread.

A gasp slips from her lips, and before I break us through the clouds, I look down at her, seeing her eye to eye for the first time with my animal at the forefront of my mind.

"You're a dragon," she whimpers. Before I can confirm or deny it, her eyes roll to the back of her head, and she passes out, taking up the smallest space against my scaled chest.

ADRIANNA

37

My tongue is heavy in my mouth, a hazy flurry worming its way over my limbs as I try to move. I manage to twitch my fingers first, and the little movement comes with a wave of relief as my toes do the same.

What the fuck is going on with me?

The moment I think about it, the last memories I have come rushing back to the forefront of my mind.

My mother.

Kenner.

Kryll.

Dragon.

All the pain and anger that came before Kryll spread his stunning white wings and flew into the air with me falls away. He was…stunning, magical, everything.

I can spend more time appreciating him later. Right now, I need to focus. Prying my eyelids open is harder than I would like, but after a few tries, I manage to open them enough to squint. My gaze instantly dips to my arm, the one Kenner ripped into, and I startle at the sight of it. Unharmed.

Why the fuck would he attack me like that if they want me to bind myself with the guys? Why would he not just try to snatch me away and trap me in a room like last time? Probably because last time didn't work out all that well for them. Maybe if I'm injured, they think they have a better chance of controlling me.

Fuck.

Basking in the relief of my arm no longer looking and feeling like a mangled mess, I take in my surroundings. Nothing seems familiar. White drapes hang a few feet away from where I'm lying, the bed beneath me is soft and warm as I snuggle in deeper. Two silhouettes stand on the other side. Whoever they are, they're deep in conversation, but their voices are nothing more than a whisper to my ears, so I don't recognize them.

What surprises me the most is that there's no looming vampire ready to tell me he told me so.

Where the hell am I?

Pressing a hand to my head, my limbs easing with each passing moment, I take a deep breath, exhaling slowly as I try to calm the confusion running through my body. Kryll will keep me safe. Unless something happened to him, too? But that wouldn't explain my healed arm. I hope.

"You're awake."

The voice comes from my right, startling the hell out of me as I whip my gaze in their direction, earning myself a groan as I pull a muscle.

Fuck.

"Nora," I breathe, squeezing my neck where it aches as I take stock of my sister.

"Hey," she mutters, wetting her lips as she offers a wave. It quickly comes to mind that the last time we spoke, we didn't part on the best of terms, and my heart aches. But more importantly than that, I need to understand.

"Nora, what are you doing here?"

She quirks a familiar brow at me. "Technically, *you* are *here*," she states, leaving me to gape at her in surprise.

Don't hate me. That's what Kryll said, and this is what he must have meant.

Taking another deep breath, I press my palm into the sheets beneath me and try to rise. I manage to shuffle back an inch before I fall backward with a grunt.

"You need to rest, Addi," she murmurs, worry storming her eyes, but I can still sense the animosity that was there the last time we spoke.

"I shouldn't be here," I admit, trying to move again to

no avail.

"Why?" Her eyebrows gather as her gaze narrows on mine, and I sigh.

"To keep you safe."

Wood scrapes across the floor as she rises from her seat, the chair discarded as she wades in on me with a pointed finger. "If you keep sprouting crap like that, you're going to need to keep yourself safe from *me* because I swear to all that might hear me—"

"Nora—"

"I am not done," she warns, coming to stand over me now. I have no choice but to look up at her. A simple nod from me, and she proceeds.

"We came here without batting an eyelid. For you." I open my mouth, but I don't get a single syllable past my lips before she puts her hand in my face, cutting me off before I can even begin. "We have done what is needed. For you. We will continue to do whatever makes your life easier, but I need you to know how hard it is for us to be away from you." Her voice cracks at the end, tears welling in her eyes, and it cuts me to the bone.

"It breaks me too, Nora," I admit. My voice wobbles as I reach for her, but she doesn't take my hand.

"Then why?" she pushes, and all I can do is be honest with her.

"Because you're all I have." My words linger between

us for what feels like a lifetime before she clears her throat.

"But what use is that when you suddenly refuse to see us?"

I try to sit up again, and this time she leans forward, helping me so my back is propped against the headboard. When she moves to take a step back, I wrap my fingers around hers, refusing to let her go too far.

"I wasn't prepared for how dangerous the people in power are." It's the truth. She knows it, but she still shakes her head.

"I spent every day of my life with you up until the day you left for the academy. I knew there would be distance between us, but not like this, and not because of people who shouldn't matter. Screw them."

I squeeze her fingers in understanding. "I wish it was that easy."

"I think you're the person making it harder than it has to be," she retorts, attempting to tug her hand from mine.

"You don't understand," I plead, releasing her hand when she tries to tug it from my grasp again.

She folds her arms over her chest, staring at me with a deepening frown. "You're right. I don't understand because you continue to give me half-assed answers that mean nothing. All I'm feeling is the loss of you. Just like we felt the loss of Mom, only this time, I don't have my sister to help me through it." Tears streak down her cheeks now, her pain coming to the forefront as my heart crushes.

Fuck.

"Nora, I'm—"

"Don't give me some bullshit apology," she grumbles with a sniff, swiping at her cheeks.

"It's not bullshit," I insist, and she scoffs.

"It's bullshit until we can be together, and you can't tell me otherwise."

Well, fuck. My lips purse as I try to wrap my head around another complex situation, but the only thing I can do is agree with her.

"You're right," I admit, and she snickers.

"I always am."

"You're also a pain in the ass," I grumble, and she offers me a watery smile.

"You're welcome." Her sass is back in full force and it warms my soul.

"I love you, Nora," I breathe, the words coming straight from the heart.

"I love you too, you big goof. Now stop thinking you have to suffer to protect everyone else," she states, wagging her finger at me once again, and I roll my eyes.

"That's too much wisdom for me right now." A yawn parts my lips, confirming my words.

"I have more loaded up," she offers with a waggle of her eyebrows.

"You always do," I muse, and a comfortable silence descends over us. Slowly, she inches back to the bed, lacing her fingers through mine in comfort, and I take the quiet moment to appreciate my sister's presence.

The two silhouettes are still on the other side of the drapes, piquing my interest. "Is Dad out there?"

"Yeah," she answers, squeezing my hand before settling her gaze on mine again. "Kryll said Mom was there?"

Well, that's not where I was aiming this conversation.

Clearing my throat, I nod. "She was."

"How was she?"

I sigh. "I don't know. I was too busy being mean," I admit, acutely aware that I really was bitchier than usual.

"Good. I taught you well," she says with a smirk, and I gape at her. "What? Just because Dad gives you the whole calm and collected speech doesn't mean it's something I live by, too," she adds, a grin spreading across her lips, and I shake my head.

"She gave me a letter."

"This?" She pulls the envelope from her cloak pocket, and I nod. "Do you want to open it?"

"Nope," I answer without missing a beat.

"Fair enough." She tucks it back into her pocket, no further questions necessary, and I silently thank her for it. Her thumb strokes over my knuckles as she smiles down at me. "You seem...different," she offers, and I sink my teeth into my bottom lip as I nod.

"I feel different."

"I can't put my finger on it, but I think the academy is changing you." That's an understatement if I've ever heard one, and I don't know how I feel about it. "Whatever it is, I think it looks good on you."

"You think?" A warmth spreads through my body as I smile at her before my eyebrows gather and my gaze narrows on her. "Something is different with you."

She sighs dramatically. "I thought you were never going to notice," she flicks her hair over her shoulder, fluttering her eyelashes at me.

My heart rate skyrockets, my mind finally paying full attention through the hazy state, and then I spot it. How I didn't sooner, I don't fucking know, but it floors me.

"Nora, how the fuck are you standing on two feet right now?" I blurt, a sob bursting through my lips as I fling myself from the bed. She cackles, taking a step back as I fall to a heap on the floor beside her. The jolt shoots from my knees to my hips, but I ignore it as I stare up at my sister. "Nora," I rasp, tears coating my cheeks as she twirls in front of me.

Fucking twirls.

My sister.

"It suits me, right?"

"Nora, how?" I rasp, watching in awe as she dances

around the room. She's been standing beside my bed this entire time and I didn't pay enough attention to realize.

Holy fuck.

"Kryll, well, his mother, but—"

"Kryll did this?" I gasp, falling backward. My back hits the side of the bed as my eyelids press closed, unable to believe what I'm seeing.

"What's going…You're awake." My father's voice carries into the room with purpose, and when I find him in the opened drapes, a soft smile touches his lips.

"Hey," I rasp, and Kryll appears beside him a moment later.

"August?" He calls my father's name in confusion, but his sights are set on me. "Princess." I've never heard a word filled with so much relief in my whole life. I have so much I want to say to him, but I can't seem to move my damn tongue. "What are you doing on the floor? Let's get you up," he insists, cutting the distance between us before he slowly lifts me back onto the bed.

"Addi," my father murmurs, walking around to the other side of the bed.

"Dad," I croak, relieved to be in his presence. I might not have wanted to come here, but now that I have, it's the best place in the world.

"Are you okay?"

"I've been better," I admit.

He nods in understanding. "It's good to see you."

"It's good to see you too. Especially Nora," I add, waving my hand in her direction as tears clog my eyes again. "You did this?" I ask, turning my attention to Kryll, who scrubs at the back of his neck nervously as he nods. "Thank you."

It's not enough. It will *never* be enough, but it's all I've got right now.

"Don't give the drama queen any more attention than she's already been getting. Her ego won't withstand much more," my father muses, earning a gasp and a chuckle from Nora, who sits at the foot of my bed.

"How have you been?" I ask, enjoying the smile lines outlining his eyes as he grins at me.

"Good. Really good."

"He has a lady friend," Nora blurts, amusement dancing in her eyes.

"A lady friend?" I push, surprise clear in my voice.

"I do not," he insists as Kryll nods eagerly.

"She makes him blush," Nora whisper-shouts, and I scoff, watching my father blush at the mention.

"Where have you brought my family, Kryll?" I ask, giving him a pointed look, but he sees the humor and winks.

I've never felt a moment like this before.

So full of love, happiness, and…hope.

"There's something different about Dad, too," Nora states, pointing a finger at him, and the man in question turns slowly.

"Your stone…it's gone."

"Stone?" My father says with a smirk, shrugging as he turns back to me, and my eyes narrow.

"Don't play dumb. You said that stone was locked in unless a…" My gaze widens as I turn back to Kryll, whose sheepish look only grows as a pink hue colors his cheeks.

"You're not just a dragon. You're an Aeternus dragon."

ADRIANNA

38

Kryll all but fled from the room, his blush almost crimson as he made his excuses and left. With my dad and sister beside me, I fell back into a deep slumber. It was calm, serene, and everything anyone could wish for. My usual torments of the night Nora was harmed turn into fleeting moments of joy, watching her spin in circles and run through the tall flowers in the meadow.

It's a different life—one we'll never get back, but that doesn't mean there isn't a chance for a similar, maybe even better one in the future.

That's my goal, my aim, my promise. To myself and to those I love.

Waking again, I find myself alone. When I try to move from the bed, it's much easier this time. With my feet planted firmly on the floor, I take in my attire. An off-white silk gown falls to my feet, spaghetti straps holding it in place. It's the softest thing I think I've ever worn, and it's for bed.

Where even am I?

Intrigue has its firm grip on me, and I inch toward the closed drapes standing between me and the outside world. Ghosting my fingers over the fabric, I pull them aside just enough to slip through, and the moment I do, my breath is stolen from my lips.

A large marble balcony stretches out before me, offering views for what feels like miles and miles, and what lies below is like nothing I've ever seen before. Clouds float around castle tops. The building's an array of colors. A mixture of pale pinks, purples, and blues. They're straight out of the fairytale books my father once spoke of. But the most awe-striking sight are the wide wings that glide through the air.

Dragons.

Not just one, or two, or ten, but hundreds.

Ferocious reds, mighty blues, haunting blacks, and every other color imaginable.

They're stunning, swooping past the balcony over and over again, but none of them are as beautiful as the one that brought me here.

Kryll.

How did I ever believe I knew him before I came here?

It's impossible.

There are layers and layers to this man that I have yet to learn, and I can't deny the fact that I want to. I want to know every part of him.

He healed my sister. He healed my father. And in doing so, he's healed a part of me I thought would be broken forever. All without telling me. I think he tried, I'm sure he did, but every time he brought anything up relating to them, I shut him right back down.

"You're up."

I startle at Kryll's voice, peering over my shoulder to find the man in question, and a soft smile teases the corners of my lips.

"How does this place even exist? It's so beautiful," I murmur, looking back out over the world beneath us.

"Isn't it," he agrees, and I feel him step closer.

"This view leaves me breathless," I gush, unable to contain the awe it strikes in my bones.

"I couldn't agree more."

Turning to him, my cheeks heat when I realize he's not basking in our surroundings like I am.

No.

He's staring straight at me.

Clearing my throat, I wrap my arms around my waist. "You helped my father."

"I did."

"You helped my sister."

"I did."

My gaze locks on his. "Thank you. I don't know how I will ever be able to—"

"Don't. Don't finish that sentence when we both know it was my honor," he breathes, stealing the oxygen from my lungs and the blood from my veins, letting it all run dry at my feet.

"You healed me," I state, lifting my arm, and he smiles.

"I did."

"How? How did you do any of this?" I ask, blinking at him in wonder, and he smiles nervously, scrubbing the back of his neck.

"My blood is rare. Rarer than rare." That's all he offers, like it explains so much, but it feels like it gives me nothing.

"Do the guys know?"

He nods. "Yes, but no one else. It's not safe for me," he admits, making my eyebrows furrow in concern.

"Why?"

Sweeping his tongue over his bottom lip, he looks out over the balcony before settling his gaze back on mine. "I'd be nothing but a tool for others to manipulate."

It is such a simple and vague sentence, but the weight of it lies heavy on my shoulders, as if it is my own secret to keep.

"I won't tell a soul," I promise, hand on my chest above where my heart is.

"I know you won't, Princess."

"How?" I cock a brow, surprised by his certainty, and he shrugs.

"Because my dragon trusts very few people, but none more than it trusts you."

"Me?" I breathe, pointing a finger at myself as his statement leaves me in awe.

He steps closer, cupping my cheek as my blood simmers with a heat that is the complete opposite of anger.

"I'm sorry I didn't get there in time to stop you being hurt at all." His brows furrow, rage and despair warring in his eyes as I gape at him.

"That's not an apology for you to make," I insist, but he shakes his head.

"It is."

"At least you don't regret letting me leave Cassian's room altogether," I muse, pressing my palms flat against his chest as he brings me in closer.

"Oh, I do, but I wouldn't change it. You're your own woman, and I respect that. If anyone understands the desire to be alone to think, it's me." His words send my pulse thundering in my ears.

I can't stop blinking at him, the air swirling with the heat that surrounds us.

"Do the others know we're here?"

"Yes."

"Are they mad?"

He gives me a pointed look, which is answer enough. "Don't ask silly questions, Princess."

"What are our chances of prolonging their wrath until tomorrow?" I have no idea what time it is now, but I'm desperate to cling to this moment. Just the two of us. It feels like I've waited forever for it.

"For you, anything."

"What if what I want is you?" My voice is barely more than a whisper, thick with my desire as I peer up at him.

"I'm already yours."

His lips descend on mine in the softest kiss that has ever existed, and I succumb to it, to him. His hold on my chin tightens as he shifts me into the perfect angle to offer him control. He can have it, all of it; I just need him.

As if sensing the need inside of me, he lifts me in the air, my feet dangling as he pins me to his chest, moving us without lifting his mouth from mine. I feel the drapes drag across my skin as the world goes dim, and it's just the two of us.

He lowers me to the bed gently, with more care than I want or deserve, but it's worth it when he releases my lips to look deep into my eyes. His hands trail under my nightdress, pressing against my thighs as I gasp, my muscles clenching beneath his touch.

"I want you, Addi."

"Are you sure?" I instantly regret asking when the panic of him changing his mind comes into my thoughts, but the way he nods settles the sudden rush of uncertainty.

"I've never been more sure of anything in my life."

Heat coils in my stomach, desperate to feel him in every way, eager to show how much he matters to me using my body since my words aren't doing it justice.

"Strip for me," I murmur, running my tongue over my bottom lip as he stands at the foot of the bed, slowly peeling his t-shirt off. The way he reaches over his head, grabbing the fabric from the back before taking it off in one swift move, has my thighs pressing together again.

He knows the effect he's having on me. I can sense it in his darkening gaze as he unbuttons his pants and strips down to just his boxers. I gasp at the outline of his cock through the black material before he discards those too.

"That's a goddamn weapon," I rasp, blinking at the sheer length of his dick as it juts toward me. "Oh, you like that, huh? Compliments are your thing," I muse with a grin, forcing my gaze from his thick length to meet his stare.

"We both know what I'd like more," he purrs. "But first, let me see you, Princess."

I shiver under his order, clambering to my feet on top

of the bed as my gaze remains locked on his.

Hot and hooded.

Reaching for the spaghetti straps at my shoulders, I tug them down my arm, and the silk material pools at my feet a moment later. I'm bare. Not an inch of fabric between us, and I preen under his stare, hyper aware of the way his pupils dilate.

His eyes rake over me, setting my skin on fire as goosebumps rise in their wake, but before he can give me another order, I sink to my knees. I bounce with the motion before I crawl the remaining distance toward him.

"I'm going to have to test the thickness of your dick with my mouth before I let you anywhere near my needy cunt."

"Fuck, Princess," he croaks, the muscles in his forearms and thighs tensing with need as his hand wraps around his cock, edging the tip in my direction.

Up close, it only seems to grow. I reach out tentatively, engulfing his length with my hand, and I struggle to get my fingers and thumb to meet.

Holy shit.

He's going to split me in two.

I wrap my other hand around him too, and there's still so much dick on display that I might cry with delight.

"You've had a feel. Now mouth only, Addi."

I shiver, flexing my fingers around him once more

before I do as he says. My palms don't go far, splaying across his thighs as my nails bite into his skin, and I run my tongue over the tip of his cock.

His muscles bunch even more as I tease him, looking up through my lashes at him to see his pupils completely blow. That immediately brings my teasing to a halt, and with my next breath, I feel the weight of him on my tongue as I take a real taste.

He groans—the only sound of encouragement I need to carry on—and I take him to the back of my throat, holding back an inch before I choke to death. Retracting, I pout, glaring at the offending appendage.

"What's wrong, Princess?"

"I'm going to need you to fuck my mouth with it. Otherwise, I'm never going to get more than the tip past my lips," I admit, earning a scoff of surprise, but he must sense the seriousness in my eyes as my gaze fixes on his.

"I can't, Addi. I need you to remember I've never fucking done this before, and I'm already skirting the edge now. The only place I want to come is in your cunt, not your mouth," he rasps, making my mouth dry with excitement.

"With the size of this thing, you can't tell me it doesn't have a double-loaded barrel," I retort, encasing my lips around his dick once again before he can tell me otherwise.

I work his cock, taking more and more with every pass, and his fingers quickly work their way into my hair, tugging at the loose strands.

"Fuck," he grinds out, his voice hoarser than ever, and when the tip of his cock reaches the back of my throat again, I gag, completely overwhelmed by the size of him, but the way he makes me swallow around him is enough to send him over the edge. "Fuck, Addi. Fuck. Fuck. Fuck," he chants, his hands curling tighter in my hair as he paints my throat with his release.

It takes a moment for his grasp to relent, and I take a deep breath the moment he does.

"Holy fuck," I breathe, my pussy pulsing in anticipation as he shakes his head.

"You missed a bit, Princess." He presses the pad of his thumb against my bottom lip, smearing the remnants of his release before easing it into my mouth for me to suck.

My eyes roll to the back of my head at the action, and when I can finally meet his stare again, his want only shines brighter. Looking down at his cock, I'm not surprised to find it just as hard as it was moments earlier, and I grin.

"What am I going to do with you, Addi?" he murmurs, shaking his head in disbelief at me.

"You're going to sit on the bed and let me ride you."

He sinks his teeth into his bottom lip as he searches his pants, retrieving a condom from his pocket a moment later. I stand on shaky legs and point for him to take his seat. He moves exactly where I guide him, with his back flush against the headboard and his legs spread.

Crawling into his lap, he plants his hand on my arm, halting me. "No. Not yet. I need to taste you, stretch you, feast—"

I cut him off with a kiss before shaking my head. "Kryll, the only thing stretching me is your cock. I won't let you deny me the pleasure," I breathe, my entire body alight with the need and excitement coursing through my limbs. He has me wound tight and ready to detonate and he hasn't even touched me yet.

"Addi—" he starts to protest, frown lines forming between his eyes, but I press my finger to his lips, effectively cutting him off.

"I want you to rip me in two. I want you to take my breath away. I want to feel so full you make my eyes water." I punctuate each statement with a kiss, each one needier than the last, as I shuffle the rest of the way into his lap.

Taking the condom from his grasp, I enjoy slowly rolling it down his length, caressing his balls once I'm done before planting my hands on his shoulders.

"Are you sure about this?" he asks, grabbing my waist before I can line myself up with his cock.

"Are *you* sure?" I fire back, and he nods.

"I told you, I've never been more sure in my life."

"Then shut up, and please, let me die on your dick," I

groan, blindly finding the tip of his cock with my core.

We fall silent, all the humor fading away, leaving the two of us open and bare with one another. Our breaths mingle between us, our eyes wide and searching as our fingers explore each other. My desire leaves me slick against the tip of his cock as I sink a little, our gasps barely audible over the ringing of my pulse in my ears.

A little farther.

Gasp.

A little more.

Breathless.

A little more.

I see stars.

A little more.

My body clings to him like my life depends on it.

He fills me up, and just as requested, my eyes water. I attempt to take a few deep breaths, which come out as little more than heated pants, before I flex my hips and grind against him.

"Fuck, Addi," he moans, fingers tightening around my waist before he leans forward and engulfs my nipple with his mouth.

I slam back down on him, harder this time, and our moans tangle in the air.

Again, and again, and again, we lose ourselves in each other, all while finding a piece of one another along the way.

As he rakes his teeth over my sensitive flesh, I cry out, my muscles coiling tightly around his cock before I detonate at his trigger.

My eyelids threaten to fall closed as I ride out the waves of electricity, but he calls my name sharply, springing them back open.

"You are mine now, Princess," he states, his voice distorted. Darker, huskier, deadlier.

I blink at him, my orgasm still rippling through my bones as his eyes shift before me. Yellow-framed slits replace his usual black orbs, making me gasp.

"Your voice."

He shakes his head, but his grip on me only tightens as he lifts me up and down on his cock, working his own release into my body before he collapses back against the headboard.

Gaping at him, I struggle to remain seated as his hold loosens and I slump against his chest. I tilt my head back, trying to meet his gaze, and watch as he blinks, the movement repeating a few times before he finally peers down at me with jet-black eyes again.

"What was that?" I whisper, and his chest rumbles.

"It was me, Princess. All of me, and no matter what life throws at us now, Adrianna, I'll be right at your side every step of the way."

ADRIANNA

39

My limbs ache in the best possible way as I stretch out, starfishing across the sheets that are still warm beside me. Turning with a huff, it quickly seeps into a sigh as I pull the covers tighter against me.

"Princess Adrianna."

"Ah," I yelp, eyes widening as I blink at the man standing beside the bed.

I've never seen him before. He's dressed in what I can only describe as a black dinner suit, with a bow tie fitted perfectly over his shirt and the tail of his blazer hanging low beneath his knees. His silver peppered hair is swept back off his face, and his beady blue eyes feel intrusive as he peers down his long nose at me.

Holding the sheets even tighter, I clear my throat.

"Addi is just fine," I rattle, and his lips purse. I can't quite decipher the look on his face, but it's something between irritation and disappointment, so either way isn't looking good for me.

"Princess, your presence is expected for breakfast," he states, ignoring my request, but I let it slide since I'm in no position to argue with this guy, with only the thin sheet shielding me from him.

"Of course," I murmur, rubbing my lips together nervously as I try to find the right thing to say to excuse him without being too rude.

Anywhere else, and I would be as blunt as ever, but this isn't just anywhere; it is Kryll's home.

"Gerald, do we really need to be so formal?" Kryll grumbles, suddenly waltzing into the room. He doesn't look at the man beside the bed, though; his attention is locked on his cell phone.

A fucking cell phone in a place like this. It shouldn't exist.

"Always, Prince Kryll."

I balk, sitting upright as I tug the sheets tighter around my chest. "Wait, prince?" The words barely make it past my lips from the lump lodged in my throat.

Kryll's gaze snaps to mine as he presses his lips together, and I sense the sheepish look in his eyes immediately. "Hi," he breathes, taking a step toward me with his lips tipping up in a small smile.

"Hi...prince?" The word feels strange on my tongue, but what concerns me more is that he doesn't correct me, just like he didn't correct Gerald.

He rubs the back of his neck nervously as his cheeks turn pink. "I guess you're not the only one with a royal secret."

What the fuck?

"You're...a prince?" I say the words slowly, hoping to make them make sense in my brain, but I'm coming up short.

"You're freaking out," he states with a nod as Gerald continues to flick his gaze between the two of us.

"Of course I'm freaking out. Why did he call me princess?" I point an accusing finger at Gerald, who doesn't falter under my narrowed eyes, and Kryll rubs his lips together, another wave of nerves drifting from him. "Kryll," his name is on my tongue, and I can't decide if it's a warning or a plea, but he sighs, almost defeated, as he turns to Gerald.

"We'll be down in a few minutes. Please insist my mother starts without us. We won't be long," he murmurs, waving the man off, and he exits the room without a backward glance as Kryll walks around to my side of the bed.

He doesn't meet my gaze until his fingers are laced

with mine, and I'm certain he can feel my racing pulse.

"Do you want to have this conversation now, or—"

"Now seems like the most suitable time, Kryll," I interject, jaw growing tight with anticipation as he nods in understanding.

Clearing his throat, his gaze softens on mine as he breathes out the next words so softly, I barely hear them. "Because you are a princess."

My heart gallops in my chest as I shake my head. "Why do I get the sense you're not referring to me being the fae princess, the wise offspring of King August Reagan," I mutter, a tremble running through my body as he nods.

"Because you are *our* princess."

He says it like it's as simple as that, like five little words form a complete explanation of the situation I've woken up to. All I've done since I arrived here is sleep and take Kryll's virginity, but…

"Is this because…" My words trail off. I have balls and willpower, but I'm not saying the *V*-word out loud right now in case Gerald or anyone else can hear us. My gaze shoots to the door, confirming it's shut, but it doesn't ease the stress building inside of me.

He nods, scrubbing at his jaw. "My mother is the ethereal queen of dragons."

"Which makes you…"

"Prince Kryll of the dragons, at your service." His grin

spreads, pride shining in his eyes as he gives me the peace sign, and I can't help but roll my eyes at him. Those are some Brody level dramatics right there.

"How charming," I muse, earning a wink.

"It's a little embarrassing," he admits, his cheeks brightening with a pink hue again.

"It's still leaving me wondering why he referred to me as a princess because of you."

"Yeah, about that."

My fingers flex around his when he glances away, and only when his dark pools settle on mine do I speak.

"About that…" I encourage him with a soft tone, and it seems to ease whatever concern he's struggling with.

"My dragon chose you."

The memory of his eyes last night just before he found his release flashes in my mind and I shiver, unsure whether I want to see that happen again so soon or not.

"Which means…"

"It chose you."

"Spell it out, Kryll. Get crayons and construction paper if you need to," I insist with a pointed look, and he grins despite the glare.

"I told you. You are mine."

My eyes widen. "I didn't know that meant I was signing up for…that," I admit, and he nods, bringing my hand to his lips to press feather-light kisses against my knuckles.

"Honestly, me neither. Naïve, I know, and I'm sorry, but I—"

"There's no reason at all for you to apologize," I interrupt, unsure where the words are coming from, and I think it surprises him too.

"There isn't?"

"No," I breathe, releasing a shuddering breath as I seemingly accept this new damn title in my life like it's nothing.

"Good," he whispers, leaning close to press his lips against mine, and I melt under his touch. "Now that you've said that…"

"What did you do?" I rear back, eyebrows raised and ready for whatever he's about to say. Not more. There can't be any more to this. "Kryll!" I call out, a definite warning this time, and a moment later, he pulls a cell phone from his pocket. Not just any cell phone. Mine.

"I got your number from Nora and added you to a group chat with the guys."

Frowning, I glance down at the screen, and my mouth widens in a mixture of shock and horror. "Eighty seven notifications. What the fuck is going on?"

Not just notifications, specifically text messages, all from one goddamn group chat. I already can't handle it. Before I can throw my cell phone back at him and hide from it, he's off the bed, releasing my hand and charging toward the bedroom door.

"I'll meet you downstairs," he hollers, making me scowl.

"No freaking way. You'll get back here and explain this," I retort, waving my cell phone in the air, but he ignores me.

"See you soon." The teasing smirk on his lips has my teeth sinking into my bottom lip as I bite back my own grin. This isn't funny. Not even a little bit.

"Kryll," I call out just before he closes the door behind him, and he pauses, fitting just his head through the gap that remains.

"Yeah?"

I shake my head in disbelief. "You're insane."

"But I'm yours," he replies with a wink, and I sigh, the rising tension easing from my limbs as I stare at him.

"You're mine."

"And the others?" he asks, and I know immediately that he's referring to Cassian, Raiden, and Brody. The four of them together form my Kryptos. Admitting it won't help me, but denying it hasn't helped either. So for the first time ever, I relent, throwing caution to the wind as I nod.

"All mine too."

ADRIANNA

40

"**W**hat in the holy fuck am I wearing?" The words tumble from my lips before I can even consider halting them, and the girl behind me chuckles, moving back a step as she takes in her handiwork.

"You look perfect," she muses, her smile growing with every word.

"I look nothing like me," I retort, running my fingers over the material that floats at my sides, and she snickers.

"You're about to meet the ethereal queen of the dragons; you're not *supposed* to," she states, her eyebrows raised, but it still does nothing to ease the fact that I'm dressed so…excessively.

"This seems…ridiculous," I grumble, avoiding her gaze, but she pulls at the lace tied at my back, making me stand taller. My eyes narrow, the warning clear, and she offers me a teasing salute before getting the hell out of here.

Looking at my reflection, I cringe. My long blonde curls are loose, but tamed, cascading over my shoulders. A far cry from the braids I'm used to. Fine pink material floats around me in layers, making me appear cute and angelic, while the silver heels encasing my feet feel like death traps sent from Hell.

I hate it. With every fiber of my being, I hate it, but she's right. I'm about to meet the queen on her territory as the apparent new 'princess' and I guess I should probably look like one. I just have to remind myself to never come back here ever again because I'm only doing this once.

My cell phone vibrates on my nightstand, pulling me from my thoughts and away from the mirror with a sigh. The screen lights up and my eyes widen.

One hundred and two notifications.

That's ridiculous. Not as ridiculous as this dress, but it's up there.

The longer I leave it, the more messages there will be. Despite my better judgment, I relent, opening the group chat so I can prolong joining everyone for breakfast.

My eyes widen in a mixture of horror and disbelief as I run my thumb across the screen, scanning through the messages that await me.

Raiden:

I still don't know why you left campus.

Kryll:

I told you.

Raiden:

Yeah, but I don't understand why we couldn't come with you.

Brody:

There wasn't time. He's already told us this.

Raiden:

I know, but I want Adrianna to see what we're dealing with.

Cassian:

I'm muting you all.

I shake my head at Raiden's controlling nature.

Brody:

Okay. It's been forever. When are you coming back?

Kryll:

She's sleeping.

Raiden:

A picture or I don't believe you.

Kryll:

Don't be a creep.

Raiden:

Please, I can do creepy if needed.

Brody:

It's not needed. Honestly.

Cassian:

I regret looking at this mess. I'm double muting your shit now.

Brody:

Good luck with that.

A ghost of a smile touches the corner of my lips as I digest their version of chaos, even in text form, when my phone buzzes as a new message comes through.

Brody:

*Hey, Dagger. I see you in here. **Eyes emoji** **heart emoji** **eggplant emoji***

I roll my eyes, searching through the emojis before I hit send.

Adrianna:
middle finger emoji

I tuck my cell phone in the top drawer of the nightstand before I hurry to the door. The quicker I get this over with, the quicker we'll be heading home and the sooner I'll be able to see them in person because the reality is...I miss them.

My nose scrunches at the thought, but it doesn't make it any less true, which only serves to unsettle me even more.

Pushing the thoughts to the back of my mind, I focus on my surroundings and recall the directions I was given. *Turn right at the end of the hall, take the second left, and the stairs will lead to the patio.*

The halls are wide and tall, framed with stained glass windows looking out on one side, while pretty framed art lines the opposite wall. Even in my dress, I feel sorely under-dressed among the magnificence of it all.

I find the stairs a little too quickly for my liking, and as I descend, I find those gathered.

"And this must be Adrianna." My gaze latches onto the woman with her hand raised in my direction and I gulp. Her eyes are black, just like Kryll's, and her red hair is the same shade as his, cascading over her shoulders in a similar style to mine, but the main difference is the huge crown that sits on her head. A white gown bunches around her waist, the frilly sleeves making my gut clench in relief that I'm not wearing something of that size.

A tight smile touches my lips, but it eases as my gaze darts to Nora and my father, who are already seated at the table with her. When my eyes land on Kryll, a shy tilt to his lips warms my heart as he stands, dressed head to toe in a white suit.

Holy fuck.

I'm definitely in Heaven if he's casually looking like that.

His black ink looks darker against his tanned skin, beckoning me closer.

"It is," he breathes as I approach, answering his mother's introduction of my arrival, and it forces me to be present instead of tucked away in my head.

"It's lovely to meet you," the queen murmurs, eyes assessing me as she remains seated.

Kryll pulls my chair out, across from my father and Nora, as I clear my throat. "You too."

It's not a lie, it's nice to meet her, it's just awkward as fuck.

"I hope my son has been a gracious host," she states as I take my seat.

"Uh—"

Kryll chuckles, quickly interrupting my stumbling as he drapes an arm around the back of my chair. "She's kidding, but of course I am," he insists, and I attempt to take a deep breath. In the process, my gaze snags back to Nora and my father, who I find dressed casually. She's literally wearing jeans and a tee with a black cardigan while I'm dressed like…this.

As the queen turns to a server, murmuring for them to bring drinks and food, my eyes narrow on my sister.

"Why aren't you dressed like this?" I whisper shout, my eyebrows pinched with a slight hint of irritation, and she grins.

"What's wrong, dear?" the queen interrupts, pulling my gaze to hers, and I gulp.

"Nothing," I quickly insist as she raises her eyebrows at me, and I feel Kryll's hand squeeze around my shoulder. It's not with an unspoken warning, though; it's filled with reassurance.

I sigh, leaning into his touch as I find the right words to speak the truth as politely as possible, or as politely as possible for me, at least. "This place is beautiful, stunning even, but the attire, not so much." My nose wrinkles, continuing to display my discomfort, and a smile spreads wide across the queen's face.

She snaps her fingers, and in a blink, the glitz and

glamor disappear, the dresses, the suits, everything. One blink, and I'm wearing jeans and a fitted white t-shirt, with a charcoal-gray hoodie in my lap. Kryll's white suit is gone and he's now relaxed in his seat in a black tracksuit. The queen, however, still manages to look just as regal in a pair of fitted pants and striped silk shirt.

"Thank goodness. It's the law to invite guests under such pretenses, but it's fake as shit if you ask me," the queen states, a relaxed glimmer in her eyes. Nora chuckles at her choice of words while Kryll swipes a hand down his face.

"Mom."

"What? It is," she insists with a nod.

"I like you," I blurt, my cheeks heating under her gaze, and I quickly reach for the glass of water the server brings.

"I like you too. It's Meredith, by the way. If you even think of me as the queen and not Meredith, then my personality will shrivel up and die, and we can't have that now, can we?" She winks, and I nod.

"Thank you, Meredith."

"You're welcome. But I guess this meeting is all down to my son, who seems to like you even more than I do," she muses, and if I thought it was impossible for my cheeks to grow any hotter, I was wrong.

I make use of the glass of water again, hiding my face behind it as I down half of it in one go.

"This is fun. I never get to see my sister embarrassed," Nora snickers, earning a glare from me, but she does nothing to shy away from it.

"Well, I don't mean to bring the tone down, dear, but I would really like to understand what happened. How were you harmed?"

I wet my suddenly dry lips as I place the glass on the table. Kryll's hand moves from my shoulder to my lap as he opens his mouth to speak, but before he can say a word, his mother lifts her hand, pausing him.

"I already know what you said, but I want to hear her account of the events. You played your heroic role, son," she says with a dramatic and playful eye roll as she taps him on the shoulder. "But she felt the pain, and with that crinkle in her brows, I'd say it wasn't just physical."

Wow.

That's some assessment.

I clear my throat, tucking a loose tendril of hair behind my ear. "My mother appeared," I admit, and she nods.

"Ah, that ghastly bitch." I gape at her as my father chuckles and Kryll splutters on the water at his lips. "I never liked her, August; what did I say to you? Tell her." She waves her hand in my direction with a nod as my father shakes his head.

His eyes land on mine, a new-found softness dancing in his pools as humor crinkles the corners of his gaze.

"She said...that's one ghastly bitch," he repeats, making even Nora snort a laugh at the statement, but the chuckles quickly die off.

"I'm sorry, I shouldn't say that. She is your mother, and that was in bad taste. I—"

I wave my hand and shake my head. "Don't apologize. I just, well, she just...I don't even know."

"It's okay, dear. Take your time."

Kryll's hand tightens on my hold, offering me the strength I didn't know I needed.

"She seemed troubled, pained, and filled with regret," I state with a shrug. "But who knows if that's true when she did such a fine job of pretending so many years ago," I add, earning a hum from Meredith.

"Did she seem startled by Kenner's arrival?" she asks, and I tilt my head.

"Yes, but again..."

"Good acting," she finishes when my words trail off, and I nod.

I don't know why, but I can't bring myself to look at my father as I speak of my mother. Things are different now, but once upon a time, he loved her. Before all the lies, deceit, and pain, there was love.

"Is this a reunion without me?" I startle at the new voice, but I take a quick glance over my shoulder to find Professor Tora striding toward us.

His arrival disburses the awkward pain that lingers along my skin, and I'm thankful for it.

"Beau," Kryll murmurs as Meredith stands.

"If it isn't my terrible son," she says with joy, and he scoffs.

"Don't wound me," he says with a pout, placing a hand against his chest before hugging his mother tight. She presses a kiss to his cheek before he steps back, running a hand through Kryll's hair, tousling the ends in an attempt to irritate him. "What's up, shithead?"

"Fuck off, Beau," Kryll grumbles with a grin as a server brings a chair from nowhere and places it between Meredith at the end of the table and Kryll beside me.

Beau ignores him, glancing around his brother to settle his eyes on me. I can sense the grin before it comes. "Did he tell you about the prince thing before or after—"

"Stop, Beau," Kryll blurts, planting a hand over his brother's mouth as Nora laughs.

Beau waggles his brows, a complete contrast to the man we see at the academy. The moment Kryll releases his hold, Beau continues to push, despite my father and his mother being present. "Well?"

"After," I grumble when I realize he's not going to stop, and he scoffs.

"Smart, man. Real smart." Beau shakes his head, the teasing easing as he meets my father's stare. "It's good to see you, August. And Nora, causing any more trouble?"

"Trouble?" I parrot, sitting forward in my seat as my eyes narrow on my sister.

"Ignore him. He thinks he knows everything, but he forgets that he's an uptight asshole who believes breathing out of sync with him is chaos enough," she retorts, making Meredith's head snap back with a laugh as my father chokes on his breath.

"Nora," my father warns, but she shrugs.

Beau rolls his eyes at my sister, the irritation clear as he rounds his stare back to Kryll. "I'd like to say this is a visit sent with love, but alas, it's not."

"How so?" Kryll asks, his thumb trailing patterns on my thigh as my spine stiffens and I sit taller in my seat.

"I'm here for you, and you," Beau states, pointing between Kryll and me as the humor dissolves and the guy I'm familiar with from the academy sits in the same seat.

"Why?" I dare ask, already bracing for the answer.

"Word got around that a new ethereal princess has been declared."

"It did not," Kryll grunts, his nostrils flaring as he glances at his mother, but she lifts her hands in surrender.

"Did too," Beau retorts like they're both little kids, but I settle on the realization.

"Bozzelli sent you."

"Ding ding ding," he sings, all traces of humor

completely gone now.

"I'm guessing her joy is at zero?" I confirm before tugging the hoodie from my lap over my head.

"Less, if that's even possible," he answers, and I sigh.

Turning to Kryll with my eyebrows bunched in confusion, his eyes find mine. "I thought you said it was a secret?" I murmur, and his grip on my thigh tightens as a soft smile touches his lips.

"The fact that I'm a dragon and my mother is who she is isn't the secret, Princess," he explains, and I nod in understanding.

"No, just the fact that he's rare as fuck. Lucky bastard," Beau states with a slight smirk before he stands, losing the teasing as he does.

"Beau," Kryll bites with a warning that feels as though it's been muttered a hundred times before.

"What? You love it," Beau retorts with a raised eyebrow, and Kryll snickers.

"You're right. I do."

Meredith stares at them with hearts in her eyes, a sense of adoration that I feel when I stare at my father. Kryll is loved. Wholeheartedly, for the right reasons, and not because they want to use him.

Not like Brody, Cassian, and Raiden's families. There always seems to be a task for them to complete at the hands of their parents.

The thought of them, and the mention of Bozzelli, has me antsy to get out of here.

Standing, Kryll's hand slips from my thigh, but he quickly laces our fingers together.

"I guess it's time to face the music," I state, and Meredith's eyes narrow.

"There should be no music to face. I will—"

I wave her off with a tight smile and a shake of my head. As nice as it would be for Bozzelli's bullshit to be nipped in the bud as soon as possible, that's not how this works, and I know it. Instead of leaning into her aid, I take a deep breath, taking a moment to meet the eyes of everyone at the table as I savor the harmony of this moment before the chaos begins.

"Thank you, but truly, if we want to win their game, we have to be in the thick of it and playing along."

ADRIANNA

41

Kryll cups my cheek, the awareness that our moment is over, our space away from reality brought to a sudden halt, hangs in the air around us.

"Do you want me to fly us down or—"

"No flying for you, asshole. There's a high chance of an audience awaiting your arrival," Beau interjects, forcing a sad and irritated smile to my dragon's face as he nods in understanding.

I desperately want to run back inside the palace and find my family. The goodbye didn't sting as much as it usually does, but seeing Nora with a new lease on life makes my heart clench with joy. I want to witness it all with her, and I will once I'm done with all this bullshit. When I'm done winning back my crown.

Without a word, the world shifts around us, and a moment later, we're standing in Beau's office. A heavy weight settles on my shoulders at the change, but the knowledge that I'll see my men soon makes it all worthwhile.

My men.

I scoff at myself. Those words in my mind feel bizarre, and I'm still on the verge of denying them, but something tells me I don't have a choice.

"Let's go, lovebirds," Professor Tora states, waving for us to follow him, and it's insane how swiftly his name shifted in my thoughts with our arrival. His walls are up, his softer side buried away as we head out into the hallway, following him through the corridors until we step outside.

The moment we do, a gathered crowd halts our tracks, and all of their eyes turn our way.

He wasn't wrong about the audience.

"Excellent, the ethereal prince and princess have joined us." Bozzelli's voice cuts through the air, tightening my chest with the way she says it.

Instead of giving her a piece of my mind and worsening whatever is about to come our way, I squeeze Kryll's hand tight, my knuckles whitening as we join the crowd. Movement catches my attention, but a blink later, Raiden, Cassian, and Brody surround us.

I exhale, unaware of the breath that was lodged in my

throat, but with their close proximity, I feel stronger. Which is insane because it's awkward as fuck with everyone staring at us.

"Now that everyone is present, it's important I share the latest news with you," Bozzelli states, running her hands over her pastel lilac suit jacket. "The decision has been made to lockdown the academy."

My eyes widen as gasps and protests ring out around us.

"Is it because of this bitch?" Vallie growls, finger pointed in my direction from where she stands on the other side of the crowd.

"I wish it was," Bozzelli grunts with a sneer. "I wish it was because some were off fighting frenzied vampires or because they were traveling to the land of dragons, but alas, it's because it seems we have had some unwanted guests on campus. The lockdown is in place to protect you, not discipline you." Her teeth are clenched for every word, her anger and despair aimed right at me, and I take it.

"This is because of my mother and Kenner," I mutter, and Kryll nods.

"Yeah."

"No one can go in or out until the lockdown is lifted. To make up for that, a ball has been organized for next weekend as we have had some frantic parents who aren't too happy with the situation. It also falls perfectly before your next trial. That is all. Have a wonderful day in class."

She saunters off without a backward glance as four mage professors stand in a circle, chanting under their breath as a flicker of magic dances in the sky. All too quickly, they're on their way too, leaving us to stare at the magic that now invisibly seals us in.

Frantic parents? What the fuck is this? We're here to be the future leaders of our kingdom, it's not a daycare.

"Stupid bitch," a girl grunts as she walks past, but instead of lowering myself to her level and pummeling her in the face with my fist, I tamp down my rage and pretend she doesn't exist. I have bigger things to deal with than an upset girl on campus.

"Please let me go and trip her at least," Brody murmurs under his breath, and I grin.

"I'm good."

"Yeah, you are," he breathes, cupping my cheek as he draws my stare to his. "I missed you, Dagger, but I'm glad you're okay." He pulls me in tight, tugging my hand from Kryll's as he wraps me in a warm embrace. I hug him back, basking in his warmth as he places a kiss on my temple.

Before I can speak a word back to him, Raiden tugs me from his arms, enveloping me in his own. He holds me close, resting his face where my neck meets my shoulder as he breathes me in. "Fuck, Adrianna," he murmurs before raking his teeth across my flesh. A shiver runs down my spine, and I remember Brody's mention of his need for blood. My body tenses, reliving the pain from Vallie, but it wouldn't be like that with Raiden. That's what Brody said. No poison makes a difference.

My lips part, ready to ask him about it, when I'm yanked from his grasp too. Cassian grips my chin, his gaze raking over me as a growl vibrates low and quiet from the back of his throat. All I can do is gape at him until he descends, kissing me with a ferocity I wasn't prepared for.

I match his need, but he pulls away too quickly.

"When you've all stopped being assholes, I would like to see my friend," Flora hollers, making Cassian roll his eyes, but to my surprise, he takes a step back so we can embrace.

"I'm so glad you're okay," she whispers against my ear, and I smile.

"You too. I can't believe you helped with the vampires."

"It was nothing," she insists as she takes a step back, and I shake my head.

"No, it was everything. I'm sorry I'm only just saying it now," I insist, and she preens under the praise.

"Where's my hug too?" Arlo asks, but before I can take a step toward him, Raiden's at his side.

"No."

"What?" Arlo questions, rearing back in surprise as Brody wags a finger at him.

"Nope."

"But—"

"No fucking way," Cassian snarls, folding his arms over his chest.

"Addi," Arlo persists, looking at me with wide eyes, but it's Flora that interjects.

"She likes them when they're grizzly, Arlo. You have no chance," she says with a snicker, linking her arm through mine as she starts to tug me along.

"I didn't really want one anyway," he grumbles, and Kryll steps toward him.

"I'll give you one, buddy," he offers, hugging him tighter than necessary.

"Yeah, thanks," Arlo splutters, rushing out of Kryll's hold the moment he has a chance.

"Are you ready for class?" Flora asks, taking me in that direction as the others follow.

"Class? Hell yeah. That sounds so normal," I muse, eager to get lost in it all.

"You mean boring," Arlo retorts, and I scoff.

"No, normalcy is exactly what I need," I reconfirm, and Brody's hand comes down on my shoulder.

"Whatever you say, *Princess.*"

"Do not," I warn, giving him a pointed look, but his grin widens.

"I can't help it, *Princess.*"

"You're annoying," I grumble, rolling my eyes at his bullshit, but his hold tightens, forcing me to look at him.

"And you're my fucking Dagger."

BRODY

42

It feels like an eternity since I last laid eyes on her. I'm too scared to blink in case she disappears again. Kryll and our girl were off living their best lives while we were dealing with the weight of the academy in their absence. Next time, I call dibs on vacation time.

I know she was injured, and I'm certain there's a part of me that's jealous I wasn't the one to heal her, but I'll get over it. Eventually. There's definitely a piece of me that *is* jealous right now, though. There's no denying it. The mere mention of another ball has us diving into another dance class, but this time, she's not my partner.

Cassian crowds her space instead. He looks down at her with a sense of awe, which I know reflects in my eyes too. She's everything. I've known it all along, and now the others are finally catching up.

"Brody, participate or get out," the professor snaps, pulling me from my thoughts. I glare at him, my dance partner sighing as I hold out my hands.

"Surely, you can pair me with someone better," she states, hand on hip as her lips twist, and I roll my eyes.

"You're not my first choice either, Vallie. Actually, you're not even my last choice. That's how vile you are. Get the fuck over yourself," I say, irritation coursing through my limbs. Of course I got paired with the she-devil herself.

I know I need to be the bigger person and see past her shit so I can focus on the class, but that's easier said than done.

"Are you okay?" Addi's at my side in a beat, ignoring the snarling vampire in front of me as she puts her hand on my shoulder.

"I'm good," I breathe, nodding for extra confirmation, more for myself than anyone else, but she sees right through me.

"Are you sure?" Her gaze shifts to Vallie for a brief moment before circling back to me, and I nod.

I should tell her now, mention the phone call she missed while she was away, but I just want to bask in her presence for a little longer. I want to enjoy a moment with her without my father tainting everything once again.

Shit, I could have sent it in a message already, now that I have her number, but I'm not about that kind of thing. I want to be able to read her expression as I speak.

If she senses the swirling in my mind, she doesn't utter a word. Instead, she leans up on her tiptoes, planting a kiss to my cheek before she sashays back off to Cassian.

I watch her go. Every step. Earning another grumble from my unwanted partner.

"Get over yourself, asshole," Vallie snaps, and I snicker.

"Oh, wow, Vallie. Your words wound me." I plant a hand to my chest and take a step back, eager to put some distance between us.

"Brody, if you're not going to do this, then I—"

"I am, Professor. You just happen to have partnered me with the worst person possible," I state, giving him a pointed look.

His chest rises and falls with a heavy breath as he looks between us. "You're my best dancer, Brody." I grin at the statement, my shoulders rolling back as I stand taller. "Fine, choose your partner."

"Wait, what?" Vallie says with a gasp, but she goes ignored as I point my finger at the one I want.

"I should have known," the professor grumbles, pinching the bridge of his nose as he sighs again. Apparently I'm a handful today, but I want my girl, what can I say?

"You're screwing me over, asshole," Cassian growls, eyebrows furrowed in irritation, but my smile doesn't waver.

"What can I say? I'm the best dancer. He said so," I

insist, pointing at the professor. "And I'll dance the best with my favorite partner," I add, watching Adrianna's cheeks turn pink as she rolls her eyes at me.

"Trade," the professor calls, before turning away to watch the other students.

"You owe me for this," Cassian mutters as he shoulders past me, and I nod.

"I do."

I don't glance back, my eyes trained on Adrianna as I approach. Her hands immediately lift to my chest when I'm close enough. I place one hand on her hip and the other reaches for hers as I lace our fingers together.

"Hey, Dagger."

"Hey," she says with a smile that instantly makes my chest ache. "This is great. Now you can tell me what's going on," she states as we start to follow the steps of the rhumba. The professor likes to set the bar high with little time to practice, but it just means I get more time up close with my girl.

"Nothing's going on," I murmur, turning us, and she follows my lead perfectly.

"Bullshit," she says with a scoff, giving me a deathly pointed look, and my shoulders slump.

"Obviously, you know me too well. I can't discuss it here though. But more than anything, I just can't take my eyes off you." It's the truth, and even though her features soften, she sees right through my crap.

"You're a sweet talker."

"For you I am," I reply with a wink, and her rich laugh wraps around us.

"We both know that's bullshit too. Your charming player ways—"

"When I was trying to play you, did I say anything like that?" I interject, my turn to give her a pointed look, and her eyes narrow.

It takes a moment, but she quickly shakes her head. "No."

I walk us through the steps of the dance slowly, our gazes focused on our feet, before I look back at her. "Exactly my point. I never pretended it was anything other than what it was."

Her eyebrows crinkle with confusion. "But—"

My hand slips from her waist to press a finger against her lip. "I've never felt what I feel for you about anyone else. I told you that already. I've told you from the first moment I was inside you that once wasn't enough. It never will be."

I don't know who moves first, and I'm not entirely sure I care when our lips meld together. My body ignites at her touch. I tilt her head back, desperate to deepen the kiss, and just as my tongue slips past her lips, a huff of frustration vibrates down the back of my neck.

"That's it, Brody—"

"Okay, okay. I'm good," I insist, leaning back from Addi with a sigh. She smirks at me as the professor saunters off once again, and we fall into step with the box moves.

"So," she starts, searching my eyes for something, anything, and even though I can't go into detail on my father, there is something I *can* offer her.

"So, while you were gone, I was doing some research."

"Research?" she questions, eyebrows raised as I nod.

"It's a lot, want to help?" I ask, and she tilts her head at me.

"What's it on?"

I clear my throat, nerves quickly creeping up my spine, but I manage to mutter the words. "Spells used to suppress a wolf."

She gapes at me, eyes widening as she nods. "I'd like that," she rasps, our steps faltering again as she smiles up at me.

"Good." My chest warms, leaving me pleased with myself, when she presses her lips to mine. It's quick, fleeting, and over way too quickly, but not too quickly for the professor it seems.

"Again?"

"I'll stop. It was me this time," Addi insists, not moving her gaze from mine.

"Actually…" another voice interjects, pulling our

attention to where a girl stands beside the professor.

"What do you want now?" Addi asks with a sigh, tension rippling from her, and I frown.

"I was just wondering if you were aware of the new moon two days ago."

New moon? My gaze narrows. Ah, fuck, this is the girl who muttered bitch under her breath earlier. I knew I should have hurt her then. That's what I get for being a nice guy.

Addi rubs her hand against my chest before stepping away from me.

"Let's get on with it then," she grumbles, patting her hair to make sure it's all tightly fixed to her head.

Cassian quickly rushes through the crowd that instantly stops their dancing to focus on the drama unraveling before them.

"No, I'll—"

"No you fucking won't," Addi retorts, raising her hand to stop him in his tracks. His mouth opens, ready to object, but she doesn't give him the chance, and it's hot as fuck. "You can fight for your own shit when I don't have so much pent up tension desperate to be released."

Addi turns to the girl, who audibly gulps once she has my girl's full attention, and I grin.

"Let's go, bitch. Say it," Addi snaps, shrugging out of her cloak as she faces off with the wolf.

It takes the girl a moment, all eyes set on her, giving everyone a chance to step closer. Raiden and Kryll included, who step between Cassian and me to watch.

"I challenge you to a duel for Cassian Kenner."

The maniacal grin that spreads across Addi's face is venomous, and I love it. "It will be my pleasure to bring you down a peg or two."

"You won't," the girl bites back, finding her strength, and Addi scoffs.

"Do you want to commit to hand to hand combat only or are we using our abilities?" She quirks a brow, waiting for an answer, and the girl wets her lips nervously.

"I'm not scared of your abilities," she states, standing tall as her eyes beam amber, her wolf letting its presence be known.

"Good."

Addi lifts both hands as she takes a deep breath, summoning her magic before she launches them at the poor, delusional girl.

Wind whips her off her feet, her cry of panic echoing around the gathered group as the professor stares in horror, but keeps his mouth shut. Once the wolf girl is dangling upside down, Addi blasts a wave of fire in her direction, stopping the burning inferno a mere inch from her face.

"Concede?" she asks, voice bored as the girl's screams grow wilder.

"Never!"

"Are you sure? I can burn you to death until all that remains of you is the smell of roasted bitch," Addi warns, cocking her head at the challenger.

Tears stream down her face, panic consuming her. A few grumble at the mention of burnt flesh, but I grin like a manic fool. She's everything, and I am in awe of her.

Even now, when she wields such magic, she pauses, offering her enemy a way out. Whether the girl takes it or not is her problem, I'm going to love my girl either way.

Love?

Do I?

I blink, my throat drying as I watch her.

All of the sounds disappear as I feel my world tilt.

It's all because of her.

The wolf girl taps out and Addi withdraws her magic, but all I can do is stare in awe at her.

Love.

I love her.

I fucking love her.

I'm so screwed, but I wouldn't have it any other way.

She's the sharpest fucking dagger on campus. Screw that, she's the sharpest fucking dagger in the kingdom.

And she's all *mine*.

ADRIANNA

43

"**I** think that was the longest day of my life."

Like, hands down. It's gone on forever, and I've lived through some shit. One lesson fell into another, each one stretching out longer than the last, like a never-ending vortex hell-bent on melting my brain.

Bozzelli's little announcement did nothing but piss me off. What's the point in organizing a lockdown and arranging a ball for the week after? Those people we're trying to keep out will be right back on campus in a flash. That's probably her intention. I don't think it was Bozzelli who pulled the trigger on the lockdown, especially when it's to "keep us safe." That's not her usual approach. She probably likes all the death, it means less competition. Whoever called the order isn't seeing eye-to-eye with her, which only reminds the bitch that she's not as in charge as she likes to think she is.

"Imagine what the past few days were like when you weren't here. It was even worse," Raiden mumbles, his head downcast as we leave the main academy building. There's something off with him. There's something off with all of them—except Kryll—and I can't help but worry that it relates back to me.

I was off with Kryll in the dragon kingdom, realizing how much I like them and how important they are to me, all while they were stuck at the academy, probably over all my drama and bullshit.

I internally roll my eyes at myself. Self-doubt doesn't look good on me; it doesn't feel good either, but I can't deny that I'm out of my element with these guys.

"She's not even sorry about it," Brody sings, a grin spreading across his face as he winks at me.

"Of course, she's not," Cassian grumbles, jaw ticking as he stares straight ahead, and just when I start to talk myself out of the worry threatening to consume my thoughts, it's back again.

"What's everyone's plan for the evening?" Kryll asks, and I release a breath.

"We're doing that *now*?" I ask, peering at the four of them.

"Doing what?" Brody asks, eyes crinkling with curiosity.

"Making evening plans together?" My heart skips a beat, uncertainty tingling down my spine as time seems to come to a stop.

"I've been waiting forever for this," Brody replies, hands raised high above his head as he tilts his face back and grins up at the sky.

"Count me out. I actually don't feel the best. I'm exhausted," Raiden states, turning to me. He offers me a timid smile as he presses a featherlight kiss to my cheek before strolling off without another word. I watch him head straight for the vampire building and my gut twists.

"What's going on with him?" My chest tightens with worry, confusion rooting itself deep in my bones as I watch his every step. He's not even using his vampire speed like usual.

"He's weak. He has been since the night that frenzied fuck got ahold of him. It's just progressively getting worse," Brody admits, scrubbing the back of his neck.

"Weak?" The word feels foreign on my tongue, especially in relation to Raiden.

"The blood thing." A memory of him bleeding out, his blood coating my fingers, flashes to the forefront of my mind, stealing my breath as I turn back to my vampire, earning one last glance at his back before he disappears around the corner.

"Oh…" I manage, at a complete loss. "Should I…"

Should I what? Fuck.

"You shouldn't be doing anything. You only just got back. Besides, he has to come to you. Raiden is all about his pride, and we both know he'll blow a gasket if we make him feel anything other than regal." The corners of my mouth tip up at Brody's assessment, but it doesn't stop the pain from twisting in my heart. I don't like the stress that comes with these men.

"How am I supposed to focus on anything when he's like this?" I ask. I'm not stupid. I know Brody's words are accurate. Raiden needs to come to me. Fear clings to my body at the thought of it, but I'd try…for him, I'd try. That doesn't stop the tension from clinging to me as I wait for him to come around.

"Well, I was wondering if you wanted to help me with some more research…" Brody offers, and my teeth sink into my bottom lip. That could be distracting enough, but it doesn't ease the emotions swarming inside of me.

"Are you sure he's okay?" I ask, folding my arms over my chest, and Cassian nods.

"I'll go and get him some stuff from Janie's."

"But we can't," I blurt, and he's standing toe to toe with me a moment later.

"I can do what I want, Alpha. Besides, I think I'm the last person you want to be around right now." He lifts a hand to cup my cheek but stops a breath away.

"Huh?" I frown at him, desperate to understand. His gaze narrows as he searches my eyes until he realizes I have no clue what he's talking about.

"My father," he grunts.

"Is a dick. We know this," I state slowly, and he shakes his head.

"He's the one who hurt you, Addi."

"And?"

"And nothing," he bites, his jaw clenching tighter.

"And everything. That was your father, not you."

"I know, I just—"

"You just what?" I cock a brow at him, the tension reaching its peak between us. It came out of nowhere, but now it's everywhere. It's always zero to one hundred with this guy. He stares, and stares, and stares, until I relent. Lifting my hand to his cheek, I can sense Kryll and Brody watching us, but they opt to keep out of it. "Go and help him if you can, but your dad mangling my arm and being a cunt is not your fault. Not now, not ever."

He gulps, his jaw flexing beneath my touch before he tilts his head to press a kiss to the center of my palm. "Okay," he rasps, repeating the motion once more before disappearing after Raiden.

I sigh, turning my attention to Brody and Kryll. The latter offers me a soft smile as he takes a step toward me. "I've hogged you enough. I'll share. For a little while at least," he breathes, tilting my chin up to plaster a kiss to my lips. He steals my breath, pleased with himself, before he disappears, too.

"And then there were two," Brody muses, reaching for my hand, and I nod. "Ready to get smart?" he asks, and I cock a brow at him.

"I am smart," I retort, and he rolls his eyes.

"Of course. I meant smarter."

"Of course you did."

"I did," he insists, squeezing my sides and making me giggle. He has a way of easing the constant stress that bubbles beneath the surface, and it's exactly what I need.

"Bring it on, oh, wise one."

ADRIANNA

44

"This one here says if they burned sage into your foot, it would…ew, no, nevermind," Brody grumbles, his nose scrunched in distaste as he shakes his head at the book in his lap before turning the page swiftly. Searching for information on suppressing powers, my inner wolf, or anything remotely in that realm of documentation feels surreal, and I'm not entirely sure I'm committed to it, but here we are.

Amusement hums beneath the surface of my skin as I stare at him. "Don't stop there, I'm intrigued," I muse, giving him a pointed look, and his lips stretch from a thin line into a huge grin.

"Admit it. You're nerdy."

I roll my eyes, refusing to talk about this again. I'm not sure how many times he's said it now, but every time he does, the sparkle in his eyes gets brighter. Shining like stars in a dark and dreary night sky.

"Fine, don't tell me," I mutter, waving a hand at him as I drop my gaze at the book I'm nursing.

"It's not a bad thing, Dagger. You can be hot, feisty, *and* nerdy. Your secret is safe with me."

My gaze whips to his, eyes narrowing as I give him my best death stare, but it doesn't hit the mark I intend.

"You're only making my dick harder when you give me that look."

Ass.

Rolling my eyes *again*, I turn my focus back to the book in my hand before I close it with a thud. "This one is a dud," I grumble with a sigh. The stack of books we've been through is growing taller than those we haven't gotten to yet, and it makes concern swirl in my gut.

Concern. Worry. Tension. Three feelings I sense more than usual at the moment, and there's a part of me screaming that it's leading to something big, but I'm quite sure our situation can't get any messier than it already is.

Wordlessly, Brody stretches, grabbing a book from his desk to hand to me. His room is lost to the stacks of leather binders, old books, and tattered papers. When he said he had gathered some research, I don't know what I expected, but the mage in him definitely took over.

I'm sure we've got half the library here.

A yawn takes over my mouth as I settle back into my spot on his bed. I open the book to the content page to see if anything worthwhile stands out.

"Do you want to call it a night?" Brody asks, pulling his cell phone from his pocket as I shake my head.

"No way," I insist, suppressing another yawn as I turn the page.

"You should eat."

"I'm good."

"If I don't feed you, I worry my balls will be cut from my body, and I rather like them where they are." His random statement draws my attention to him. His arm is already extended, his cell phone in hand as he flashes the screen my way.

Raiden:

Have you guys eaten?

Brody:

Not yet.

Kryll:

It's been hours.

Brody:

Our girl says she's good.

My cheeks heat at the mention of *our girl*, but I don't linger on it; I focus on the next line and bite back a scoff.

Cassian:

Feed her. Now.

"Fine, I could eat," I relent, watching him visibly relax in his spot on the floor with a sigh.

"You're a lifesaver, Dagger. Is there anything in particular you feel like?"

"I'm not fussy, but I want snacks, too," I decide, nodding eagerly. If we're going to make it through all of this, snacks are definitely needed. Maybe I should have gotten Flora involved. She's the queen of snacks.

He doesn't pester me any further for an answer, and I smile, turning back to my book, knowing the decision has been taken out of my hands. I've reached my limit of decisiveness for one day, and having someone else take the reins is nicer than I want to admit.

"Whatever the Princess of the Dragons wants, she gets," he sings, tucking his cell phone away as I grab the pen at my side and throw it at him.

His eyes narrow, but he manages to catch it with little effort. "I'm watching you," he warns, raising his eyebrows at me, and I scoff, turning away again.

"I know. I can feel your eyes on me."

"You can?" The lilt to his voice reveals a degree of surprise that I don't expect.

"Always," I confirm with a nod, feeling it even more than ever as I skim my finger over the text before me.

"Look at me." His words are soft, but the order is firm.

Glancing at him, my throat dries out when I find an intensity in his eyes that only darkens the longer I look.

"I'm going to spend the rest of my life looking at you." My teeth sink into my bottom lip as my neck warms, the feeling creeping up to my cheeks, and I turn away. "You like that, don't you?"

I can't even bring myself to imagine the color of my face as the heat increases, but I keep my eyes glued to the book in my grasp.

"You need to focus on the books," I mutter, earning a snicker from him. I wave my book at him for good measure and he hums.

"Hmm, whatever you say, Dagger."

We fall into a comfortable silence again, only the sound of turning pages echoing around us as we consume page after page. If Brody is irritated with me declining the music he offered, he doesn't show it. I just can't concentrate with anything on in the background. Although, it leaves me acutely aware of everything the man next to me is doing.

A hand sweeping through his hair, his tongue flicking out over his bottom lip, his legs spreading as he gets comfortable, revealing the outline of his…

Nope.

Focus, Addi.

It feels hopeless at this stage, but we have to find something. *Anything.*

Done with another book, I add it to the discard pile, and Brody silently offers me another. I take it from his grasp with a soft smile, watching as his attention goes back to the book in his lap.

Clearing my throat, I instantly have his attention. "Are you going to tell me about earlier?"

"Earlier?" he queries, line marks gathering between his brows.

"Whatever you were holding back in dance class," I explain, and he goes still.

"Ah." He scrubs at the back of his neck nervously.

"Ah," I repeat, trying to bottle up the concern that instantly bubbles to the surface so I don't overreact. I'm not sure if it works or not; either way, his shoulders sag and he speaks.

"I heard from my father while you were gone."

No beating around the bush, then. It leaves me slightly impressed. "That sounds…joyous."

He scoffs, sensing the sarcasm that attempts to hide my uncertainty. "Yeah…definitely not," he retorts, running his hand through his hair with a sigh.

"I get the feeling what he said involves me," I admit when he doesn't explain straight away, and it earns me another scoff.

"You would be right. It's actually what led me here," he clarifies, tightening my chest as he still withholds exactly what was said.

"Here?" I ask, needing full disclosure, the book in my lap completely forgotten as my eyes drill into his.

"To the research." Tension radiates from him and I can't contain it any longer.

"Tell me."

He nods, accepting my demand as he clears his throat, looking up to the ceiling for a brief moment before his gaze settles on me again. "He seems to think that if you continue to suppress the wolf in you, the chance of them forcing the fated mates has a higher success rate."

His words hang in the air for what feels like an eternity before I finally remember how to use my tongue.

"So, if I find my wolf…"

Brody shrugs. "It's no guarantee, but I wanted you to have options."

I blink at him. One simple word and it makes me falter. Heat creeps over my skin again, but this time, it's not with shyness or desire. No. It feels a little like embarrassment.

"Options. I've never had those before," I blurt, slapping my hand over my mouth quickly to stop anything else from slipping out. Brody's eyes soften, along with his smile, but before he speaks, I drop my hand. "I don't know if I'll want to go ahead with whatever we might find." Another blurt, another truth, and it's accepted with a simple nod.

"I know, and that will be your choice," he states, and I know without a shadow of a doubt that he will stay at my side no matter what I choose, no matter where our fate falls, he's always going to be there.

"Thank you," I breathe, unable to expand on my appreciation, but he doesn't seem to mind as he winks.

"You're welcome."

I nod, my gaze drifting back to my book, but something pauses me from going back to the passages. "Why did he call you with that information?"

"To get me to do the opposite," he answers immediately, and my eyebrows crinkle. "He wants me to be on high alert with you to ensure you don't find your wolf."

There it is. That's the issue. What a fucker.

"Thank you for telling me."

"Always," he says with a firm nod, sealing the promise between us. With a lingering smile, we turn back to our books.

Flip, flip, scan, pass. Flip, browse, sigh, flip, pass. Flip, flip, flip, scan, scan, pass, double sigh.

The cycle continues, the desperate need to find something—anything—grows.

"Oh," Brody hollers suddenly, making me pause.

"What?"

He scrubs the back of his neck, his eyes narrowing on whatever he's reading.

"What?" I repeat when he doesn't answer quickly enough.

"I'm trying to confirm the sources," he offers, but I shake my head.

"I swear, Brody, if you don't tell me what it says—"

"It says if you mate with your fated other, it could lift the spell or whatever it is that's suppressing you."

My heart rattles in my chest. "Mate?"

"Yeah." He finally lifts his gaze from the pages to look at me, to find my eyebrows crinkled.

"You know what that means, don't you?" he says, wagging his brows, and my throat dries. I struggle to gulp. "Do you like the idea of that?" he pushes, placing the book beside him as he rises to his knees.

"Of sex? Obviously—"

"Not just sex, Addi—"

A knock at the door startles me and halts whatever Brody was about to say. He groans, rushing to his feet and charging toward the door. As quickly as he swings it open, he slams it shut, but when he turns to me, there are two bags of food in his hands.

"Who was that?" I ask, discarding my book carefully.

"Kryll," he answers with a shrug, and I gape at him.

"I could have said hi."

"You're mine right now." The pointed look he offers leaves me rooted to the spot.

"Am I, though? We're discussing me fucking my true mate. I'm going to assume that's a wolf, not—"

He cuts the distance between us, slamming his palm against my mouth before I can say another word. "Don't finish that sentence while you're with me. There's teasing, Dagger, and then there's playing with fire. You're off the Richter scale with words like that." His eyes darken with every word, leaving me speechless. "Do you like that? You like my warning?" he breathes, keeping his hand firmly in place as he kneels over me on the bed. I nod, unable to deny it, and he grins. "I love that you're not shy."

I grin against his palm before I open my mouth and sink my teeth into his flesh. He groans, his hand slipping from my mouth and dropping to my waist as he slowly shuffles down my body.

"Brody." I don't know what I want or need but his name parts my lips nonetheless.

"We should eat," he breathes, and I freeze, but when he looks up at me through his lashes, the heated gaze sends a shiver up my spine. "And I'm not talking about food, Dagger."

"Brody?"

His hands smooth down my thighs, pausing at my knees before he spreads my legs apart.

"I think I want to start with dessert."

BRODY

45

"Brody."

My name on her lips is a prayer, shooting straight through my cock and leaving me to tremble before I've even had a chance to strip her out of these goddamn pants.

"That's it, Dagger. Remember who's feasting on you tonight," I breathe, slipping my palms up the inside of her thighs before I reach for the waistband. Her breath hitches as she lifts her ass off the bed, just enough for me to discard her pants.

Red lace covers her pussy and I bite back a groan at the sight.

Skimming my hands over her skin, I feel the goosebumps rise in my wake. Her back arches when my hands slip beneath the hem of her t-shirt, and her gasp is like a sweet melody in my ears.

I can't hide my groan this time. Not when I find her tits encased in the same red lace that frames her pussy.

"You're a fucking sight to behold, Addi," I rasp, my eyes consuming every inch of her as I commit it all to memory.

"You're overdressed," she whispers in return, and my gaze finally meets hers.

I can change that.

Lowering my head, I press a kiss to her stomach, just above her belly button, and I feel her muscles clench.

Fuck.

Desperate, I rush to my feet, knocking a stack of books over as I go, but I ignore it all, my focus set on her as I drag my t-shirt over my head and quickly shake out of my pants. Her eyes drift from my face, scanning down my chest and fixating on my dick. Following her line of sight, I find the tip of my cock peeking out of the waistband of my black boxers.

Dragging my gaze back to her, I find her stare unmoved.

"Like what you see, Dagger?"

"You know I do," she purrs, running her tongue over her bottom lip as she finally meets my gaze again.

"I fucking love what I see," I reply, my voice dropping down an octave or two as my desire creeps to the surface. Her smile spreads wide and her nipples peak beneath the red lace.

"Come prove it." She lifts up, propping herself on her elbows, her red lingerie drawing me nearer.

I feel like a damn bull, with my damn heart, body, and soul all set on chasing down the red flag. All for the damn prize.

Her.

Grinning, I reach for the bags of food on the bed, set on moving them when something catches my attention.

"What are you doing?" she asks, and my lips twitch in a smile.

"Seeing what treats he chose," I answer, her sharp intake of breath clinging to every fiber in my body.

"I thought—"

"Ice cream," I blurt, pulling the tub from the bag.

Her gaze shifts between my face and the vanilla ice cream in my hands. Her throat bobs as she swallows, but I notice her pupils dilate.

She's something else.

"What are you going to do with that?" she asks, rubbing her lips together nervously, and I grin, placing the bags on the floor before crawling between her spread thighs. I open the tub and take a scoop from the top layer with the spoon Kryll was clever enough to remember.

"Adrianna Reagan, I'm going to eat it off your pussy. What else would I do with it?" I say with a snicker, and her eyebrows shoot up.

"Brody—" she starts, but her words are cut short as I slide her panties to the side and rest the underside of the cool spoon against her skin. "Fuck," she croaks, legs trembling as I slowly move the spoon around and let the ice cream drip onto her folds.

My tongue darts out just as quickly, feasting on the classic flavor as it warms at her core, and I think I've just found my new favorite snack.

"Holy crap," she groans, breathless, as I swirl my tongue from her core to her clit, taking every last sweet drop of ice cream with me.

"You taste like Heaven, Dagger," I murmur, setting the tub beside her as I inch up her body, my eyes fixated on her taut peaks pleading for my attention beneath the red lace.

Swooping the thin fabric from her tits and settling it beneath the swell of her breasts, I scoop ice cream onto each of them. Addi's head falls back with a groan, anticipation heightening between us before I lean in.

The moment I do, her moans of pleasure fill the air, making my cock jut toward her with need. Her skin feels hotter, the ice cream melting against her touch instead of cooling her.

"It's too much," she rasps, her chest rising in short, sharp bursts as she looks down at me through hooded eyes.

"It's not enough," I retort, and she huffs a laugh.

"That too."

"Come for me, Dagger, and I'll stop," I offer, trailing the melting ice cream through the valley of her breasts, over her stomach, and down to her core.

I discard the tub and spoon with a clatter on my nightstand as I follow the path with my tongue. Her back arches off the bed, desperate for my touch as her fingers fist into the sheets beneath her writhing frame.

The second I lap at the remnants at her entrance, I thrust two fingers inside her core, feeling her walls spasm around me.

"Fuck, Brody, fuck," she cries out as I suck on her clit, raking my teeth over the tight nub as I rub my fingers precisely in her center, finding the electric spot that has her bucking against me. Her chants fall to whispers as her hands twist in my hair, giving her the purchase needed to ride my face.

And ride she does.

I feel her muscles coil tight, the touch almost deathly, before she detonates, painting my tongue with her release as my fingers dance over her sensitive flesh.

"Brody," she groans, low and slow, making me curse under my breath before I look up at her.

"That's it, Addi, say my name."

"Brody," she whispers, and my eyes roll to the back of my head.

She knows exactly what she's doing to me, and she loves it.

"I'm not done with you yet, Dagger," I promise, grabbing her waist. My fingers flex against her flushed skin, making me grin before I spin her around. She lands on her knees, her face a mere inch from the sheets as she tries to find balance on her elbows, but I push down against her back, bringing her cheek flush with the bed.

Her ass is stunning, raised in the air, eager for me to claim her. I run my fingers over her heated skin, and she shivers at my touch. When I trail a hand between the apex of her thighs, finding her clit once again, she moans.

"What would it feel like to mate with someone?" I ask, trailing my hands all over her from head to toe as my cock brushes against her core.

"I don't know," she rasps, the same answer as me.

Grabbing at her hips, I pull her core flush against me, making us both groan in delight.

"It would be earth shattering," I breathe, and she sighs with wonder.

"You think?"

"Fuck, Dagger. Skin on skin? It sounds like a gift from above," I admit, the tip of my cock teasing at her entrance before I slip through her folds, teasing the both of us. I repeat the motion again and again, basking in her heat, inching a little deeper every time, and even though it may only be millimeters, it's still pure ecstasy.

"Brody," she whispers, my name a warning or a plea, I'm not sure.

"Imagine," I repeat, "Fuck, Addi. Just once, one little go, please, before you tell me to stop?" I all out beg, with the head of my cock lined up with the home it so desperately wants, and Addi scoffs, making me freeze.

"You better not stop," she bites, peering over her shoulder at me with a feral glare in her eyes.

"What?" I hear her words. I just need her to confirm them. She doesn't use her voice. Instead, she lifts her left arm, pointing to the little star marked against her skin in the crook of her underarm. "The imprint of Ceres." My heart ricochets in my chest, my need for her only growing at the revelation. "Are you sure?" I croak, my skin heating with the impending pleasure dancing across my body.

This girl has been walking around with birth control all this time and I've been using condoms? We're going to have to rectify that.

She keeps her words to herself as she plants her palms flat against the sheets, coiling her fingers into the fabric as she pushes back against my cock in one swift move.

Fuck. Fuck. Fuck.

Our groans intertwine when her slick core doesn't stop until I'm nestled deep in her pussy. My hands clamp down tighter on her hips, pausing her as I try to find my breath.

"Don't fucking move, Dagger. Not unless you want me to fucking blow right now," I grind out through clenched teeth, and she hums.

"I like the sound of that," she mutters, the humor tingeing each word before she rolls her hips, not waiting a single second for me to bask in the sweet heat of her pussy.

My grip on her tightens in warning, but it does nothing to stop her. "Fuck, Dagger," I snap, slipping my hand from her waist to her neck, flexing my fingers tighter as I push her back down into the mattress.

She falls with the movement, her hips tilting even more to keep me buried in her core. Taking a deep breath, using it to my advantage as I retract my cock until only the tip remains before I slam back into her at full force.

Her cries of pleasure are muffled by the sheets as I repeat the action desperately, urgently, and hungrily.

"You wanted to tip me over the edge, Addi? Well congrats, you did it," I rasp breathlessly as I piston into her core at the perfect angle that has me hitting her g-spot with every thrust.

"Brody…fuck, Brody," she cries into the sheets, her hands balling tighter as she holds on for dear life. I feel the moment she reaches the apex of her climax, her pussy clenching around my cock so tight, it steals my breath before she shatters.

I see stars, feeling her release coat my cock, and my

movements become longer as I absorb every ounce of it until I can't hold off anymore, and I quickly follow her off the cliff and into the heated pools of ecstasy.

Every pulse from my dick earns another ripple of pleasure from her body, leaving us to ride out every last drop until I fall flat against her.

Perspiration holds us together, mingling between us as we try to catch our breaths.

"Fuck, Brody," she mutters, the first to break the silence, and I press a kiss to the curve of her neck.

"You're welcome," I reply with a grin, earning a rich laugh from her lips.

"I didn't say thank you," she retorts, and I run my nose over her sensitive flesh.

"You didn't have to."

"You're insane." She shakes her head, but when our eyes meet, it's like I've found a beacon in the darkness. I know where home is, I know where I'm meant to be, and it's with her.

Everything links back to her.

"You love it," I state, pushing up off her back as I reluctantly slip my cock from her center.

"Maybe," she breathes, a soft smile on her lips as she continues to shake her head at my antics.

Before I can tease her more on the subject, her stomach grumbles, effectively cutting me off.

"Pizza, then more books?" I offer, and she shakes her head again.

"Pizza, but no more books."

"No?" I ask, not bothering to find my clothes as I grab the bag with four small pizza boxes inside. I place them on the bed beside us, and Addi waits until she has my full attention before she speaks again.

"No, I want to do that again."

CASSIAN

46

The familiar scent of Janie's hits my nose the second I slip through the back door and hide in the dark corridor that leads straight into the kitchen. I take a moment, listening to my surroundings, but all I can hear is the sound of the steak grill sizzling. It's talking directly to my stomach.

Remembering why I'm actually here, I run my tongue over my bottom lip and push through the doors.

"It's been too long," I state, locking eyes with Jake, Janie's husband, and he leaps out of his skin as he whirls around to face me. His spatula is raised and aimed in my direction. I cock a brow at him and he waves me off.

"Warn a man, Cass," he gripes, and I scoff.

"I don't know what you're talking about. You like it when I keep you on your toes," I insist, stepping farther into the room as he works through the order on the ticket in front of him.

"If you say so," he grumbles, a hint of a smile on his lips.

I take another tentative step toward him. The quiet that surrounds him isn't laced with calm. I can feel the tension rippling from him.

Clearing my throat, I cut the remaining distance between us so I'm standing by the grill with him. "How have things been?"

He pauses but doesn't lift his stare from the steak that has his full attention. "You want the everyday bullshit or the truth?"

"The truth, always the truth," I breathe, stealing a breath as I brace for his words, but he keeps them clipped.

"It's fucked, man."

I sigh. "I had a feeling it would be. What can I do to—"

"You will do nothing, Cass," he interjects, turning his spatula in my direction again.

"But—"

"The way you care, the way you think, it's the way of a leader. Not like…" His words trail off, refusing to admit that my father, his alpha, is not fit for the job. He doesn't have the best interests of the pack at the heart of his actions. Just himself and his fully inflated ego that seeks more and more power.

"I can't keep leaving you all to this," I admit, scrubbing the back of my neck, and a second later, he pats me on the back, spatula forgotten.

"You're not, man. You're preparing us for a better future. We'll feel the benefits of it eventually," he insists, his words taking root in my bones.

"But what if I don't—"

"What if you don't what?" he interrupts again, eyebrows raised as he waits for me to spit it out, acutely aware that I have his undivided attention.

My gut twists as I think about my pack and the innocent people I left behind. "What if I'm not the new heir?"

Thoughts of Adrianna shoot to the forefront of my mind. My gut knows who the true heir is, who it should have been all along, but what does that mean for my people?

"You thinking about that fae girl Janie keeps rambling on about?" he asks, eyes searching mine as the door to the main dining area swings open.

"I do *not* ramble," the lady herself says, wagging a finger at her husband before her concerned eyes flit my way. "What are you doing here? It's not safe," she rushes out, cutting the distance between us to wrap me in her arms.

I bask in her familiar warm embrace as she rocks me from side to side.

"Raiden is struggling," I mutter, refusing to let go just yet.

"The vampire?" Jake clarifies, and I nod in his wife's embrace before she leans back, holding me at arm's length.

"What does he need?"

"He needs blood, but he's refusing to ask for it. So I need something to tide him over," I state. Janie nods, but it's Jake who speaks.

"Give me two minutes," he insists, plating the steak from the grill before disappearing into the walk-in fridge.

After a beat, Janie turns her attention to me again. "I could sense you were here. I could hear your conversation with Jake. If I did…" Her muttered words trail off as I nod.

"Then others did, too."

"Yeah, and Dalton is out there," she mouths, pointing over her shoulder to the main dining area, and I curse under my breath.

"We haven't got much, but hopefully, this will help," Jake states, bustling back into the room with a bag in his hand.

"Thanks for this," I murmur, unsure what it is I'm even grateful for, but I am nonetheless.

"Always," Janie states, patting me on the arm.

"Thank you," I repeat, unable to show my gratitude enough. "I'm sorry I'm not doing anything, or not enough, at least," I add, earning a deathly glare from Janie.

"You are. I swear it. You are, but you need to go," she insists, nudging me toward the back door, and I nod.

Jake waves as Janie guides me to the door, but before I step outside, her hand tightens around my arm.

"How's Addi?" she asks, and I immediately smile. A knowing look washes over her features as she peers into my eyes. "You love her."

"I do not," I say with a scoff, and she cocks a brow at me, daring me to deny it again. Fuck that. "I came for some bloody meat, not a therapy session," I add with a grumble, and Jake snickers from across the room.

"Oh, I'm far from qualified to deal with your fucked up shit," Janie adds with a grin, and I huff, highly aware of the truth in her words.

"Thanks." I reach for the door handle again and she pats my back.

"You're welcome."

"When you want to talk about losing your balls to a woman, I'm here, man," Jake hollers. I mutter my thanks at the same time Janie calls out her protest.

"Thanks."

"Hey!"

Janie pulls me in for a final hug, cursing her husband out as he chuckles in the background.

"I miss you. Stay safe," I whisper, squeezing her extra tight, and she hums.

"I miss you too. *You* be safe," she retorts.

She releases me all too soon, it feels. I give myself a beat. Just one before I nod and slink out into the night.

I take a deep breath, exhaling slowly before I move, but I don't make it a whole step before movement in the shadows halts me.

"Surely you know I'm going to be aware of my disgraceful son's arrival on my compound."

I look up to meet eyes so similar to mine, it hurts. "I didn't assume otherwise," I state, my tone bored while my body tries to uncoil from the surprise of his sudden arrival.

My father assesses me, breaking me down without a word like he always does, and my gut twists when he finally speaks. "I have a job for you."

I shake my head. "I'm not a part of this pack. I don't take any jobs from you."

He knows that, he just doesn't care.

"Listen here—" he starts, and I raise my free hand, refusing to deal with any more of his shit, especially after his recent attack on Addi. Again.

"I think you've made your presence in my life known already. The answer is no. It's always going to be no," I bite, unable to hide the emotion from my voice. Even if it is anger, I don't want him to see that he can get to me, but he already knows he can.

My hands ball into fists, desperate to unleash the fury

that threatens to creep higher to the surface as he tilts his head at me.

"Ah, how is the little fae anyway?" he asks, knowing exactly what I was referring to, and that only seems to piss me off further.

"I don't know who you're talking about," I grind out, trying to act unfazed, but he scoffs.

"Your skill at playing dumb is poor, son," he states, rolling his shoulders back as if working off the aches and pains I know Kryll caused.

"So is your ability to be a good alpha, but here we are," I snap back, unable to stop myself. Instead of raging at the comment, he smirks, taking a step back.

"Don't worry about my job," he advises, making my brows furrow as I shake my head.

"I wasn't."

"I'll be seeing you at the ball either way," he declares, the corner of his mouth turning into a wicked smile as his eyes roam wildly before he snatches the bag from my grasp.

Then he's gone.

His ability to get under my skin will be my downfall, especially when he knows my Achilles' heel is Addi. He's not done with us. He's not done with me. It's going to bite me in the ass soon enough, I just need to hope and pray I can keep Addi out of his line of sight as best as I can.

I owe her that.

ADRIANNA

47

The dregs of sleep cling to every achy limb as I stir awake. A distant knocking sound makes my eyelashes flutter, but I ignore it, pleading with the darkness to claim me once again.

A nudge at my core halts the sleep from taking me and I freeze. Prying my eyes open, I see nothing, but I feel everything. I gasp, sweeping my tongue over my bottom lip as the nudge comes again.

"Brody?" I rasp, my body heating as I feel the weight of him pressed against my back.

"Yeah?"

I have to wet my lips two more times before I can make my tongue work. "Is your cock still inside me?"

His smile spreads across my skin, leaving goosebumps across my neck as his cock flexes inside of me.

"Yeah."

Holy fuck.

The man is insatiable at the best of times, but take the barrier from between us, and he's even needier. My muscles ache in the best way possible, and I expect to tremble with a hint of pain as he slowly works his stiff cock inside me again, but to my surprise, my pussy tightens around him, desperate for more.

Another knock rings in my ears, but it sounds closer this time. Much closer.

"I think someone's at the door," I croak, and I feel him shrug behind me as his hands find my waist and his dick swirls against my walls.

Fuck.

"I'm not moving. I'm happy exactly where I am." He punctuates each word with a little thrust of his hips, his cock growing harder with each movement until he's filling me to the brink again.

"Brody," I mutter again when the knocking becomes more insistent, and he grumbles.

"Fine." I expect him to move, to whimper at the loss of the warmth between my thighs, but instead, he slows his pace. "Who is it?"

I gape at him in surprise when a gruff call comes from the other side of the door.

"Me."

"I don't know a me," he retorts, making my body heat as he continues to wreak havoc on my pussy in slow, delicious strokes.

"Fuck off, Brody."

My eyes widen. Raiden?

I shift to move, but Brody's hand tightens on my waist, rendering me helpless in his grasp as he uses his magic to open his bedroom door. The muttered chants are inaudible with the sound of my pulse ringing in my ears, but a moment later, a pale vampire steps through the threshold.

He's panting, eyes wild as he blinks at me. His mouth opens, but nothing comes out. He tries it a few times to no avail before I relent.

"What's wrong?" Any attempts at moving are restricted by Brody, but I manage to prop myself up on my elbow to get a better view of him.

"I need your help," he rasps, his eyes bleak in the dark room as Brody shakes his head from behind me.

"She's busy."

"How?" Raiden grunts, eyes narrowing at us. Brody flips the sheets off my body.

He accentuates every roll of his hips as he fucks me, putting on a show as Raiden falls to his knees with a curse.

"Fuck, Brody," I mutter, feeling exposed, but it only serves to bring me closer to the brink of ecstasy.

Brody's lips trail over my neck as he keeps a steady

pace fucking me. "Tell him, Dagger," he whispers against my ear, and I shiver.

"Tell him what?"

"Tell him that he can." My nerves instantly spike, adrenaline coursing through my veins as understanding washes over me. "It'll be so good, Addi. I swear. Especially with my dick inside you," he explains, making Raiden groan from his spot on the floor.

"I thought Cassian was going to help?" I croak, goosebumps rising across my skin from head to toe as Raiden shakes his head.

"Kenner."

One word, one barrier, one fucking asshole.

"Is Cassian okay?" I ask, worry building inside me, but it's quickly calmed by a nod from my vampire.

"See? He needs you, Dagger. Otherwise, he wouldn't be here, down on his knees and desperate." Brody's words are acting as an aphrodisiac as his cock sinks into me again and again. "Tell him. You know you want to find out," he adds, nipping at my ear lobe, and I gasp.

"Raiden." His name falls from my lips, and his gaze meets mine. "Please," I croak, and he frowns, his tongue sweeping across his bottom lip as his uncertainty holds him in place. Clearing my throat, I stretch my hand out toward him. "Please, whatever you need, I can help."

My words hang in the air, heating the space between

us, fueled by the sound of skin slapping against skin as Brody groans and ups his pace.

"That's it, Addi. Fuck, you're perfect," he moans against my ear, making my muscles coil with desire.

Raiden's eyes don't stray from mine as he shuffles across the floor on his knees, not stopping until he's right beside me. Hope swirls in his eyes as his gaze flicks down. "Your throat?"

I gulp, nerves mingling with curiosity as he curses again.

"Fuck, watching your throat bob like that only makes me want it more," he admits hoarsely, desperation clinging to every word.

Brody strokes the loose tendrils of hair that cling to my skin out of the way, offering Raiden a better view before digging his fingertips into my hips again.

"Taste her while I fuck her, Raiden," Brody orders, and Raiden rises up on his knees for better access, but he waits for me to nod before he moves any closer.

"Are you sure, Troublemaker?" he asks when his lips are against my flesh.

"Yes."

He rakes his teeth over my skin.

Once.

Tremble.

Twice.

Tremble.

Three times.

"Do it, Raiden," I plead, anticipation clawing at my skin, and a breath later, his teeth sink into my throat.

I cry out at the sharp bite against my flesh, the sound quickly morphing into a groan as he sucks desperately.

All I can feel is Brody's cock buried in my pussy and Raiden's tongue lapping at my neck.

All I can see are the colors bursting across my vision, painting the world in a kaleidoscope of rays.

All I can hear are moans, from who, I'm not entirely sure, but I'm certain mine are mingled among them.

It's all too much and not enough at once. Everything shifts as I feel Raiden press his thumb against my clit, pulling the trigger on the sensations glossing over my skin, and I fall apart between them.

My shudders ripple through my body, and a beat later, Brody curses in my ear.

"Fuck, Dagger. Fuck." His movements stagger as he finds his release. "Painting your pussy with my cum is my new favorite thing to do," he rasps, pleasure leaving his voice light and airy.

Raiden's assault on my throat pauses as he leans back, looking me dead in the eye. "Adrianna."

My name on his tongue is a combination of wonder and need.

Without a word, Brody slips from my core, grabbing my waist and maneuvering me around until he's nestled against his headboard with me between his thighs, legs wide and inviting for my vampire, who looks entirely different from the guy that walked in the room. He gropes at my chest, tweaking my nipples as Raiden watches, eyes darkening with every passing moment.

"Please," I croak, chest heaving like I didn't just chase an orgasm off the cliff already.

He crawls onto the bed, not bothering to discard a single item of clothing as he unbuttons his pants, tugging the zipper down enough to release his cock before he's at my entrance.

Brody keeps my thighs spread for his friend while Raiden's hand reaches for my throat, sweeping a thumb across the blood trailing over my skin before he brings it to his lips. The second he sucks the crimson stain from his thumb, he thrusts his cock deep into my core, no barrier between us, in one swift move.

"Fuck, Adrianna," he bites through clenched teeth, reaching for my ankles as he shifts his angle, forcing me to lean back onto Brody even more as he takes me.

Sweat clings to me as Brody plays my body with precision, matching the pace of Raiden's hips as they spread me wide and wring me dry. I feel the orgasm coming this time, stealing my breath as my eyes fall closed. It starts in my toes, making them curl with insatiable desire as it zips up my legs, coiling tight in my stomach and nestling deep in my core before I implode.

"You're fucking perfect, Troublemaker," Raiden growls with a ragged breath and his hips flush against mine, finding his own release as he pulses inside of me.

All I can do is hum in acknowledgment, words failing me as I try to catch my breath, my eyes still glued shut.

I feel the loss of him slipping from between my slick thighs before I'm manhandled into another position, but this time, it's delicately against the sheets before a sheet is drawn over me.

"What are you doing?" Brody asks from my left as Raiden scoffs from my right.

"Sleeping here," he retorts, sounding a lot more like his usual self than he did earlier. That fact calms me in a way I can't even express, but Brody protests.

"No—"

"Sharing is caring, Brody," Raiden sings as someone trails their hand over my cheek, but I don't have the energy to pry my eyes open to see who.

Instead, I embrace the ghost of a smile clinging to my lips as I pass out, completely content.

ADRIANNA

48

My lips purse as I run my hand over the material of my dress. "I don't have a good feeling about this," I admit, disappointed that releasing the words doesn't ease the weight on my shoulders.

"About the dress? It's gorgeous," Flora states, frowning at me in the mirror, and I shake my head with a sigh.

I wish my worries were about the dress.

"No. The ball. Bozzelli has something up her sleeve. I can feel it," I grumble, turning away from the mirror as I search for my shoes.

"Hmm. Maybe, or maybe she wanted a good time." Her voice lilts higher than usual, attempting to have a positive outlook on the whole thing, but it's bullshit and we both know it.

"That woman has never experienced a good time in her

whole life. I don't envision it happening now," I say with a haunting snicker, and Flora nods.

"That's true. Maybe we don't go then," she offers, and I shake my head.

"I wish, but being there is exactly what's going to give us the information we need if she is actually up to something."

"You're too wise," she says with a grin, tapping her chin. "But maybe if you weren't there, she wouldn't be up to anything because we both know if she is, it involves you."

I hum in agreement. This damn ball has been weighing on us all week. Raiden feels it, Brody feels it, Cassian feels it, and Kryll feels it. Shit, even Flora and Arlo sense something. Especially after Kenner's comments to Cassian when he took off to Janie's.

A knock on the door pulls me from my thoughts and Arlo's voice comes from the other side a moment later.

"Are you guys ready?"

"Ready as we'll ever be," Flora murmurs as I lace up my boots, opting to avoid any kind of heel, just in case.

One more glance in the mirror and I'm good to go. I'm slightly impressed. Since we weren't able to leave campus, Flora worked her magic and dyed the dresses we wore last time. Now, I'm draped in black, and she's rocking a forest green that makes her hair look deeper in color.

My hair is braided into a crown on my head like usual, which seems to accentuate the smoky eyes Flora did for me. I feel good, but ready for combat, just in case. At the thought, my magic coats my flesh, reminding me that we're not restricted this time. Not like the last ball when I had the amethyst nestled between my shoulder blades.

Flora opens the door and I move to leave, but my feet freeze in place as I gape at what awaits me on the other side of the threshold.

My wolf comes into view first, his arms folded over his chest as his eyes rake over me from head to toe. He's dressed in black, shirt, tie, and all, and he's never looked so deadly. It's sinful.

My mage grins from beside him. He wears a charcoal suit fitted perfectly, a pristine white shirt, and a matching tie. The tempting smirk on his lips is sent straight from the devil, a promise of mayhem in his eyes.

My dragon prince leans against the opposite wall, his black ink traveling over his neck and down beneath his white shirt. My mouth runs dry, appreciating the navy suit that molds to his muscles, and my thighs press together.

My vampire is last but certainly not least. His black-on-black suit matches Cassian's, except for the blood-red tie that he wears. He flashes his teeth as he offers a rare smile and I feel like I'm about to melt on the spot.

"I think we could skip the ball and—"

Brody's husky words are cut off by Flora's scoff as she steps over the threshold to where Arlo is waiting for her. "You wish. Her investigation mode has been activated. So, unfortunately for you, she's focused."

"You can focus on my dick instead if you like," he offers with a wag of his brows, and I shake my head at him.

It's tempting, *really* tempting, but not when my gut tells me lives could be at stake. He rolls his eyes, not uttering a word as he offers me his hand, accepting Flora's statement as we head down the hall. I can feel four sets of eyes on me, making my skin tingle.

I'm fucked.

They're going to be the death of me, and I'm their willing victim.

RAIDEN

49

Blonde hair, smoky eyes, blood-red lips, and a sensual black dress.

Four descriptions, a handful or so words, but put it all together and you get the captivating woman before me, yet they do nothing to convey just how fucking beautiful she is.

Stunning doesn't come close, either.

Alluring. Attractive. Gorgeous. Elegant. Exquisite. Pretty. Ravishing. Sexy. Divine. Dazzling.

Ten more words, and still, none of them are good enough.

Her bedroom door clicks shut behind her and I elbow my way forward to grab her hand, lacing our fingers together before I tug her to my side. The corner of her mouth tips up, amusement dancing in her eyes as my tongue sweeps over my lips.

All I want is to pull her in the opposite direction, slip behind her bedroom door, and block the rest of the world out as I get lost in her. There's a strange...feeling in the air this evening, one that's only grown thicker this past week. The quicker we get this over with, the better.

Heading down the stairs and into the night air, I take a deep breath, willing the cool breeze to deflate the semi trapped in my pants, but with Adrianna at my side, there's no chance of that.

Mindlessly, I lift her knuckles to my mouth, ghosting my lips across her skin, and she sighs.

"Are the media going to be here again?" she asks, immediately invoking a memory of the last ball we attended. My gut twists, recalling the moment I slipped from Adrianna's side to head inside with Vallie in hopes of easing the stresses that surrounded us. I scoff. It did nothing. Nothing at all.

"I imagine so," I admit, turning to look at her with my eyebrows raised. "Want me to hide you?" I offer, but she shakes her head.

"There's no point. They'll find me regardless."

"That's the truth," I mutter, earning a sound from her lips that's a mixture between a huff and a laugh.

A sense of high alert sweeps over us as we all head toward the impending doom that awaits. Quicker than I would like, the red carpet dazzles in the distance. Without a word, she tugs her hand from mine, rolling her shoulders back as she stands taller, like she's ready for battle. I let her go, slipping my hand to the small of her back as she takes a step ahead, presenting herself as the leader that she is.

Media lines both sides of the red carpet, and every pair of eyes whip her way the moment she nears, forgetting the other students who held their interest a moment earlier.

"Princess Adrianna Reagan, how are you surviving the campus?"

"Have there been any threats against you?"

"Where is your father, Adrianna? Tell us."

"Is it true you're now the princess of the dragons?"

"Where is the prince of the dragons?"

They all try to speak at once, making my eyes narrow as I assess each and every one of them. Adrianna, however, tilts her head from side to side, smiling at each of them demurely before she saunters down the carpet without a fucking word. Her head remains high, chin up, and smile plastered in place. It takes me a second to move after her, but a quick shove from Cassian resumes my march forward.

I storm the carpet, ignoring everyone and everything except the sway to Adrianna's hips as she slips inside without a backward glance. She really shouldn't be allowed to be this fucking hot and sinful. I can't handle it. Every member of the media is fixated on her, snapping pictures and throwing more questions, even though she's no longer here. I wonder if they realize the presence of greatness they're in when she's around.

Following her inside, I find her hand again, and she laces her fingers with mine. Brody swoops in on her other side, draping his arm around her shoulder, and she relaxes between us.

"We won't be separated this time," Cassian grunts, rounding on us to give us all a pointed look, and I nod. There will definitely be no separating this time.

Thankfully, as we step into the ballroom, I notice the difference between tonight and the last. There aren't large tables set out with our names organized by origin. There's a buffet to the left, an open dance floor in the center of the room, and a podium along the far wall. The guests already in attendance mingle in the remaining space around small bar tables.

It's better yet worse all at the same time.

"Something feels off," Kryll states, acknowledging exactly what I feel as Adrianna hums in agreement.

"Yeah, something isn't right."

"You feel it too?" I ask, my hand clenching tighter around hers, and she nods. "What are you catching that's setting you off?" I'm intrigued to know what's knocking us all off-center.

"Not here," Brody murmurs, guiding Adrianna off to the small alcove to the left, and we all follow after them. Flora and Arlo included.

It's a rather tight squeeze, but we all nestle in. Cassian and Kryll are watching the crowd around us, but I set them aside and keep my gaze locked on the hot fucking fae that infiltrates my nightmares and my dreams all at once.

Brody chants under his breath, and Adrianna watches his lips move until a grin spreads across his face, earning a smile from her sweet mouth too.

"My father is here. He keeps nodding his head for me to follow him," Brody states, keeping his back to the rest of the ballroom, and Cassian scoffs.

"My father is here. He's pretending I don't exist, but that's worse than his demands. That means he's up to something and he doesn't want me to get a read on him."

Wolves.

All fucking assholes.

They're no damn better than vampires, even if they like to think they are.

"My mother is always here, but she's not standing with my father," I say with a sigh, not bothering to look away from my girl. "Which means she'll be with Vallie's uncle, hanging off his every word and up to no good," I grumble.

Vallie is watching us, which means whoever her uncle is, he's up to no good too.

"Wait, wait, wait," Flora blurts, waving her hands to get all of our attention before she taps her ear.

I frown, along with everyone else, the sound of jazz music ringing in my ears before I hear it.

"Kenner," I rasp, glancing at Cassian, who nods in acknowledgment.

"Repeat the plan, Bozzelli."

"Is that really necessary? We've been over this enough times."

"Not with me, you haven't. Let me hear it."

"Fine. The plan is for me to announce the immediate trial, which will allow you time to slip away and set up by having the students give surprise speeches."

"And then?"

"And then the trial begins. You can gather the students you want, and no one will be any wiser."

"Excellent, and then we'll have the luxury of the future fated mates under our control. Make it happen, Bozzelli."

"You're a genius, Kenner."

Fuckers.

I can't decide who sounds more cunning. Bozzelli will have definitely been the one who looked the most smug, but Kenner will definitely have been giving her a run for her money.

"They're talking about us," Adrianna states, confirming what I'm sure we're all sensing.

"How do they expect us to fall under their control?" Cassian bites, his jaw tight with anger, and Brody sighs.

"Because when fated mates are linked, they're in a weakened state immediately after," he offers, pinching the bridge of his nose as I smash my molars together in irritation.

"Which means?" I give him a pointed look, my question going unheard until he finally lifts his head up.

"Which means they would have time to cast a puppet spell."

"A puppet spell?" Adrianna repeats, frown lines forming between her eyes. I want to sweep them away, but I know they'll only return over something else the moment I do.

"I've heard my father talking about it. It basically places you under the control of the one casting the spell, and there would be nothing we could do about it."

"Fuck that," Kryll blurts, squeezing the back of his neck in anger as his nostrils flare.

"What he said," I add with a nod, my gaze finally flicking to the rest of the ballroom as I try to observe the situation from all angles.

"We can't let them win," Cassian grinds out, and Adrianna stands taller, channeling her inner goddess as she nods once. Firm and decisive, like a queen.

"What can we do?"

Brody looks her dead in the eye, nibbling at his bottom lip before he speaks. "There may be something."

ADRIANNA

50

Fuck. Fuck. Fuck. Fuck. Fuck.

I know what he's saying without uttering a single word.

"What?" Kryll asks, glancing between Brody and me with a bewildered look on his face.

"I'm not ready for this," I ramble, swiping my damp palms over my dress to no avail. "I haven't even considered…" My words trail off, my chest tightening as I try to take a breath.

"Considered what?" Cassian prods, inching closer as I feel my temperature rocket with panic.

"Spoiling their plan," Brody murmurs, his hand finding the small of my back as he draws small circles. He still isn't saying it, likely in hopes of allowing me to find the right words, but my tongue is like lead in my mouth as my pulse thunders in my ears.

"How?" Raiden asks, stroking his thumb over my knuckles and reminding me he's here, but all I can do is gape at him.

Fuck. Fuck. Fuck.

Brody takes a deep breath, exhaling slowly before pressing a kiss against my temple. "By finding her mate to try and activate her wolf."

My next breath lodges in my throat, refusing to budge as I blink, my gaze fuzzy as Cassian scoffs.

"There is no finding," he grunts, squeezing around the small space so he's standing toe to toe with me.

"What?" Kryll asks, thankfully echoing my thoughts, despite my inability to speak.

"It's me." Cassian speaks the words so matter of factly, so calmly, that all I can do is frown at him, my jaw slack as I stare in shock. "I fucking know it's me," he repeats, fiercer this time. I shake my head, lost in the turmoil swirling in his eyes. "Do you want to stop them or not?" he rasps, stroking a thumb down my cheek as I gulp, dislodging the lump in my throat enough to croak out a few words.

"Yes, but that doesn't mean you're my—" He effectively cuts my words off as he grabs my waist and hauls me over his shoulder. "Cassian," I squeak, hearing the chuckles coming from Arlo and Flora.

"Stall them," Cassian snarls before he cuts through the

ballroom with me firmly in place.

"Cassian," I repeat, slapping his ass as discreetly as possible so we don't garner a bigger audience than I'm sure we've already got, but he completely ignores me.

Fucker.

Now is not the time for this.

The music dulls down as he heads out into the hall, and a few moments later, the women's bathroom door swings shut behind us. He lowers me to my feet and reaches for my chin. The touch is gentle and sweet. It makes my walls fall away, but my body tightens in the next breath when he spins me on the spot, turning me toward the mirror over the vanity.

"Look at us," he grates, his grip on my chin tightening as he meets my stare in our reflection. "Look at me and tell me it's not me. Tell me I'm not the one because I sure as fuck know you're my alpha."

"Cassian," I breathe, my chest heaving with every ragged breath. I don't know what he wants me to say. I don't know the answer, but more than that, I'm scared that he won't be. Then what? I can sense my thoughts, but conveying them is something else entirely.

That doesn't mean anything to Cassian, though. He shakes his head, dropping his chin to his chest as he releases me. I move to turn and face him, but his hands shift to my waist, locking me in place.

"Say it, Addi."

I gape at him, blinking as I will the words to come, but all I can manage is his name.

"Cassian…"

He shakes his head, baring his teeth as he flicks up my dress, every single layer, before he snags on my panties, the material falling at my feet. I lean forward with a gasp, planting my hands against the vanity as he palms my ass.

"Tell me, Alpha. Fucking tell me," he snaps, his eyes practically black as he glares at me in the mirror. "I've told you time and time again that if I took you without… if I felt you with no barrier, I know…"

"Cassian…"

"Tell me you don't want to find your wolf or that you don't want to stop their plan, but you have all of five fucking seconds to do so."

He spreads my ass cheeks, revealing my pussy to him as I continue to gape at him in the mirror. Tingles zap up my spine, the hairs on the back of my neck standing on end as he silently counts me down.

I shake my head as every second stretches between us while I try to find any other word, until he leans forward with a snarl. "Time's up, Alpha."

He punctuates his nickname for me with one swift thrust of his hips. I lurch with the movement, a strangled moan parting my lips further as he groans.

"Cass," I whisper, goosebumps burning over my skin, my body trembling as he retreats all the way before slamming into me again, with more intensity this time. "Cassian, we can't be sure, we can't…"

He ignores me, plowing into me with a ferocity that makes my knees weak and my pussy clench with every thrust. He spreads my walls with every breath, and all I can do is succumb to the pleasure. To him. To the possibilities.

"Tell." Thrust. "Me." Thrust. "Now." Thrust. "Alpha."

"Cassian." His name is a plea, a prayer, a wish.

He retracts, filling me once again as our skin connects over and over again.

"I can't hear you, Alpha."

"Cass—"

My breath is stolen and my body tenses as my eyes latch onto the mirror just in time to see the change, the shift. The flickering green of my eyes swirls into golden beams with flecks of emerald sprinkling the edges.

"Cassian!" My pupils dilate as he meets my stare and his do the same, swirling with a new color before a salacious grin spreads across his face.

He doesn't relent, he doesn't question it, he doesn't falter for a single moment.

Instead, he fucks me harder and faster as I cling on to the vanity like my life depends on it.

The tingles down my spine grow more prominent, leaving me gasping as I watch my life unravel. "Cassian, I can't breathe," I manage through weighted breaths as my body heats.

"Tell me, Addi. Tell me, and everything will be okay," he promises, squeezing my chest as the words part my lips without thought or caution.

"I'm yours, Cassian. I'm yours."

The climax that rockets through my body is like nothing I've ever felt before, burning like an elixir through my veins from head to toe, forcing my eyes to slam shut. My lips part, Cassian's name on the tip of my tongue, but nothing comes out as I crumple to the floor.

Before I can call my asshole of a wolf lover out for letting go of me, I curl in a ball, riddled with excruciating pain as I scream.

I can't see. I can't feel. I can't hear.

It's all-consuming, and I'm at its mercy.

It feels like an eternity, but just as quickly as the pain takes over, it disappears, depleting to nothing as I try to catch my breath. Rising up onto my hands and knees, I sway, blinking my eyes open slowly to find Cassian hovering above me.

A whimper bursts from my throat, the phantom pain lingering in my bones as he stares down at me with wide eyes.

My mouth falls slack, but even when I will his name to my lips, nothing happens.

Cassian gulps, his shoulders relaxing as the corner of his mouth tips up, and a moment later, he shifts. One moment, a man, another a wolf. So beautiful, so mysterious, so mesmerizing.

He inches closer, nuzzling his face into mine, and I lean into the touch, basking in the sensation until I freeze, realization dawning on me. I jolt back, blinking at the wolf before me, but when I look down at the floor, the paws that I see don't match the color of his fur.

They're white.

Whiter than white.

A huge contrast to the black fur that covers his body.

Lifting my hand, the paw moves and I jump back in shock.

It's me.

I'm...*I'm* the wolf with the white paws.

Me.

A wolf.

My wolf.

Cassian is quick to cut the distance I created, resting his forehead against mine as we stare into each other's eyes. His presence, his close proximity, is calming; it keeps me grounded as my mind whirls at high speed.

"I am yours, and you are mine. Now, forever, and

always."

My eyes widen as my breath lurches.

He just fucking said that…in my head.

"How are you doing that?"

"The same way you are." I can hear the amusement in his voice, but it's laced with awe too.

"I don't know how I am."

"It's natural in our wolf form."

In *our* wolf form.

Holy fuck.

"What now?" I think, the thought drifting between us as he takes a small step back.

"Now, we take the kingdom and fuck up their plans along the way."

My chest rises and falls in heavy breaths as I nod, enraptured by his words when the door slams behind him.

The calmness that clung to my limbs moments ago is gone, lost in the wicked smile that taints Kenner's features.

I take a step back, heart in my mouth as I start to panic. I may be a wolf, but it's not familiar to me. I don't know what the fuck I'm doing and I feel defenseless.

"Excellent," he says, beaming from ear to ear as Cassian moves to stand in front of me, blocking me the best he can from his father's direct view, but Kenner makes no move to come closer. "You did the job I wanted of you without even trying, son. And you, Adrianna, I knew you would seek out your wolf the moment you were told not to, just as I planned."

AFTERWORDS

Wow. Just wow.

This series is in my veins, it's the only way to explain it.

My heart is full, my smile is wicked, and that ending was written by a cunt.

Hahaha.

Truly, I hope you love these guys as much as I do. They're giving me all of the feels, and it's cementing a level of happiness and joy in me that feels so special, I'm grateful you're here with me.

Did you hear the offer has confirmed this is a five book series?

I know, she's dramatic, but I'm beyond excited for my first five book series to be with these guys. We should have the series completed by the end of the year, it'll be an early christmas gift haha

Much love!

THANK YOU

Michael. You never read these, but the pride you have in me, the unconditional love, it gives me strength every day. You are me, and I am you. Today, tomorrow, forever. Thank you for seeing my shine even when all I see is darkness. I love you, so much it makes my chest ache.

My angel faces, you give me air, you give me love, you give me excitement. I want to make you proud every day, just like you make me proud. Thank you for showing me patience, thank you for showing me love, and thank you for brightening my life.

Nicole and Jeni, my gals, my peas in this pod. I love you guys so hard it's embarrassing, but here we are. I'd hug you, and we all know how I feel about showing emotion, which is secretly hilarious. Thank you for supporting these characters just as much as you do me. You make being in a girl tribe extraordinary.

Kirsty, you're a dick, and I love you. Don't tell anyone. Ever. You Aries/Pisces cusp peeps are alright, I guess. Haha.

My beta readers, thank you for the comments, they light up my life and instill enough confidence in me to last a lifetime!

Lily and Sarah, the gals with the goods, making me look pretty with your hard work. Thank you!

ALSO BY KC KEAN

Featherstone Academy
(Reverse Harem Contemporary Romance)

My Bloodline

Your Bloodline

Our Bloodline

Red

Freedom

Redemption

All-Star Series
(Reverse Harem Contemporary Romance)

Toxic Creek

Tainted Creek

Twisted Creek

(Standalone MF)

Burn to Ash

Emerson U Series
(Reverse Harem Contemporary Romance)

Watch Me Fall

Watch Me Rise

Watch Me Reign

Saints Academy

(Reverse Harem Paranormal Romance)

Reckless Souls

Damaged Souls

Vicious Souls

Fearless Souls

Heartless Souls

Ruthless Brothers MC

(Reverse Harem MC Romance)

Ruthless Rage

Ruthless Rebel

Ruthless Riot

Silvercrest Academy

(Reverse Harem Paranormal Romance)

Falling Shadows

Destined Shadows

Cursed Shadows

Unchained Shadows

Heirborn Academy

Kingdom of Ruin

Reign of Blood

Hunt of Night

Fate of Eternity

Printed in Great Britain
by Amazon

46919099R00301